After a successful career in advertising, working as a media buyer, Rod Reynolds took City University's two-year MA in crime writing, where he started *The Dark Inside*, his first Charlie Yates mystery. He lives in London with his wife and two daughters.

Praise for Rod Reynolds' *The Dark Inside*:

'A seriously good debut. Rod Reynolds depicts the dark heart of 1940s Texas with terrific punch and authenticity, achieving the rare trick of combining fearsome grit with real heart.' Anya Lipska, author of *Where the Devil Can't Go*

'Evokes the same shadowy, phantasmagoric atmosphere as the first series of [*True Detective*].' Barry Forshaw, *Financial Times*

'Reads like an authentic piece of good old-fashioned Southern noir . . . There are echoes of Chandler in washed-up journalist Charlie Yates's terse, cynical narration but this is more than a mere pastiche: it's subtle, original and enthralling.' Jake Kerridge, *Sunday Express*

'A fascinating web of intrigue and deception; readers will find there can be no turning back until the last page has turned. Stylish, assured and perceptive, *The Dark Inside* is a remarkable first novel.' Pam Norfolk, *Lancashire Evening Post*

by the same author

THE DARK INSIDE

Black Night Falling

ROD REYNOLDS

FABER & FABER

First published in 2016
by Faber & Faber Ltd
Bloomsbury House
74–77 Great Russell Street
London WC1B 3DA

Typeset by Faber & Faber Ltd
Printed and bound by CPI Group (UK), Croydon CR0 4YY

The right of Rod Reynolds to be identified as author of his work has been asserted in accordance
with Section 77 of the Copyright, Designs and Patents Act 1988

Epigraph: lines from Nietzsche's *Beyond Good and Evil*, translated by Helen Zimmern (New
York: 1917) with minor emendations

A CIP record for this book
is available from the British Library

ISBN 978–0–571–32321–0

2 4 6 8 10 9 7 5 3 1

To my daughter, Isabel; my love always.

He who fights with monsters should be careful lest he thereby become a monster. And if you gaze long into an abyss, the abyss will also gaze into you.

Friedrich Nietzsche

CHAPTER ONE

OCTOBER 1946

It was almost dark when I landed.

The DC3 rolled to a stop and I climbed down onto an asphalt runway. I was the only passenger disembarking in Hot Springs – the other dozen or so on board staying on to Little Rock or Memphis – so the ground crew dragged the steps away from the aircraft as soon as I was clear. I looked back and watched as the co-pilot pulled the door shut, wrenching it as though he couldn't get out of there fast enough. Made me think about the risk I was taking; that being here was a mistake.

The control tower was the only structure on the airfield, a metal and glass box atop a low concrete building. I started towards it. The sun was below the hills in the distance, casting them in shadow, the trees that carpeted them appearing black in the low light. There were no porters or carts, no one in sight at all, so I carried my bag by my side and made for the front of the building, hoping that Jimmy Robinson was good to his word and had a ride waiting for me.

Robinson was my reason for coming to Hot Springs, and the reason I was so damn hinky about it. It was six months since I'd seen him last – six months that felt like a lifetime.

Texarkana never left me. The worst of the wounds I suffered, mental and physical, never closed; but time and

1

distance wore down at them, and the memories were fading – bleached, like a photograph left in the California sun.

Having Lizzie at my side helped. My singular fear about taking her to Los Angeles had been that we'd always serve as a reminder to each other of the hell we endured; that we'd never be able to put aside those four weeks last spring. But like most things, it turned out different than I expected; rather than being a scar that brought to mind the cut, Lizzie was the salve. The one good thing that came of all that business.

And I knew she felt the same way. At least I did the day she'd agreed to be my wife.

I'd proposed marriage the same day my divorce papers from Jane came through. Even as I'd slipped the ring on her finger, I wasn't sure what Lizzie's response would be. She told me after that I was crazy to think that way – but that kind of certainty is a blessing of youth, one that withers with experience. Since Texarkana, it felt like most every thought entered my head came loaded with doubt.

We'd been living together three months in California, renting a rundown bungalow in Venice Beach. The canals had been overrun with oil wells since I'd last been there, but the town still had a honky-tonk feel to it that Los Angeles looked down on, and that was part of why I liked it. Our neighbours had assumed we were man and wife when we arrived, so we said nothing and acted like we were. Part of me figured to leave it that way; coming off a broken marriage, seemed like the smart move was not to rock the boat. But pretty soon I recognised that was a faint heart talking and that being afraid of driving Lizzie away was no way to start something together. Jane's father was using his stroke to hurry the divorce along, and that was just fine with me. When the papers arrived, I'd blown a month's paycheck on a ring, taken Lizzie to the beach at sundown, and asked her to be my wife. We'd been standing in sight of the abandoned amusement pier and I remember my eyes flitting to the gulls circling the top of the big dipper track, their cries magnified in my ears as I waited for her answer. My hand hadn't stopped shaking even when she said yes, and the smile didn't leave my face for a week.

At the time, that day had felt like a demarcation point. The day when our pasts took a backseat to what was still to come. And now I stood here, on a desolate airfield in the Arkansas wilderness, a stone's throw from Texarkana. Darkness drawing in on me. Cross-country to see a man I never imagined seeing again. On the strength of one desperate telephone call.

*

Some reason, I wasn't surprised when I got to the front of the airfield and found no one waiting for me. Robinson had promised to send a car to carry me into town, but like everything he'd said, I'd been suspicious; now it felt like a portent – the first proof that I was on a fool's errand.

I had no reason to trust the man. The last time I'd seen him in Texarkana, he'd tried to help me – but that was only when the weight of his own guilt got to be too much. He'd pulled a gun on me twice before that; we weren't friends, and I damn sure didn't owe him any debt of gratitude.

I found a telephone kiosk inside the control building and asked the operator to connect me with a cab company. It was more than an hour before a car showed up.

The ride into Hot Springs took twenty minutes. Night had fallen and the roads were unlit most of the way, so I got no sense of the terrain I was passing through. The smell of pine trees came to me intermittently – both familiar and foreboding at the same time. My mind ran to the same safe haven it always did, and I thought about Lizzie. But the image that came to the fore was the shadow that'd crossed her face when I first told her about Robinson's call. I remembered standing across from her in our dinette, unable to meet her gaze, as she implored me not to go. Me telling her I had to.

I stared out the cab window into the darkness. The driver tried to strike up a conversation, asked what brought me to Hot Springs. Truth was, I didn't have a good answer for him. I pretended not to hear him and he let it alone after that, starting in on what sounded like well-worn patter about the thermal springs that gave the town its name, and how they drew visitors from all over the country. I let him talk, his words washing over me, and thought about his question. Just what the hell was I doing here?

Robinson had tracked me down through my work. Lizzie and I had arrived in California with almost nothing – me with the few clothes I'd bought as I drifted west, her with a bag full of hand-me-downs from the cousin she'd run to in Phoenix. That made finding a job my first priority. I figured I'd have a hard time convincing anyone to take me on, seeing how I couldn't tell why the *Examiner* had canned me, or what had really gone on in Texarkana – how I'd shot a man and fled, even though it was an act of self-defence. So I tracked down my old editor from the *LA Times*, Buck Acheson; he was running a third-rate outfit in Santa Monica called the *Pacific Journal*. My fourth day on the coast, I doorstepped him outside their building – call it a joke from one old legman to another – and asked him for a reference. Could have been the three-highball lunch I could smell on his breath, but he said he'd go me one better – come work for him, the City beat. *'The pay's lousy, and our name won't open any doors, but it's yours if you want it.'*

I'd started the next day. The work was dull; Santa Monica politics was corrupt as hell, but it only ran as far as arguments over beachfront zoning codes, so no one really gave a damn. Me and the other three legmen spent most of our time finding bigger stories to chase down in LA proper. Acheson loved scooping his old bosses at the *Times*, so he was happy to let us off the leash. It smarted to have slipped so far, all the way from the New York City crime beat to the California bush leagues, but I threw myself into the job to leave myself as little time as possible to dwell on what had passed.

Lizzie fell hard for California. She loved the beach; the first time she saw the Pacific, she'd stood watching the waves roll in for more than an hour, neither of us speaking, just enjoying being there. The salt-spray on our faces and the crash of the breakers was like an incoming tide that washed against the dark memories, pushing back at them.

Our bungalow was nothing to look at, but it was three blocks from the oceanfront and was all we could afford until Lizzie could bring herself to sell her parents' house in Texarkana. The bungalow was spartan when we moved in, but Lizzie made a home of it: bouquets of wild bush sunflowers to distract from the drab olive walls, handmade drapes and

5

curtains, fresh white linen for the creaking walnut bed. On the sideboard, a small silver picture frame – the picture of Alice that she carried in her clutch, the only one that she'd had with her when she fled Texarkana. Lizzie talked about her sister more as time passed, and from experience, I knew it was a sign the pain was slowly ebbing. The stories she recalled were of happy times they'd spent together, rather than those nightmare days leading up to Alice's death.

Before the attack on Alice, Lizzie had spent eighteen months teaching farm kids at a two-room elementary schoolhouse in Miller County. By her own telling it wasn't her calling in life, but she'd enjoyed it enough to want to keep at it. But it only took a few weeks of searching to see she wouldn't be able to score a similar position in California without proper training or a diploma. Playing homemaker would never be enough for her, so after a month of needling Acheson, I landed her a secretarial position at the *Journal*. The work was too easy for her, but she enjoyed it all the same, the novelty of the big city and the newsroom enough to make everything exciting at first.

We'd gone on that way for months. We never spoke about what happened in Texarkana, only sometimes about Alice.

Then a week ago, sitting at my desk at the *Journal*, the telephone call came. The caller hadn't given his name, and it'd taken me a moment to place the voice.

'Been a long time, New York.'

'Robinson?'

'Thought you might have forgotten me a minute there.'

I wrapped the telephone cord around my hand, saying nothing while I let the surprise pass. If I'd thought of him at all before then, it was figuring he'd have drunk himself into oblivion. 'How did you get this number?'

'We newsmen, New York. Ain't hard to find a man has his name in print every day.'

I looked around the office, searching for Lizzie, suddenly needing to have her in my sight. 'What do you want?'

'You don't wanna shoot the breeze none? "How you been, Jimmy? What's—"'

'It's been six months. You didn't call to reminisce.'

He sniffed. 'Always straight to the point – you ain't changed none.' A noise came down the line – him sucking on a cigarette and exhaling. 'How you feel about making a little trip?'

'What are you talking about? A trip where?'

'Town called Hot Springs, in Arkansas. Ever hear of it?'

'Never.'

'Ain't your kind of place, but there's things would interest you here.'

'What the hell is that supposed to mean?'

'Means you and me got to talk. Face to face. How soon can you get yourself on a airplane?'

The notion was ludicrous enough I almost laughed. 'Fly halfway across— You're out of your mind, Robinson.' Lizzie was talking to one of the sub-editors, smiling, some papers in her hand. She hadn't noticed me looking at her. 'If you're holding some kind of grudge—'

'I ain't holding no grudge, the hell are you talking about? Is that how you think on me?'

'Then what's this about?'

He was quiet for a moment. Then he said, 'This about dead girls keep turning up. Unfinished business.'

The hairs on my neck stood up. There was a buzzing sound

in my ears like an off-frequency radio. 'Texarkana is in the past. I don't want anything to do with it. It's over.'

'Not from where I'm standing.'

I looked down at the desk, saw I'd scribbled *Hot Springs, AR* on the scrap of paper in front of me. I turned it over and pushed it away. 'I don't want any part of your problems. I'm hanging up—'

'Hold up.'

I held a breath in my lungs, waiting for him to speak.

'Yates?'

Lizzie walked back to her desk at the front of the room and sat down. Something made me turn away from her. 'I'm here.'

'Do you still care?'

The line crackled and I said nothing. He took another drag on his cigarette, and when he spoke again, his voice was shaky. 'Look, Yates, I need your help. Please. I made a mistake and ain't no one else I can turn to.'

It was a glimpse of the real Robinson, the scared man underneath the braggadocio. 'Help with what?'

'To stop this.'

'Stop what?'

'Goddammit, I can't explain it on the telephone. I got a trunkful of evidence you need to see. Three dead girls, more on the way if I'm right. Get yourself here and I'll lay it all out for you.'

I scratched at the indentations on the desk. 'Why come to me?'

There was a jittery silence and I wondered what he was thinking. Then he said, 'It was me you called from Winfield Callaway's house the night you blew Texarkana. Why'd you do that?'

I thought back to that day, six months before. Three corpses in the room with me, gunsmoke in the air, blood still trickling down the carved leg of the cabinet where Sheriff Bailey had gone down. A snatched telephone call to the man before I ran – a hope that Robinson would tell the story I couldn't. I closed my eyes and willed the memory away. 'Because I figured you'd do the right thing.'

'There's your answer.'

*

The cab passed through the outskirts of Hot Springs, and I saw shades of Texarkana all around me. The streets were dotted with white clapboard houses, captured in the dull glow of their yellow porch lights. Most were two or three storeys high, with pitched roofs and tall, thin windows. Every so often we passed a Baptist church, recognisable by the white steeple – the type I'd seen all around Texarkana. It felt like I'd travelled back there and the nightmare was starting all over again.

Then everything changed. We turned onto a four-lane boulevard, bookended by two immense buildings at its northern end and one at the south, and lined with magnolia trees planted at precise intervals. Pedestrians filled the broad sidewalks, and motor vehicles streamed up and down the street. To my right, set back from the road, stood a row of ornate buildings, the architecture a mix of different classic and colonial revival styles. One sported Italianate cornices and friezes, another Spanish Mission-style arched windows and terracotta detailing. I saw domes and decorative towers. All were fronted by elaborate entranceways set in landscaped gardens. The street

9

sign said Central Avenue, but the driver said this stretch of it was called Bathhouse Row – the grand buildings we were passing being the bathhouses of the name.

Even so, my eyes were quickly drawn to the other side of the street. Ritzy-looking clubs with neon signs and striped awnings stood on every block, patrons in eveningwear, some even dinner suits, filing in and out. I read the names as we passed: the Southern Club, the Ohio Club, the Indiana Club. The scene was like something out of a twenties flick.

The cab driver watched me in his rearview. 'You a gambling man, sir?' He gestured to the row of nightspots. 'Any of these places happily take your money.'

'Not really.'

'Just need to find your game is all. Slots, dice, cards, anything you want.'

I touched the window glass. 'I've had enough trouble with the law.'

'Law won't trouble you none. Anything goes here.'

'It's legal?'

'May as well be. Ladies too, you want them. Right upstairs.'

I looked up at the windows above the clubs. 'I have a wife.'

'That won't offend them none.'

I fixed his eyes in the mirror. 'Not for me.'

'Just telling you how it is, sir. This here's The City Without A Lid.' He blazed the rearview with a crooked smile as he said it, proud of the moniker.

A backwoods town full of gamblers and prostitutes – like something out of the Old West, but with fancy architecture and neon signs. I wondered what the hell could have brought Robinson here. Figured, again, I'd loused up by coming.

For four days after Robinson's call, I'd done my best to lay it aside. Told myself he was a drunk and what he was asking was crazy. It'd worked at first, or so I thought, but his words took root in my mind and gnawed at me; they came to me in my dreams at night, and were still with me when I woke in the morning. *Dead girls. Unfinished business. The right thing.*

The more they stuck with me, the more I'd railed against doing what he asked. I came up with explanations for his true motivations: that he was playing me somehow, or worse, baiting me into a trap. Hot Springs was no distance from Texarkana; I'd made enemies there and, at a stretch, I could see Robinson having made a deal with them to lure me back.

As much as I tried, I couldn't make those notions stick. For all his faults, Robinson wore his heart on his sleeve, and I didn't think him capable of masking his intentions that way. His plea had struck me as earnest, and in the end I came to believe he needed my help.

When I'd stripped the rest of it away, all that was left was cowardice. Same as always. The thought of going to a place so close to Texarkana terrified me, and once I'd recognised what was holding me back, I had no choice but to go. I was done with letting fear dictate my course.

I'd first talked to Lizzie three days ago. I'd said nothing before then because I saw no point in troubling her with it when I'd dismissed the whole stupid notion from the get-go. It hurt to tell her what I was intending, just as she was starting to see a future that wouldn't always be tainted with darkness.

Lizzie had kept her own counsel while I talked, letting me

tell it at my pace. The telephone call. Going back on my decision. My reservations. My fear. When I was through, she'd said I was crazy.

'If he's in trouble, you don't have to be the one to ride to the rescue.'

'It's more complicated than that. You remember what he was like, he's not the kind to ask for help for himself. He talked about girls turning up dead, evidence to show me.'

'And that's enough for you to come running?'

'Listen to what he's saying.' I stood up, rubbing the back of my neck. 'What if it's connected?'

Her eyes were locked on mine. 'Connected to what?'

'To Texarkana. That was the implication. Why else would he come to me?'

She turned away, and I caught her glance at the picture of Alice. 'We're here now. That's behind us.'

I recalled the way the newspapers had reported on the killings after the fact – Richard Davis as the lone crazy, responsible for all the murders. No mention of Winfield Callaway or Sheriff Bailey's involvement, or their past crimes; the cover-up in place. Their deaths were written up as being the result of a robbery gone bad. No connection was made between the two happenings. I never knew if Robinson went to Callaway's house that morning. Someone in Texarkana had to have orchestrated the lies that came after, and it was alarming to question now whether Robinson had ever tried to piece together the truth – or if he'd gone along willingly with the fabrications. 'Doesn't mean it's over.'

'Then that just speaks to the risk you're taking. They have long memories over there—'

'I'm not going to Texarkana. It's not the same thing.'

'You just said it's connected.' She watched me, waiting for me to say something.

'I said it could be—' She gave me a hard stare that stopped me trying to back away from my own words. 'Look, I know there's a risk,' I said. 'But it's a small one—'

'And still you're willing to go? Everything we've built here . . .'

'It doesn't have to change any of that. I'll be back in a few days.'

'You can't know that.'

I walked into the dinette, Lizzie following after me. 'Whatever's going on there, I can't just stand by if people are dying.'

'How do you know you can trust him? You know what that man did, he's a liar and—' She cut herself off, her emotions starting to bubble over. She smoothed her skirt, buying a moment to compose herself, then took my face in her hands and kissed me. 'Don't go.'

I hugged her, held her body against mine because I couldn't bring myself to look her in the eye. 'I have to.'

*

Coming to the end of Bathhouse Row, I asked the cab driver where I could find a public telephone. He veered across two lanes and drew up in front of one of the giant buildings at the north end of the street – a hotel he called the Arlington – and said there were kiosks off the lobby. I stepped out of the car and looked up at the two towers atop the hotel above me, stretching into the night sky like battlements. There was a staircase leading up to the main entrance. I climbed it and went inside.

The interior was as grand as the exterior, all art deco elegance: pastel walls jazzed up with colourful murals depicting some kind of jungle scene; chandeliers and rotating fans that dropped miles from the high, domed ceiling; sweeping staircases with wrought-iron balustrades that led to a mezzanine lounge.

I crossed the lobby and found the telephones, pulled out the number Robinson had given me, and dialled. Strange: the operator came back to say she couldn't connect me because the line was dead. I asked her to try again, but got the same result.

I ran my hand over my face and checked my watch. Close to eleven, Central Time. Fourteen hours since I left home. Dog-tired.

Robinson had promised to fix me up with a room, but he never told me where. We'd spoken only twice, and he'd been cagey both times. The first call had ended with him reeling off a number to contact him at, and telling me to be sure to ask for Jimmy – no surname. *'That's how they know me here.'* The second time we spoke was when I'd called to tell him that I'd agree to come. That was when he'd promised to arrange lodging for me. He'd been adamant it wasn't safe for me to stay in the same place as him, and refused to tell me where he was at. I'd chalked all of it up to his paranoia, and now I was kicking myself for playing his games. I went back outside into the night and asked the cab driver to take me to a motel; somewhere away from all the neon.

*

The Mountain Motor Court was a mile north of downtown, a horseshoe-shaped building around a gravel and dirt parking lot. There must have been twenty rooms, but only three were occupied, judging by the cars in the lot. I went into the proprietor's office and paid for two nights. I asked him if there was a telephone I could use, but he shook his head, said they'd take messages for me but that they didn't allow guests to make calls on their line. I went out to pay the cab driver and asked him to pick me up at seven the next morning.

My room was at the far end of the parking lot. It was dark inside even with all the lamps turned on, the pine board walls stained a rich brown. There was a wooden chair tucked into a table, two beds, and not much else in the way of furniture. The carpet was olive green – a reminder of home. Bare as it was, it was clean and warm. I walked to the window at the back and cracked the drapes; it looked out onto dense pinewoods, hard to make anything out in the haunting darkness of the trees. I went to the bathroom to wash my face, then I lay down on the nearest bed and thought of Lizzie. For just a moment, the chatter of the katydids outside sounded like the ocean on a calm night.

*

Hunger woke me at six the next morning. I realised I hadn't eaten since the layover in Dallas the day before. The small breakfast room next to the motel office had warm biscuits and bad coffee, and I tucked into both before the cab showed up to collect me.

We drove back to downtown and the driver dropped me

just along from the Arlington. Daylight stripped Central Avenue of its air of neon vice, and the grand bathhouses looked picturesque in near-silhouette, a watery sun rising behind the mountain that backstopped them. The magnolia trees along the street were verdant in the morning light.

I went inside the hotel and tried Robinson's number again, but the line was still dead. I asked the operator what address it connected to; I took it down when she gave it to me, then went back to the car and handed the scrap of paper to the driver.

'This where your friend is staying?'

'I think so. You know the place?'

He turned in his seat to face me. 'Sure, this here a bar and boarding house, name of Duke's. You spoken to your friend the last day or more?'

I was reaching to pull the door shut. Something in his voice made me stop. 'No, why?'

He cupped his hand over his mouth before he spoke. 'This place burned down three nights ago.'

CHAPTER TWO

Robinson's boarding house was a half-dozen blocks away down Central Avenue – *'near the black section'*. The driver talked as we drove, but his words offered no reassurance.

'Fire started in one of the rooms upstairs. Believe a man died – what I heard.'

'You know his name?'

'No, sir.'

'What about a description?'

He looked at me in the rearview, shaking his head. 'Sorry.'

Questions came to me all at once. 'Are the cops involved? How'd it start?'

'Way it was told to me, was supposed to be an accident, but I don't know no more than that.' He glanced back at me, said, 'Could be it wasn't your friend.'

I looked out the window and said nothing.

We pulled up at the address a minute later and I jumped out. Duke's ran to three storeys, the bottom floor occupied by a saloon. The windows on the second floor were boarded up, the brickwork around them blackened where the flames had licked at it. The front door was ajar.

Inside, the smell of smoke was overpowering; the floor and furniture were covered in wet ash and soot, and the ceiling was scorched and cracked from the heat above. Grey water stains ran down the walls, but the mirrored backbar was still standing, liquor bottles intact. It seemed the fire had been mostly contained upstairs.

A man in filthy overalls was sweeping wet ash into a pile in one corner of the room. I called out to him from the doorway. 'This your place, friend?'

He glanced over but didn't stop sweeping. 'What's left of it.'

I picked through the debris halfway to him, coming to a stop by the bar. 'I'm looking for someone – Jimmy Robinson.'

'Ain't know no Robinson. You mean Jimmy Clark?'

I frowned, then remembered Robinson telling me to ask for him by his first name only, and I wondered if he'd given a false surname. I described him briefly, and the man stilled his broom.

'That's him. He a friend of yours or the like?'

I nodded, the truthful answer too complicated to broach. 'Yes.'

He looked over to me again, meeting my eyes this time before he looked away. 'I'm sorry to be the one has to tell you this, but Jimmy passed in the fire.'

I steadied myself on the bar rail, my thoughts thrown into chaos. 'Goddammit—'

I felt a twitch in my stomach telling me to run, to wheel around and get as far away from Hot Springs as I could. Go back to California, to Lizzie and the *Journal* and a safe life. But the feeling was cut with guilt – a sense that things could have worked out different if I'd been as quick to act in the first place. That maybe Robinson would still be alive if I'd come sooner.

The man leaned his broom against the wall and went behind the bar. He produced two cups that looked clean enough, turned and poured coffee into each. He spooned three sugars into one and handed it to me. 'Here, you come over pale.' I pulled some money from my pocket but he pushed my hand away. 'On me.'

I nodded and gulped down two mouthfuls. Even given the hour, I wanted something stronger. 'What the hell happened?'

He held his drink with both hands, staring at it. He wore a rough denim shirt, unbuttoned at the collar, and the sleeves rolled back. His hair was black and unkempt, greying around the temples. There was a tattoo on his forearm, just above his wrist – a small heart with a word across it too faded to make out. 'There ain't too much I can tell you. Fire started sometime overnight Tuesday. Jimmy – he was drinking down here like always, and when I closed up for the night he took himself up to his room. Had a half a bottle of bonded with him – but it ain't like he never done that before. They suppose he passed out with a cigarette in his hand, dropped it, and that's what set the fire.' He took a sip, his mug now dirtied by soot-blackened fingers. 'That's what the fire department told me, anyhow. They said the smoke would've done for him before he would've come round.'

I reached a hand to my throat. The taste of smoke seemed to coat my tongue and the inside of my mouth. I saw Robinson lying on his bed suffocating, never having a chance to escape, never even knowing. It seemed impossible that I'd spoken to him only days ago. I closed my eyes to shut it all out. When I opened them again, the man was watching me.

'How long was he staying here?' I said.

'Going on three weeks.'

'You have any idea what he was doing?'

It was a direct question too many, and the man straightened.

'You a friend of Jimmy's you said?'

'A friend, yeah. He asked me to meet him here, I came in from California last night.' I offered my hand. 'Name's Yates.'

He hesitated before he shook it. 'Clay Tucker.'

I waited, my last question hanging there.

He took another mouthful of coffee, trying to see out the silence, but he gave up when he realised I'd wait all day. 'Didn't much concern myself with his business.'

I glanced around the bar, taking in the damage; water was still dripping from the ceiling in one spot. 'Did he associate with anyone while he was here in town? Is there someone else I could ask?'

He splayed his fingers on the bar surface. 'No one I know of. Kept to himself pretty much. Don't mean this as a slur, but he wasn't the sort to invite conversation.'

It sounded like he was brushing me off, but I couldn't tell if it was just cussedness at not wanting to talk to me. I drained the rest of my coffee; my mind was racing, casting around for any kind of footing. 'Can I take a look at his room?'

He shook his head. 'They had it boarded up, and the staircase ain't safe. What you want to do that for, anyhow?'

I still hadn't marshalled my thoughts enough to give him an answer. 'Was anyone else hurt in the fire?'

He set his cup down, shaking his head. 'No – and it's a god-damn miracle. Wasn't no one else staying here, praise Jesus.'

I got up to leave, a nasty feeling prickling in my gut. 'Sorry about your bar.'

'Not as damn sorry as I am.'

I caught the edge to his voice and turned back to him. But instead of anger, his face was drawn with regret, and he was staring at the wall behind me. His eyes darted back to mine. 'Look, you might could try the diner a couple blocks down.' He pointed to indicate which way. 'Jimmy went there most mornings. Maybe . . . I don't know.'

I nodded in acknowledgement and made for the door.

*

I wanted to go back to the Arlingon Hotel – call Lizzie, tell her I'd be coming home. She'd be relieved, and I wanted to hear it – a measure of comfort in a town that felt even more hostile and isolated now than it had an hour earlier.

I started walking, but the sense of unease inside me festered. I felt bad for Robinson. Most of the time I'd known him in Texarkana, I'd wanted to knock him on his ass, but by the end I'd come to understand that it was fear made him the way he was. He didn't deserve to die like that – alone in a strange town, in a room above a dive bar, suffocating on black smoke. Maybe no one gets what they deserve in this life.

I looked up and saw the diner Tucker had mentioned was a few yards along from me. The lot between it and me was vacant, had been flattened and cleared to use as a makeshift parking lot; without thinking, I started making my way across it, weaving between the automobiles towards the entrance.

The smell of grease and eggs hit me as soon as I walked inside. The counter stools were full so I went to the chipped service hatch and hooked the counterman. I forked over a dollar and dropped the name *Jimmy Clark* on him. Blank look. I tried *Robinson* then too, but got the same empty stare. When I described him, though, the man nodded his head.

'I think I know the fellow. Keeps him some strange hours.'

His use of the present tense jarred. 'What do you mean?'

'Comes in all times of the day and night. I see him here at four in the morning some days, and back again at seven for coffee. Other times it's the middle of the afternoon before he shows up, or not at all. Never eats a bite, always black coffee.'

'You ever talk to him?'

The man crumpled his face. 'Some folk ain't much for talking. I got him pegged for a gambler, way he lives. What you want him for?'

My mouth curled down, sensing I was at a dead end, no appetite for re-hashing the details of Robinson's death with another stranger. 'He ever come in with anyone else? Or talk to any of your waitresses? The other customers?'

'No, no, nothing like that. Keeps to his own self.'

'Just drinks his coffee.'

The man nodded along. 'Always got a pen in his hand, scribbling away. I thought as likely he was keeping a ledger. What he won and lost – all the serious ones do that.'

'Gamblers.' I said it under my breath; it was as good as any description of the man I'd known.

'What's your name, fellow? I'll remember you to him next time he's in.'

I saw Jimmy surrounded by flames. Lifeless. 'Don't trouble yourself.'

'You want me to pass him a message for you at least?'

I stepped away from the counter to leave, but something made me stop and go back. 'Yeah. Tell him I'm sorry I was late.'

*

Double-timing it back to the Arlington, I followed Central Avenue north, passing a parade of seedy hotels, dime-cigar stores and liquor holes. After a few minutes walking, Bathhouse Row came in sight and I started noticing electioneering posters affixed to the utility poles, urging support for the 'GI Ticket' in the upcoming election. I got the gist quick enough – they were a band of war veterans that were running for office on an anti-corruption platform. I wondered what chance they had in a town that set the bar as low as this.

I kept going, battling my own thoughts. Part of my brain saw motive in everything. If Robinson was investigating a spate of murders like he told me, then it stood to reason there was a party out there with reason to want him stopped. And that was without giving consideration to the trail of blood that led all the way back to Texarkana. I thought again about having tipped him to the slaughter at Winfield Callaway's house the morning I'd left town. If he'd gone out there and saw what happened, the knowledge made him a danger to whoever was telling the lies that followed. And that was true whether he was complicit in the cover-up or not.

I told myself to pull back the reins. It was no more than an hour since I'd learned of his death, and already I'd come up with two theories for why it wasn't an accident. I thought about it another way. Could be my first instincts were right – that Robinson was working against me and had brought me here on behalf of whoever was calling his tune. If that was the case, maybe the fire was just what it seemed – a nasty accident that played in my favour and saved me from the trap. If that was so, the smart thing to do was to hightail it back to California.

Still, I was torn. My gut said Robinson wouldn't set me up

like that. And besides, if that was his aim, it meant the timing of the fire that killed him was a coincidence – and I always had a hard time with coincidences. And that was to say nothing of all the clandestine bullshit he'd been pulling – the fake name, hiding from me, all of it.

By the time I reached the Arlington, the doubt was nagging at me bad. I decided to make a different call first – to Sid Hansen, one of the sub-editors I'd known at the *Texarkana Chronicle*, to get the skinny on Robinson's recent past. It was a risk having anyone in Texarkana know I was back in Arkansas, but given the situation, it felt like a shortcut worth taking.

The operator couldn't get a circuit to the *Chronicle* at first, so I waited in the booth, looking around the grand lobby of the hotel. The centre of the room was filled with guests taking breakfast, most every table occupied. I looked from one to the next, seeing sharp suits and gleaming shoes – money in every seat. As my eyes flitted around the scene, three men passed through, heading towards the street. The one in the middle caught my eye – something familiar about him. He was short and slightly built, wearing a newsboy cap that partly obscured his face, and a suit that was cut baggy. I couldn't put a make on him, and he went out the doors before I could get a better look. I wondered if it was a face I knew from Texarkana. The thought made my pulse trip.

I was still staring towards the exit when the operator called back. I waited for the connection, and then Hansen's voice came on strong over the newsroom hum.

'*Chronicle*, Sid Hansen.'

'It's Charlie Yates, Sid.'

He gave a little whistle. 'Not a voice I was expecting to

24

hear from again. The operator said this call's coming from Hot Springs – the hell are you doing there?'

Seemed like he didn't know that's where Robinson had been. 'I came to meet Jimmy Robinson. He told me he was working a story here and needed my help.'

'Jimmy? What story?'

'That's what I was hoping you could tell me.'

He grunted. 'Beats me. Jimmy took off a few weeks back. Said he had family business needed taking care of. I ain't heard from him since. You best tell him the bosses are fixing to serve him his papers— Wait, why ain't he told you all this?'

I took a breath. 'Sid, Jimmy's dead. The room he was staying in caught fire three nights ago, before I got here. I'm sorry.'

He started to say something, couldn't get anything out. Finally he said, 'A fire? You mean like an accident?'

'That's what they're saying here. Passed out and dropped his cigarette.'

'What? Why the hell ain't no one called?'

'I don't know.'

'What about the police? The coroner . . .' His voice broke.

I said nothing, but his question made me think. The saloon owner, Tucker, would have identified him to the authorities as Jimmy Clark – but what about his papers? Robinson must have carried some identification with him. Unless the fire claimed it all. 'I'm sorry, Sid. Truly.'

He sighed and said something that sounded like *goddammit, Jimmy*, under his breath, then fell silent. When he spoke again at last, his voice was fractured. 'Where's his body at? What condition?'

'I don't know, I just found out an hour ago. First thing I did was call you.' I waited, hearing voices in the background on his end, then said, 'I don't like the way it looks – that's why I'm calling. You have any clue what made him come here like that?'

'What do you mean *the way it looks*?'

'The whole picture is off. Him coming here, calling me out of the blue, the fire. I just want to be sure.'

He lowered his voice. 'What are you saying, goddammit? You think someone killed him?'

'Hold on, I'm not saying anything right now; I'm just asking questions. Same thing Jimmy would do in my shoes.'

'Ain't my recollection that you two were friends. You got no right to talk like you know what he'd do.'

The rebuke stung because it was true. 'I didn't mean anything by it.' I had my hand up, as if he could see me motioning for him to take it easy. 'I'm just saying I owe it to Jimmy to figure out what happened.' I paused, in my head weighing how much was safe to tell him, not knowing whose ears my words might reach. Suddenly Texarkana felt a lot closer; I didn't mention the dead girls Robinson had spoken about. 'What about before he left? You know what he was working on the last few months?'

'The hell should I know?' He thought about it, maybe taking a second to simmer down. 'I ain't know of him doing anything out of the ordinary until he upped and went. He filed everything late, but that was just Jimmy.' He started talking slower again, the first wave of shock passing. 'I'll speak to some people here, see if anyone knows different.'

'I appreciate it.' I was about to tell him where I was staying, then thought better of it. 'I'll call again in a day or two.' I rubbed my hand over my face and a different image of Robin-

26

son came to me – that stupid grin he wore like a mask. It felt like Hansen and me were the only people knew or cared he was dead, and it didn't sit right. 'Sid, did he have any family? I never asked him about that before.'

His voice was hollow, distracted, like he was already making memorial arrangements in his mind. 'Not much of a one. His folks died years ago, and he ain't got no brothers. Got a sister somewhere near Wichita, Kansas – I thought that's where he'd went.'

'You think maybe someone should call to let her know?'

He took a long breath. 'I'll find out her number and see if I can get a hold of her.'

'If you speak to her, would you give her my condolences?'

'Yeah. I can do that for you.'

I thanked him and told him I'd be in touch. I placed the receiver back in its cradle. At my remove, it felt as though his reaction was a genuine one. At the same time, that didn't mean he wouldn't be straight on the line to whoever might care to know Charlie Yates's whereabouts.

I looked at my watch, realised it was still too early in California to call Lizzie – and that I wasn't certain what I was going to say to her any more. I found an empty table near the bar and ordered a cup of coffee, watching the waiters in their black bowties and high-collared white shirts buzzing between tables. My mind jumped back to Clay Tucker earlier that morning. His version of what happened was spare – especially concerning Robinson's movements and who he'd been talking to. Good lies are peppered with enough detail to give them credibility, so either Tucker really didn't know anything, or he was a bad liar.

I sifted through what he'd said again and realised that in fact there were two details he'd let slip: that Robinson went to bed with a half-bottle of bonded the night of the fire, and that it wasn't unusual for him to do so. The only things he'd kicked loose, and they both helped buttress the idea that Robinson drank himself into a stupor, then started the fire that killed him.

A waiter placed my coffee in front of me, the clink of china meeting the wooden tabletop bringing me out of my thoughts. I took a sip, the coffee scalding hot and bitter, and made my mind up. If Robinson's death was somehow linked to Texarkana, then I was putting myself in danger by staying here. But it also meant I couldn't just let it go on. I gave myself forty-eight hours to get a lead on what Robinson was doing, and what really happened to him. If I had nothing after that, I'd catch the first flight out of there.

CHAPTER THREE

The sun was still climbing when I left the Arlington, and the morning was fresh. It was at odds with how I felt. Opposite the hotel was an art deco skyscraper, the inscription above the door naming it the Medical Arts Building. Most of the structure was still in shade, but the highest floors caught the sunlight, and the yellow-brown bricks glowed almost white in the glare.

I flagged a cab to the Hot Springs Police Department. I checked my wallet as we rode, aware that I was running short of cash. The *Journal* gig paid well enough, but nothing like the *Examiner* had in New York, and the cost of flying to Arkansas had drained my savings. I'd convinced Acheson to let me have a week off to attend to a personal matter out of state, and he agreed on the condition that he didn't have to pay me. I'd conceded the point so as to forestall too many questions. As I thought about it now, I realised I'd used the exact same pretence as Robinson to excuse my absence; I wondered if we were more alike than I realised and tried not to think that I might be following him down the same path.

*

The officer behind the receiving desk of Hot Springs PD was balding and had a moustache that covered most of his mouth. I told him I was looking for information about a friend who died in the fire at Duke's and he glanced up at me without lifting his head. He gestured to a pair of wooden chairs against the far wall, one missing its back, and told me to sit while he went to fetch someone. He came back a couple minutes later with a detective who introduced himself as Harlan Layfield.

'Charlie Yates. I'm here about the man died in the fire three nights ago.'

'So Browning said. I'm real sorry about that.'

I nodded. 'Do you happen to know what caused it?'

He linked his fingers together. 'There ain't a way to sugar coat it, so I apologise if this seems coarse. Seems the gentleman in question dropped a cigarette in his room – most likely when he fell asleep. What I understand, he was too incapacitated by liquor to wake up, and the smoke suffocated him.'

Corroborating stories. 'That's what the owner of the place told me. Are you investigating?'

'Fire department were on the scene right away, and their report states they satisfied that's what happened. That being the case, there's no call for us to get involved. You say you spoke to the owner?'

'Clay Tucker, yeah.'

'Well then, there's not a whole lot more I can tell you. Sorry.'

'So there are no suspicious circumstances, that's what you're saying?'

He tilted his head. 'That's right. Why, you know of something we should be aware of?'

I thought about the question, but had nothing of substance to say in response. 'No. I'm just not sure what my friend was doing here in town.'

'Most everyone comes here for the baths and the nightlife.'

'That doesn't sound like him.' I rubbed my neck, starting to wonder if I was paranoid, seeing cause and motive where there was only the hand of chance at work. 'Listen, are you investigating any murders right now?' His face changed when I said it, like I'd crossed a line. 'Reason I'm asking is my friend told me he was working a story about three girls that got killed. Figure the least I could do is pick it up for him.'

'You a reporter, Mr Yates?'

'That's right, same as Jimmy.'

'What outfit?'

'It's in California, you wouldn't have heard of it.'

He looked at me the way a dog sizes up a bone, deciding whether it's worth chewing on. 'Sir, this town's known for relaxation and recuperation, and we real careful to keep it that way. We maybe get two killings in Hot Springs in a bad year, and there ain't none on the books at the moment. I don't know what your friend was doing here, but he wasn't investigating any murders.'

I glanced to one side. 'Has anyone spoken to his family?'

'No, sir, they have not. We didn't know who all to contact. Clay Tucker gave us the deceased's name, but that was all he had. Any identification Mr Clark was carrying must have burned up in the fire, wasn't nothing we could find.' He produced a pencil and notebook. 'You have the name of a relative you could furnish me with?'

I gave him Hansen's name at the *Chronicle*. 'He'll be able to put you in touch with the family.'

'Obliged.'

Hearing the name *Clark* again tweaked me, and I realised

I'd overlooked something. 'So you haven't made a formal identification yet.'

Layfield looked at me like I was simple. 'Clay Tucker confirmed the room was occupied by Mr Clark at the time of the fire. That'll do it until we can bring his family down here to confirm it for the record.'

'I'd like to see the body. I can tell you for sure.'

'Procedure requires a family member—'

'I know that. But you want to take the risk of bussing in the wrong family? At least I can confirm it's the man you know as Jimmy Clark.'

He creased his forehead. 'The way you say that suggests you knew him by some other name.'

'Let me see him and we'll talk about it.'

He slipped his notebook back into his top pocket, then tilted his head to look at me. 'He was in rough shape when they found him . . .'

'I've been around the block.'

He thought about it for a beat, then shrugged. 'I'll meet you out front in five minutes.'

*

The Gresham Funeral Home was on Central, a couple blocks south of Bathhouse Row. The drive there only took a few minutes. Layfield parked out front, giving me the side-eye as he did. 'How'd you come to know Mr Clark?'

'We worked together one time.'

'In California?'

'Texarkana.'

He set the parking brake. 'And now he's brought you out here on account of these supposed dead girls.'

I nodded.

'But you don't have no names or nothing about them, that it?'

'That's it. He wanted to tell me about it in person. You're sure you can't think what it would pertain to?'

He shook his head and looked down at his hands. 'I ain't wanna talk ill of the dead, but he must have got his wires crossed somewhere along the way.' He popped his door and climbed out, and I did the same. He looked at me across the car roof. 'What you said before about his name – you care to elaborate yet?'

It felt like I was betraying Robinson's trust to tell it, but I weighed that against the confusion and false hope it could cause Robinson's sister when Layfield made the call to her. 'His name was Robinson. Jimmy Robinson. He was from Texarkana.'

He tipped his hat to signal thanks and led me across the sidewalk up to the entrance to the building. He was small for a cop – a full head shorter than me, and barely medium build. He took clipped steps as he walked, his jacket snagging on his holster with every pace. He must have called ahead because when he opened the door, the undertaker was waiting inside the small hallway.

He offered his hand and introduced himself as Mr Gresham. 'My condolences. I've prepared Mr Clark as best I can.'

Gresham led us through the home to a small room in the rear. The temperature was appreciably lower inside there, and the mortuary refrigerators droned like wasps. There was a

33

metal table in the centre of the room, a white sheet covering the body. Gresham positioned himself on the far side of it, but Layfield hung back by the doorway. The temperature dulled it, but the smell was unavoidable: burnt flesh and smoke. Or maybe it was in my mind. Gresham looked at me, holding the corners of the sheet, waiting; I nodded and he drew it back as far as the shoulders.

Any hope of a mix-up vanished. I swallowed hard and held it to stop my stomach from turning inside out. The skin on his face was blackened and charred, mottled in places with patches of pink and red. His teeth were strangely prominent, his lips shrivelled or burned away – a death grin that was a cruel reminder of the one he wore in life. His hair was all but gone. Despite the damage, I was in no doubt it was Robinson.

I looked away. Gresham replaced the sheet and I stepped outside and took three deep breaths, trying to purge my lungs. Layfield followed me out and came around so he was stood in front of me. 'Fire's always the worst. You want some water?'

I shook my head.

'Can I take it that's your man?'

'Yes.'

Layfield took his hat off and stared at his feet like he didn't know what else to say. I couldn't get the smell out of my nose and mouth. I felt the anger stirring inside me – the idea someone might have done that and skated on it. I looked back and nodded to Gresham and headed out through the building again, Layfield trailing behind me.

When we were back on the sidewalk, he said, 'You need a ride somewhere?'

I shook my head, still dazed.

'What's your plan now?'

I looked along the street, squinting. 'I don't know yet.'

He offered his hand. 'Well, you think of anything else you need, be sure to come by again.'

I took a look at his face and the offer seemed sincere. We shook and he walked back to his car.

I stood on the sidewalk, gasoline fumes dislodging the smell at last, trying to make sense of it all. *No murders on the books*, Layfield said – so what the hell was Robinson doing here? I wondered if his story had been a pack of lies; no dead girls, just a tale to bait me with. I remembered the familiar face I'd spotted in the lobby of the Arlington, the man in the newsboy cap – wondered if he was a part of it somehow. If I was in danger. I didn't want to believe it of Robinson.

Certain facts were at odds with that theory. There was no identification found in his room – no papers, no driver's licence, no press card. It was plausible that the fire could have claimed it all, but wasn't it just as likely Robinson had ditched it sometime beforehand? It jibed with him staying under a false name – trying to pass himself off as someone else. Why bother with all that just to get at me? The better explanation was that he was trying to hide from someone.

I ran that thread out some more, thought about his car. If they had it, the police would have been able to identify Robinson through his registration plate; the fact they still believed his name to be Clark indicated they hadn't located it yet. So either he'd travelled to Hot Springs by some other means – or he'd stashed his car somewhere away from Duke's. I thought about his frame of mind – paranoid, drunk, living under a false name in a flop above a bar – and it wasn't a stretch to imagine him wanting to keep his valuables somewhere safer. Somewhere like his car.

The trouble with that line of thought was that it also sounded like the kind of man who could conjure up a bunch of lies about dead women and maybe even delude himself into believing they were true.

Then his own words came back to me, and I saw something I'd missed. 'A trunkful of evidence' to show me: maybe not the exaggeration I'd taken it for, but instead a literal description. I let the notion play in my head a minute, and it felt solid. My blood was pounding through my veins now, a familiar sensation – the rush at having a lead to run down. As long as no one had beaten me to it.

*

The saloon bar was locked up when I got to Duke's, no sign of Tucker. I banged on the doors, rattling them in their frames, but the joint was still. The smell of smoke and damp was potent even on the outside, and I backed away.

There were cars parked all along the street, forty-five degrees to the kerb, a few of them black Fords similar to the one Robinson had driven when I was in Texarkana. I couldn't be sure if any of them were his – and that assuming he'd kept the same one. Duke's adjoined a drugstore on one side, but was separated from the building on the other by a narrow alley. I walked down it a little way to see if there was a parking lot out back, but it led all the way through to the next block. I stopped and put my hand on the side wall of Duke's, my finger tapping double-time against the redbrick, frustrated at stalling so soon.

The smell of the fire was masked there, overpowered by rotting food.

I hurried back around front and looked up and down the street again. There was a click in my mind as I did – couldn't say what prompted it. I set on going car to car, knew it would be futile, but felt I had to try. I made to start, but then I saw the sign on the diner down the street. The click became bells in my head, and suddenly I had an idea where Robinson had stashed it.

I ran down to the diner, and the parking lot next to it. Close enough to Duke's that he could get to it whenever he needed, hence the visits to the diner at all hours, but anonymous enough that no one would take notice of it. I scanned the lot, saw a dirty black Ford between five other cars in the middle row. It had an Arkansas plate, and the dashboard was buried under various pieces of detritus – newspapers, a soda bottle, a flattened cigarette carton. It was how I remembered Robinson's car. I went to the back of it and tried the trunk. Locked.

I circled around to the front of the car. One of the news-papers was a copy of the *Texarkana Chronicle*.

I glanced around, my heartbeat like a piledriver now. From outside the diner looked busy, but I was alone in the lot. I moved on instinct, adrenaline carrying me. I grabbed a rock, wrapped my jacket around my fist, and caved the passenger window. I popped the door latch and used my jacket to brush the broken glass into the footwell, then slid across the bench seat behind the wheel. I hit the ignition switch and took off.

*

I made one stop on the way out of Hot Springs – a hardware store close to the Oaklawn Race Track – then pushed on past the limits. Clear of the town, I kept going, following an empty rural road a good distance until I found a turnoff among the trees where I was confident I wouldn't be disturbed. I parked there. The crowbar I'd purchased at the store was next to me; I took it up and stepped out to go to the trunk.

I jammed the crowbar under the lid and wrenched, metal screeching on metal. My palms were clammy. I whispered under my breath, imploring the damn thing to give – and for my instinct to be right.

The lock snapped and the trunk lid came loose. I threw it open wide.

The inside was like a snapshot of Robinson's mind. It looked like it had been rifled, papers scattered everywhere, three overflowing notebooks laid among them – but his desk had been the same way in Texarkana. I snatched up one of the journals and sifted through it. At first glance it was impenetrable. Robinson used his own mix of shorthand and cursive, all of it a messy scrawl that was almost illegible. I recognised some of the entries as interview notes, dates and times recorded in the top corner. No names, only initials – cautious Jimmy protecting his sources. There were details cribbed from reports – newspaper or official, hard to tell. There were lists of things to do: *Quiz F. re. H*; *C.B. – AGAIN*. One item that jumped out: *Call C.Y.*

Read individually, none of the pages made sense, but I was getting the feeling there was truth in what he'd told me – and then came the clincher. A photograph fell from between the pages; it showed a young woman in a light-coloured print dress sitting at a table. She had dark, shoulder-length hair, pinned back from her face and tied with a ribbon just visible at the back. Her jaw was square and she wasn't smiling, but there was a hint of joy in her expression, as though she'd been told to keep a straight face and couldn't quite hold it. I flipped it over, found the note Robinson had written on the back – not his usual scribble but block capitals, obvious care taken over the lettering. It made my guts sink, the proof that what he'd told me was true:

THEY KILLED HER APRIL 8 1946
YOU OWE IT TO HER

CHAPTER FOUR

I used the crowbar to clear the remaining glass out of the passenger window. I had to keep my side rolled down to match it; the weather was just warm enough that it wouldn't look unusual. Robinson's papers were still in the trunk, but I kept the woman's photograph in my inside pocket. The attention he'd paid to making the note legible had me wondering if it was meant for my eyes. I'd never seen her before, so it seemed unlikely; best I could come up with was it was a reprimand to himself he didn't want to forget.

I raced back to the Mountain Motor Court and parked right by my room. It took two trips to get the contents of the trunk inside; I dumped it all on the floor, closed the drapes and then stood there looking at it.

Robinson's *evidence*. The dead women.

I set the notebooks to one side and started organising the heap of loose papers. I plucked sheets to read at random as I stacked them in two piles. Nothing made sense. I flipped through the books – pages and pages of scrawl. I skim-read for an hour. My eyes blurred. The little that was legible meant nothing without context or a place to start. Or Robinson to guide me.

A few sets of initials recurred, and I made a note: *J.R.* and *C.Y.* – easy enough to crack. Less obvious: *E.P.* and *N.G.* When I'd been through them all, I set the notebooks aside and rested my head against the wall. I had the sense the notebooks were summaries of what was contained on the loose papers, but it was only a hunch. I took the picture of the print-dress woman from my pocket and studied it. For some reason it brought Lizzie to mind, and I wanted her to be close. I wanted to call her, hear her voice, but I knew the relief wouldn't be there now when I did, because I couldn't tell her what she'd want to hear.

Only this instead: that I thought someone had murdered Robinson, and I couldn't come home until I knew for sure.

*

The photograph and its inscription were the closest I had to a lead. Next morning, I drove to the public library and sought out the archives. The paper serving the town was the *Hot Springs Recorder*; I pulled out every edition from April 8th to the end of that month and whizzed through each copy, looking for a picture of the dead woman, or at least a murder story. My hope for easy answers drained as I got to the bottom of the stack. My hands were grubby with ink, but I found nothing – no murders reported at all.

I remembered the cop, Layfield, telling me there were only two killings in Hot Springs in a bad year. If that was the case, I couldn't make sense of how this woman's murder didn't garner some ink.

Two murders a year – seemed a good chance he'd remember the woman in the picture therefore. But showing it to him would throw up all kinds of questions about where I got it from, and I had no easy answers for that.

Then I figured on a smarter way to come at matters.

The address for the *Hot Springs Recorder* located the paper just off Bathhouse Row. When I got there, I found a squat red-brick warehouse with offices at one end of the building. The other end was taken up by a loading bay, two flatbeds waiting half-inside of it, ready to roll out with the next edition. The *Recorder*'s premises took up a block on their own, and were overlooked by the towering building that marked the southern end of the main drag.

My press card got me into the newsroom as a professional courtesy. The receptionist wasn't sure what to do with me once she'd led me inside, eventually depositing me with an apology at the desk of a hack named Clyde Dinsmore. Dinsmore was tall and rangy when he stood, his arms hanging slack at his sides. I introduced myself and we shook hands. It was like shaking the branch on a sapling.

'I'm here to see about a friend of mine, died in the fire at Duke's the other night.'

'Sorry to hear that. What can I do for you?' He surprised me when he spoke, his mouth working a mile a minute, in the way smart people's sometimes did.

I described Robinson – giving his name as Clark – and asked if he'd come by the paper at all.

'Doesn't sound familiar. Hold on.' He called out to two of his colleagues and repeated the name and description; both men shook their heads. He turned back to face me. 'Not ringing any bells.'

'You hear any talk about someone sniffing around town? He had a way of making his presence known.'

'Bar talk you mean? Nope, nothing like that. What was he doing here?'

'On the level? That's what I'm trying to figure out. He told me he was investigating three murders, but I don't have any more details. The police tell me they've got nothing on the books right now.'

He was nodding along. 'Can't say anything springs to mind. Had a Garland County Sheriff killed here a few years back, that got a lot of play – no one was ever charged for it.' He looked to the man at the desk next to his. 'Sheriff Cooper was shot in 'forty-one, right?' The man nodded and Dinsmore turned back at me. 'Biggest story since I been working this rag.'

I shook my head. 'I think it's something more recent. To do with dead girls – my friend was talking about three dead girls.'

A woman popped up in front of Dinsmore and handed him two typewritten pages to read, then loitered by him, waiting for his approval. Dinsmore shook his head distractedly as he skimmed over the sheets, saying to me, 'Like the cops told you, nothing to report. Sorry.' He handed the papers back to the staffer and told her they were fine to run.

'Would you take a look at something for me?' I reached into my pocket for the photograph and held it up. 'Do you know who this woman is?' He took it from me, examining it. 'I think she was murdered. Back in April.'

He shook his head – slowly at first, then with certainty. 'No. I've never seen her before. Who is she?'

I took the picture back from him. 'That's what I'd like to know.'

'Sorry, Yates, but I've never seen the broad.'

I looked around the office, seeing white-grey walls and

pea-green linoleum on the floor, the desks arranged around a central bank of tall flatplanning tables like spokes on a wheel. 'What about the fire, anything about that come across your desk?'

'Not to sound like my needle's stuck, but nothing at all.' He tilted his head. 'What makes you ask?'

I spread my hands. 'I'm always suspicious. Comes with the job, right?'

He flashed a smile. 'Sometimes. Depends what deadline I'm working to.'

I mirrored it, irritated by his glibness, but trying to keep on terms with him. 'I hear that. But a man died – doesn't that warrant a cursory pass?'

'We ran it, sure. But the fire department report said it was an accident. That gets three hundred words on an inside page. Unless you know something I don't? In which case I'm all ears.'

I shook my head, nothing to tell beyond a hunch.

Dinsmore tapped his finger on his desktop. 'Now, I'll grant you the fire department were always going to call it that way.'

I focused on him again. 'How come?'

'With the election coming and all. The mayor's fighting for his life against these GI boys – last thing he needs is a suspicious death right before folk go to vote.'

'The mayor could make the fire department change their report?'

'Be ironic what with the corruption allegations they're tossing around, but why not? He's got a band of war heroes trying to kick him out of office, maybe even indict him if the prosecuting attorney has his way. Getting a little fire glossed over would be small potatoes – especially at a dive like Duke's.' He held his hand up. 'No offence.'

I waved it away. 'What are the corruption charges? He's done this kind of thing before?'

He screwed his face up. 'No, not so I know of, but he's never had cause like this before. But the corruption talk is just politics. It's easy to level at Teddy Coughlin because he's been mayor going on twenty years and the casinos and cathouses survive on his say-so. But they were here long before him – Hot Springs has always been a wide open town.' He reached for a mug on his desk and took a drink, holding it against his chest when he was done. 'Don't get me wrong, Coughlin takes his piece of the action, I'm sure, but that's the same in any town – you ever seen a mayor lives in a shack? Calling him out for allowing casinos is like calling the Pope out for allowing churches. Hell, it's what he campaigned on.'

'I hear you, but taking dirty money isn't the same as covering up a man's death. That's a different ballgame.'

'Is it? It's a word in someone's ear and a stroke of a pen. It's not as though I'm accusing him of starting the fire himself – it's just protecting his image. You think there's an elected official anywhere wouldn't do the same if they were losing their grip on office?'

I rubbed my face, thinking Coughlin sounded like a walking story. I'd want to pursue it if I was in Dinsmore's shoes, and I wondered why he wasn't more interested. Could be it was just a symptom of the sordid town he lived in. 'How could I find out if someone got the fire report changed? Who can I speak to – off the record?'

He laughed the idea off. 'Out-of-town reporter? No one's going to give you the time of day.' He saw my face, must have seen me tense my jaw, because he tried to make nice. 'Look, I'm just flapping my gums here. Chances are it went down just like they said. But I'll ask some discreet questions, let you know if I get a sniff of any scuttlebutt.'

'Think I could get a carbon of the report at least?'

He put his hands on his hips. 'Let me see what I can do. No promises.'

I nodded, held my hand out to shake.

He took it. 'You know there's a quid pro quo, right?'

I grunted, should have seen it coming. 'Try me.'

'You dig up anything suspicious about the fire or what your friend was working on, and it looks like a story, you give it to me. You're playing in my sandbox, after all.'

I nodded and let go of his hand. 'I'm not working a story here, this is strictly personal. I find something, you can have it.'

I thanked him for his time, but it struck me he was being disingenuous about his side of the deal. Dinsmore was the local; he'd have the inside track on any story to be had here. I wondered if what he really wanted was the opportunity to bury anything I turned up. Who knew what sources or connections he wanted to protect? He wouldn't be the first hack with a private agenda.

I turned to go, then thought to throw out one last pitch. 'Hey, Dinsmore, do the initials *E.P.* or *N.G.* mean anything to you at all?'

'In relation to what?'

'Anything. Names, maybe.'

He scratched the side of his face, considering it. 'No. Not a thing. What's it about?' I watched his expression but it was deadpan.

I shrugged like it wasn't important, then headed for the street. I didn't trust the man enough to tell him anything more.

*

I drove back to the Arlington, this time noticing Teddy Coughlin's election signs and posters. The mayor's bills took the form of a list of questions for his opponents to answer, most of them accusing the GI Ticket of pandering to the Negro vote. Bathhouse Row was busy now, droves of out-of-towners ogling the sights and crowding the sidewalks. I eyed the Ohio as I passed, figuring these clubs – and what they represented – had to be what the election fight was really about. Money and power, same as anywhere else. The Ohio's plain green awning was like a sun visor, hiding its face. Above it, bay windows protruded from the building, topped with an Ottoman half-dome. The architecture was an extravagant mishmash, and the opposite of how things would be in New York or Chicago. In either city, a gambling joint or brothel would do everything to keep a low profile; a place looking as garish as the Ohio would be raided inside of five minutes. But somehow the rules were different in Hot Springs. I thought about Robinson and what he might have got caught up in here; whether he'd stumbled into something without understanding how this town worked, and it'd got him killed.

I cut short thinking along those lines, the parallels to what I was doing too obvious.

I parked outside the Arlington and went inside to the telephone kiosks, deciding what I was going to tell Lizzie. Secrets and half-truths had destroyed my first marriage, so after

Texarkana, I'd made a promise to myself that I'd always be honest with her – even about the things I was ashamed of. Except this time, I had nothing to hide for my own benefit; at issue was how much I could tell her without making her worry.

I called her at work. One of the *Journal*'s subs answered and put Lizzie on the line; just hearing her speak gave me a lift.

'I'm glad you called. I was starting to think maybe you'd gotten sidetracked along the way.'

'No, I made it just fine. I was going to call yesterday but I got caught up in some things.'

'Is everything all right? Your voice – you sound tired.'

'Yeah, I'm swell, doll. It's—' She'd know if I was equivocating, so I came right out with it. 'Jimmy Robinson is dead.'

'What? How?'

'There was a fire in his lodgings before I got here. He didn't make it out.'

She said nothing at first and I could tell she was conflicted. She hated Robinson for the way he'd treated her sister, but she'd accepted his motivations when I told her the full story, and she knew his confession to me went some way to helping expose the truth in the end. More than that, she was too good a person to be vindictive. 'That's awful. Was he— Was it an accident?'

'That's what the fire department say.'

She let out a breath, sounded like relief. 'I'm sorry, Charlie. I know this trip was important to you.'

I pressed my hand against the side of the booth, the varnished wood tacky under my palm. 'I'm not convinced.'

She met it with silence, the way I knew she would. She was no fool, seeing through me right away.

'I can't prove it, but I think there's more to it.'

Her voice had acquired an edge when she spoke again. 'What do you mean?'

'I don't know yet.' I braced myself against the kiosk. I told her about the car and the papers in the trunk. I told her about the photograph. 'Far as I can tell, they're his case notes on the murders he was investigating.'

'I don't understand. How does that prove the fire wasn't an accident?'

'Instinct.' I closed my eyes, feeling the conversation getting away from me.

'That's all of it?' She sounded incredulous.

'No. I can't put it into words. Something's not right here. The evidence he's collected, the murders – what if Robinson got close to uncovering something and they killed him for it?'

'Who are you talking about when you say *they*?' Static came over the line. 'You're talking like—' She took a breath. 'You're talking like you're back in Texarkana.'

'Lizzie—'

'Please don't try to tell me that's not how you're thinking, Charlie. I can hear it in your voice.'

'I have to know.'

'Why? Why can't you just leave it in the past and walk away?'

'It's all too convenient. Robinson told me he made a mistake, and now he's dead in an accident? You don't buy that any more than I do.'

'I have no opinion on it, Charlie. I don't care. I just want my husband to come home safe.'

'If there's nothing going on here, then I'm in no danger.' I regretted saying it straightaway, not sure how I'd slipped into trying to checkmate her with logic. 'I'm sorry, I didn't mean to come off like that.'

She took a slow breath and I knew I'd hurt her – too proud to let it show any other way. 'Are you calling to tell me you're not coming home?'

'Two days. I'm taking two days to see what I can dig up. If I don't have anything by then, I'll come right back.' I felt disingenuous as I blurted it; yesterday's resolution, made redundant by what I'd found out since. Already playing games with the truth.

'On the strength of a hunch? You don't have to be the hero this time. You have nothing to prove.'

'I need you to know—'

'Charlie, you have nothing to prove to me.'

I started to say that I owed it to Robinson, but I clammed up because that wasn't it. I thought about why I was so determined to chase this, and I realised my wife had come to it long before I had: it was because of Texarkana. Because it was all connected; if not directly, then at least in how I saw myself. I'd nearly died six months ago trying to prove to myself I wasn't a coward; if I walked away now, how much of that was I giving back again? 'Nothing could stop me from coming home, remember that. I'll call you soon.'

I didn't hang up, wanting to hear her tell me she understood, or at least she wasn't mad. When she didn't say anything right away, I thought she was going to wait me out with the silent treatment, but instead, after a few seconds passed, she said, 'I love you, Charlie. Please be safe.'

CHAPTER FIVE

Clay Tucker told me Robinson had been in Hot Springs almost three weeks. What did he do in that time? Who did he talk to? And how did it relate to the woman in the photograph? Still wary of showing my hand to Layfield, I decided to go back to Duke's to press Tucker on those questions, certain he knew more than he was letting on.

When I got there, though, the doors were still locked and there was no sign of him. I looked along the street; aside from the diner where Robinson had stashed his car, it was a mix of bars, low-rent hotels and private residences. Not content to kick my heels, I started working along block-to-block, asking if anyone remembered Jimmy.

I had no photograph of him to show, and the only description I could give was sketchy – and months out of date. I flashed the picture of the woman in every joint I stopped in, but got bupkis on her – no signs of recognition at all. Most every establishment I went in had an upstairs parlour or rooms, offering gambling or girls.

I was almost to the end of the street when I hit on something. It was in a bar called the Keystone; the tender gave his name as Leke, and nodded along when I reeled off Robinson's description.

'Yeah, I know the man,' he said. 'Came by here on occasion.'

'You have a conversation with him ever?'

'Not worth a damn, he wasn't no talker. Besides, what he did say was fair bleak.'

'Are you thinking of something specific?'

The man leaned on his elbows over the bar top. 'I'd seen him around a couple weeks, and he'd been in before, so I asked him what all brought him to Hot Springs. Wasn't meaning to pry – most folk don't stay in town that long is all, couple days, so I was curious, you know?' He rubbed his nose with his knuckle. 'Anyhow, when I did, he put his glass down and said, *"I'm fixing to drink until it does for me."*

'I thought he was fooling, so I asked him why in the world he'd want to do that. He put a look on me would cut glass, and that's when I knew he weren't.' He pointed at his own eyes with two fingers, for emphasis. 'Said to me he'd seen too many bad things and he was through with it all. I told him to put the whiskey away, see how it looked in the morning, but he didn't look like he was listening. Tell by the smell of him he was liquored up already, so I let him alone after that. I thought maybe he was a veteran still getting his head turned up the right way.'

'When was this?'

He scratched his left cheek. 'Three, four days ago.'

I started to think about a timeline of Robinson's movements. 'Can you say which?'

'Today's Saturday?' he asked. I nodded. 'Then Tuesday, I think.'

'What time did you see him? Approximately?'

He closed one eye, thinking. 'It was light outside so I'd hazard at afternoon.'

Tuesday was the day of the fire. Robinson on a mid-afternoon drunk, supposedly talking suicidal, hours before he died in the blaze. A third possibility emerging: could Robinson have set the fire in his room on purpose?

I tried switching gears. 'You said you saw him around some. Ever see him talking with anyone?'

'So many questions, mister, must make you thirsty. You oughta take a drink to keep your throat oiled.'

I took his meaning and slipped a bill across the bar, asked for a coffee.

He folded it into his shirt pocket, placed a blue mug in front of me and poured. 'You say this fella died in the fire down at Duke's?'

'Yeah.'

'So what's behind all these questions? He owe you money?'

I tried the coffee. It was cold and stewed. 'Something like that.'

'Have to ask you to elaborate on that "something".'

'What's it to you?'

'Answer the question first.'

I pushed the coffee slowly to one side. 'He was a friend of mine. I want to know what he was doing here and what happened to him.'

'All right.' The bartender looked at me hard as if he was trying to make me confess something. Then he said, 'Reason I ask, I seen him with someone and I ain't of a mind to put a stranger onto her if I think you gonna bring trouble to her door.'

I leaned forward, my forearms on the bar. 'I didn't come in here shouting the odds, did I?'

He rose up to his full height, easily topping six feet. 'No, sir, you didn't. But now you been fair warned.'

'Noted.'

'All right. I was outside taking the liquor delivery, so this would be Monday. Saw your man coming down the street talking with Ella Borland, used to work around here. I only took notice because I know her a bit – he was just another face at the time. Wasn't till he came in here the next day I remembered it was him I seen her with.'

I had my notebook out and was scribbling the name. 'You know where I can find her?'

He pursed his lips and shook his head. 'Nope. You could try Clay Tucker. Owns Duke's, he might tell you. Maybe.'

'Why him?'

He looked at me as if I was being stupid. 'She used to work there.'

I knocked on the bar as a thank you. 'You know where I can find Tucker? He wasn't there a while ago.'

He shrugged. 'He ain't there, who knows?'

I took the photograph of the dead woman from my pocket. 'Any chance you can tell me who she is?'

He squinted, then shook his head. 'No one I know. What's it to you?'

'Forget it. Thanks for the pointer.'

*

I steamrolled back to Duke's determined to wait out Clay Tucker, feeling like he'd been playing games with me. I wondered if he knew about Robinson stepping out with this Borland woman and that's why I'd got the feeling he was holding out on me. I tried not to let anger take over, put myself in his shoes – I was a stranger asking questions about a dead man; why would he drag her name into it?

Turned out there was no call to wait on him. The saloon was open when I got there and Tucker was inside, pushing a broom again. He looked up when he saw me come in, startled, as though I'd caught him doing something he shouldn't.

'You back again,' he said, his tone flat.

'I'd appreciate five more minutes of your time. Couple things I forgot to ask you earlier on.'

'Look, I don't mean to be inhospitable, but I got my hands full here right now.' He gestured to the debris all around him. 'Don't know what else I can tell you.'

'The name *Ella Borland* familiar to you?'

He hesitated and it looked like he was thinking to say no, but then he got smart and said, 'Sure.'

'I heard tell my friend might have passed some time with her. I'd like to talk with her about it.'

He shrugged, pulled a face as though he didn't know what it had to do with him. He was more jittery than when I'd seen him earlier. 'What I told you before, about the diner. You try that place already?'

The change of subject didn't go unnoticed. 'Yes.'

'You find out anything?'

I shook my head. 'Turns out Jimmy drank a lot of coffee.'

He bulged his cheek with his tongue as he nodded along. 'Sorry about that.'

He wasn't, and the muscles in his face relaxed just enough to suggest relief.

'What about Ella Borland? I'd appreciate if you could tell me where I could find her.'

'Best I can do is tell you she used to live out by the water somewhere. But that was a time ago.'

'When she worked here?'

He blanched, obviously surprised I knew that part. He gave a small nod. 'Long time ago.'

I had a thought to grease him with a five spot, but remembered the state of my finances and decided to try another route. 'Why do I get the feeling you knew Jimmy was talking to this woman?'

'What?'

'Did you see them here together?'

'Why would you think that?' Tucker laid his broom against the wall and went behind the bar to pick up his coffee. I wondered if he just wanted to put the bar between us – or if he had a weapon stashed back there for protection.

'Because you coiled up like a spring soon as I mentioned her name.'

He eyed me as if he was deciding what to do, the tension in the room sparking now.

'I'm not here to cause anyone trouble,' I said. 'Tell me where I can find her and we can all go about our day.'

His hands dipped out of sight and I readied for him to come at me. But instead of reaching for a weapon, he braced himself on the counter under the bar and hung his head. 'Look, I seen them here together, so what? I didn't want to tell you nothing because I ain't one to put the bad word on a dead man.'

'How's that?'

I heard him drumming his fingers. 'Used to be them rooms upstairs was for a different purpose. Ella worked up there, back then – you catch my meaning?'

Robinson and a working girl. Maybe something, maybe nothing – but the only living lead I had. 'Yeah, I understand just fine. How can I talk to her?'

He looked up again now. 'I'm telling you straight, I don't know where she lives no more. Your friend brought her here one time, but I ain't seen her since.' He held his hands up in frustration. 'And to save you asking, I'll just tell you I ain't spoke to her when she was here.'

'Tell me how I find her. Give me a place to start.'

He sagged and I knew I had him on the run. 'You might could try Maxine at the Star-Vue Hotel.' He blew out a breath. 'That's as good as I can do. But don't tell her I sent you, right?'

'What does Maxine look like?'

'Brown hair, had it pinned up last time I saw her. Too much rouge.'

'Nothing more than that?'

He shrugged, spreading his hands.

A description that matched half the women in the state. I searched his face; his nerves were shot over something, and everything that came out of his mouth sounded like a lie – made him hard to read. 'All right.' I rubbed my nose, the smell bothering me again. 'Can you tell me when you saw Robinson and Borland together?'

'Yeah, I can tell you that. It was last weekend – Saturday night.'

I tried to get it all straight in my head. Last Thursday was when I'd first heard from Robinson. Saturday and Monday, he was seen with the Borland woman. I'd spoken to him again on the Monday afternoon, telling him I'd come to Hot Springs. He'd sounded relieved. Then by Tuesday he was supposedly talking about drinking himself to death in the Keystone bar, and hours later he was dead.

I couldn't get a fix on his state of mind. My first thought was could something bad have happened late Monday or sometime Tuesday? 'What about Tuesday, the night of the fire,' I said, 'you speak to Jimmy beforehand when he was down here drinking?'

He hooked a thumb behind the strap of his overall, edging back towards composure. 'We been over this.'

'Anything? Think about it.'

'Beyond "Howdy" and "What'll you have to drink?" not a damn thing.'

'He didn't say anything strange to you?'

'He didn't say nothing at all.'

'How was his mood?'

'Mister, you can ask me a hundred times and a hundred ways, but I can't tell you what I don't know. He sat here, he drank, and I ain't barely paid him no mind. Long as I see the president's picture on a bill, I keep the drinks coming and no more.' He turned his back and plunged his mug into a sink of water.

Robinson talking about taking his own life on the same day he died was troubling – but I couldn't imagine him doing it. And there were surer ways to take your own life than starting a fire. For his part, seemed like Clay Tucker wanted to wash his hands of the whole mess – but I couldn't decide whether he was holding anything more back.

I whipped the photograph from my pocket and held it up so he could see it in the mirror behind the backbar. 'You're going to tell me you don't know who she is, but I want you to think hard about it before you do. Take a real good look.'

He looked at it in the reflection, then turned and studied it up close. He shook his head. 'You already know what I'm'a say, so what you want me to tell you?'

'My friend was here three weeks. The way you talk, you'd think he was a ghost – never uttered a word, never left a mark. Floated through walls.'

'Case you ain't noticed, I had a lot on my mind.' He looked at the ceiling and ran his hand through his hair, leaving a greasy tuft standing. Then he shook his head, his eyes downcast as though he were reconsidering. He took the pen from his shirt pocket, held it out to me. 'Leave your particulars. I remember anything more, I'll be in touch.'

I ripped a scrap of paper from my notepad and scribbled my name and the name of the motel on it. I placed it on the counter, pinning it with my finger. 'You do that.'

I went out the door and walked a little way down the street, feeling uneasy about the whole conversation. My instincts made me double back. I peered through the window of Duke's, staying out of sight. The broom was on the floor now, as if it had been thrown there, and Clay Tucker was leaning on his elbows on the bar, rubbing his temples.

CHAPTER SIX

I set off looking for Maxine, desperate to track down the Borland woman through her. The Star-Vue Hotel was three blocks down, the neon sign out front advertising 'Entertainment and Fine Food', same as most all the other places around Duke's. I saw little evidence of it inside. *Entertainment* seemed to be the agreed-upon byword for what was offered in the upstairs rooms.

It was early evening when I walked in, and there was only a thin crowd inside. They looked young and, by their dress, local, the tourists keeping to the glitzy joints up on Bathhouse Row; this strip was for hometown drinkers and gamblers. I wondered if Robinson had managed to blend in here, or if he just thought he had. If he was making waves without realising it, he would have been an easy target – no protection in a false name.

The downstairs of the Star-Vue was little more than a dive bar, a cut below even Duke's. The bartender was a kid playing at being tough, the pockmarks on his face undermining the act.

'I'm looking for Maxine, know where I can find her?'

'Whores are upstairs.'

I held his gaze for a moment longer than he was comfortable with. 'Watch your mouth.'

The staircase was in the far corner of the room, climbing back towards the front of the building. I crossed over to it. At the top, a heavy in a threadbare suit and creased shirt stood in front of a black door. He wasn't trying hard to hide the bulge in the left breast of his suit coat – packing some kind of heat.

'Money up front, friend. Ten dollars.'

'I just want to talk. Looking for a girl named Maxine.'

'What you do through the door is your business. Whether you get through the door is mine. Ten bucks.'

I reached for my wallet and pulled out two fives, my cash reserves almost shot. The man handed me a poker chip with a Red Indian's head on it, and pulled the door open for me to step inside.

Through the doorway was a small waiting room decorated with red floral wallpaper and matching carpet that had once been plush. There were two couches set around a low coffee table. One was occupied by a man in a suit, his necktie pulled away from his collar, and he looked away when I entered. Two doors led off from the room. There were no women in sight.

I stayed standing and took a spot against the near wall, eyes moving between the doors, wondering if I should let myself in. I was still thinking on it when the one to my left opened, and a young woman in a silk dressing gown came out. She had brown hair, worn in victory rolls at the front and grazing her shoulders at the back. The man on the couch stood and handed over his poker chip without being asked – not new to this. She took him by the arm and led him towards the door.

I called out to her. 'Miss, I'm looking for Maxine . . .'

She carried on through the doorway, and as she closed it, said over her shoulder, 'Your turn next, hon.'

Then she was gone and I was alone in the room again. I couldn't tell from her appearance or reaction if she was Maxine. I already felt dirty from a night trawling through the gutter of Hot Springs, and now it felt like I'd slipped down the drain. It was getting on top of me, being in that room, and I thought about throwing doors open and kicking out the degenerates so I could talk to Maxine and get the hell away from there. The thought of the minder outside, and the piece inside his jacket, made me hold steady. My hand was in my pocket, turning the poker chip in circles.

Finally the other door opened and the John took his leave – red-faced, his collar unbuttoned and tie loosened. He didn't look at me as he passed. I stepped to the middle of the ante-chamber and waited for the woman inside to come out.

The woman appeared. She wore a thin lick of makeup on her face that looked like it had been slapped on in haste. I held out the poker chip. 'Maxine?'

She hesitated as she took it from me. 'You been here before, soldier? Don't remember your face.'

I shook my head. 'I just want to talk to you.'

Her eyes flicked to the main door, as if talking would bring the heavy outside down on her. Then she jutted her hip out, one hand on it, trying to look sassy again. 'Sure, we can start with some talk. Come on in.'

I followed her into the small room, hoping she'd be more likely to spill in the confines of whatever privacy it afforded. The flop was only just big enough to fit a bed and a small dressing table; it smelled of coupling and sweat, under a spritz of too-sweet perfume.

The woman reached past me when I didn't shut the door. 'You born in a barn?' She turned her back and started to take her robe off.

'Keep it on. Please.'

She turned to me again. 'Oh, right, talking. Look, it's your dime, but so you know, you gotta be out in fifteen minutes, or—'

'I'll be out in one. I'm looking for someone. Ella Borland.'

She stopped moving, hands clutching her robe over her shoulders. She studied my face, saying nothing, and I wondered what she was weighing up. The silence held a beat too long, then she turned it back on me. 'What do you want her for?'

I suddenly felt like Borland might be within my reach. 'A friend of mine spent some time with her. He died a few days ago, before I could get here. I wanted to talk to her about him.'

'You sure like your talking, huh?'

The line brought an unexpected smile to my face. 'Beats fighting.'

Maxine stepped over to the mirror on top of the dresser and examined her own reflection. She picked up a puff and powdered her cheeks with rouge. 'Sorry about your friend. How'd he die?'

I had the feeling like I was being tested, and a wrong answer would see me back at square one. 'In a fire.'

She put the powder down. 'That so? Had a fire not too far from here a few nights back.'

'That's where he died.'

'Huh.'

I stared at her reflection, her face filling the small mirror. It was obvious she was keeping some card close to her chest, so I said nothing, let her take the lead.

She turned around to face me again. 'Where you from, mister?'

63

'California. Los Angeles.'

'First time in Hot Springs?'

'Yes, ma'am.'

'Figures. You don't know how it goes here.'

I put my hands in my pockets. 'I'm starting to get the picture.'

She shook her head. 'I have my doubts about that.' She sat on the edge of the bed and chewed the nail on her little finger. 'You wouldn't be in here asking for Ella if you did. You know who she works for now?'

'I'm all ears.'

She gave a nervous laugh and shook her head. 'No, you look like a good sort, so I ain't about to do that to you.' She stood up, too close to me now in the cramped room, the scent of her perfume overpowering. 'Give me your number and I'll tell Ella you're looking for her. She decides she wants to talk to you, she'll holler.'

I ran my hand over my mouth. 'I appreciate it, but I'm short on time. If you could see your way to telling me where I can find her—'

'Mister, I'm looking out for you here. If I liked you less, I'd do exactly what you're asking.'

She was sure in her tone; it felt like the end of the road. I wrote my name on a piece of paper, along with that of the Mountain Motor Court. 'Ask her if she'd leave a message for me at the desk if I'm not there.'

She took it and slipped it in her clutch beside the dresser.

'Tell Miss Borland my friend's name was Jimmy. Tell her—' I froze up, blindsided by the image of Robinson in that room again. Except this time he was awake, flames all around him, the heat peeling the skin right from his face. He was screaming, the kind of terror only a man facing death knows. The Robinson I saw in my imagination was the one I'd uncovered only at the end in Texarkana – the scared man who'd been running from his fear too long but saw it catch him up anyway. In that moment, I was certain that he'd been trying to do some good here and that someone had killed him for it. I wanted to convey that scene to Maxine, get her to tell it to Ella Borland exactly as I saw it, an appeal to her better angels, but the words were bitter and mangled in my throat and made me feel like I was choking. I couldn't get them out.

'Mister?'

I stepped back from her, startled. 'Just ask her to call me. Please.'

She nodded. 'Sure, I'll ask.'

'There's one other thing.'

'There always is with your type.'

I took the photograph from my pocket. 'Do you happen to know this woman?'

She took it from me and frowned. 'She's a little plain Jane for my crowd. Sorry . . .' She handed it back, and when I took it, she reached for the button of my suit jacket, twisting it. 'I'll talk to Ella for you. It's not right what happened to that man.'

A vein in my wrist pulsed. 'What do you mean? It was an accident.'

'You wouldn't be here if you believed that.'

'If there's something you can tell me . . .'

'I don't know anything, I just got eyes and a brain. And even if I did have information, I wouldn't tell you. This isn't our town.'

'What do you mean by that?'

She let go of the button. 'Ella wants to speak to you, that's her choice.'

I stared at her a moment, weighing whether to push it, but all I saw was a girl with more bravado than experience. I turned to go.

She touched my arm. 'Mister – you already paid, don't you want to get your money's worth?'

I stopped and looked at her. She glanced to the door and back to me, a nervous look in her eyes, as though she'd be in trouble with the man outside if she let me go without disturbing the sheets. I shook my head, almost apologetic. 'That's not me, sister.'

CHAPTER SEVEN

It was past nine when I arrived back at the Mountain Motor Court that night – fourteen straight hours spent scrapping for information on Robinson, with little to show for it. I stopped at the office to check for a message from Ella Borland. It was too soon, but I did it anyway, got zip.

Back in my room, I took my suit off and laid it out on a chair, caught a whiff of cigarettes and liquor coming from it – like the lingering stink of a party I hadn't been invited to. I was weary, but my mind was still running hard. I sat on the floor in front of the uneven piles I'd made of Robinson's papers, and started to read. The material was as indecipherable as earlier, and frustration set in fast. My thoughts wandered – to Robinson, and what he'd been doing in Hot Springs, and how far I was willing to take his fight when I wasn't even certain what the cause was. I thought about the woman in the print dress, and how he came to be investigating her murder, and Ella Borland and what she might be able to tell me – if she made contact.

When all of that fell away, I was left with thoughts of Lizzie. I worried I'd already driven a wedge between us by coming here, and that notion scared me – the damage I might have done to my marriage, and for god only knew what reason. I'd promised to go home if I had nothing inside of forty-eight hours – but that was already out of the question. I worried how she'd react when I blew my own deadline, and I wanted to kick myself for making a promise I knew I couldn't keep.

I stared at the papers, the words mashing into one, and a new face came into my head – Maxine's. I remembered her offer before I'd left, about getting my money's worth, and the way it had made me pity her. I pictured her in that dingy room, so scared of whoever ran the joint as to be inured to selling her body to any man with enough coin. Hot Springs flaunted itself as a good-time town, a place anyone could get their kicks; that reputation came with a price, and it was exacted on young women like Maxine. From what I'd seen, it wasn't one worth paying.

I put the papers aside and went to the bathroom. As I touched the doorknob, I heard a noise outside. A scraping sound on the wall. I stopped still.

I looked to the back window, saw movement in the crack between the drapes. Sudden, like someone ducking out of sight. I glanced around the room, looking for a weapon – nothing. I darted over and pressed my face to the glass. To the right I saw a dark shape scrambling away through the trees. I felt my skin go drum-tight around my bones.

I hesitated, shallow breaths fogging on the pane. The shape disappeared from view and the thought of not knowing sparked me to action. I ran to the door and threw it open, then pelted all the way across the parking lot, jagged stones under my bare feet. I reached the street and looked left. There was a pickup parked on the verge two hundred yards away, its lights on. I started sprinting towards it. As I came nearer, I could make out a man on the driver's side. He glanced back, saw me, and leaned across to throw the passenger door open. When I was thirty yards away, a man stumbled out from the trees behind the motel, running from the direction of the back of my room. He threw himself into the pickup. The driver gunned the engine and the truck took off, slamming the door shut. I kept going, chasing, straining to get the plate, but in a second they were gone.

I stopped and doubled over, panting with my hands on my knees. My feet were ripped to shreds, the asphalt warm against my bare skin. I was in the middle of the road, everything around me shaking and still at the same time.

CHAPTER EIGHT

No sleep came. Nervous hours spent staring at the shadows on the ceiling, listening for noises outside, waiting for dawn.

When morning showed up, I got out of there early as I could and drove Robinson's car to the Arlington so I could call Clyde Dinsmore at the *Recorder* and pay too much for eggs and coffee. I got the food first; I had no appetite, but expected another long day. I tried to shut out the incident the night before and focus only on Robinson. It was easier said than done.

The hotel lobby was busy again, breakfast service in full swing. As I ate my food, my eyes set upon the table in the far corner, drawn by the racket the men around it were making. I watched the occupants. The table was in its own small section, on a platform that raised it a little above the others. There were five men, but I straightaway zeroed on one – the same man I'd seen the time before, strolling through the lobby. The same familiar face.

He was far enough away not to notice me looking. The other men wore suits, two of them smoking cigars, but he was sporting golf attire – a cream-coloured shirt and beige slacks, two-tone brogues on his feet. He was the only one not talking, instead buttering a piece of toast, glancing up to smile every now and then when one of the others cracked wise, It was a cautious smile, isolated from the rest of his expression. He seemed alert, although not on edge, regarding the other men the way a politician does at a fundraising drive.

I left my food half-finished and rounded the edge of the restaurant to get a better view, being careful not to be caught staring. I took up a spot near the bar that afforded me a good look at his face and tried hard to place it. I thought back to Texarkana, ran through lists of the people I'd encountered there – cops, reporters, victims. No one made the nut.

I buttonholed a passing bellhop.

'Sir?'

'Who's the gentleman at that raised table?' I indicated with my thumb.

'Do you mean Mr Tindall's table, sir?'

Tindall. The name and the face came back to me all at once. 'Tindall as in William Tindall?'

The bellman scratched his wrist. 'Yes, sir.'

I nodded to send him on his way, my eyes locked on the man now. William Tindall. Not from Texarkana. A name I knew from back in New York – one of the most powerful racketeers the city had known. A bootlegging kingpin from twenty years back, with an empire that had been rumoured to extend into real estate, boxing, breweries and numbers. His public face was boss of the Cotton Club – the Harlem nightspot that brought black jazz talent to white crowds. His reputation in the underworld was that of a vicious mobster who went by the handle 'Bill the Killer', who'd toughed-out ten years in Sing Sing on a manslaughter beef.

And now he was taking breakfast a few yards from me. In a town where gambling and prostitution flourished.

I closed my eyes, not sure what it all meant. Then I opened them again and stepped away from the bar, glancing back at

Tindall's table one more time. The man next to him had the attention of the group, animated, recounting a story of some kind and looking over at Tindall every few moments as if to check he was getting his approval. Tindall was stirring his drink with a spoon, paying the man just enough attention so as not to appear impolite.

I went to the telephone kiosks and called Dinsmore, on the pretext of chasing up the fire department report. I doubted he'd have it yet – and that assuming he hadn't just paid lip service to the request so as to get me off his back – but I wanted him to know I wasn't going away. I couldn't believe three murders could go unnoticed, even in a place like this, and I had the feeling he was snowing me.

Turned out it was a wasted nickel; Dinsmore hadn't made it to his desk yet, and his colleague didn't know what time he was expected. I held the receiver after I put it in the cradle, thinking about my next play. I called the desk at the Mountain Motor Court, eager to see if Ella Borland had made contact. The proprietor answered, but before I could say anything, he started asking about my plans.

'You fixing to check out tomorrow?'

I had a spare nickel in my hand, started tapping it against the telephone casing. Thoughts of money nagged at the back of my mind; the trip was going to leave me flat broke. 'I haven't decided yet. I'll come by the office later on and we'll straighten things out.'

He cleared his throat. 'All right. But if you want to stay on, each night is payable in advance. House rules.'

'I understand.' I closed my eyes, feeling as if the decision was going to be made for me. I had enough to pay my airfare back to California, but at this rate, I'd have to dip into that just to stay, and pride wouldn't let me call Acheson to ask for an advance on my salary. 'I was calling to see if you have any messages for me.'

'Yes, sir. Hold a minute till I find it.' There was a rustling sound as though he was shuffling papers around the desk. 'One for you, called just a few moments ago. Dame by the name of Borland. Didn't leave nothing but a telephone number—'

I snatched a pen out of my pocket. 'What is it, please?'

He read the number out to me and I thanked him and hung up. I slotted the nickel I had in my hand into the phone and dialled, pressing the receiver to my ear as if it would make her pick up faster.

Instead, a man answered. I could hear voices in the background – people in conversation. I asked for Ella Borland and the man didn't respond. It was a second or two before I realised he'd gone to get her.

Then a new voice came on the line.

'Ella Borland speaking.' Husky but soft. Her accent more Texas than Arkansas.

'Miss Borland, this is Charlie Yates. Thank you for returning my call.'

'Mr Yates . . . you sent me a message. Maxine told me. What is it you think I can do for you?'

'I think we know someone in common – Jimmy Clark.'

She hesitated. 'May I ask what this is about?'

'Jimmy died a few days ago, were you aware of that?'

Her tone hardened. 'What's the meaning of this?'

'I'm sorry, I didn't mean to come off blunt. Jimmy was a friend of mine, and I want to know what happened to him. I wondered if you could help me.'

'Are you a policeman, Mr Yates?'

'No, nothing like that, ma'am, I'm a reporter. We worked together some.'

'A reporter.' She said it to herself and then was silent a few
seconds. I couldn't get a read on what she was thinking. 'I heard
about Jimmy, it upset me a lot.'

'Can I ask how you came to know him?'

'We were acquaintances.' At first I thought she was going to
say something more, but she held her tongue.

'The reason I'm calling is I was hoping you could shed some
light on what he was doing here. Jimmy asked me to come to
Hot Springs to help him, but by the time I got here, he was
dead.'

'Oh, I'm— That's awful for you. I'm sorry, Mr Yates, truly.'
The emotion in her voice sounded genuine, but she was still
guarded.

'He only told me a few details about what he was working
on because he didn't want to discuss it over the telephone—'

'He was like that. Old fashioned.' For the first time, there
was a hint of fondness in her voice.

'So if there's anything you can tell me, I'd be in your debt.'

The line went quiet, and then she drew in a long breath.
Some kind of commotion kicked up across from me, the sound
of a plate smashing on the floor. I turned away from the din just
as she started to speak again.

'A friend of mine was killed some months back and
Jimmy—' Her voice trembled and she took a moment to compose herself. 'I'm sorry, it's still difficult for me to talk about
this. Jimmy was looking into it.'

My skin prickled – on the verge of something now. 'What was your friend's name, ma'am?'

'Jeanette Runnels. Jeannie.'

I scribbled it down awkwardly, pinning my notebook to the wall and writing with the same hand.

'Jimmy came to me some months ago and said he was writing a story about her. He wanted my help and I obliged, and we became friendly over the course of those conversations.'

'My condolences on your loss, ma'am. Both losses.' A rush of questions came to me, but I was mindful of not pushing so hard that I scared her away. 'Can I ask when you last saw Jimmy?'

She thought about it, then said, 'Monday, I think.'

'How did he seem to you?'

'You know what he was like – he could be up one minute and down the next. He was always that way.'

'Did he seem troubled at all?'

She gave a rueful laugh, no humour in it. 'Always. But no more so than usual.'

'Do you know if he had any enemies here? I know Jimmy could rub people wrong.'

'None that I know of. If you'll allow, why are you asking me this, Mr Yates?'

I thought about how to respond. 'I'm trying to know his frame of mind before he died.'

'Forgive me, but that sounds a little hollow.'

'Pardon me?'

'I was told his death was an accident, but unless I'm mistaken, you have doubts that it was.'

I kept my tone even, surprised at how perceptive she was. 'I have some questions I'd like answered, that's all. Would you

75

consider meeting with me in town? I don't want to cause you upset, but I'd like to ask you some more about Jimmy.'

'What kind of questions? Are you suggesting I was involved in his death?'

'What? No, not at all. That's not what I meant.' The thought had never occurred to me, but I wondered now if it should have. 'I have questions about whether the fire was an accident. Until I figure out how he spent his time here, I can't know if someone might've had cause to do him harm.' I dropped another coin in the slot. 'Please, ma'am.'

I heard her light a cigarette. 'But I don't know anything. I don't see how I can be of any help to you.'

'Then I'll be out of your hair in ten minutes. Spare me that, at least.'

She took a drag. 'I'm sorry, Mr Yates. I spent a lot of time raking over things for Jimmy, I don't think I can put myself through that again.'

'Wait. Just let me—'

'I'm sorry. Goodbye.' The line went dead.

I stared at the receiver, feeling uncertain. The conversation was one-sided – it felt as though I'd given up too much inform-ation without getting anything in return. Then I took a step back from it, realised I was being an ass. The woman didn't know me from a hole in the ground, and I was asking her to dish about two dead people she knew. How else was she sup-posed to react?

I looked at the notebook in my hand again. The name she'd given me, Jeannie Runnels – a place to start, but something more than that: a wrong assumption. I turned back a page and looked at the recurring initials I'd jotted down from Robinson's notes. *J.R.* – what I'd assumed to denote *Jimmy Robinson*, but could just as surely be *Jeannie Runnels*.

Both Dinsmore and Layfield had told me there were no open murders Robinson could have been investigating. I couldn't see how they could both lie or make the same mistake, and it made me suspicious as hell.

*

The girl at the front desk of the *Recorder* didn't recognise me from the day before, but she went to summon Dinsmore anyway. He showed no surprise when he came through the door and greeted me, and I wondered if he knew I'd be back. 'More questions?'

'I've got a name for you, maybe the murder my friend was working on.'

'Shoot.'

'Jeanette Runnels. Seems like she went by Jeannie, too.'

'Runnels? Yeah, I remember that one. Strangled four or five months back.' I felt my blood rising at the man's barefaced cheek. I swallowed, tried to keep my temper in check and let him talk. 'Horrible story. They found her in her bedroom – son of a bitch used her own nylons to garrotte her.' He scratched his cheek. 'Hell, what was the other girl's name . . . ?'

'What other girl?'

He held his hand up, gesturing to give him a minute, his head tilted back to the ceiling. I waited, fighting to keep a lid on my temper. 'Bess something, like the president's wife – some of her regulars called her the First Lady on account of it.'

'"Regulars" – you're talking about a working girl?'

He snapped his fingers. 'Prescott, that's it. Bess Prescott.' He turned his gaze to me again. 'Same thing happened to her about six weeks later. Strangled in her own home, the same perp. Police chalked it up to some manner of sex maniac.'

'Was Jeannie Runnels a working girl as well?'

'Sure. Right out of the gate, the cops figured they were looking for one of their Johns, someone they had in common, but you start turning over those stones in this town and a lot of folk get uncomfortable real fast. That's why the police didn't spend a whole heap of time investigating; that and the fact it was a couple dead whores, so who cares, right?' I felt my fists clench up. He saw it and spread his hands. 'I'm not saying that, you understand – just telling you what the prevailing thinking was.'

I closed my eyes, the picture coming clear now. Two dead working girls – embarrassment looming for anyone who'd paid for their services if the cops started knocking on doors. Family men with wives. Maybe men with influence. It was a bum deal for the dead women, but easier all around just to hush it up and move on. Made me sick to my stomach. I looked at him again. 'Who was the third?'

'The third what?'

It felt like he was still trying to stall me, my patience about shot now. 'The third victim, Dinsmore. My friend told me before he died there were three murders.'

He looked puzzled. 'That's what I was going to ask you about. I remember you telling me that, but there were only two.'

I pointed at his chest. 'Quit messing with me. Yesterday you said there weren't any murders, now you're telling me there're only two – what game are you playing?'

He took a step back, a look of surprise on his face. 'Hold on now, Jack. You're the one told me your friend was investigating these murders.'

'What's that supposed to mean? Why didn't you tell me—'

'They got the man that did it.' His face was red with exasperation, veins showing in his neck. 'Why the hell was your friend investigating a case that was already solved?'

CHAPTER NINE

Dinsmore slid into the booth and signalled the waitress for a coffee without waiting for me to even sit down. I wore it – suppose I'd earned the slight. He leaned back and took a Lucky Strike from his pack and held it upside down between his thumb and forefinger. 'You got some nerve, I'll give you that.'

The diner was a half-block from the *Recorder*'s offices, just south of the point where Central Avenue shed the last of its glitz. Dinsmore had been all set to ditch me in the reception to go back to his desk, but I'd talked him down with the offer of buying him lunch. I'd never known a newsman to turn down a free meal, but figure what he really wanted was to watch me eat crow.

The booth was cramped, my knees butting into his as I sat down. He stared at me, tapping his smoke on the table to tamp the tobacco down.

'Cut me some slack,' I said. 'You can see how it looked.'

'That I was holding out on you? Why would you assume that? Seems like a dumb way to go about your business, you ask me.'

'Enough, already, I'm buying you lunch, aren't I? You can drop the wounded soldier act.'

His eyes twinkled, celebrating scoring a point off me. 'You know, I feel like steak all of a sudden.'

'Sure. Live it up.' I looked off to one side, towards the counter, tapping my thumbnail on the table. Only half the stools were taken; all of the occupants were men, and most wore blue shirts and work pants. I turned back towards Dinsmore. 'All right, let's start over.'

He shrugged and clamped his cigarette between his front teeth. 'Okay.' He lit it, blew a stream of smoke sideways from the corner of his mouth; it curled against the window pane and came back towards us. 'Where'd you turn up Jeanette Runnels' name?'

The question caught me off guard. I didn't see what it mattered, unless my first instinct was right and he was trying to keep tabs on who I was speaking to. 'That's not important.'

He stuck out his bottom lip. 'No, I guess not.' His tone said he wasn't satisfied with that answer.

I pulled out the photograph. 'You're sure that's not Miss Runnels or Miss Prescott?'

He took it to look at, then slid it across the table to me again. 'Sure.'

'Who killed the two women?'

The waitress set his coffee down in front of him, the mug gleaming white but chipped around the rim. She asked for our order, but Dinsmore surprised me by waving her off. 'A nigger lowlife called Walter Glover. He already had a rap sheet full of minor offences, then sometime last decade he broke into the big leagues when he assaulted a woman in his car. He claimed she'd gone with him willingly, but the jury didn't believe him.'

'Any chance he was telling the truth?'

'The dame was white, so what do you think? Anyway, they convicted him and he served eleven-and-change for it, got out in June. He'd only been free a couple weeks before he killed Runnels. Parole board had shaved his sentence some because he found Jesus in the clink. Made them look real bad, in light of what he did next.'

'You said the cops soft-pedalled the investigation into the murders.'

'Uh-huh.'

'So how'd they get hip to Glover?'

'Hot Springs PD didn't want anything to do with it, but the Garland County Sheriff's Department decided to involve themselves.'

'For what reason?'

'Hot Springs is the county seat of Garland County, they can do what they like.'

'I meant why did they get involved if the city cops ignored it?'

'Who knows why?' He held his hands up as he said it. 'Sheriff was a hoss by the name of Cole Barrett; he got a tip to look at Glover for the killings and he went after him. Tracked him to a dogtrot cabin out by Lake Catherine and gunned him down. Afterwards, Barrett said Glover confessed to the murders on the spot but tried to draw on him, so he had to shoot him in self-defence.'

I had the first thought I always did with anonymous tips: who was the tipster? 'Did he kill him?'

He tapped his chest. 'Sure did. Put two right in his heart.'

'You believe Barrett's version of events?'

Dinsmore pursed his mouth and spread his hands. 'I have no reason not to.'

He saw the look on my face.

'I know, I know, there are parts that sound fishy. Could be the case they're not giving us the whole truth, and that's why, but that wouldn't be unusual. What's done is done.'

'Were there any witnesses to the shooting?'

He shook his head. 'But there's no reason to disbelieve Barrett. He was sheriff six years and a deputy a long time before that. He was well respected and never known as a gunslinger. And besides, why would he lie?'

'Because he shot a man in cold blood?'

'Come on, Yates, think it through – what cause would he have to do that? When backup arrived, the deputies found Glover with his gun in his hand. I'm inclined to believe it went down how Barrett said.'

'When did this happen?'

'Couple months back – August, around then.'

August. Prior to Robinson's time at Duke's. I traced my fingernail absently across the tabletop, back and forth, wondering what the hell had drawn him to this mess. Seemed like Cole Barrett was someone I needed to talk to. Hearing Dinsmore speak about him brought to mind another sheriff – Horace Bailey, late of Texarkana. I wondered if that was the link – if Robinson had heard about Barrett, got a line on some dirt on the Glover shooting, and decided another crooked sheriff was more than he could stand.

Thoughts of Bailey summoned to mind my last image of him: his corpse on the floor of Winfield Callaway's study, his hat fallen next to him, a smear of blood on the crown. My gun arm still shaking. The memory made my hands tremble again now; I folded them in my lap, out of sight. 'Where's Barrett's office?'

Dinsmore tapped his cigarette on the chrome ashtray. 'Forget it, he's retired.'

'Retired?'

'Yeah. He was forced out, the rumour goes. Seems like you and our prosecuting attorney-elect think alike; he made it known he wasn't buying Barrett's story and that he'd be looking to empanel a grand jury when he takes office in January so he could bring unlawful killing charges against Barrett. From what I heard, the mayor stepped in to broker a deal – Barrett retires immediately and gets to keep his pension. In return, Masters – that's the prosecuting attorney – promises he won't go after Barrett. At first I couldn't see why Masters agreed to it – he's leading this GI Ticket, says him and his boys are going to clean the whole town up, but then he's doing deals with Teddy Coughlin before he's even in the door. But then you think about it, and realise it's a smart move; Masters got what he wanted all along – Barrett out of office, clearing the way for one of his own men to be elected sheriff come November. For all his talk about justice, he didn't give a damn what Barrett did or didn't do. He just wanted him out of the way so he could—'

I held my finger up. 'Why would Barrett take the deal if he had nothing to hide?' I imagined Robinson hearing the same story I just did, and having the same thoughts – that Barrett was dirty as hell. Another lawman above the law. His blood boiling as he heard it.

Dinsmore shrugged. 'Avoid the embarrassment. Protect his pension. Who knows?'

'Anyone from your outfit think to ask him about it?'

'Who, Barrett? Sure – I tried a couple times, but he wouldn't talk to the papers.'

'Maybe I'll go ask him for myself.'

He laughed, billowing smoke as he did. 'Good luck with that. Retirement's done nothing to brighten his disposition.'

I looked him in the eyes. 'I've dealt with worse. Where's he live?'

'Y'already owe me lunch, Yates. How many markers you want to build up here?' He smiled when he said it, but it quickly faded when he realised I was serious.

He checked his watch, slid along the bench seat and stood up. 'I oughta scram. Take some time to cool off. You'll thank me for it.' Then he stepped back from the table, cracked a smile. 'And don't think I'll forget about lunch.'

When he was gone, I slumped back against the booth and closed my eyes, all of it dancing around in my mind. Political warfare and dirty deals. A dead sex fiend, supposed murderer. A sheriff forced from office under a cloud. Dinsmore playing coy, like it was for my own benefit – perking my suspicion about him. At the centre of it all, Jimmy Robinson and all those dead women.

CHAPTER TEN

The idea came to me late so I had to race out of the diner, start-ling a waitress in the process. I made it outside in time to see Dinsmore pass by the *Recorder* offices and disappear around the corner of the next block. When he was out of sight, I went in the main entrance of the newspaper and hurried over to the girl at the front desk. 'Miss, Clyde Dinsmore said I could trouble you for directions to your archives. Could you help me out?'

She nodded and sent me to a large file room in the base-ment. My luck held; when I got there, I had the place to myself. I found a table in a corner and started pulling issues of the *Recorder* until I found what I was looking for. The June 20th edition: one column on Jeannie Runnels' murder. The story got short-shrift, almost no detail provided beyond the fact that her body was discovered in her bedroom after a neighbour called the police. It made no mention of how she was killed – the details presumably too indecent to print – stating only that authorities had confirmed foul play was involved, but had no suspects at time of going to press. There was no mention of her line of work, but the lack of column inches told its own story about how interested the paper was in Miss Runnels' fate. I flicked through the next week's worth of issues, but found no follow-up on the story.

Dinsmore said Bess Prescott's murder was around six weeks

after Runnels', so I jumped forward to the start of August and started looking through the papers from then. I found it in the copy from August 11th. She was referred to by her full Christian name, Elizabeth, and I belatedly made the connection to the other set of initials I'd cribbed from Robinson's notes – *E.P.*

Just as with Runnels, they short-changed her – this time a half a column in the gutter of page eleven. The report noted that she had been found on the floor of her bedroom, and that a friend had raised the alarm when she hadn't heard from her for several days. The friend wasn't named. The story ended abruptly by saying police were investigating.

I raced through the remaining issues from August, looking for coverage of Barrett's shootout with Walter Glover. It wasn't hard to find – the story made the front page, sharing top billing with a claim by US intelligence officers that a million former German soldiers were now Commies. I read through the *Recorder*'s account and it came across pretty close to how Dinsmore told it – Barrett had tracked Glover to a remote cabin in Garland County and managed to wrangle a confession from him, but Glover had drawn a firearm when Barrett moved to take him in. Runnels and Prescott were named as Glover's victims, but beyond their names, ages and places of birth, nothing more was said about them. It felt like another indignity for the dead women – Barrett gets lauded for killing their murderer, but the victims themselves barely warrant a mention.

Dinsmore's name wasn't on the piece – a Clifton Elliot got the byline – and I noticed he'd been off on one of the details: this version stated that Barrett had fired twice at Glover, striking him once in the chest. The other bullet wasn't mentioned again, and I figured Barrett must have missed, but that detail didn't fit the heroic picture Elliot was trying for, so it got ignored. The article continued on page two, recounting Barrett's 'years of distinguished service', and Mayor Coughlin weighed in with a quote praising his dedication to justice. There was a photograph accompanying the piece that showed a grandee pumping Barrett's hand, a crowd looking on, smiles all around. It was no surprise when I saw the caption identified the other man as Coughlin.

It was all real tidy in the way everything was presented to show Barrett as snow-white as possible. Even Dinsmore's talk about *two bullets in the heart* felt like him getting carried away glorifying the sheriff.

I skimmed the report a second time, more interested now in what didn't make the page than what did. I looked at the following day's paper as well, but there was nothing new, just retread. I jotted notes as I went, putting myself in Robinson's shoes, searching for insight into his thinking.

Glover was written off as an ex-con with a troubling criminal history, but there was no mention of what had led Barrett to suspect him. Dinsmore had said it was a tip-off, but that nugget wasn't reported here. I wondered if it was another product of Dinsmore's creative licence and, if not, if the tipster was ever identified; I scribbled down to ask him.

Also: was there any evidence against Glover, aside from the confession? Men confessed to crimes they hadn't committed all the time. Surely Barrett would have looked for some confirmation of Glover's guilt in the wake of the shooting – if nothing else, to be sure he had the right man?

And then the big question: did Glover kill a third woman? There was no hint of it in the stories I'd read, but it could have come out later – or maybe not at all. Maybe Robinson got wind of it in the course of his own enquiries. But if Glover had only killed twice, who the hell was the woman in the photograph?

I went back upstairs to the front desk and asked the girl if she could find out an address and telephone number for me. She looked put out at this latest request, but called the operator anyway, gave the name I'd written down for her, and scribbled the information I needed on the same piece of paper. When she finished writing, I motioned for her to pass the receiver over, and asked the voice on the other end to connect me to the number she'd given.

It rang a moment, and then a man with a raspy voice answered. 'Cole Barrett.'

Now I knew he was home, I hung up without saying a word.

*

Barrett lived ten miles outside of town, close to Lake Catherine state park. It was mid-afternoon by the time I set out, the sun high in the clear sky as I drove south-east out of Hot Springs. The Ouachita River circled around the town from west to east and I crossed it near Carpenter Dam. From the road I caught a glimpse of the white-water torrents thundering through the concrete barrier downriver.

Past the bridge, I was plunged into the backwoods. The highway was lined with a dense mix of pines, sycamores and elms, punctuated by the occasional farmhouse or creek. As I drove, I mulled over everything Dinsmore had told me, and wondered again if Robinson had confronted Barrett. It was easy to imagine him careening down this same road, fuelled by bonded liquor and righteous anger, determined to get the truth about the murders from him. Seemed the simplest way to connect all the dots.

But as the idea swam in my head, I realised there was another connection: the mayor, Teddy Coughlin. Dinsmore had said it was Coughlin who brokered the deal to save Barrett from the grand jury investigation, and he'd also speculated that the mayor's office could have coerced the fire department to change the report into Robinson's death. I wondered if Robinson had spooked Barrett somehow, enough to give him a motive to start the fire at Duke's – knowing that the mayor had protected him once already, so why not a second time?

I told myself to pull back, aware that I was getting way ahead of the facts. I knew why I was doing it, too: time. My forty-eight hours were almost up, and it felt like I was still fumbling in the dark for Robinson's trail. I was forcing the little I knew to fit a theory held together by conjecture and rumours, a desperate attempt to bring some kind of closure to matters. It was amateurish, and I knew as much. When I thought about it in that light, the whole notion of doorstepping Barrett seemed rash – but it was too late to turn back now.

*

After twenty-five minutes, I drew up to a cabin on a low rise overlooking a muddy pond. The land around the house was studded with trees and shrubs, their leaves sprinkled with reds and browns, fall and its colours taking hold. There was a grey pre-war LaSalle parked out front, and my pulse quickened some when I saw it, at the thought of what was to come. I carried on past the house and parked a little way down, on the far side of the track. I stepped out onto a patchwork mulch of grass and fallen leaves.

The cabin was in two sections, the main building two storeys tall, built on a fieldstone base, and with windows in the shingled roof. A smaller, single-storey structure had been tacked on to one end, and that was where the front door was. Off to one side, a little way from the main structure, stood a tumbledown woodshed, its door hanging from its hinges.

I walked up to the house and rapped with the knocker. A dog started barking somewhere round back.

I heard a voice and then footsteps from inside. The door opened and a fiftyish man with sandy hair stood across the threshold from me. 'What?'

I took my hat off. 'Sheriff Barrett?'

He looked at me in a manner that said if I had to ask, I wasn't worth answering. From the way Dinsmore had called him a hoss, I'd expected an imposing figure, but Barrett was rake-thin and no taller than five-eight. He wore tan trousers held up by a narrow belt, cinched tight, and a white short-sleeved shirt, his skinny arms accentuated by the starched arm-holes. I decided an appeal to his ego was my best play.

'My name's Charlie Yates, I'm a reporter and I was hoping—'

'I got no call to speak to reporters. Be on your way.'

I held up my pen, signalling him to wait. 'I'm writing a story about the women Walter Glover killed. I'd sure appreciate a few minutes of your time.'

'You hear me, son? I told you—'

'Please, Sheriff.' I slapped a big smile on my face, played

the star-struck newsman. 'You're the hero of the story, doesn't make for much of a piece without you. Maybe just a quote or two?'

He went to shut the door on me. I shot my arm out without thinking, bracing it open.

'Take your hand away.'

I kept up the breathless enthusiasm – anything to get him talking. 'I've been doing my research and I just had a few questions. Can you tell me how you tracked Glover to that cabin?'

A woman appeared in the hallway behind him, looking anxious. 'Cole?'

He spoke to her over his shoulder, eyes still on me. 'It's fine, go see to the dog.'

She glanced at me, her face drawn, and then disappeared from view again.

I persisted. 'Is it true you put two bullets in Glover's heart, Sheriff?'

He gave a small shake of his head and fixed me with a stare. 'You don't know the first goddamn thing about it. Get the hell off my property.'

He pushed my hand away and tried to close the door again. I jammed it with my foot and met his stare, decided to give up on the act. 'Try this, then: why did you retire? Is it true you did a deal to avoid a grand jury investigation?'

That froze him on the spot. He stopped struggling and opened the door a fraction wider. 'Who are you? Who sent you?'

'I'm just an interested party. Now how about you speak to me and tell me your side, so I don't have to write it the way it looks right now.'

'And just how is that exactly?'

I straightened my shirtfront. 'Like you've got a whole hell of a lot to hide.'

He looked at me like I'd kicked his mother. The dog out back was barking double-time now, the sound echoing around the trees. He yelled at it to shut up.

Before he could speak again, I asked the question I'd come for. 'Did a man called Robinson try to speak to you, Sheriff? Maybe something similar to what just happened here?'

He flung the door open soon as he heard the name. He planted his hand on my chest and shoved me backwards, his other hand still gripping the frame. 'I ain't a hero and I ain't a sheriff any more. Get gone. You come around here again and I'll loose the dog on you.' He turned and slammed the door shut before I could say anything more.

I stood there a moment, my pulse running so strong that I could feel it in my arms and in my neck. I knocked on the door and called out, but was met only with the sound of the dog barking. After a minute more, I went back to the car and climbed in.

I drove a little further along the track, keeping the house just in sight, then cut the engine. There were no other cars on the road, but I was far enough away to not be too conspicuous. I waited, watching the house and the grey LaSalle through the back window, wondering if Barrett would reappear. My questions had spooked him, and I thought he might panic and make a run to go see someone to unload his troubles.

I let ten minutes go by, my pulse slowing back to normal, but nothing moved. I took one last glance at the cabin, then started back to town.

The way he'd blown up when I dropped Jimmy's name told me what I needed to know. He might as well have come right out and admitted he knew exactly who I was talking about. But it wasn't just the way he reacted that stoked my fears – it was the fact that he reacted to Robinson's real name.

CHAPTER ELEVEN

I drove back to town trying to make the parts fit together. If Walter Glover had really killed those women, I couldn't see how Robinson had a story to chase. It was all done and dusted before he took that room at Duke's. Everything about the encounter with Barrett made me think he was dirty somehow, and that was what had drawn Robinson here; maybe, in his mind, a way to make good for Texarkana. Or was that just how I wanted the world to be?

I developed a working theory: Barrett went out to Glover's intending to kill him all along, but sometime after he shot him, got wind that Glover wasn't the killer and had to hush it up. That would explain why the prosecuting attorney was threatening a grand jury. It would explain why Robinson was still investigating, and what would have brought him into contact with Barrett. Maybe he was trying to expose him. Hell, for all I knew, Robinson could've been trying to blackmail him. Either explanation would leave Barrett with a motive for wanting Robinson out of the picture. And either meant whoever killed Jeannie Runnels and Bess Prescott was still on the loose.

I hit Central Avenue and traffic slowed to a crawl. People on the sidewalk were staring and pointing at something two cars ahead of me, smiles and applause rippling along the street as the commotion passed them.

The two cars in front of me turned off at the next

intersection, and I saw the cause of the blockage: a man riding a horse-drawn sulky buggy. He waved at the bystanders, soaking up the attention. I trailed behind him at five miles per hour, waiting for a chance to pass, but he slowed to a stop outside the Arlington. As I went by, I recognised the man and pulled over, wanting a better look.

The man in the buggy handed his riding crop and the reins to a black man who was waiting on the kerb. The attendant took pains not to make eye contact. The rider climbed out and straightened his straw fedora. He was wearing a white suit with a red carnation in the lapel, a getup that made him easily recognisable from the photograph of him I'd seen in the newspaper, pumping Cole Barrett's hand after the Glover shooting: Teddy Coughlin. He ascended the Arlington steps, stopping to gladhand a passer-by as he went. The black man saw me staring and looked away.

I called out to him. 'What's the occasion?'

'No occasion, sir. The mayor has a mind to parade his horses every evening. This here Scotch and Soda.' He stroked each horse on the nose in turn.

'That a fact.' I glanced at Coughlin one more time as he entered the hotel, then nodded to the attendant and drove on.

It was a slick routine, the public face of a political animal. Wasn't hard to imagine a workaday lawman like Barrett being caught in Coughlin's thrall.

*

I rose early the next day.

My forty-eight hours were up, but there was no way I could

walk away now. The call to Lizzie would be rough, but I hoped I could make her understand. Then it was a matter of twisting Acheson's arm to get him to finance my endeavour.

I walked down to the *Recorder* offices, wanting to know if a third victim was ever attributed to Walter Glover. On the way I passed the giant building at the bottom of Bathhouse Row and saw it was a veterans' hospital. Outside it, a man with a medal pinned to his gown was sitting in a wheelchair in a spot that caught the first rays of sunshine. He had no arms, and a nurse was standing over him, feeding him drags from a cigarette.

*

The front desk at the *Recorder* wasn't manned so early on a Monday morning, and I passed right into the newsroom. There was no sign of Dinsmore, but the man who sat at the next desk was pecking at his typewriter. I introduced myself and explained that Dinsmore had been helping me out with the Glover case.

'Thought I knew your face from somewhere. Something I can do for you?'

'I hope so. You familiar with the story?'

He nodded. 'Sure. Son of a bitch got what was coming to him.'

'D'you happen to remember how many women he killed?'

'Two, as I recall. Don't ask me to tell you their names.'

Dead whores – not worth remembering. I understood his implication and my hand twitched. 'Were there ever any others attributed to him? After the fact, I mean.'

He flattened his hair across his scalp, thinking. 'Not so as

I'm aware. I don't work crime, that's Clyde's game, but unless I'm forgetting something . . .'

I thought about the *Recorder* articles I'd read, Clifton Elliot on the byline; I asked where I could find him, thinking he'd have a deeper knowledge of the case.

'Clifton? He quit. Got himself a plum job up in Little Rock. Couldn't get out of here soon enough after that.'

Another break in the chain. I thanked the man for his time and hit the street again.

I started to walk towards the Arlington, feeling adrift and angry that no one seemed to give a damn about any of the dead women. I had time to kill until I could call Lizzie. A police car cruised by and it brought Detective Layfield to mind. He'd seemed eager enough to help, so I figured maybe he'd field my questions. There was still risk attached to going to him, but I was running out of blind alleys to run down.

*

I caught a break when the desk sergeant said Layfield was in the squad room, and he'd go fetch him. Layfield appeared almost immediately, his clothes creased and unkempt, his eyes blood-shot. He looked as though he was at the end of a long shift.

'Yates, wasn't it?'

I nodded. 'I think I figured out what my friend was doing here. Something to do with the Walter Glover murders.'

'Glover? That was bad business.' He raised his eyebrows indicating I should get to the point.

'Who worked the case, do you know?'

'We caught the calls and had a file open on the victims,

but it was Garland County Sheriff's Department punched his ticket. Some kind of tip-off, I believe, and it placed Glover in their jurisdiction. Sheriff Barrett rode out there himself to bring him in. You know what happened after that, right?'

I nodded. 'What about his victims, though? Runnels and Prescott – did you have any evidence to implicate Glover?'

'Is our present conversation off the record?'

'Sure.'

'He was a person of interest, yes.'

'Were there others, or did you think he was your man?'

He tried to swallow a yawn, holding up his other hand to excuse himself. 'I'd have to familiarise myself with the file again.'

'Think I could get a look at it?'

'Are you crazy? What do you think? You can't breeze in off the street and start reading police files.'

'Where's the harm?'

He scoffed. 'The chief would have my badge, for starters. Where you driving at with this, Yates?'

'I can't find a whole lot of detail about the two women that died, and I'm curious what led Barrett to Glover.'

'I told you, his name came from a tip-off.'

'Happen to know who the tipster was?'

'How should I know? Ask the Sheriff's Department.'

'A case as high profile as this and you don't know? A man was shot—'

'Hey, go spin, okay? It wasn't our case.'

I held my hands up and bowed my head, signifying an apology. He shot me a glare, but he came off more weary than angry. I waited a beat to let him calm down, then said, 'When we spoke, you told me there were no murders on the books—'

'Yes, I did.' He put his hands on his hips. 'You didn't say nothing about cases they already put to bed. Why would I—'

I raised my finger. 'Hold on, I wasn't busting your chops. Hear me out.'

He closed his eyes and took a breath. 'Sorry, long night.'

I waved it off. 'Is there a chance Glover had a third victim somehow? Either a murder that was attributed to him later on, or maybe a body that fit the profile of his other victims?'

He looked at the floor, chewing on his lip as he thought about it. Then he shook his head. 'This is on account of what your friend was saying, huh? You talked about three murders before.'

'Right.'

He shook his head again. 'Glover killed two women. That's what he confessed to Sheriff Barrett. I can't see no reason he'd have cause to lie.'

'Who? Barrett or Glover?'

He tilted his head. 'What's that supposed to mean?'

'I mean we've only got Barrett's word for it, right?'

He furrowed his forehead, looked at me through his eyebrows. 'I know you just lost a friend and you're looking for answers, but you won't find none by talking trash about a brother officer of the law.'

His reaction made me realise the futility; asking a cop to spill on another cop – even a retired one – was like trying to figure out which dog had the most fleas. 'You work closely with Garland County Sheriff's Department?'

'If you're asking me if I know Barrett, the answer's no, not well. But I know his reputation and he's as straight as a rifle barrel.' He started backing away in the direction of the squad room. 'Now, is there something else I can do for you today?'

His tone said it all, but the photograph in my pocket felt like it was throbbing, and I decided to take the risk. 'Sure,' I said, pulling out her picture. 'Is this woman familiar to you at all?'

He stepped closer again, took the photograph between his thumb and forefinger. He stared for a long moment, and I thought he recognised her. Then he shook his head. 'Who is she?'

'If I had to guess, I'd say she's the third victim.'

'You know her name?'

'No, but I'd damn sure like to.'

He looked at it again, then his eyes flicked to mine, and I knew what was coming. 'Where'd you get this?'

'A source.'

'A source that gave you a photograph but didn't tell you who all's in it?' He dropped his arms to his sides. 'Don't come that with me, if you're sitting on information—'

'I'm not. It belonged to the man who died, he gave it to my source for safekeeping.'

He stared at me, breathing hard through his nose. 'What else your *source* give you?'

'That's it. It might not even be related.' I tried not to blink under his gaze.

He passed the photograph back to me. 'I shown you every courtesy, Yates. I'd appreciate the same in return. Now, we on the same page here?'

'We are.'

He offered his hand and we shook. Then he walked off.

The gamble hadn't paid off, and it chafed – I worried I

might've burned Layfield as a source. But it cut both ways; I wondered how truthful he'd been about Barrett, and if the conversation would get back to him. Part of me hoped it would.

CHAPTER TWELVE

It was almost ten by the time I got to the Arlington to call Lizzie. The lobby was crowded – families checking out before heading home and diners scarfing their breakfasts. The smell of coffee and bacon made my stomach growl. A bellhop zipped in front of me with a cart overloaded with bags and cases, making for the exit.

I passed by the restaurant and saw William Tindall at the same raised table he'd occupied the day before. There was only one other person with him this time, a woman. At a guess, about the same age as him, decked out in pearls and a shimmering aquamarine dress, her fair hair intricately pinned. Tindall was reading the newspaper, while the woman picked at a plate of fruit. She said something and he laughed, his eyes dancing in genuine humour. He reached across to chuck her chin and went back to his reading.

I watched them for a few seconds, the throng around me keeping me inconspicuous. The waiters fawned over Tindall, taking his chair when he stood to shake hands with a fellow diner, and refreshing his drink every second sip. He seemed to enjoy the attention, sharing a joke with them as he sat back down and handing out tips as easy as handshakes. His presence unsettled me; the locals seemed to buy him as some kind of bigwig, but I only saw the killer reputed to have slain at least five men.

I walked across to the phone booths and placed a call home. When the call went through, Lizzie answered straightaway. It felt good to hear her voice – and it brought back a nagging doubt whether I was doing the right thing by staying.

'How are you?'

'I'm so glad you called, Charlie. It's empty here without you.'

'I miss you too.' I took my hat off and dangled it from my finger. 'Hold that thought till I can be back there.'

'Are you coming home soon?'

'I can't. Not yet.'

'What's happened?'

'I found some things out. I just can't make them fit together yet.'

'Please don't be obtuse with me, Charlie.'

I let out a breath, knew she was right to call me on it. 'The more I dig, the more I think Robinson was murdered. I just can't prove it yet.'

She was quiet for a moment as it sank in. Then came the questions. 'Who would do that? Are you in danger?'

'No, no. I'm not in any danger.'

'How can you say that with certainty? If he was killed because of what he knew – what you know . . .'

'Just wait a minute. I don't think it was to do with Texarkana – not directly anyway. My best guess is Robinson went after another crooked sheriff, and he got in over his head.'

Her breathing was ragged down the line. 'Isn't that proof enough that you should get out of there, then? Please, Charlie. We didn't come all this way just for . . .' She let the thought wither and die, too hard to finish.

The silence hung for a moment, neither of us knowing how

to persuade or reassure the other. Then I laid it out for her. 'There were two women, Jeanette Runnels and Bess Prescott. They were both twenty-four years old. They were murdered.' The words I didn't need to say: same as your sister.

'Then let the police do their work. I know why you don't trust them but they're not all like Bailey and Sherman.'

'The police killed a man they said did it. They said he confessed but no one witnessed it. I don't think Robinson believed he was guilty, and I need to know what made him think that way.'

'Why, Charlie?'

'Because if this man didn't do it, then more women are going to die.' My voice was urgent now, too forceful. Trying to convince myself as much as her. I closed my eyes and counted to five, trying to level off. 'The police don't care. These women mean nothing to them and it galls me. As far as they're concerned, they got their man and they've closed the book on it.'

'I meant why does it have to be you? This isn't your hill to die on.' She said it softly, cutting right through my anger.

I gripped the telephone cord. 'Because I'll be damned if I'm going to have any more blood on my conscience.'

It went quiet again. I listened to her breathing, could have sworn I felt it against my cheek. She said, 'Is it always going to be this way?'

'What way?'

'I know your work here bores you, Charlie, and I know you're only happy when you're chasing a story—'

'That's not true.'

'Okay. Perhaps I should have said *happiest*. But I worry that I'm always going to lose you to whatever's next.'

'That's not how it'll be.' To my own ears it sounded like I was pleading. 'I'll be back as soon as this is done.'

'And then what? What if Sal calls you from New York with a story for you? Or goodness knows who else?'

'Then nothing. This is different. Robinson came here to make things right. It cost him his life and he entrusted me to finish what he started. You can see why I have to do this, can't you?'

'Not if it's at the cost of your life too.'

I had no comeback. If Robinson was murdered, it stood to reason I was putting myself in the firing line by poking around in the same hornet's nest – and she knew it. I saw it was no use trying to convince her and made up my mind to move matters along, focus her attention elsewhere. 'Lizzie, I need you to do something for me.'

'Are you changing the subject?'

'No. This is related. It's important.'

'What is it?'

I glanced back towards the restaurant. 'There's a man here, his name's William Tindall. He used to be a racketeer in New York, a big one, but he disappeared. Now he's here acting like he's royalty. I want to know how he came to be here and what his game is. Men like him don't retire.'

'I don't understand, where does he fit into all this?'

'I don't know, and that's what's troubling me. But this place does crooked for breakfast, lunch and dinner, and I don't like the coincidence.'

'Is this busywork? Are you trying to divert me?' She sounded doubtful and eager at the same time.

'No. I'll see what I can turn up this end. I want you to cover off the background. Start with Sal. He'll be able to give you the New York dope, and he'll know who to speak to for the rest. Check the wire services too, and the cuttings files, see if you can turn up anything there. I'll square it off with Acheson.'

'Are you sure? I've never done anything like this before.'

'I know what you're capable of, and so do you.'

'All right, but only on the condition that you come home at the first sign of trouble. Do we have a deal?'

I lodged my hat back on my head. 'I'll call again soon.'

I broke the connection and checked my watch, thinking about another run at Ella Borland – not ready to give up on my best lead just yet. I pulled out my notebook and found her number, dropped a nickel into the slot. The same man as before answered, almost immediately this time.

'This is Yates calling for Ella Borland.'

Again he said nothing, and again she came on the line a few seconds later.

'Miss Borland, this is Charlie Yates – we spoke yesterday.'

'I remember you, Mr Yates.'

'I don't mean to badger you but I had one more question I was hoping you could answer for me. It's about Jimmy.'

'I assumed that was the purpose of the call. What is it you want to know?'

'Can you tell me when Jimmy first approached you?'

'I don't— Give me a moment.' I waited, not sure if she was thinking about it or about hanging up. Then she came back on the line. 'Sometime in August. Maybe towards the end of the month.'

Bingo. Confirmation that Robinson was coming to Hot Springs long before he moved to Duke's to live. The timelines jibed as well; Barrett shot Glover in mid-August – if Robinson had read about it and that had drawn his attention, it would make sense of why he came on the scene around that time. It still didn't explain why he suddenly came here to stay in early October. The obvious answer: he felt he was getting close to something. 'Ma'am, did Jimmy ever talk about Sheriff Barrett to you?'

'What's the significance of this, Mr Yates?'

I tried to keep it breezy. 'Just loose ends I want to tie up, is all.'

'I rather doubt that. I thought some more about our conversation yesterday.'

I pressed the receiver tighter to my ear. 'Yes?'

'I told you, it's still very hard for me to talk about Jeannie and what happened to her, so when you called before, it was a shock to bring it all to mind again.'

'I understand, I'm sorry.'

'There's no need to apologise. I've had time to think about it now, and if you still want to meet to talk about Jimmy, I'd be willing to consider it. What I'd like to know, however, is what your intentions are, as relates to his death.'

'My intentions . . .' I tried to bring order to my thoughts, suddenly thrown into a jumble by her about-turn. 'Look, I'll tell it straight. I want to know what he was doing and if it got him killed. And if it turns out there was foul play involved, then I'm here to see that the parties who did it get what's coming to them.'

She took a deep breath. 'I sensed that was it. So this is about revenge.'

'Not revenge. Justice.'

'You sound like you're certain he was murdered.'

'I'm not certain about anything. But I won't go away until I am.'

'You talk the same way Jimmy did. He was always talking about justice.' Her voice was distant as she said it, and I thought I'd scared her off; that the idea of gouging open the same wounds as Robinson had done was too much for her to contemplate. But then she said, 'I'll agree to meet with you, but I'll want to know what makes you think he was killed. Everything. If you hold something back, you won't hear from me again.'

'Fine.' It sounded like she'd been burned before, and I wondered if it was by Robinson – and what he would have tried to hide from her. 'Can you meet me today? Somewhere in town?'

'Very well, but not in town. Let's say five o'clock this evening at Jaycee Park. It's still under construction, so we'll have privacy enough. There's a bench at the south-east corner, right where the railroad crosses the creek. I'll be waiting.'

'I'll be there.'

I put the receiver back in its cradle and tapped the top of the unit, staring at nothing across the lobby. The amateur spook bullshit was a wrinkle I wasn't expecting, made me wonder what I was walking into. It was as though she was afraid to be seen talking with me.

CHAPTER THIRTEEN

I didn't want to risk another foray to the *Recorder*'s archives, so a return to the public library was the next best bet. The librarian smiled when I tipped my hat to greet her.

Inside, I made for stacks that held the old newspapers, pulled out a pile of *Recorder* copies, and gave myself ninety minutes to glom as much dope as I could on the political dogfight that was happening in Hot Springs.

It was slow going trying to form a picture by sifting through weeks of election stories, but an hour in, I felt I had enough that I could pitch the story to Acheson without tripping myself up. As I read, it was notable that any mention of corruption alleged against Coughlin was handled with a light touch – '*Unsubstantiated rumours of electoral malfeasance*', '*Fiercely refuted suggestions of fiscal impropriety.*' Nothing to even hint at the kind of wrongdoing I suspected him to be involved in. It was discordant with Dinsmore's speculation about the mayor's involvement, and I wondered if Coughlin's activity was an open secret the papers left alone, just like the gambling dens and brothels that flourished in the town.

I pressed on a little longer, trying to take in as much as I could about the broader issues at stake, and that's when I stumbled across a name that gave me the perfect hook. I creased the page to mark it, then walked to the telephone kiosk.

I called Acheson at home. Even at seventy, he alternated six- and seven-day weeks at the *Journal*, taking only every second Monday off; by my reckoning, today was one of those off-days. He'd been in newspapers his entire life and worked at outfits all over California. If he'd slipped some since his heyday at the *LA Times*, he made up for it with the weight of his knowledge, and he could run a rag like the *Journal* in his sleep. Above all else, he still knew a good story when it found him – if you knew how to pitch it.

'Buck, it's Charlie.'

'Charlie? To what do I owe the pleasure?'

'I don't mean to disturb you at home, but I'm going a little crazy with this idea I had for a story, and I wanted to talk it over with you.'

'What story? You're on leave, I thought?'

'I was, but I stumbled across something and I think it's a runner. You ever hear of Hot Springs in Arkansas?'

'Is that a town or a resort?'

'Both. You wouldn't believe this place, Chief. Every joint on Main Street is touting gambling or girls upstairs, and it's all out in the open. The law just looks the other way.'

'Sounds like trouble for a god-fearing man like you. But I don't think you'd Shanghai my day of rest for a morsel like that . . .' The playful tone to his voice meant I had his interest.

'Try this: the mayor's a career pol named Coughlin, been in office twenty years. Far as I can see, it's on the strength of the fact he's kept the state and the Feds turning a blind eye to what goes on here. He trots his horses right up the main drag every night, for god's sake.'

'Does this local colour lead somewhere meaningful?'

'Hear me out. The city elections are in a week and a half and there's an ex-Marine Corps officer, name of Samuel Masters, making a big noise about how he's had enough of *"business as usual"*. He's a war hero and he's put together an opposition group, decorated GIs all, and they're standing on an anti-corruption ticket. Masters got himself elected in June as prosecuting attorney for the local judicial district here, and if you believe the polls, his crew are a solid bet to take over the rest of the city government. If that happens, means you can kiss good-bye to Coughlin, the casinos, all of it. They're writing leader pieces here making out like it's the fall of Rome all over again.'

He sucked his breath through his teeth. 'So far, so quaint, but what's the angle for the *Journal*?'

I played my ace card. 'Benny Siegel.'

The Hollywood mobster, undisputed boss of the Los Angeles underworld. Bugsy's reputation was fearsome enough that Jack Dragna had been forced to relinquish control of the rackets to him as soon as he arrived in LA. I let Siegel's name hang there a moment, the hook baited now. 'He's been coming here since the thirties and he's visited a half-dozen times in the last two years alone. He was in town just last month, and the local hacks covered it like he's royalty or something. Now tell me you can't see the angle here. We run it as a reportage piece, *"War Heroes Fight Vice In Bugsy's Secret Vacation Haunt."* Break it up over a few days, make it a *"Charlie Yates reporting from the front line"* kinda deal.' I stopped for a breath, almost getting carried away by my own sell job. 'But here's the trick: I write it so the whole thing is a haymaker aimed at Santa Monica City Hall. Corrupt pols getting their comeuppance, *"A New Day Is Dawning For American Demo-*

cracy" – lay it on real thick. How's that sound?'

He muttered something derisory about the City Council, then said, 'It's a slick pitch, I'll say that much.' He took a deep breath. 'If I said no, would you listen to me?'

'No, sir. But I'd sleep better knowing you were on board.'

He scoffed. 'I somehow doubt it. All right. File two fifteen-hundred-word pieces as a starter and we'll see how it looks.'

'I'll need a per diem.'

'I thought I felt your hand in my damn pocket. I'll authorise it with Accounting.'

'Great, thanks, Buck. I could really use some walking around money, can you get them to wire it?'

He grunted, and I took it as an affirmative. 'Make sure this is worth my while.'

'You got it.' I cleared my throat, pushing my luck now, but confident I was on a roll. 'One other thing. I've enlisted Lizzie to do some research for me – pertains to the story. I said I'd clear it with you so she can work with the wires and so on. She'll see to it that it doesn't interfere with her normal duties.'

'You've put your wife on the story already, before you—' He cut himself off. 'You're some piece of work, Charlie. Any other liberties I should know about?'

'Lizzie's overqualified to be a secretary, you know it as well as I do. She could make for a real asset to the *Journal*. Hell, I should be billing you for training her up.'

He gave two stunted laughs, incredulous. 'Sure thing. Send me an invoice and see what happens.'

*

113

Knowing money was on its way was a load off my mind. I still had time before meeting with Ella Borland, so I swung by the Mountain Motor Court to extend my accommodation there. The manager insisted on taking for two nights up front, not one, the 'house rules' apparently changed just for me. I let it slide so I could go about my business and asked the man for directions to Jaycee Park. He showed me on a tattered map he took from under the counter.

'Jaycee ain't finished, so it ain't marked on here yet, but it's right around here.' He pointed to a spot on the southern fringes of town, a half-dozen blocks west of Central Avenue.

I thanked him and turned around and opened the door.

He called after me. 'Ain't nothing to see, what you wanna go there for?'

I looked back from the doorway. 'I'll tell you when I figure it out myself.'

CHAPTER FOURTEEN

There was little traffic on the roads, and I arrived ahead of time. A dirt track skirted around the edge of the park on three sides. I followed it in order to make a survey of the area and find the meeting point. I'd assumed it was a public park that was being laid out, but turned out it was a baseball field. A chain link fence surrounded the central construction site, and a banner tied to it read: *Opening May 1947: Jaycee Park, New Home Of The Hot Springs Bathers*. Beyond it, I could see where the diamond was marked out, the turf still a potato field, and a pair of half-built concrete bleachers that rose along what would be the first and third base lines. A steam shovel sat idle on one side of the site, with other digging and construction equipment scattered around. The stillness was eerie in the low light, and the place felt abandoned.

The road stopped at a narrow creek that ran all along the eastern edge of the park. The water was dark and frigid-looking, even on a mild fall evening. I left the car and followed the muddy bank along to the south-eastern corner of the field, where a raised railroad bed crossed the water on a tumbledown trestle, the criss-cross supports underneath it rotting away. I spotted the bench Borland had said to meet by, and waited there, scanning in all directions for her, the sound of gurgling water behind me.

At five minutes after five, a blue sedan pulled up next to

mine and a woman climbed out of the passenger side. The driver remained behind the wheel, and for some reason my mind reached back to the pickup truck I'd chased away from my motel. He lit a smoke, but even in the flare of the match, I couldn't make out anything of the man's face.

The woman came walking down the same way I had. The first thing I noticed was her hair – jet-black, worn in short, curled bangs that dressed her face and made for a passing re-semblance to Hedy Lamarr. She wore a maroon pillbox hat with a short birdcage veil, and a dark plaid coat that stopped past her knees. She walked towards me slowly, glancing around as she came near. I got to my feet to greet her. 'Charlie Yates. How do you do, Miss Borland?'

She offered her hand, the glove she wore not quite the same shade of maroon as that of her hat.

'Mr Yates.' Up close, the Hedy Lamarr comparison didn't hold up, but she was beautiful nonetheless. The way she spoke suggested an education level uncommon to her line of work. I'd noticed it when we spoke on the telephone, but it was even more pronounced in person.

I waited for her to sit, then took my place next to her. 'Thank you for agreeing to meet with me.'

'It seemed the least I could do for Jimmy. It's such an awful thing that happened.'

I nodded at the sentiment, and something made me look away briefly, like I was needling at her grief. 'You said something this morning – said that Jimmy talked about justice a lot. Can you tell me how he came to be interested in your friend's murder?'

She folded her hands in her lap, and lowered her eyes to

them. 'Forgive me, Mr Yates, but I came here to listen as much as talk. I told you what I wanted, and I'd be obliged if we could begin the conversation there.'

I shifted in my seat so I was angled towards her, surprised at how forthright she was. 'All right, fair enough. But you have to understand, most of what I have is suspicion, nothing more.'

She met my eyes now. 'I'd like to hear it all the same.'

I nodded and leaned forward so my elbows were resting on my knees, and started talking. I told her about Robinson's telephone call, his line about making a mistake, and him implying that whatever was happening wasn't over. I told her how he spoke about three victims; she showed no reaction to that. I dropped Clay Tucker's name and said how he'd lied to me, and that I felt he knew something more than he was saying. I described the barman at the Keystone recounting how Jimmy had hinted he was going to kill himself. I mentioned Cole Barrett, and that I wanted to know what evidence had led him to Glover, but not that I'd gone to see him. I said nothing about our past in Texarkana. I edited my story on the fly, deciding what to tell and what to hold back, my brain racing to stay a step ahead of my mouth; I had no reason to trust or distrust this woman, but no way was I giving everything up on the first dance.

When I was finished, I said, 'From the time you spent with Jimmy, does any of this add up?'

She kneaded her hands, looking straight ahead. 'A little. Clay Tucker is a contemptible man, I'm not surprised at all that he lied to you. I suppose it was him gave you my name?'

'No, ma'am. That was the bartender at the Keystone.'

'Leke?' Her eyes moved as she thought about this. 'I didn't

know he'd seen me in Jimmy's company.'

'Were you trying to keep your association under wraps?'

She shook her head, eyes still set on the distance. 'No. I just forget how claustrophobic this town is sometimes.' She turned to me. 'Did you say Jimmy talked about taking his own life?'

I nodded.

'When was this?'

'The day he died.'

She brought her hand to her face and touched the corner of her mouth gingerly. 'Do you think he went through with it? That the fire . . .'

I looked across the field towards her car, could make out her driver looking in our direction. A light breeze blew across me, carrying the smell of mud and heavy duty oil. 'It's possible.'

'You sound unconvinced.'

'I think it's unlikely.'

'Because you think he was murdered.'

'How about you tell me. Did he have reason to take his own life?'

'I couldn't say. We weren't that close.' She trailed off at the end so her voice was almost a whisper. There was a sadness to the way she said it that gave her away.

'You said Jimmy first approached you sometime in August?'

'Yes.'

'What made him come to you?'

'We had a common acquaintance, in Texarkana. I used to live there, and she suggested he speak to me.'

A judder ran through my chest. 'You're from Texarkana?'

'Not originally, but I lived there a long time.'

'When did you leave?'

'Three or four years ago. Why do you ask?'

I sat upright. 'I told you I met Jimmy on a story – that was in Texarkana. You hear about the Phantom killings there a few months back?'

'Of course – it was all over the news. People here were running to the police because they were terrified the killer was hiding in their backyard.'

'When Jimmy called me, he spoke as though there could be a link between those murders and what's happening here. You have any idea what that could be?'

'I don't understand. They found the killer, I thought? He shot himself before the police could take him in.'

That was how the Texarkana cops had told the story, and was the only version I'd seen reported in the aftermath of the killings. I knew the real truth of course; the memory of standing over Richard Davis when he shot himself was always with me, clear as day – the Phantom Killer no more, just a corpse in a rotting clearing in the woods. 'He's dead, yes. I was thinking there might be some other kind of link, something more subtle – maybe something to do with Cole Barrett. Who was your friend that put Jimmy onto you?'

'Catherine Stanton. Do you know her?'

I shook my head, a momentary surge of hope snuffed out. I lodged it in my memory anyway. 'My first question still stands: why was Jimmy interested in Jeannie Runnels' death?'

She moistened her lips. 'He never volunteered a reason, and I never asked. He told me he was writing a story about her and the other woman that was killed and he wanted to know everything I could tell him about what happened. You know how he talked – "lies" and "evil" and "righteousness", but he spoke in riddles a lot of the time. Especially after he'd taken a drink.'

I wondered if he'd spoken those words of Barrett. If whatever Robinson had learned, he was seeing it through the prism of what had gone down in Texarkana; if, in his mind, he was still trying to right those wrongs. 'Can you tell me what you told him about the murder? I know it's hard.'

She twisted her fingers together. 'I only know the little the police told me, and I don't see what good it would do. Jimmy asked about it endlessly, Mr Yates, and I would prefer not to trawl through it all again.'

I covered my face with my hands and took a deep breath, weighing how far to push her. 'I don't want to cause you undue distress, ma'am. Let me be specific – just a few questions.'

She looked at me, brown eyes searching my face. Whatever reassurance she was looking for, she must have found it; she nodded once and looked out over the construction works in front of us.

'Can you tell me how Walter Glover came into contact with Miss Runnels?'

'In what sense?'

'I mean was it a crime of opportunity? Of passion? Was she known to him?'

'If you're trying to spare my blushes, you can save yourself the trouble. You're asking me if he was a customer of hers?'

'Lady, I don't care how he knew her, I'm just asking if he did.'

Her cheeks flushed a little. 'I'm sorry, I've no reason to be curt with you. I'm not in that line of work any more, but I refuse to be ashamed of it.'

'It's none of my business. I'm just trying to figure out what angle Jimmy was working.'

'I'd never heard Glover's name before. That's not to say they couldn't have met – Jeannie was her own woman – but the police said they made some enquiries among the others, and no one recalled seeing him before.'

'Where did she work?'

'Why, at Duke's. I thought you knew?'

I closed my eyes and laughed once under my breath. Smart Jimmy, not a coincidence that he'd chosen to stay there. 'But that wasn't where she was murdered?'

'No. She kept a room in a boarding house on Quapaw Avenue. It was supposed to be her escape. That's where they found her body.'

I tried not to imagine the scene – her terror as the killer tightened her own nylons around her throat. Clawing at his wrists. Her screams. 'Were there any witnesses? Someone must have heard something.'

'A neighbour reported shouts and that's what led the police to investigate. No one else, though. None of the other boarders were home at the time.'

'Did you or Miss Runnels know Bess Prescott?'

She shook her head. 'I didn't know her. I can't say for sure about Jeannie, but she'd never once mentioned her to me.'

'She didn't work with you at Duke's, then?'

'I never told you I worked there, Mr Yates. I see Clay Tucker's discretion only went so far.'

'Like I said, that's not my concern here.'

'No. I'd never heard of her.'

I rubbed the back of my neck. 'Did Jimmy ever mention a

third victim to you? Did he say anything at all about it?'

'No, he never did. I don't know what he could have meant by that.'

I took the photograph from my pocket, expecting the same response as everyone else had given me. It was still a small disappointment when she looked at it and shook her head. 'Who is she?' she said.

'At a guess, she's Jimmy's third victim. Seems like she's a ghost.' I leaned back against the bench, feeling like the story was impenetrable. What did Jimmy see in the deaths of these women that drew him here? Where did Barrett and Glover fit into the picture? Did he even get himself killed, or was I seeing malice where there was none?

'Mr Yates, I can sense your frustration, but may I ask you a question?'

I looked at her, waiting.

'You said you thought Sheriff Barrett may have been something to do with why Jimmy called you. What makes you say that?'

I wondered if she'd sensed I was holding back something about Barrett – or if she just thought the comment was curious. 'The lawmen in Texarkana ran to their own rules, and they didn't care too much who got hurt along the way. I'm starting to think maybe Barrett's cut from the same cloth, and that's what brought Jimmy here.'

'Do you think he might have had something to do with Jimmy's death?'

'I don't know. You never answered my question on the telephone – did Jimmy ever talk about him to you?'

She took a white handkerchief from her clutch and dabbed

her nose. 'No. I don't believe he did.'

The headlamps on her car flashed twice and she looked up, startled.

'Who's the wheelman?' I said.

'A friend. You'll forgive me, Mr Yates, but it would seem he's getting impatient.' She stood up in a rush and offered her hand. 'It was a pleasure to make your acquaintance. I'm sorry for your loss; Jimmy was a troubled man, but I think that's because he had such a big heart.'

She took a step back and then turned and made her way up the path. The wind had picked up and was going on cold now. I folded my arms and waited as she climbed into the car. From what I could see, neither she nor the driver spoke. The sedan wheeled around in a circle and headed off down the road, and I watched until it passed behind the bleachers, disappearing from sight. Robinson had been living in town three weeks before he died, and visiting her for a month or so before that; what little Ella Borland had told me wasn't enough to explain why that was.

Clay Tucker told me they were together at Duke's the Saturday before last; I tried to picture them – an intimate conversation in the same place she and Jeannie Runnels had worked together. Jimmy asking about the case for the thousandth time, Borland telling him she'd already given it all up. I didn't buy it, she knew more than she was saying – about Runnels' death or Jimmy's, and maybe both.

CHAPTER FIFTEEN

When I thought about it, seemed like there was one man in town with as much antipathy towards Cole Barrett as me.

Early the next morning, I parked outside a converted real estate broker's office off Central that was listed as the headquarters of the GI movement. I expected to have to wait a while for the staffers to show up, but there was a man sitting inside already, leaning against a desk and flicking through the morning's paper.

I rapped on the window and he looked up. If he was surprised to have a visitor at that hour, he didn't show it. I held my press card up to the window and waited as he crossed towards me. When he opened up, I introduced myself and told him I was looking for Samuel Masters.

'Well, you've found him, sir.' The man flashed an uneven smile that wasn't the usual practised effort of elected officials, his eyes narrowing almost to slits.

'Mr Masters, there are matters I'd like to speak with you about, most particularly a former sheriff by the name of Cole Barrett. I think you know him.'

He looked reluctant until he heard the name. 'Barrett? What about him?'

'I'd like to know why you threatened to put him in front of a grand jury over the Glover case.'

He opened the door fully and stood against it with his arms

folded. 'I don't usually conduct my business on the doorstep. Come in.'

I stepped through the doorway and waited for him to show me inside. The office was makeshift and utilitarian; row upon row of tables served for desks, most overflowing with campaign materials and other papers. More posters and signs were piled in the corners and against the walls, which were themselves plastered with electioneering slogans and bills. I noticed there were no partitions or private offices. Incongruous among all of it was a hand bell strung from a bracket attached to the wall. I realised it was a sale bell, presumably left behind by the previous occupants.

He perched on the nearest desk and gestured for me to take the one opposite. 'We don't go in much for comforts here, I'm afraid.'

Masters would have made for a good defensive lineman. He looked to be in his early forties and was built like a fire plug, a head shorter than me, but with a barrel chest and wide torso. He had mid-length wavy hair, combed to one side and receding some along the part. He wore a clean white shirt, a pen in his top pocket, and a sober necktie that was already loose. His front left tooth was chipped. At a guess, he cultivated his appearance carefully; he looked like a blue collar Joe, with smarts enough to go toe-to-toe in a courtroom or a bar room without looking out of place in either. 'I'm fine standing, thank you.'

'If you'll pardon my speaking plain, what's a California man doing in Hot Springs? I knew our little revolt here was making waves, but I didn't think they'd travelled that far.'

'A friend asked me to come. He died in the fire at Duke's last week.'

He unclasped his hands and rested them on his thighs. 'I know about that fire. My sympathies.'

I nodded to acknowledge him. 'He was investigating the murders committed by Walter Glover. I've been looking into the case some and the way Cole Barrett gunned Glover down. The scenario as it was reported sounded curious to me.'

'That's interesting.' He picked up a mug of coffee and took a sip. 'Struck me the same way when it happened. Suspect offers his confession, then tries to shoot his way out of it. Not your usual chain of events.'

'You have a theory on what might have really went down?' I answered my own question. 'I mean, you must have if you were fixing to put Barrett in front of a grand jury.'

'A theory? I wouldn't say anything as complete as that. *Concerns* is maybe a better way to put it. Cole Barrett has been running bag for Teddy Coughlin for years, so when I heard he'd killed a man, of course it got my attention, and even more so when I heard the particulars.'

Barrett as bagman for the mayor. I held onto my surprise, not wanting to look a naïf, the casual way he said it making it sound like no big secret. 'Are you saying Coughlin had something to do with the shooting?'

'We're off the record here, right?'

'If that's what you want.'

'It is. Now, sorry to disappoint, but I'm still not going to answer that question in the affirmative. Don't misunderstand, I would love to be able to hand you some evidence to show Teddy was involved somehow, but there isn't any. Me and my men raked through it because when a dog bites a person, you don't scold the dog, you look to the man holding his leash,

126

you understand? But truth of it is, I didn't expect to find much of anything because I just couldn't figure out why Coughlin would have cause to bother himself about a sewer rat like Glover.'

'Is Coughlin that dirty?'

'Enough to have a man killed?' He took his time drawing in a breath. 'I'd go as far as to say nothing would surprise me.'

'You're thinking of something specific.'

He wrinkled his eyes and tilted his head, reluctant.

'Off the record, I swear. If you know something . . .'

He swelled his chest taking a breath and held it. Then he talked. 'Before Barrett, the Garland County Sheriff was a man name of Cooper. In nineteen forty-one he was shot dead in the street in the middle of the afternoon. No witnesses came forward, no one was charged or even arrested. He'd been in the job nine months.' His eyes were fixed on mine, unblinking. 'The rumour – the persistent rumour – is that Teddy had him killed because he refused to enforce his protection business for him and threatened to go talk to the state boys in Little Rock if Teddy didn't let him alone.'

'Was Coughlin ever investigated?'

He flicked his hand. 'By who? Teddy got Barrett elected as his replacement and Garland Sheriff's took charge of the investigation. Six weeks later Pearl Harbor happened and no one gave a damn about a dead lawman any more.'

I straightened on the desk. 'Was it Barrett pulled the trigger?'

He shook his head. 'He was at the courthouse escorting a suspect at the time. His alibi's solid – maybe because Teddy wanted to ensure there was no suspicion on him. So far as I know, no one's come up with a name for the shooter.'

My mind was racing, too many connections being made at once, jamming the switchboard. There was Teddy Coughlin's name coming up again; I saw a jagged line from Robinson's burnt-out room all the way to the mayor's office, but couldn't begin to guess the route that line took. If nothing else, it cemented my feeling that Robinson had gotten into something way over his head. 'Then why did you pursue the grand jury angle if you had nothing on Barrett?'

He held up his hands, the lopsided grin back on his face. 'Sometimes, you just have to march on into the cornfield to see what startles. Even if Teddy wasn't involved, Barrett's version of events didn't hold water to me, and as it turned out, there must have been something to it, because the next thing I knew, Teddy was calling me to work out a deal to have Barrett step down. *Retire*, as he had it.'

'And you let him.' The words sounded sharp as they left my lips, and I cursed myself for risking putting the man's back up.

In the event, Masters just shrugged. 'I'm fighting a dozen electoral races here – having one break my way by getting the incumbent off the ballot paper was worth it. But indulge me and go back a step – what does this have to do with your friend?'

I opened my mouth to speak but instead took a breath, deciding which version of the truth to tell him. Masters had an easygoing manner about him that somehow engendered trust, but his eyes were as hard and sharp as razors. I could imagine men following him into a fire fight – just as easily as I could imagine him putting a bullet into an enemy soldier. It convinced me to play it straight. 'I think he was murdered.'

He scratched his top lip with his thumbnail. 'I'd like to know what makes you say that.'

I gave him a précis of Robinson's call to me, ending with his line about making a mistake. 'That was a week before the fire. If nothing else, doesn't the timing strike you as suspicious?'

He jutted out his bottom jaw and looked to the ceiling, considering it. Then he looked at me again. 'There's nothing wrong with your instincts, buddy, but do you think you might be adding two and two and getting five?' He slipped off the table's edge and stood facing me. His posture was rigid, shoulders square, still carried a military bearing.

'I don't follow.'

'I had some men I trust look into that fire. Hell, I've got men looking under all sorts of rocks just now, and something like that we'd look at as a matter of course. The man who runs the joint is a lowlife by the name of Clay Tucker—'

'I spoke with him.'

He nodded. 'Assumed you might have. The day after the fire, we got a titbit saying Mr Tucker is behind on his payments to Teddy Coughlin's people. A long way behind, at that.'

'Coughlin again? Why does his name keep cropping up no matter what I'm asking about?'

He put his hands on his hips. 'Because he's a cancer that has a hold on every part of this town. If you haven't got the picture yet, nothing gets done here without his say-so. He takes a cut of every dollar that gets spent in every casino and every bordello. He's got cops in his pocket. Judges. He controls thousands of votes – anyone who works for the city, the casinos, their families, all of them.' He was talking like a zealot now, stabbing his finger into his other palm to emphasise each point. 'He decides who gets what office, and he has done for twenty years, and I've had my fill.' He stared at me and swallowed, composing himself again. 'I didn't drag my carcass around every goddamn island in the Pacific, in the name of democracy, to come back to America and be told my vote didn't count. That no one's did. No way in hell.'

His conviction was evident, and the way he expressed it hinted at the power and violence I'd sensed in the man. Straight away, though, his face softened again and he clapped me on the shoulder, the soldier giving way to the politician. 'Sorry. You didn't come here to listen to me stump. The point I started out to make was that if you think Duke's burning down was no accident, Clay Tucker being behind on what he owed is where I'd focus my enquiries.'

I put my hand in my pocket, the whole conspiracy I'd built starting to crumble around me. Robinson's death not an accident after all, but nothing to do with him or the dead women. 'But the fire started in my friend's room. Why would...' I trailed off and looked to one side, still working through the implications.

'I'm told the fire department put the blame on your friend for being careless with a cigarette, is that right?' I nodded, my eyes still on the wall, thinking. 'Well, that makes for a pretty good cover story, doesn't it? Teddy's group are having to tread real carefully right now, because they know we're watching every move they make, waiting for a misstep. That's why I was surprised they'd be as bold as to do something like this now. No matter how well they covered their tracks, it's not the kind of thing you want happening around election time. Got me to thinking that maybe Clay Tucker set the fire himself.'

I felt the blood pounding in my temples. 'Tucker? Why?'

He held up his forefinger. 'I'm speculating now, you understand, but it would sure solve a bunch of his problems, wouldn't it? The insurance money lets him pay back what he owes and gets Teddy off his back. I don't mean to trivialise what happened to your friend, but could be he just got caught in the middle.'

I gripped the table, telling myself it was just talk, but seeing Tucker's face in my mind nonetheless. Seeing him lie to me. Bullshit me and make me for a fool. I remembered how tightly wound he was when I'd started poking around, and it suddenly took on a new perspective – the man worried I was about to expose him for being complicit in some way.

Masters put his hand on my shoulder again, leaving it there this time. 'I can see that look in your eyes, buddy, and I'm gonna tell you to just take a breath here. Whatever Clay Tucker did or did not do – and I stress that last part – you charging off after him won't make anything right.'

'I'm a reporter, not a brawler. If I go after him, I'll have a pen in my hand.'

'Is that why you're gripping the table like you're about to fall off the edge of the world?' He nodded to my knuckles, spotting white. 'Listen to me: aside from the fact that if something were to happen to friend Tucker, I'd be obliged to bring a charge to your doorstep soon as I take office, there's the small matter that he's still assuredly under the protection of Teddy's men. Either because he's paid up, or more likely, because they won't want any harm coming to him until he has. Don't underestimate what these men are capable of, Mr Yates. Teddy's in a tight squeeze, so he's getting desperate, and desperate men are unpredictable.'

131

I shrugged his hand off my shoulder. 'I don't need your permission to go have a talk with Tucker.'

He rubbed his forehead with his fingertips. 'You're lashing out at the wrong man. Whatever happened in Duke's that night, if you stick your neck out, you might just find a blade against it. You'd be making a mistake to underestimate the thugs you're dealing with here.'

I spoke with my teeth clenched. 'What would your suggestion be?'

'Leave these matters alone, let me and my men handle it. We'll get Teddy Coughlin – at the ballot box first, then in the courtroom, god willing.'

I made for the door. 'I didn't hear you say anything about Clay Tucker.'

'We'll get to them all, in time.' His tone was calm and assured, like a teacher talking to a student. 'Rash undertakings seldom turn out the way we expect. Think on that.'

I glanced back from the open doorway. 'I'll bear it in mind.'

CHAPTER SIXTEEN

I knew there was sense to Masters' words about acting rashly; it was the same rap my editor in New York, Tom Walters, used to lay on me. I knew as much, and still I didn't care.

I raced across Central towards Duke's. The anger in my chest felt like a buzz saw was loose in there, and my fists gripped the steering wheel.

I tried to reel myself back in. I didn't have any evidence against Clay Tucker, but that just made my temper worse – as though he'd lied to me and thought he could get away with it. All I had were my suspicions and the speculation of a man I'd just met – but something made Masters' words carry weight with me; he spoke with a heartfelt anger that reminded me of Robinson.

I pulled up by Duke's and jumped out, leaving the car at an angle to the kerb. The doors to the saloon were locked. I checked my watch, saw it was only eight-thirty. Too early for a bar to be open to the public, but not too early for Tucker to be there working on his cleanup. I looked around. The drugstore next door was open and I went inside and found the store clerk, asked him if he knew where Tucker was.

'At a guess, he's probably sleeping one off. He's had one heck of a rough week.'

'Do you happen to know where he lives?'

'Sure, right upstairs from the bar. Until the fire.'

'And now?'

The clerk opened his hands. 'I haven't a clue, sorry.'

'Have you seen him this morning?'

'No, sir. Haven't seen him since Saturday.'

'Not one time?'

He shook his head. 'Doors haven't been open once.'

I balled my hands and planted them on the counter. 'And you're sure you don't know where he's staying now? Think about it before you answer.'

The clerk took a step back. 'No, sir, I don't. What do you want him for, exactly?'

The tremor as he spoke made me pause. Another voice came into my head, that of Ella Borland, speaking to me the day before, asking me if this was a matter of revenge. I'd told her it wasn't, that it was about justice, but now I wasn't convinced. I took in the clerk's face, his discomfort at having me bawl him out in his own store, and realised my temper was out of control. It jolted me, bringing to mind everything that weakness had cost me before. Justice wasn't served by me laying my hands on Clay Tucker, and much less by running a two-bit intimidation number on this man. I took a breath and unclenched my fists. 'I'd like to talk to him, is all. I'll stop by again.'

I beelined it back to the street, feeling a smaller man than when I went in. I leaned on the hood of the car and tried to bring some order to my mind. Because it dawned on me then that Ella Borland had been right – at least in part. That a need for revenge was driving me as much as any desire for justice. That didn't sit well; I had no right to lay claim to anger at Robinson's death. It hadn't escaped my attention that somewhere along the line I'd started referring to him as my friend –

a useful shorthand at first, but now used almost by way of explanation. As a justification. *We weren't friends* – those were my own thoughts when I'd arrived in Hot Springs, and now they served as a testament to my hypocrisy.

I closed my eyes. If I was going to pursue this, it had to be in the name of finding the truth of what happened to Robinson – not some reckless crusade for revenge, anger holding my reins. Nothing good was served by that.

I got back into the car and sat there, cooling off by trying to figure out my next move. My gut told me Clay Tucker wasn't coming back. He'd been gone for three days, and if his debts were as bad as Masters made out, chances were he was in the wind. There was merit in what Masters said about the simplest explanation usually being the right one. But even knowing that, my thoughts kept tracking back to Barrett and Coughlin. I had a firm link between the two men now; Barrett running bag explained Coughlin's motivation in intervening to protect him from a grand jury. And the rumours about Coughlin ordering the murder of the previous sheriff elevated him to a whole new level of criminal.

Favours owed and favours repaid. Had to make for a nervous situation between the two men now – both counting on the loyalty of the other, just as Masters' campaign made the price of that loyalty skyrocket.

Jimmy Robinson had been wading around in the Glover case for weeks before he died; what if he'd turned up some evidence to incriminate Barrett? If so, and Coughlin or Barrett had got wise to the fact, it was the start of a motive for why they might want him dead. A panic move, but a necessary risk, even in the glare of Masters' spotlight.

As a theory it was a long way from watertight, and I knew it. I kept moving the pieces around in my mind, trying to figure out who was more compromised, who had the most to gain from silencing Robinson, but I just didn't have enough to see the picture. Maybe there was no picture, Clay Tucker the target all along. Jimmy unfortunate to be in the wrong place at the wrong time.

Businesses along the street started to stir, but Duke's remained dark and still. I figured I had little chance of catching up with Tucker before Coughlin's men, but then I had an idea for a long shot. I drove up to the Arlington and placed a call to Ella Borland's number. A voice I didn't recognise from the previous times said she hadn't been in that day and to try the Southern Club. I thanked the man and hung up.

The Southern was right across the street from me. The frontage was less garish than that of the Ohio, but not by much; it sported the familiar striped awnings, a candy-cane green and white in this case, but the structure was more understated – a grey concrete facade with minimal flourishes.

I went inside and found myself in a deserted restaurant. The tables were laid and ready for service – the lights glinting off buffed silverware, the smell of parched white tablecloths – but all stood empty. I spotted a waiter in the far corner. I went over and asked for Ella Borland.

He nodded to the grand staircase at the back of the room. 'She's rehearsing.'

I climbed the stairs and garnered a nod from a heavy seated on a stool on the landing. Open double doors led into a large room that evidently served as the casino. There were three roulette wheels, a half-dozen dice tables, a chuck-a-luck cage and three rows of slot machines. Even at that hour on a Tuesday morning, one of the dice tables had a thin crowd around it, and the slots were seeing action, the continuous dinging of bells like a fire truck.

At the far end was a small stage. Ella Borland and two other women were on it, walking through the steps of some kind of dance routine. I moved closer and watched, waiting for a chance to talk to her.

The stage wasn't lit and the women moved at half-speed, stopping to re-do a step every few seconds. It was apparent that Borland was no natural; her movements were stilted by comparison to the other two women, and she struggled to keep pace with them. Even so, she moved with a certain grace, and was mesmerising. She kept her eyes on the back of the room, and where the other two wore smiles that were too wide to be mistaken for real, Borland just seemed to shimmer, in a way that could buckle your knees.

She stopped abruptly when she caught sight of me, and the spell was broken. She looked uncomfortable at noting my presence; she said something to the others and then slipped off the stage and came over to where I was standing. 'Mr Yates, what are you doing here?'

'As it happens, I was looking for you.'

'Why? We don't have anything more to talk about. I'm certain I made it plain when we met that I don't care to trawl through everything again.'

I held up my hand. 'I'm not here about Jimmy. I need your help – I'm trying to track down Clay Tucker. He's not been seen at Duke's since Saturday. You happen to know where else I could try?'

'Clay Tucker? I wouldn't have the first idea. I have nothing to do with that man.'

'I understand that, but I'm wondering if he had any family in the area, something along those lines.'

She glanced back at the stage, the other two dancers now in hushed conversation to one side of it, then looked back at me. 'He talked about a brother, sometimes. Leland, I think. I remember him saying he lived out by Stokes Creek.'

I memorised the place name to look up after. 'Do you have anything more specific?'

She shook her head. 'I have to get on.'

'I appreciate it.'

She started to walk to the stage, then stopped and turned back. 'What do you want with Clay Tucker, Mr Yates?'

I stepped closer to her again. 'I spoke to Samuel Masters earlier and he had some interesting things to say. The more people I talk to, the less it seems like that fire was an accident. I think Clay Tucker knows what really happened, and I'm going to make him tell me.'

She frowned. 'Why, what did Mr Masters say to you?'

I put my hands in my pockets. 'That Clay Tucker is behind on his debts to some serious people. I'd like to know if that had some bearing on what happened.'

Her hands were by her sides and she splayed them, but only for as long as it took her to realise she'd done it. 'If you find him, you won't mention my name, will you?'

I shook my head, wondering why she looked so worried. 'No, of course not.'

She nodded and then turned and went back to the stage.

I watched her a moment longer, thinking she looked rattled.

But it was fleeting, and in a moment she was moving fluidly again. The casino sounds came back to me and started to grate. I wheeled around and crossed the room heading for the stairway.

Halfway there, I stopped in my tracks. William Tindall was standing with one of the pit bosses, his eyes moving around the room, taking everything in. Before I could think, I'd ducked out of sight behind a bank of slot machines. I let a second pass before I peered over to watch. The pit man was trying to argue a point, but his words just seemed to bounce off Tindall. He persisted, each sentence rolling into the next, until something he said caused Tindall to look him straight in the eyes.

Right away the pit man fell silent. His mouth parted and his head tilted to one side, like he'd just missed the last lifeboat. Then he held one hand up and backed away. From what I could tell, Tindall hadn't even spoken a word.

Keeping out of sight, I slipped along the row of slots towards the exit.

CHAPTER SEVENTEEN

Stokes Creek was a long and narrow inlet off the Ouachita River, running along the southern edge of the airfield I'd first flown in at. I could see houses spaced all around the U-shaped shoreline as I drove towards it, the opposite banks of the waterway no more than three hundred yards apart. I stopped at the general store at the eastern tip of the creek and asked for directions to Tucker's brother's place – a half-mile down the road it turned out.

The house was a sprawling wooden structure near the water's edge, with flaking green shutters and a shady porch that ran the length of the bottom storey on the landward side of the property. There were four rocking chairs spaced along it, Clay Tucker sitting in one wearing a yellowing white shirt, and a man who looked like him sitting in another. I'd driven out there to grill Tucker's brother on Clay's whereabouts, assuming there was no chance he'd be hiding out from Coughlin somewhere so obvious, and yet there he was, bold as a Halloween lantern. It was another wrinkle that didn't make sense.

I stopped the car out front, and as I did, I saw two pickup trucks parked on the far side of the house. The closer of the two looked like the one I'd chased outside the Mountain Motor Court that night.

Tucker saw me as soon I opened the car door. He jumped out of his chair, sending it rocking wildly. He bolted along the porch and disappeared around the side of the house. I ran after him. The second man darted towards me and tried to block me off, but I had the momentum and barged him out of the way, sprinting full pelt after Tucker.

I rounded the house and saw him in a small boat, ripping the starter cord on the outboard motor. I splashed into the shallows, water kicking up all around me, and shoved him over the side, nearly toppling myself as I did. He clawed his way up to all fours in the brown water, spluttering and panting.

'Why'd you run, Tucker?'

The second man jogged down the bank but stopped short of the water. 'Clay?'

Tucker turned his head, water dripping from his hair. 'Go on inside. Get the shotgun.'

I shouted over to the brother, still pointing at Tucker. 'You bring a gun out here and I'll break it over your head. Stay there.'

The brother looked at me and must have seen a madman – knee-deep in the muddy water, suit trousers soaked through, balling my fist. There was doubt on his face and he didn't move.

I waded around the boat so I was standing over Tucker. 'The fire was no accident, was it?'

He pushed himself up so he was on his knees. His face was white as a sheet. 'I don't know what you're talking about.'

'You're in hock to Teddy Coughlin. Start there.'

He got to his feet and called out to his brother. 'Leland, will you go inside and get the goddamn gun?'

'DON'T MOVE.' I turned back to Tucker. 'Who started the fire, them or you?'

He started to make for the bank, but I stood in his way.

'You don't know the first damn thing, do you?' he said.

'So tell me.'

'And wind up like your friend? No way.'

I stepped closer to him. 'What does that mean?'

He was shaking and it spilled into a scared laugh. 'It means talking to you'll get me killed.'

'Why? By who?'

He stumbled around me and out of the water and flopped down onto the mud. He hung his head. 'Why's this have to land on my doorstep? I ain't never wanted nothing to do with this.'

'Answer the question, goddamn you.'

'I don't know, already.' He held his arms out. 'Ain't like no one sat me down and explained anything to me. The man calls me and says, "*Get outta your bar or you're gonna burn*," so I did. Next thing I know, I got two goons bouncing my head off the wall and telling me to keep my mouth shut. I tried to tell them, I can't say nothing 'cause I don't know nothing—'

My brain fritzed. He was warned in advance. He could have stopped it. 'Who? Who called you?'

He shook his head. 'Walk away, city boy. Get the hell out of here while you can.'

I jumped on top of him and had my hands at his throat before I knew what I was doing. 'Why didn't you warn him?' I pressed him into the mud. 'Why didn't you tell—'

There was a shout behind me. I lifted my head and saw Leland advancing on us with a shotgun aimed from his hip. 'I said, get off of him.'

I let go of his throat and staggered to my feet. Tucker reached for his neck, gasping.

'You left Jimmy to burn. You could've saved him.'

Leland picked his way down the bank until he was standing close to Tucker.

Tucker screwed his face up. 'Jimmy's the one they wanted. I try to warn him and they'd have killed us both. It was him or me. I never wished no harm upon him, but I got kids, I got a wife.'

'So you saved yourself.'

He looked along the water, squinting.

I eyed Leland and his shotgun, no inkling how close he was to pulling the trigger or not. 'Who killed him, Clay? Give me that and I'll take my leave.'

He fixed me with a look now. 'I swear to you, I ain't know what's going on.'

'Who warned you?'

He shook his head, drops of water shaking loose from his hair.

I knelt down so I was at eyeball level with him. Leland tracked me with the gun barrel. 'I know you're afraid. I can help you. Give me the name.'

He scoffed. 'How you gonna help me? You got an army behind you I don't see?'

'Samuel Masters is looking for ways to get at Teddy Coughlin. If you tell him what you know—'

He slapped the mud with the flat of his hand. 'Fink on Big Teddy? Y'all dumber than you look. Masters is a flash in the pan, Teddy ain't never going away. Everyone knows it too, and that's why ain't no one gonna open the book on him.'

'Don't be naïve. There's always a weak link. Always. Someone'll be desperate enough to talk, and he's the only one going to get a pass. This is your chance to—'

'No one ever crossed Teddy and walked away.' He pushed a strand of wet hair from his temple. 'No one.' He reached up without taking his eyes off me, gripped the shotgun's barrel and pointed it at his own head. 'I'll make Leland pull the damn trigger before I rat Teddy out. It's the same damn thing.'

I looked away over the water, the fear on his face contagious.

'Anyway, I done told you I don't know nothing. I don't know what Jimmy done to end up like that.'

'Who called to warn you? I'm not going away until you spill on that.'

'Are you confused about who's side Leland's on?'

I looked at Leland, saw his finger wasn't touching the trigger. I took a swing in the dark. 'Leland's not a killer, he's not firing that gun. Neither of you are.' My heartbeat ran triple-time. 'Tell me.'

'I can't, goddammit.' His eyes welled up. 'I never wanted this. I never wanted none of this.'

'You want money?' I took my wallet out. 'You owe Coughlin, right? How much?'

'More than you got.'

I drew my sleeve across my face, taking the sweat from my forehead and leaving creek water in its place. 'Try this then: I'll go have a talk with your insurance adjuster; figure he'll be interested to hear how you knew about the fire and let it happen.'

He was still then.

'Think I won't?' I said.

'Goddammit, leave me out of this, can't you? You gonna get us all killed.'

'You left an innocent man to die. Don't try me for sympathy.'

He looked at his brother, uncertainty writ across his face. 'Son of a bitch.' Then he closed his eyes. 'Cole Barrett.'

It shouldn't have been a surprise to hear his name, and still it shocked me. I rose up slowly, feeling water seeping up my trouser legs like a creeping panic. Barrett set the fire – so whatever Robinson had on him was serious enough to kill for. 'Did Coughlin order it?'

'That's what I'm telling you, I ain't have a clue what was behind it. On our mother's grave.' His eyes were wide, pleading. Afraid.

Leland had let the gun sag below his paunch, his fight all but gone. They would have been pitiful in other circumstances.

'That was you at my motel room window the other night, wasn't it? Your pickup truck.'

Tucker offered no denial.

'What were you doing there?'

He let his head loll back, his arms still wrapped around his knees. 'See what all you was up to. You come around asking all them questions . . . made me nervous as hell.'

I stared at him, deciding what my next move was.

Tucker must have sensed as much. 'You can't go to the cops and you can't go after Barrett,' he said. 'Do like I told you and walk away. For all our sakes.'

I tried to marshal my thoughts. I thought about Robinson's notes sitting back in my room, wondered if the truth about Barrett was in there somewhere. And what he'd do to me if he knew they existed. 'Never.'

CHAPTER EIGHTEEN

I left Tucker staggering back into his brother's house and drove away from Stokes Creek. I wanted like hell to drag them to the authorities to see them punished, but as limp a pair as they were, it was still them had the shotgun, and it spoke for them.

It felt like my guts were lodged in my throat. If Barrett killed Robinson to keep something buried, then it stood to reason he'd kill me too if he thought I was a threat. I thought back to my theory, that Barrett found out Glover wasn't the murderer sometime after he shot him. Was that motive enough – or was it something even more sinister?

I parked outside my room at the Mountain Motor Court and sank my head against the steering wheel. My soaking trousers clung to my calves, and my skin felt cold and stained with dirt. The snatched memory of another conversation came back to me, Dinsmore speculating about the fire report being falsified by Teddy Coughlin's office; what was pure guesswork at the time now seemed a real possibility – and it indicated a conspiracy that went so high, there was no way I could penetrate it. It felt like the walls were closing in on me.

I dragged myself out of the car and unlocked my room door. I stepped inside and froze cold. Cole Barrett was standing in the far corner.

'We need to talk. Shut the door.' He looked me up and down. 'The hell happened to you?'

A tremor ran head to toe through me. I glanced at his hands – empty, but he was wearing a hip holster. His wicker Stetson was on my bed, thrown there like he was home. I weighed making a run for it, but then I remembered Robinson's papers – and then saw they were gone. 'Where are they?'

'Where's what?'

'The files. You cleared them out already?'

'You're talking double Dutch. Bring yourself inside.'

I pushed the door over without taking my eyes off him. 'What do you want?'

'You need to quit playing detective before you get yourself hurt.'

My chest tightened like a drum. 'Don't threaten me.'

'I ain't threatening you. Clean your ears out, you'll hear I'm offering you a warning.'

'Same way you did with Jimmy Robinson?'

He uncrossed his arms, looked at me through narrowed eyes.

'Did you set the fire at Duke's?' I said.

'What? No, course I didn't.'

'I know you knew about it.'

'Ain't the same thing.' He stepped out of the corner and set himself in the middle of the room. 'You been talking to Clay Tucker.'

I said nothing, imagining Tucker squealing to Barrett the minute I left. Every muscle in my body was tensed. 'Who did then?'

He closed his eyes and exhaled. 'The more you know, the quicker it'll get you killed.'

'I'll take my chances.'

'Then you sure as hell gonna end up like your friend. A little bit of knowledge is a dangerous thing.'

'You condescending son of a—'

'You think there's safety in the truth, is that it? I'm here to tell you it got your friend killed. Hell, the man that wore the sheriff's badge before me was shot in broad daylight because he didn't know when to zip his mouth, and wasn't no one even arrested for it. That's how truth goes in this town.'

'Sheriff Cooper. Your boss had him killed, didn't he? Put you right in the dead man's shoes.'

He glared at me, his jaw muscles bulging.

'My friend came to see you, didn't he? Jimmy Robinson.'

He ran his tongue over his teeth. Then he nodded. 'He did.'

'What did he want?'

'He'd arrived at a wrong conclusion.'

'Which was what?'

He shook his head. 'For your sake, you don't want me to get into it. Just know that he was wrong, and so are you if you think I killed him.'

'You came here for his papers, then. Dressing it up as some bullshit warning to me doesn't make you any different to a common thief.'

He twitched. 'I told you once, I ain't know what papers you're talking about. Now, I'll see myself out, but so I can leave knowing I made it plain, hear this: get out of town today. Right now. I'm sorry for your friend, but ain't no good can come from you ending up the same way.'

He picked up his hat and placed it on his head, started towards the door.

'Did Teddy Coughlin send you to deliver that message? He

must be in worse shape than I thought if you're the best he's got.'

He stopped in front of me. 'Ain't no one sent me.' He blew a breath out, frustrated. 'I tried my damnedest to warn your friend and he still wound up dead. I got no use for seeing history repeat.'

He opened the door, but I slammed it shut again. 'You're not leaving with those papers—'

Before I could finish the sentence, his pistol was out of his holster and in my stomach.

I couldn't hear anything, and for a heartbeat I thought he'd pulled the trigger and I was already falling. Then the sound of my own breathing broke through – shallow, distorted – and I felt the blood rushing back into my limbs. His face was inches from mine.

'I don't scare that easy, Barrett.' I tensed my gut to still a tremble as I said it.

He looked at me, held it, his eyes a watery blue that, strangely, betrayed no malice. 'I believe you. And it's a damn shame.'

He stepped around me and out through the door. I watched from the doorway as he crossed to the far end of the parking lot, hand on his gun, glancing back at me as he went. The grey LaSalle was parked among other cars there, same one I'd seen outside his house, and I kicked myself for missing it on the way in. He climbed inside and pulled away.

The fear started to subside, and in its place came the familiar surge of rage. I braced myself on the desk, shaking, fighting not to snatch up the chair from the floor and put it through the window, disgusted at my old weakness: finding bravery in anger only once the danger had passed. I took a half-dozen deep breaths, determined to control myself and not to slip back down the path of surrendering to my basest impulses.

The white heat passed, and all that was left was a hollow feeling, like taking a gutful of liquor on an empty stomach. I couldn't make any sense of it. Barrett admitted he'd known about the fire, but was adamant he wasn't behind it. Clay Tucker loomed in my thoughts, and I wondered if he'd bought me off with half the story – if he'd set the fire after all, but told me about Barrett's warning to let me jump to my own conclusions. But then there were Robinson's files – why would Barrett steal them if they weren't incriminating? How the hell did he even find out about them? And why was I still alive if it was him killed Robinson—

A knock at the door snapped me out of my thoughts with a start. I peered out the window, expecting I'd find Barrett, come back to finish the job. Instead, I saw the motel manager. I opened up.

'Mr Yates, got a message for—'

'Did you let someone into my room?'

'Pardon me?'

'My room. Did someone get a key from you?'

He blanched. 'Of course not. I don't know what you're referring to.'

Maybe I was a sucker, but I believed him. The lock was a simple one, easy enough to pick. Hell, Barrett could have had master keys for the whole town for all I knew. 'Forget it. What's the message?'

He looked shaken, struggling to keep up. 'It's— Your wife, she said it was urgent, so I thought I should come right over.'

'What did she say?'

'She sounded upset. She asked you to telephone as soon as possible.'

The floor lurched under me. I pushed past him and ran across to the office, yanked the door open. The telephone was on a desk at the side. I ducked under the counter and snatched it up. The operator got me a circuit to the *Journal* and I counted the seconds as I waited for the connection. The manager came in after me, panting, started a half-hearted protest about me using their line, but I shot him a look that shut him up.

Acheson's secretary answered and I asked for Lizzie.

'Mr Yates, is that you? She's gone home.'

'What's wrong?'

'You should talk with her.'

I broke the connection and asked the operator to put me through to our home line. When the call finally went through, Lizzie answered straightaway. 'Charlie?'

'I'm here. What's happened?'

Her voice was strained. 'We've been robbed. They— Our house, they've torn it apart.'

'Are you okay? Were you at home?'

'No, no, I'm all right. I was at the paper. Charlie, it's . . .' Her voice broke.

I closed my eyes, relief the first sensation flooding me at the knowledge she wasn't hurt. 'Tell me.'

'They've ransacked our home. It's ruined. Clothes, the furniture. Everything.'

'What did they take?'

'I can't be sure, it looks like a bomb went off. They broke all the windows.'

My head was pounding, blindsided by another haymaker. I tried to think what we had of value that they could have taken. 'When?'

'Sometime this morning. They must have come right after I left for the office. The police called to tell me they were here and it was a mess. They told me the neighbours telephoned it in.'

'Did they catch anyone?'

'No. No.'

'What about a description? They must have heard—'

'They told the officers it was two men, but the details they gave could be of anybody. Dark clothes, dark hats, stocky builds. They said they looked out in time to see them smash the last of the windows and then they took off towards the marina. They must have been inside the house for such a long time – they've wrecked everything.'

'I'm coming home. I'll get the first flight I can. Take a room in a hotel until I can get there. If you need money, get Acheson to float you an advance – I'll call him to—'

'Charlie, hold on a minute.' She snatched a breath. 'I will not be chased out of my own home again, not after Texarkana.' The indignation in her voice reminded me that my wife was tougher than she looked, and twice as wilful. It was one of the things I loved about her. 'I've called a locksmith and he's going to be here soon.' She faked a breezy tone. 'Besides, it's not like they left any reason to come back.'

'You'd be safer—'

'My mind's made up, Charlie. And I thought about it before you called, and I don't think you should come home. Not if you're not ready.'

'What? I need to be there. I need to know—'

'Hear me out.' She took a breath, as if she'd been preparing what she'd say next. 'What you said the other day struck a chord with me. You could have walked away at any point in Texarkana, and no one would have thought any less of you, but you didn't. That's who you are, and it's why I love you. I can't ask you to change now. If you can stop someone else having to go through what I did . . .'

I leaned on the desk, surprised by her candour – adrenaline and emotion loosening her tongue, everything spilling out together. The more she told me to stay, the more I wanted to go to her. 'Will you reconsider on the hotel, at least?'

'I'd sooner buy a gun.'

I smiled despite myself. 'I'll call you again tonight.'

'I'll be here.'

*

Gravel dust clung to my damp trouser legs as I made my way back across the parking lot. The urge to blow town walked with me. Lizzie was scared, maybe even in danger. Robinson's notes were gone. I could still feel where Barrett's gun touched my stomach. I put my hand on the doorknob and thought about just walking away. Lizzie's words echoed in my ears then, and it shamed me to think she held me in higher esteem than I ever deserved.

I went inside to change into dry clothes. I pulled a new shirt on, thinking about Robinson's notes and wondering if Barrett had already destroyed them. Figure he must have. I pictured him taking the call from Tucker and racing over here to threaten me. Busting into my room and finding the papers stacked there. How long was he in here for? At least long enough to skim-read the notes and realise what they were. He had to assume I'd done the same, and that made it even stranger that he'd left me alive after that. Maybe only the fact that he wasn't prepared for what he found saved me – for now. He swore he didn't start the fire, but everything he'd done said that was a lie. If he killed Jimmy for what he knew, punching my ticket was the logical next step. Unless—

Unless something he found out was more pressing. His words came back to me: '*You been talking to Clay Tucker.*' The inflection in his voice – a hint of uncertainty; a question, not a statement. And then I saw I'd got it all wrong.

Tucker never squealed to him – Barrett put it together on the spot. No one else could have clued me in. Which meant I'd given Tucker up to Barrett—

I ran to the car.

CHAPTER NINETEEN

I skidded to a stop in almost the same spot as before outside Leland Tucker's cabin. I snatched a look each way along the road, saw no other cars there. The afternoon was bright enough, but with the sun lower in the sky than when I'd visited that morning, the scrub in front of the house was in shade, and the place felt dank. The rocking chairs on the porch were empty and still.

I ran to the front door and hammered on it, the sound reverberating around the clearing. There was no answer. I looked over, saw the two pickups were still parked at the side of the house. The breeze caught the trees and dappled sunlight moved and shimmered across the ground. I walked along the porch, peering through the windows, looking for movement, listening for sounds from inside. I came to the end and went around the corner of the house, followed the gentle slope down towards Stokes Creek. I felt my skin gooseflesh. 'Tucker?'

I followed the wall to the far side of the building, had a view of the water now. I stopped still, keeping one hand on the corner of the house, as though there was some safety in that tether. I could hear the faint slap of the water against the bank. I called out again. No response.

I took two tentative steps towards the creek. Then I saw what the water was washing against, making the slapping sound. Not the bank. A figure, lying motionless, his lower half in the water. Clay Tucker.

I ran over, my stomach like a sack full of pins.

I crouched next to him and reached down to check for a pulse. His hair and face were wet, his neck too, but it was the greasy damp of water on lifeless skin. Dead.

I lifted my head, panic rising up in me. 'Leland?' His brother was nowhere in sight. I examined Tucker's body for signs of injury, couldn't see any. I shot to my feet and looked around.

I caught a glimpse of something back towards the house. It was on the ground between the pickups, hidden from view when I'd come down from the road. I moved towards it, a sinking feeling dragging on me like my blood had turned to lead, getting wise early to what I was going to find.

Leland was face down in the leaves. He was motionless.

I checked his pulse, knowing there wouldn't be one. There was blood on his cheek, looked like it'd streamed from his mouth. He was gripping something in his hand. I bent close, saw it was a car key. A nightmare made real – seeing his own brother killed, then suffering the same fate as he tried to flee.

I heard a sound and jerked my head up, realising late that the killer might not have left. I stayed low, backed away from the body so I was shielded between the two pickups. I looked all around, watching for movement and listening hard.

Nothing happened. The trees kept swaying in the wind, and small waves rippled on the water. I could feel the pounding of my own heartbeat. I counted off two minutes, then made a break for my car. I jumped in and started the engine, glancing outside for any sign of danger.

The house was still.

'You been talking to Clay Tucker.'

Barrett's words haunted me as I sped away from the carnage at Tucker's place. I envisaged him going straight from my motel to Tucker's cabin; the terror in Tucker's eyes when he saw him arrive, fearing the worst about Barrett's intentions, then having all those fears met. I slammed my hand on the steering wheel, sickened by my own failings. The blood on my hands.

I pulled over at a diner on the road back from the creek, a dirty swill of anger, guilt and fear pooling in my guts. I used the telephone to call the police, told them there was a body in the water at Tucker's address and hung up. I didn't want my name taken down in connection with the call.

I was about to go when I remembered Masters' warning from that morning – that if anything happened to Clay Tucker, he'd know to come looking for me. I braced myself against the wall, a new sense of anxiety rising in my chest, seeing everything with fresh eyes now: stopping at the general store to ask for directions to Tucker's. My footprints in the mud around the bodies. My fingerprints on the window glass. I searched my memory, tried to think if a neighbour could have seen me scuffle with Tucker. None of the houses along the bank were in view of his – but then I remembered the houses on the opposite shore. At least three had a clear view across the narrow waterway.

I picked up the phone again and asked to be connected to Masters' campaign office. I barely recognised my own voice as I spoke. A staffer picked up and called Masters to the line.

'Twice in one day, Mr Yates; to what do I owe the honour?'

'Clay Tucker is dead. His brother too.'

Masters let out a stunted breath. When he spoke again, his voice was a gruff whisper. 'Please tell me you didn't kill him.'

'No, of course I didn't. That's what I'm calling to tell you.'

'How do you know this?'

'I found the bodies. At his house. I telephoned it into the cops just now.'

'Goddammit, you went there after what I said this morning? You expect me to believe you went on out there and just happened to find—'

'He was alive. I went there this morning and he was alive.'

'And then you went back and he was dead? Buddy, what kind of a fool do you take me for?'

'There's more to it. Tucker told me Cole Barrett—'

'Stop. Stop. Listen to me good: I'm not your attorney, if you tell me something incriminating, it's not protected, and I sure as hell don't want to hear it without due process.'

'Jesus Christ, I know that, I don't need an attorney. Tucker told me Barrett warned him about the fire the night it happened. When I got back to my motel, Barrett was waiting for me. I called him on it, and he knew it was Tucker who told me. Then he pulled a gun on me. Now you tell me that doesn't make him suspect number one.'

'No, that would be you. If your story's true, I'll grant he's got some questions to answer, but right now, you need to drive yourself to the nearest police station and hand yourself in.'

'I can't. I'm onto something here, I know it. Jimmy Robinson was killed because he got close to it. It's all connected – Walter Glover, the women he murdered, Coughlin, Barrett, the fire. I don't know how, yet, but I will do.'

'NO. Let this alone, Yates. If there's something to find out, we'll do it. Give yourself in and clear your name, that's your best course of action.'

'To who – Garland Sheriff's? Barrett's old running buddies?'

He exhaled. 'Try Hot Springs PD. They'll book you at their offices and you'll get a chance to tell your side of the story. You can get out in front of this.'

I thought about Detective Layfield, wondered if he'd give me a fair shake, then remembered being suspicious when he said he wasn't well acquainted with Barrett. 'I can't do that. Just know that I'm innocent.'

'Yates, tell me where you are and we can—'

'I'll call you again when I've got the answers.'

*

I figured Masters would be on the horn to the cops as soon as I hung up, so going back to the motel was out of the question. Didn't bother me. The burglary back home had made me realise I hadn't owned anything of value in a long time. Lizzie was the only thing I cared about.

All I could think to do was run. Highway 70 skirted the top of Stokes Creek and carried me west out of town, crossing the Ouachita River. Cold air rushed through the open windows as I drove, the highway in front of me desolate. I kept the panic at bay by planning, weighing up what the hell to do next.

A murder suspect. A fugitive from the law.

I drove with no destination, waiting for some respite in darkness. When evening fell, I pulled in at a truck stop that was little more than a slash of asphalt through a break in the pinewoods. The sky was a dark shade of purple, the moonlight filtered and refracted by low clouds. I got out and leaned on the car roof, the engine ticking and creaking as it cooled. I closed my eyes and tried to make sense of it all.

Barrett had been adamant it wasn't him killed Robinson. Not two hours later, Clay Tucker was dead. It wasn't proof, but it was damning as all hell.

Barrett had warned Clay Tucker the fire was going to happen. Had to be him that killed Tucker, for telling me as much. Play devil's advocate for a second: say Barrett didn't set the fire – how else would he come to know about it? And the follow-up to that: who else would have a better motive than Barrett to kill Robinson and Tucker?

I picked through it in my head. Robinson was reinvestigating the murders of three women – Jeannette Runnels, Elizabeth Prescott and an unknown third – presumably the woman in the photograph. I took it from my pocket without thinking, looked at it again, her features hard to make out in the dull light.

Just what the hell did you have, Jimmy?

I thought about the initials I'd cribbed from Robinson's notes: *J.R.*, *E.P.* and *N.G.* – the first two now identified, and decent odds that the woman in the picture was *N.G.* Yet no one seemed to know who she was. I lingered on that thought, getting the feeling I'd missed something. I'd shown the picture around plenty, got nowhere – although there was always the chance someone had lied to me—

That wasn't it. It came to me then, the oversight. I'd made an assumption without recognising it before – that all the murders Robinson was investigating happened in Hot Springs. But Robinson's note on the back said she was killed in April – long before he started travelling here. Maybe I was asking the right questions in the wrong place. Maybe Robinson had started out closer to home.

I climbed behind the wheel again, two bad options crystallising: stay in Hot Springs, lay low, try to clear my name; I made the cops as heavy favourites to catch up with me if I did. Or go back to the last place on Earth I'd want to be. But it felt right somehow that Robinson's trail would start there, and the more I thought about it, the more I saw it was the only move that made sense.

I guided the car back onto the blacktop and realised my scattergun course had already taken me some distance towards where I had to go. Maybe it was inevitable all along; drawn back, like a desperate wolf to a rotting carcass. I drove south, heading cross-country until the road joined up with Highway 67. The road to Texarkana.

CHAPTER TWENTY

The road was the same bleak highway mile after mile, lined by towering pines, but the sense of familiarity grew with my sense of discomfort. When I'd fled Texarkana before, I'd killed a man and was running for my life. I never imagined I'd go back. Here I was, under a different cloud, the fear just as real. I had the sense that I was still being battered by the waves set in motion all those months ago.

I arrived in the early hours, the roads deserted. Recognition made me recoil. The Hotel Mason; the Federal building; the *Texarkana Chronicle* offices. Innocuous edifices that nonetheless served as triggers for memories I'd done everything to bury. A dark expectation filled me, the fear that a cop would pull me over at any moment. I didn't know if it was reasonable or not, whether the authorities even knew I'd been in Winfield Callaway's house that night. There was a bleak irony in realising that, if they did, it would likely be because Jimmy Robinson had informed them.

Union Station was my first stop – enough people there, even at that hour, that I wouldn't be conspicuous. I parked in the lot and went inside looking for a telephone kiosk. I was surprised to see GIs in uniform on the concourses – sleeping, smoking, waiting. Not in the numbers I'd seen before, but there all the same; the last stragglers making their way home from a war the rest of America was trying to forget.

I called home to check on Lizzie. It was close to midnight in LA, but I knew she'd be awake, a little needle of guilt pricking at my neck as I waited for her to pick up – the thought of her scared and alone, me not being there. It coloured my thinking, made me resolve not to tell her about Tucker's murder, or coming to Texarkana – another retreat from my promise to always be honest with her.

'I didn't know if you'd call,' she said. 'It must be so late there.'

'Are you bearing up?'

'I've turned on every light in the house. The neighbours will think I'm a crank.'

'Did the locksmith come?'

'He came. I had the windows boarded up too. It looks like ... my god, our home looks like a derelict. Why would someone want to do this to us—' She stopped abruptly after she said it, trying not to let me hear her distress.

'Did the police turn up anything?'

She took a breath, her voice thick with emotion when she spoke. 'They said they're investigating. I don't think they've got anything much to go on.'

'They'll keep a file open and never look at it again. Burglaries don't rate.'

'I got that impression. Charlie, what are we going to do?'

I rubbed my eyes. 'I'll be back as soon as I can—'

'I wasn't trying to make you feel bad. I meant what I said earlier.'

'I know.' I looked up and checked around the station concourse, annoyed I'd forgotten where I was and let my guard down. 'Did you figure out if anything's missing?'

'Some. I'm still sorting through the mess. They took the

twenty you kept behind the coffee jar, a few pieces of jewellery – nothing worthwhile for all this. I keep thinking they can't have satisfied themselves with twenty dollars and some trinkets and they might come back because of it.'

'Don't think like that. These kind of lowlifes just move on.'

She was silent a beat too long – not reassured. Or maybe sensing my doubt. 'Are you any closer to being finished there?'

I wanted to come clean about everything, have her tell me that things would turn out all right. But I knew it wouldn't go that way; that she'd tell me to get away while I still could and catch a flight home – and I wasn't sure I had the resolve to tell her no this time. 'I know the fire wasn't an accident. The proprietor was warned before it happened.'

And now he's dead too.

'What? Who was he warned by?'

'The sheriff I told you about before.'

'The man you think Robinson was suspicious of?'

'The same.'

'How can that be? I mean, if he knew . . .'

'I don't know. That's what I'm working on.'

She drew a deep breath. 'Are you safe there, Charlie?'

I eyed the group of GIs nearest me, three of them slumped back to back against their tote bags. 'Safe enough. Try to get some sleep, I'll call you in the morning. I love you.'

I set the receiver down and rubbed my neck, the needle there now a spike. How could it be that a man's best intentions led him to betray his own promises?

I dropped another nickel and called the *Texarkana Chronicle*, catching a break when the voice on the other end said Hansen was working the night shift. He came onto the line.

'No one had spoken with Jimmy's sister.' His opening shot reminded me that this was still a fresh wound, and the hurt in his voice was plain. 'First she knew of it was when I talked with her. Hardest goddamn conversation I've ever had to have. The woman was torn up.'

'I'm sorry, Sid. That's a tough gig to have put on you.'

'You're damn straight it is.'

'I gave the detective in charge your name as a way to reach the family. Harlan Layfield – you didn't get a call from him?'

'Ain't no one called me. You tell those jackals up there that they ain't fit to call themselves men.'

'You're more right than you know.' I pulled my collar loose, tiredness advancing on me, surprised Layfield hadn't been in touch. 'Sid, did you manage to speak to anyone there about Jimmy? What he was working on?'

'We ain't barely talked about nothing else but Jimmy, it's a goddamn miracle we got a newspaper out these last days gone.' He sounded spent. 'I don't know what to tell you. No one I spoke to knew he was in Hot Springs. He was filing stories like normal right up until he went away. I checked and the last couple was about a liquor store hold-up at a place near State Line, and a spate of robberies at the new subdivision out on Washington Street. Routine stuff. Hold on—' There was a sound like he was spitting tobacco juice into a cup, then he spoke again. 'Only thing came up was that apparently he kept disappearing on his days off. Far as I knew, Jimmy spent his free time drinking in Hamblyn's or Finnigan's. He ain't never had much of what you'd call a personal life, but the talk is, these last few months he ain't been seen at neither. No one knows where he was at instead. You think maybe he was taking off for Hot Springs?'

Ella Borland had told me as much. 'Yeah. I got a source says he'd been showing up there since August.'

'You any the wiser about what he was doing there yet?'

'Did anyone mention murders Jimmy might've been working?'

'Murders? Ain't been nothing like that since . . .' He trailed off, the killings that past spring still raw.

'Listen, Sid, there's something I want to show you.' I was nervous about telling Hansen I was in Texarkana, unsure how much he knew and if he could be trusted – and who else might be interested to know I was back. But I had no choice. 'When do you get off?'

'What is it?'

'A photograph. It belonged to Jimmy.'

'Of what?'

'A woman.'

'If I'm reading between the lines right, you gonna tell me this a dead woman.'

'Yes.'

'Who is she?'

'That's what I want you to tell me.'

He grunted. 'All right, I get off at six this morning. What time can you be here?'

'I'll meet you at six. The coffee shop opposite Union Station – you know the one?'

'Course I know it.'

*

I managed three hours of broken shuteye in the backseat of Robinson's car, woke up feeling like I'd slept in a suitcase. It all came back in a violent onslaught – Tucker, his brother, Barrett, running. A state of hyper-alert that made it feel like I'd never slept at all.

It was still dark as the clock approached six. I moved the car to the other side of the station's parking lot to get a better view of the coffee shop, and waited.

Hansen showed at ten past. He walked alone. I strained to see as he arrived, looking for him to signal or glance around at someone, but he kept his head down and went straight inside. I waited a few more minutes, but no one appeared to follow him in.

I pulled my hat low, crossed over and went inside. I saw him first but he recognised me quickly and waved me over, stood to greet me when I reached his booth.

'You look like you been driving all night.'

'I didn't want to lose any time.' I sat down and he did the same.

He raised his arm to signal someone. I whipped around, feet planted to run, but saw he was just hailing the waitress.

'Didn't never expect to see you round these parts again,' he said.

I turned back slowly, wondering if he was testing me. 'Makes two of us.'

The waitress came over. She wore a faded pink uniform. She placed a coffee cup in front of me and filled it, then topped Hansen's up. Neither of us said anything while she poured.

When she was gone, he leaned on the table and swiped his palm over his face. 'What the hell happened to him, Charlie?'

'I don't know.' I moved the coffee aside and linked my fingers on the chequered tablecloth. 'I want to know.'

'What's these murders you was asking me about?'

I held his gaze, trying to get a read on him. 'I think that's what took him there. Dead women.' It felt like there was danger in every grain of truth I gave up.

He took a dip of tobacco from his pouch and wedged it in his lip. 'In all the years we worked together, I never heard him mention Hot Springs once. Who are they? The women.'

I ducked the question. 'I can't make sense of it. That's why I came here.'

'Let me see it then.'

I took the photograph from my pocket and held it in front of his eyes, watching his expression.

He took it from me and examined it, pinched between his thumb and forefinger. 'You say you have no idea who she is?'

I shook my head.

He turned it over and saw the inscription. 'Answers my next question – how you knew she was dead if you don't know who she is.' Then he placed it on the table in front of him. 'You said this was Jimmy's?'

I nodded.

'How'd it come to you?'

On a better day I'd have seen the question coming and had an answer ready. I took a sip of coffee, stalling. 'He left it for me. With a friend.'

Hansen said nothing at first, recognising the lie for what it was. To my surprise, he let it pass. 'Hate to tell you, but I think you done wasted a trip.'

I closed my eyes and felt my heart sink.

'What makes you think she's from Texarkana?' he said.

'It's guesswork.'

He stabbed at Robinson's scrawl. 'See the date? Right around the Phantom killings. Ain't no way I'd forget another gal got killed around then.'

I spun it towards me and stared, couldn't believe I hadn't made the connection. I thought back; April 8th was two days after I'd left Texarkana; I was still running west then. I rested my head on the leather seatback and stared at the motionless fan blades above me.

'Level with me, Charlie: what was Jimmy doing up there?'

I sat up and studied him again. Was he pumping me for information? On his own behalf or someone else's? Nothing in his bearing hinted at it. His face was criss-crossed with deep worry lines; he looked like a man who'd lost a friend and was desperate for answers. 'He was investigating the murder of two dead working girls. I don't know why.'

He tapped the photograph, eyes still on me. 'She one of them?'

'No. When we talked, he told me there were three dead women. I don't know where she fits in. I don't know anything about her.'

He turned his mouth down, thinking about it. 'Don't make a lick of sense to me. Jimmy got no business being up there.' He folded his arms. 'What you said the first time you telephoned me, about the fire being suspicious – you of the same mind now?'

I looked off to the side, torn between protecting myself and wanting to assuage his grief with the truth. I backed away at the last moment. 'The police have closed it. They're satisfied it was an accident.'

'Why're you dodging the question?'

I spread my hands. 'I don't know what else to tell you.'

'You always believe the cops?' He'd sat forward and was staring at me, unblinking.

My chest tightened and suddenly all I could hear was his voice, his question, no sounds around me. It felt like he was daring me to ask him about Robinson and the cover-up in the aftermath of the Phantom murders. 'You know of a reason someone might want Jimmy dead?'

He held my stare a second or two, my pulse racing, time stretching. Then he shook his head once and dropped his eyes to the table. We sat in silence, my legs jittery, until, finally, he said, 'All the bodies we had this year . . . Jimmy ain't deserve to be one of them. Not for a second. He could drive you crazy, but that's just because his heart was bigger than his brain.'

'It took me a while, but I worked that much out.'

'That why you're doing this?'

'Doing what?'

'Trying to figure what happened to Jimmy. Lot of folk would've just packed up and gone home. You figure you owe it to him?'

'He helped me, before. At the end. This is my last chance to pay him back.'

'"*The end* . . ."' He pulled his mug towards him and stared into it. 'You sure took off kinda sudden.'

'The story was over.'

'When Richard Davis died?' He looked up.

I nodded, mind racing. 'What was it like afterwards?' I said.

'At the *Chronicle*, you mean?'

'All of it. Texarkana.'

He twisted his cup through a half-turn. 'It was the only story for weeks when it was all over, but it died down after a time, same way it always does. Folk started getting back to normal. The Greenbeck people put a new editor in after Gaffy . . .' He swallowed, his eyes clouding over. Too many dead. 'They dropped in some hotshot out of Austin. Put a lot of noses out of joint, but that ain't all his own fault.'

'I read what happened to Horace Bailey and Jack Sherman. Out at Winfield Callaway's place.'

'A tragedy.' His voice was flat as he said it.

'They ever catch anyone for it?'

'No one. Supposedly some nigger bandit.'

'Who led the investigation?'

'Ward Mills, the Texas-side police chief.' Sherman's old boss and Bailey's partner in crime. All along, the man I considered most likely to have initiated the cover-up. 'What you ask for?'

'Just filling in the blanks.'

He fixed me with a look and broke it again just as quickly. I wondered if he was trying to coax me into an admission, or maybe himself. All the truth lay in things unsaid.

Then he slid the picture back to his side of the table. 'Let me show this to some of the others at the paper. I wouldn't hold your breath, but maybe someone else'll know something.'

On reflex, I shot my hand out to stop him from picking it up.

He looked up, shocked by the sudden movement. 'What?'

I studied his face and his eyes, looking for a clue to his intentions. His expression showed only surprise. 'How about I come with you?'

'Come with me? I just got off, I ain't going back there now.'

'Please, Sid. It'll take you a half an hour.'

He took a deep breath. 'Goddamn. All right, but you ain't coming with me.'

We stared at each other over the tabletop, the picture frozen between us, and I felt like I was inching towards a canyon's edge.

'Don't worry,' he said, 'I'll get it back to you safe.'

I lifted my fingers to free it. 'How soon?'

He took the picture, slipped it into his breast pocket and glanced at his watch. 'Let's say eight. Here again.'

I nodded and thanked him, slipping out of the booth.

CHAPTER TWENTY-ONE

Ninety minutes. Enough time for him to set any kind of trap, if that's what he had in mind.

I ran lists in my head – trust him or don't. In his favour: he'd known I was in Hot Springs – he could have alerted the Texarkana cops and sent them after me any time. And his reaction to the picture seemed genuine – a stranger to him. Still I wasn't convinced. He spoke in elliptical terms, seeming to prod at my secrets. And he addressed me with a warmth that invited disclosure – and wasn't in keeping with our previous dealings.

I cruised the streets, trying to keep my nerves under control by staying mobile. I ended up at Lizzie's old house. I couldn't say what made me go there; maybe I was just looking for comfort in the place that had the strongest connection to her. The drapes were closed and the yard overgrown; a decaying shell that had once been a loving home, its inhabitants picked off by fate until only my wife was left. I thought about her, stuck in our shattered bungalow in California, and wondered how much more she could endure.

I was torn about calling her when it was pre-dawn still in California, but standing in the shadow of the life she'd had ripped away sent my feelings haywire. I went back to Union Station ahead of time and grabbed a telephone.

She surprised me by answering right away.

'Did you sleep any?'

'Not so well. I was . . . Well, anyway.'

'You can say it. Anyone would be unnerved after—'

'I won't let these men have control over me that way. I'm fine.'

I closed my eyes, all the things I wanted to say lost in my guilt.

'Anyway, distract me. Tell me what you're doing now.'

I could see the sign on the Hotel Mason in the distance; it felt like I was rifling her room while she was making coffee in the kitchen. 'Same as always, chasing down leads.'

'You're terrible at ducking me, Charlie.'

'I'm not ducking you. I'll tell you everything when I have it. On my life.'

'I don't care for that expression.'

A train sounded its horn, a dying moan. I stared out across the crowds, agitated, fearful of what the next meeting with Hansen would bring. 'I should keep moving. I'll call again—'

'Wait a moment. With everything going on I forgot to tell you yesterday – I started looking into that man you asked me about.'

'Tindall?'

'Yes. I spoke to Sal, he was very helpful.'

I looked at the clock above the platform entrances – still a half-hour to burn. 'Give me the gist.'

'Sal said he remembered some of it and he checked the archive for the rest.' She took a breath, as though getting it all straight in her head. 'He said the way the *Examiner* reported it, Governor Roosevelt ran Tindall out of the city a dozen years ago – part of his crackdown on racketeering. Sal didn't sound impressed with that and said to tell you, "*The whole jive was*

174

bogus, just a springboard for FDR's White House run." There was amusement in her voice as she reeled the line off, and it heartened me. 'He said the real story was that this Tindall fellow was forced to leave after he murdered a rival of his, a man he said was called "Mad Dog" Vincent Coll. Sal speculated that the authorities conspired with certain criminal figures to see him gone.'

I was impressed with how assured she came off. Suggestions of collusion between the authorities and criminal bosses should have been shocking, but when I thought about what she knew, what she'd seen firsthand, I realised it was nothing new to her. 'That's good work. Did he say anything else?'

'Only that it seems he accepted his removal because he dropped out of sight after that. No one could recall his name featuring in the New York papers after about nineteen thirty-three. I've enlisted Mr Edwards at the *Journal* to help me see if I can turn up anything on what he's been doing in the intervening years.'

'Bunny Edwards? What did that cost you?'

'A week's worth of pot roasts – he doesn't know I can't cook worth a lick. He's been very accommodating, actually.'

I looked towards the station entrance. 'Look, don't trouble yourself with any more for now. Take some time—'

'Wait, there was one other thing. When I told him where you were, Sal said the name of the town was familiar. He checked and he said Charlie Luciano was arrested there in 'thirty-six. He asked if that was pertinent.'

She said the name with familiarity. 'Lucky Luciano? How do you come to know who he is?'

'He worked for Arnold Rothstein, that man who fixed the

World Series. I'm from Texarkana, Charlie, not the moon.'

'Sorry.' The most famous gangster in America, picked up in a backwater like Hot Springs. The same town Bugsy Siegel had been visiting for a decade or more. A confluence that screamed there was a story there – just not the one I was chasing.

The clock moved to twenty before the hour. 'I should go. I'll call again as soon as I have news. Will you be all right?'

'You don't need to worry about me, Charlie. I'm doing enough of that for two.'

She didn't mean it to, but the line stung way past when I hung up.

I went outside to the lot and moved the car to where I could monitor the coffee shop again. I watched for anything unusual, swearing to myself that I'd blow the meet and get out of town at the first sign of a trap. A city police black-and-white rolled by and I started the engine, ready to take off, but it kept moving, never slowing or stopping.

Hansen came down the street on time and went inside. He was carrying a large satchel. I let a few more minutes tick by, then went into the station behind me and called the coffee shop. The waitress who answered didn't know Hansen by name, but she managed to pick him out when I described him, and called him to the phone.

'Who's that?'

'It's me, Sid. Change of plan. Meet me in the station, at the ticket office. Right now.'

'What the hell?'

I hung up and ran back outside. I peered from behind the car, watching for him. He came out of the coffee shop and turned towards the station, looking irritated, then crossed the street. He was alone, and did nothing to make me suspect the cops were waiting nearby. I watched until he entered the ticket hall, going in the Arkansas-side door, and then I made my own way through the Texas door and followed him across the concourse at a distance. The station was busy now, lines forming by the ticket windows, men hurrying to catch trains, and he didn't see me.

I looped around and came up on his blindside. 'Sid.'

He whipped around, startled. 'Hell, Yates, what you creeping around for? What was wrong with the last place?'

I put my hand out. 'Where's the photo?'

He tilted his head as he reached into his pocket, thrown by my urgency. He pulled it out and forked it over. 'Here.'

I glanced at it, making sure it was the same one, then put it away. 'Any luck?'

He rubbed the corner of his mouth with his forefinger. 'Some. I ain't got a name for you, don't get your hopes up.'

I looked around, nerves stretched. 'Go on.'

'But I got a lead on her for you. One of the fellas recognised her, told me she used to work at Pine Street Hospital.'

The name resonated; the last place Lizzie's sister, Alice, was seen alive. 'How can that be? What you said before, about remembering if there'd been—'

'I know, and I'm at a loss to explain it. I asked two of the other subs, making sure I ain't crazy, but they said the same – there weren't no other murders then.'

An echo of what I'd encountered in Hot Springs when I first picked up Robinson's trail. Solved murders and non-existent murders, no apparent connection between them. I thought about my actions that morning, fear and paranoia riding me, and wondered if this was how Robinson behaved in his final days. 'Thanks, it's a help anyway. I'll see you.'

As I turned to go he stopped me, his hand on my forearm. 'I got something else for you.'

The satchel he'd been carrying was by his feet; he picked it up and shoved it into my chest, making me take it.

'What's this?'

He swiped the back of his hand over his mouth. 'It's everything was in Jimmy's desk. Ain't much, but ... I don't know, maybe it'll be some help.' I unfastened the bag slowly and looked in. I saw a mass of papers, the top one showing Robinson's familiar scrawl. 'Just do me one favour and don't tell no one it was me gave it to you.'

I looked up from the bag and saw he was glancing around, nervous. 'Why are you giving me this?'

He moistened his lips. 'Soon as you told me about that fire, I knew it weren't no accident. Ain't a doubt in my mind.' My skin tingled. 'I cleared his effects out the day you called, and I been sweating on what to do with them.'

'Have you been through it all?'

He shook his head. 'I ain't a fool; I know there's more to certain stories than what was told, and there ain't a chance Horace Bailey and Jack Sherman went out to Winfield Callaway's house in the middle of the night on account of a goddamn burglary.' He paused, his jaw muscles tensing. 'Someone left a message for Jimmy, tipped him to go out there that morning. Someone I think knew what was really going on.'

My message. He was staring at me hard and I fought to keep my legs still. 'Did he go?'

He didn't answer. He glanced down at the bag then locked

178

on my eyes again. 'I got a wife, I got children, I got a home, so I don't care to know any more than what made the papers. But that don't mean I can stomach it when a man like Jimmy winds up dead. You understand me?'

I looked at him, his emotions showing at last – fear and anger, but relief as well, airing thoughts he'd clearly been holding close. 'Did Jimmy ever talk about the murders afterward? Or about Callaway and Bailey?'

He shook his head, his eyes still roving around the concourse. 'Not much. Sometimes when he'd taken a drink, he'd start talking oblique, saying things ain't made a lot of sense to me, but . . .' He took his hat off and ran his sleeve over his eyes. 'Like I said, ain't proud of it, but some of us put our own concerns first and didn't want to hear no more.'

'Do you remember any of what he said?'

'No.' He took a step back from me. 'Look, I'm not like you and Jimmy, I'm about as far out on a limb as I can handle. I hope you figure out what happened.'

He turned and disappeared into the crowd.

I stood there clutching the bag, faces swarming around me, a blur of civilians and soldiers, all going about their *own concerns*. If what Hansen said was true, the cover-up was nothing like the monolith I'd imagined, everyone that mattered in on it and working to maintain the fabrication. The reality I saw now was simpler, more human – a lie crafted by someone at the top, and enough people looking the other way, out of fear or self-interest, to let it perpetuate. And when I thought of it that way, Jimmy Robinson felt more and more like the last person you'd want loose with an inkling of the truth.

CHAPTER TWENTY-TWO

I hightailed it to Pine Street Hospital with my eyes glued to the rearview, looking for cops or anyone else following me, a feeling like I was getting deeper and deeper into the woods.

I parked on the street out front and looked at the satchel on the seat next to me. I dragged it over and opened it, finally feeling like I had a few seconds' breathing space to do so. I shook the contents out, a stack of photographs spilling over into the footwell. I reached down to pick them up first and found myself looking at pictures of a face I knew: Ella Borland. They were candid shots, Borland apparently not aware she was being photographed. One showed her going into Duke's, another her walking along the street – looked like Bathhouse Row. In another she was talking to a man outside the Southern Club. Different outfits suggested different times and places – dolled up like a dime store starlet in one, wearing a sober green dress in another. I looked through them again, realised they were all summer numbers she wore – must have been taken earlier in the year. I studied the last image and recognised the newsboy cap on the man she was talking to – William Tindall. I gazed at it a moment, remembering the two being in the Southern Club at the same time when I saw her dancing there. I closed my eyes, mulling the thought, trying to get a fix on what Robinson would have seen in these shots. Then I set them aside and started picking through the rest of the pile.

The papers were a mix – some typewritten, some in cursive. There were drafts of pieces Robinson was writing, office memos, meeting notes – no names or details that leapt off the page at me at first glance. One discrepancy I did notice: these notes included full names, not initials, and identifiable headings – *Jennings Robbery, Beating on 4th*. I started to get the feeling this was everyday business he'd left behind when he took off for Hot Springs.

Which made the Borland photographs even more incongruous. I found more as I picked through, a similar style to the others, her not looking at the camera in any of them. A variety of outfits and locations. He'd been following her for weeks, capturing her movements on film. The only reason I could think for why he'd do that was that he was suspicious of her.

At the bottom of the pile, a different set of pictures – older, showing creases and frayed corners. There were ten or so, most blurry, a hand partially blocking the lens in some. Scenes of commotion. The images I could make out showed a crowd of men, some of them identifiable by their uniforms as police officers, a building in the background. I leafed through, my thoughts still on the Borland shots. I was about to put them back in the bag when recognition came to me. Not a building – a house. Winfield Callaway's. Photographs from the scene of his murder. Proof that Robinson did go there that morning. A question lingering as to how much he saw and what he did with it.

I stuffed the papers and photographs away and got out, the bag slung over my shoulder. I crossed the grounds in front of the hospital, the whitewashed walls a dull grey under the heavy sky.

Past the entrance, I followed a corridor until I came to a ward off to the right – a long room with six beds on either side, five of them occupied. There was a nurse stationed behind a desk at the far end; I went up to her, taking the picture of the unidentified woman from my pocket. 'Ma'am, my name's Yates. I'm looking for information on this lady. I'm led to believe she worked here. Do you happen to know her at all?'

The nurse looked at the picture, then at me, shaking her head. 'I'm sorry, sir, I only started here a couple weeks ago.'

I thanked her and moved on, went back out into the corridor looking for another nurse. I repeated the same rigmarole three more times before I found someone who recognised her.

'That's Ginny.' The nurse set her pen down and looked up at me. 'Are you with the police?'

'No, I'm a reporter. I'm—'

Her eyes darted back to the papers she was working on. 'We're not supposed to talk to reporters.'

'On who's say-so, miss?'

'It's hospital policy.'

'Please, if you have any information at all about her, I'd sure appreciate it. What was her surname?'

'Sir, Ginny died some time ago, I really don't think—'

'How did she die?'

She looked up at me again now, frowning. 'She took her own life. That's as much as I know about it.' I went to press her, but she cut me off. 'Please, you should take this up with hospital management.'

'If you could just tell me her surname, I'll be out of your hair.'

A second nurse appeared at the side of the desk. She was older, had a bearing about her that said she was in charge. 'Nurse Henley, is everything all right here?'

The nurse in front of me reddened. I turned to the newcomer. 'I was just asking about the woman in this picture.' I held it up. 'Did you happen to know Ginny, ma'am?'

The younger nurse looked up again, about to protest, but the boss nurse held a hand out to silence her. 'What is this about?'

'I'm a reporter. A friend of mine was investigating your colleague's death—'

'Reporters are asked to direct their enquiries to the manager's office. The *Chronicle* men all know that, I'm surprised you don't.'

'Time is against me, ma'am.'

'That may be the case, sir, but it doesn't change procedure, so please see yourself out. Otherwise I'll have someone escort you.'

A man in one of the beds behind me cried out in pain, and the younger woman took the opportunity to escape. The boss nurse had her hands on her hips and was glaring at me; I was about to move on when she checked over my shoulder, then mouthed, '*Outside, two minutes,*' her expression never changing. I inclined my head, her movement so quick I wasn't certain I'd lip-read it right, but she raised her eyebrows just enough to underscore the point. I whipped around and made for the exit.

Coming out into the daylight, I looked back inside for the nurse, but there was no sign of her. I wondered if she'd played a neat trick to get rid of me. I turned and looked out across the grounds, jumpy, giving her a minute more to show, trying to untangle the implications of the woman in the photograph taking her own life. Not murdered. As I stood there, my eyes laid upon my car and I flinched: a police cruiser was idling behind it.

I slid back into the shadow of the entranceway and watched as the officer stepped out, double-checked the registration plate, and walked around to the driver's side. He carried on, circling the car, then looked up and over towards the hospital and where I stood.

I froze. He was fifty yards or more away, and still it felt like he was looking right at me. He looked away again and pulled out his notebook, scribbled something down.

My heart kicked in again and I started to move my feet, my legs like stilts. Then I felt a hand on my arm. I pulled away on reflex, about to run.

'Who are you?'

A woman's voice. I whirled around and saw the boss nurse, standing close. I glanced from her to the cop and back again, stepping to the side so I was completely out of sight from the street. 'I'm a reporter.' I was about to say my name but I stopped myself, trying to remember if I'd given it to the younger nurse before, picturing the cop sauntering inside looking for me. 'I'm here about your colleague Ginny, I want to know what happened to her.' The words came fast, running into one another.

'You look unwell. Is something the matter?'

'I'm fine, ma'am. Ginny – did you know her at all?'

'I won't have you troubling those girls in there. Not after what happened.'

'Ma'am?'

'Your friend that was investigating her death – he have mousey blonde hair, head like a cinder block? That the one?'

Jimmy Robinson. 'Yes.'

She grimaced and looked away, shaking her head. 'Why is he interested in her death?'

'I don't know, ma'am. How did you come to know him?'

'I don't know him, but I remember him bugging Ginny plenty. He showed up here all the time, even after all the other reporters stopped coming, never let her alone. He's hard to miss.'

Lightning went through me, *'other reporters'* jolting the connection into view. 'When was this?'

'Earlier in the year. You know about the killings we had here?'

Her face went out of focus and her voice seemed to fall away, the connection whole and complete now, my breath running short. I said the words: 'Did Ginny nurse Alice Anderson?'

She nodded once, her face a question mark. 'I think you ought to tell me just what your interest is here.'

The conversation with Jimmy was seared into my memory. A telephone call with him shortly after Alice had disappeared. Him telling me one of the nurses at the hospital had seen a man she swore was a cop hanging around Alice's room that day. A man I figured was sent to snatch her. Ginny had to be Robinson's source – and now she was dead. 'Why did Ginny kill herself?'

'How would I know? I'll tell you this much, though, I always thought it had something to do with that man hounding her. Smelled of liquor, all the time, and—'

'He's dead.'

She stopped with her mouth half-open. I glanced over to the cop again; he'd climbed back into his cruiser and was moving it around the corner. Smart – wait me out instead of come hunting. I turned back to the nurse. 'You won't ever see me again, I promise. Just tell me her surname.'

She looked at me a long moment. 'What happened to him?'

'He died in a fire.'

'An accident?'

'No.'

Her eyes darted to one side, and she blinked in rapid succession. 'Does that strike you as a coincidence?'

'No, ma'am, it doesn't.'

She brought her hand to her mouth and touched her lip. 'Kolkhorst. Ginny Kolkhorst. She hated having a Kraut name.' She looked at me again now, all her surety gone. 'I always thought there was something strange about her passing like that. That's why I didn't want anyone to see me talking to you back there.'

'Why do you say strange?'

'It's not something normal folk do, is it? Throw themselves off of a bridge and . . .' She reached for the wall, steadying herself.

'Do you have reason to doubt she took her own life?'

'Only the common sense the Lord blessed me with. What does this mean?'

'I don't know, but that's what I'm trying to figure out. Did Miss Kolkhorst have any family?'

She hesitated, her expression making me realise she was suddenly afraid of me. 'I don't . . . I don't know.'

'Ma'am, my only interest is the truth. I promise.'

She looked at me a long moment, then said, 'I think she lived with her folks. I don't know the address.' She took hold of my shoulder. 'Mister, are we in danger?' She inclined her head to the hospital building.

'Not if you go back inside, and go about your business like this conversation never happened. Tell the other nurse to do the same.'

'Why? Who would come asking?'

'The men who killed my friend.' The words I left unspoken: and who may have killed yours.

CHAPTER TWENTY-THREE

I made it to Olive Street on foot, skirting the edge of the hospital until I found a path leading from the rear of the building across the grounds. I looked back as I hit the sidewalk, but the cop wasn't behind me.

My luck turned, a cab coming down the street before I'd even made it thirty paces. I flagged it and prayed the driver wouldn't recognise my face, not knowing how intensive the search for me was.

In the event, the man never bothered to look back once. I asked him to take me to a car rental joint, and he said the airport was the closest. The route took us along State Line Avenue a few blocks, and I sat low in the seat, my hat pulled down, my mind in tumult at what I'd learned. The connection between Kolkhorst and the dead women in Hot Springs eluded me. So did the significance of the last set of initials – *N.G.* Not compliant with *Ginny Kolkhorst*, even though I now knew her to be the woman in the picture. The possibilities got on top of me – I'd assumed Robinson's inscription on the photograph meant Kolkhorst was murdered, but what if that had been wrong from the start? If that was the case, who was the third victim? Was Kolkhorst's death related at all? It was like viewing a painting from too close – the image becoming more obscure the nearer I got to it.

My thoughts turned on me then, Hansen's words prompting a realisation. I'd sent Jimmy to Callaway's house that morning to pick up my story, and maybe he was dead because of it.

I closed my eyes and tried to shut it all down. When I opened them again, I noticed a police black-and-white overtaking us in the next lane, headed in the direction of the headquarters building downtown. I went to avert my face, but as I did, I noticed the markings on it: Hot Springs PD.

*

The clerk didn't look at my licence too close – the dollar tip I slipped him across the counter at the same time distraction enough. He handed my paperwork back to me and I stashed it fast.

I waited outside while the clerk went to fetch my rental, thinking about the cops that were on my tail. I couldn't make sense of how they caught up with me so fast. Even if the Texarkana police had known to radio Hot Springs PD to dispatch a car, it couldn't have got here that quick. So it had to be they were already here.

That opened up its own slew of questions. It was conceivable someone got a look at Robinson's licence plate since I'd been driving his car and was therefore able to connect me to it. Cole Barrett sprang to mind then. Maybe an outside chance that some other party had noted it down while it was parked outside Tucker's cabin.

What I couldn't figure is how the cops from either place knew to look for me in Texarkana.

*

I found a single listing in the name of Kolkhorst in the city directory and decided I wouldn't risk a telephone call in advance.

The address was on the Arkansas side of town, the street dotted with young pines and sycamores, the houses a rag-tag mix of low-rise fieldstone bungalows and newer clapboard dwellings – a working class neighbourhood.

I stopped at a light just before the Kolkhorsts' block, their house in view now – a corner plot, neat yard out front, cleared of leaves, freshly painted white walls and a tiled roof adorned with a little brick chimney.

I looked up at the stoplight on its wire above me, still red, then back at the street. I realised I was drumming my fingers on the wheel. Something felt off. I looked along the road and checked my mirrors, but there was no other traffic around me. I looked ahead again and cottoned to what was bugging me: a little way down, a midnight blue coupe was parked on the other side of the street, facing the Kolkhorst place. A man was sitting up front, but I couldn't make him out. My eyes flicked from him to the stoplight and back, my nerves jangling now.

The light changed and I drove on. Instinct told me not to stop, so I cruised by the house and on past the coupe, stealing a look at the man inside as I went by. He watched me go, his head swivelling as he followed my progress. I didn't know him, got the feeling I didn't want to know him. I carried on driving, checking the rearview. When I was thirty yards past him, he peeled away from the kerb and pulled a U-turn, falling into step a few car lengths behind me.

I carried on to the end of the block, straining against the urge to stamp on the accelerator, and made a right. I drove on, making turns at random, the coupe staying with me. Then the street I was on ran out where Highway 67 cut across it, the raised bed of the railroad tracks visible beyond that. I reached the junction and saw a chance.

I pulled out onto the highway. There was a steady flow of vehicles coming in the opposite direction. I picked up speed slowly, biding my time, the coupe matching me.

Then there was a break in the oncoming traffic. I slammed the brakes and spun the wheel to make a sharp U-turn, my back end fishtailing out onto the verge. An oncoming truck had to swerve to avoid me, the sound of his horn blaring in my ears.

Now I slammed the accelerator, sped away as fast as I could, the coupe trapped travelling in the other direction by the stream of oncoming cars. I watched in the rearview until the other car disappeared from sight, my heart pounding, trying to get as much distance between us as possible.

I raced down the blacktop, trying to marshal my thoughts. Someone was one step ahead of me at every turn: finding Clay Tucker dead, the Hot Springs cops showing up in Texarkana, and now a man watching the Kolkhorst place. Waiting for me. It made me scared and it made me mad. But it also told me it was all related – that Robinson had stumbled into something that ran further and deeper than either of us could have imagined.

*

A telephone call wasn't ideal, but it was the only choice left to me.

I found a gas station with a kiosk. A man answered, softly spoken and with accented English – traces of the old country.

'Am I speaking with Mr Kolkhorst?'

'Yes, who is this?'

'My name's Yates, I'm calling with regard to Ginny Kolkhorst. May I ask if she was family to you, sir?'

'The name we gave her was Geneve. My daughter.' He coughed, a heavy smoker's hack. 'What of it?'

'I apologise for calling you on the telephone; I wanted to visit with you in person, but there are matters that won't permit me to do that.'

'What do you want?'

'It's not an easy subject, but I wanted to ask you about the circumstances of your daughter's death.'

'What is *circumstances*? You are an American, Mr Yates?'

I hesitated, the question unexpected. 'I am, sir.'

'Well then, it is correct to say it was your countrymen who killed her. They killed her because her papa is a Kraut, and they broke her mother's heart for ever in so doing. This is your *circumstances*.'

He said it with such quiet anger that I thought he was about to hang up. But the connection stayed open. 'You believe she was killed? I was led to understand she had ended her own life.'

'Yes, of course, this is what they tell us, the police. The doctors say to us it was guilt – the girl she was caring for at the hospital who ran off and stepped in front of a train. Geneve felt responsible for it in some way, maybe.'

Alice Anderson – snatched and murdered but made to look like suicide; lies dogging her even in death. Then a leap, my blood curdling as I realised the parallels: Kolkhorst saw the cop that snatched Alice from Pine Street Hospital; days later, Alice was dead, a faked suicide. What if they'd done the same with

Kolkhorst? It all happened in such close proximity of time and location, it was hard to dismiss the similarities. 'But you believe otherwise.'

'What I believe does not matter. What does it matter? She is gone and this is what they tell us.'

'It matters, sir. To me. Do you know who would've had reason to harm your daughter?'

He scoffed. 'All of you. Geneve was born in this country, she was *Ami* – the same as you. And still you call her *Kraut* and *Nazi* and tell her to go back to Germany. We say to her, tell them, "*This* is your home." But of course it makes no difference. In the end. Only hate and ignorance.'

I closed my eyes, his words heartbreaking; but at the same time, disappointment was settling in my stomach – my hopes that he had solid evidence dashed when in fact he was just a father wracked with anger and sadness. 'When did she die, Mr Kolkhorst?'

'April.'

'Do you recall the date?'

'They cannot tell me for sure. The 8th is the day she disappeared. She was not found until the 10th.'

The 8th – the date Robinson inscribed on her photograph. 'Where was she found?'

'Lake Hamilton. "*A nice place to do it at least.*" Can you believe one of the officers says this to me at the time?'

'I don't know it. I'm sorry.' The word sounded incongruous to the conversation, not something I'd meant to say, but somehow necessary. An apology for intruding in his life and trampling all over his suffering.

'It is in Hot Springs. The back country, you would say. Why

does she think to travel all this distance, Mr Yates?'

My spine went rigid. 'Hot Springs? Why there?'

'My question precisely.'

'Would she have cause to go there?'

'No. She spent time there, for her training, but that was many months ago, a year or more.'

'Who found your daughter, sir?'

'The local sheriffs.'

'Garland County?'

'Yes.'

'A man named Cole Barrett?'

'No. I don't remember the name, but not that.'

Barrett's turf, Barrett's men. Maybe naïve of me to think he'd involve himself in person. 'Did they investigate? How did they conclude she took her own life?'

'They say they had a witness who saw her throw herself from a bridge, and that the coroner finds she is heavily intoxicated at the time. They take only two days to tell me this is the explanation. "*There is nothing to indicate foul play.*" This is what they tell me.'

Ginny Kolkhorst died in Hot Springs. Suicide on the record, murdered according to Robinson. The other two victims were garrotted in their own homes. It fit and it didn't – but the proximity meant the likelihood of a connection between Kolkhorst, Runnels and Prescott was suddenly greater.

'Why are you asking me these questions?' he said. 'Still you have not stated your purpose. You are working with the other journalist?'

'The other?'

'Yes. Mr Robinson. He approaches me too, asking questions

like you. He says to me they were friends – "*Nurse Ginny*" he calls her and says she was helping him with important matters. He believes me, that she was murdered. He tells me this.'

The nickname clicked immediately. Nurse Ginny – *N.G.* So simple, and yet I wasn't sure I'd ever have seen it. 'Robinson and I were colleagues. I have to tell you that he died several days ago. He asked me to help him with his investigation, but he passed away before I could get to him, so if there is anything you can tell me about what he said—'

'He is dead? My god, how?'

I told him about the fire, calling it an accident so as not to cloud matters any further. 'Please, if there is anything you can remember about your conversations . . .'

'He came only two times after she died, I remember all of it. He was like you, he never tells me his purpose, but he asks so many things about her. What schools did she attend, the names of her friends, all about her life. He was most particularly interested in her training – because of Hot Springs, I suppose.'

'Do you remember what you told him?'

'What could I tell? I say to him she completed her training in Hot Springs, and he asked me all manner of questions about this, but this was when our daughter was becoming a woman, and she stops telling her papa everything. He says it is helpful to know nonetheless.'

'Where did she train, sir?'

'There is a veterans' hospital there – for the very worst cases, you understand?' I thought of the giant building looming over the bottom of Bathhouse Row, the wounded servicemen I'd seen in passing. 'This is what makes me the most angry – not only was Geneve *Ami*, but she wanted only to help others – the victims of that mad fool Hitler. And still they killed her. The wrong kind of *Ami*, yes?'

*

I raced away from the gas station with a renewed sense of purpose. Kolkhorst may have been mistaken about what caused his daughter's death, but his pain was all too obvious. At the very least, he deserved to know that there was more to it than the lies he'd been fed. The responsibility for finding him that peace of mind was mine; if Ginny Kolkhorst's death was linked somehow to Alice Anderson's, then the blame was at my doorstep, for failing to finish the job when I had the chance.

I took the rental car back to the airport, intending to switch it for a different model – guessing that the watcher at the Kolkhorsts' place would have my plate now. But as I pulled up outside, I realised I'd gained an advantage, and that doing so would be to squander it. It was just a question of eluding them long enough to cash in.

I cruised by the rental offices and saw there was a different clerk behind the desk – the break I needed – so I drove back into town and parked around the block from a cab stand, then I ran back to it and paid for a ride back out to the airport. I made it to the hire car office just before closing time.

The clerk was rushing to shut up shop, so he took no care over the paperwork. I paid him with the money I'd stashed for my airfare home, half-gone now, hoping like hell that Acheson was good to his word and had sent more cash. For my part of the bargain, whatever story I could cobble together for the *Journal* would have to wait.

When we were done, the clerk handed over the keys and hustled me out the door. I climbed into the new rental, dropped the satchel Hansen had given me on the seat, and set off, taking the highway north-east, into the coming dusk.

Whoever was watching for me knew I was in Texarkana now. And if they found the old rental, parked two blocks from State Line, they'd take it as a sign I was still in town. A little diversion; let them think they were still closing the net on me.

CHAPTER TWENTY-FOUR

Driving into Hot Springs for the second time, I experienced almost the same feelings of dread I had going back to Texarkana, the two places almost as one in my mind now; the sense that they were bound together by a common evil.

I found a fleapit motel on the east of town, its only attraction that cash up front would avoid any need to show identification. It was midnight by the time I got into the room. I hunkered down with Robinson's papers and photographs that Hansen had given me and pored through them – all of it spread across the floor by necessity, the motel too cheap to provide even a table.

It took me more than an hour to leaf through everything. The handwriting was no easier to read than in the earlier notes Barrett had stolen, but the contents were less cryptic, and it was as I'd feared – all of it the mundane notes of a working hack. By the end, I was worn out and no closer to the truth.

I climbed onto the bed with the small set of photographs in hand. I looked through the prints of Ella Borland, my vision double from reading too long, questioning why Robinson was shadowing her. I thought back to my own feeling she was hiding something and wondered what made him suspicious enough of her to go to such lengths. She looked subtly different in each of the shots – not just the outfits she wore, but her whole countenance, like watching the ocean in shifting sunlight, colours and shades changing from one glimpse to the next.

I set the pictures of Borland down and looked at the older photographs – Winfield Callaway's house on the night my life changed for ever. When I'd killed a man. I flipped through them, my eyes heavy, feeling like I was eroding the last vestige of remove I'd built up between myself and the events of that night. I passed out, the pictures still between my fingers.

*

I woke a little before seven with the photographs scattered around me, the bed sheets torn apart by my thrashing. I gathered everything up to stash in the car, then stood under a cold shower trying to wash the night off me. When I couldn't take the icy water any longer, I towelled off, shivering, and dressed in the same clothes I'd been wearing the day before. All I had left.

*

The veterans' hospital was imposing enough before I knew of its links to Ginny Kolkhorst. Walking inside now, the place felt as though it was cloaked in gloom, an oppressive silence shrouding its corridors. The men there seemed to move aimlessly, the final reckoning of the war on display. A man with bandages covering his eyes, a nurse guiding him along the hallway; a man with stumps where his hands used to be. One man had burn scars over the entirety of his head – his features lodged in a sea of melted skin that covered all of his face and scalp. My thoughts right away ran to Robinson – the way he'd looked in Gresham's funeral home. Alice Anderson had told me *'death ain't the worst thing can happen to a man'*, and it sickened me to think how many times since I'd seen things that called her words to mind again.

The Personnel office was on the second floor. I knocked and poked my head around the door without waiting for a response, saw a fat man behind a desk in the corner. I looked both ways around me, as though I were disoriented, noting the row of filing cabinets along the wall to my left. The fat man moved to stand up, but I muttered something about it being the wrong room and stepped outside again. I retreated along the hallway and found a place to sit where I could see the office, then hunkered down behind my hat and a discarded newspaper.

It was only twenty minutes until the fat man opened the door and headed off the other way down the corridor. As soon as I saw him go, I dropped the paper on the seat next to me and fast-walked back to his office, then slipped inside.

I went along the filing cabinets until I found the one marked *H–L*. I pulled the drawers in turn until I came to the Ks, rifling through them until I found Ginny Kolkhorst's employee record. I glanced over my shoulder to check the door – no movement. The file was a slim brown folder, a single sheet of paper inside of it. I took it out and slipped it into my pocket, returning the folder to the cabinet, then went out the door again, glancing down the corridor to check I hadn't been seen.

It felt like I didn't draw breath until I made it back to the car, apprehension a constant companion whenever I moved in daylight now. I'd left it parked under a magnolia tree on the street running along the side of the hospital, shade just creeping over it as I returned. I set myself behind the wheel and took the precaution of starting the engine before I unfolded the file to read it.

Ginny Kolkhorst was twenty-seven years old according to the birth date shown at the top of the record, and she'd worked at the hospital for one year, from August 1944 through August 1945. Heinrich Kolkhorst was listed as her next of kin, at the same address in Texarkana he still inhabited now. Underneath the personal details, the main body of the record was a list of training rotations she'd completed – burns patients, amputations, facial disfiguration, along with the accompanying dates. Mundane items all.

The one line that stood out was at the bottom of the sheet. It read:

Cited for improper conduct. HS PD queried, allegations unsubstantiated. Employee censured, recommend future behaviour be observed keenly.

It was dated to June 1945, a signature next to it that I couldn't decipher.

I turned the sheet over, but the back was blank. I lifted my eyes, checked up and down the street – the movement so familiar now it was like a nervous tick. Ginny Kolkhorst in trouble with the law. Not what I'd expected, but surely relevant. I pulled away from the kerb and went to find a telephone.

*

'*Hot Springs Recorder*, Clyde Dinsmore speaking.'

'Dinsmore, it's Yates.'

'Yates?' There was a frantic shuffling sound, and when he spoke again, his voice was almost a whisper. 'Where are you? Your name's all over the radio.'

'Fame at last.' I flattened myself against the side of the booth, trying to make it so I couldn't be seen from outside. The kiosk was one of three out front of the bus station, and the place was mid-morning busy, the air laden with diesel fumes. 'Listen, I need your help with something.'

'Help? Yates, the cops are looking for you. They're saying you killed Clay Tucker and his brother—'

'Wise up, I didn't kill anyone.'

'What I'm hearing, the evidence is pretty damning.'

'Hearing from who?'

'Garland Sheriff's.'

'Figures. Cole Barrett is up to his neck in this, guess I'm a nice scapegoat.'

'Still singing that song? I'd be real careful who hears you . . .'

'I found my third victim. The one my friend was investigating. She was a nurse by the name of Geneve K-O-L-K-H-O-R-S-T. Ginny to her friends. She worked a year at the veterans' hospital up there. They pulled her out of Lake Hamilton in April of this year.'

'The photograph you showed me?'

'The same. You write about it at the time?'

'First I'm hearing. Why are you telling me this?'

'I told you, I need your help.'

'How about you help yourself and turn yourself in?'

'Come on, Dinsmore, there's no mileage in that for you. You

wouldn't still be talking to me if you weren't curious to know what I've got.'

He didn't respond, and I knew I'd got him.

'Garland Sheriff's wrote her death up as suicide,' I said. 'I want to know who took charge of the investigation—'

'This is starting to feel like a witch-hunt against Cole Barrett, Yates.'

'Isn't it strange that you never heard about this at the time? Why would he keep it from you?'

He exhaled. 'That's a straw man and you know it. They don't serve stories up on a plate, they make us do the work. An out-of-town suicide wouldn't play, anyhow.'

'Then try this: Barrett knew about the fire at Duke's. Before it happened.'

'What? How the hell would you know that?'

'Because I'm a goddamn reporter and I know how to work a story right.'

He said nothing, the implication in my words settling between us. I butted the back of my head against the kiosk, sore at letting my temper get on top of me.

'Look, Dinsmore, I didn't mean—'

'No, hold on, you said plenty. You talk like you're a hotshot, but all I see is a crummy legman flinging mud to see what sticks. You know the only reason I didn't hang up five minutes ago?'

'Shoot.'

'Because you might just have stumbled into something – but if you have, it's only thanks to me.' He took a breath, baiting me to ask, his indignation coming across as half-hearted. I held my tongue, and he went on anyway. 'I got a look at the fire department report into what happened at Duke's. It's all there in black-and-white – an accident.'

'That doesn't mean a thing. They could have written it up any way—'

'Let me finish. I did a little more digging; I found a source at the telephone exchange, tells me an hour before the fire, a call was placed from the mayor's house to the fire chief's home line.'

Coughlin again. Lines connecting and intersecting. 'No need to change the report if Coughlin told them how to write it up in the first place – right?'

'I wouldn't be willing to go that far, but the timing is curious, I'd say that much.'

'Can you corroborate it?'

'Corroborate how? I spoke to the dame who placed the call, what more you want?'

I ran my hand over my mouth, thinking about the implications. 'So will you look into the Kolkhorst girl?'

He blew out a breath, sounded like he was emptying his lungs. 'You got any proof at all that she didn't kill herself?'

'She lived a hundred miles away from where she was found. Does that sound right to you?'

'Maybe, maybe not. If you're crazy enough to take your own life . . .'

I had Robinson's photograph of her in my mind – the hint of happiness in her expression, at ease with the world. 'I don't think she was crazy.' I wanted to say more, bring up the link to Alice Anderson, but it felt too dangerous even to voice it aloud – and despite it all, I still couldn't gauge how far to trust him. 'There's something else. You have any ins with Hot Springs Police Department?'

'I haven't agreed to the first thing yet.'

'Kolkhorst got into some kind of trouble while she was working at the veterans' hospital, and Hot Springs PD were brought in. Nothing came of it, but I need the skinny on what happened.'

There was a slight hesitation before he spoke again, and I could tell he was scribbling down a note. 'When was this?'

'June of last year.'

'How can I get back to you?'

'I'll call you.'

I cut the connection and checked outside, nervous at being in the same place for longer than I was comfortable with. The bus from Little Rock had just pulled up, a mob of passengers emptying onto the tarmac.

I faced inside again, dialled, and waited for the call to connect. When Lizzie answered, her voice was heavy with sleep.

'Did I wake you?'

'That's okay, I hoped it would be you. No one else would think to call at this time of the day. I need to get up anyway, I'll be late.'

'You're going to the *Journal*?'

'Sure, why wouldn't I?'

'Are you up to it? You need to rest.'

'I'm not unwell, Charlie. I won't shut myself away indoors. Besides, one of us has got to be there to keep the place from crumbling.' I smiled, for what felt like the first time in forever. 'By the way, Mr Acheson asked how your story is coming along. Care to tell me what that's about?'

I switched ears. 'I had to find a way to make some money while I'm out here. There's an angle that might play. Stall him for me – I'll put something together when I get back.'

'I wish you'd told me. I looked a little foolish when he asked me and I had no idea what he was talking about.'

'I'm sorry. With everything that's going on . . .'

'What *is* going on? I meant it when I said I want you to stay there for as long as you think is right, but I'd feel better if I knew what was happening. I can hear the strain in your voice.'

I started to say something, dissembling, but stopped before I finished a sentence. She deserved better than that, and I knew it; whatever trouble I was in, adding to the lies and omissions I'd placed between us served no benefit. I started over, and once I set the ball rolling, it gathered steam on its own. I told her about Cole Barrett jumping me in my room and stealing Robinson's files. Him warning Clay Tucker about the fire. Tucker's murder. Running from the police. Even the parts I wanted to protect her from, like being a suspect in the killings, came pouring out. Lizzie was silent the whole time.

Before I told her about going to Texarkana, I asked, 'Do you remember any of the nurses that cared for Alice?'

The question caught her off guard, and she hesitated getting the words out. 'I don't— I mean, perhaps if I saw them there's a chance, but . . . Why are you asking about this?'

I told her. I told her about Ginny Kolkhorst being the woman in Robinson's photograph, and the inscription saying she was murdered. About her body being found in Hot Springs, and how that made a link to the Glover killings more feasible. About being in Texarkana and seeing Hansen. His implication that he'd always suspected the truth had been covered up, but he was too afraid to speak out. I even told her about him giving me the contents of Robinson's desk, and his photographs of Ella Borland that somehow haunted me. When I was through, I felt as though I'd gone fifteen rounds with Joe Louis.

'I don't remember the nurse.' Her voice was hollow and distant. 'I'm sorry, Charlie, I can't . . .'

'It's not important, don't trouble yourself.'

'Don't say that. I can't remember her face. She cared for my sister and now she's dead because of it and I can't even remember—'

'Slow down—'

'When is this going to end, Charlie?' Her voice rose, anger coming now. 'When the hell is this going to end?'

'It's going to be all right. I'm going to make it all right.'

'How? Look how much blood there's been, and still it goes on. You can't keep fighting this, it's too big.'

'Don't let yourself think that way. I can make this right.'

She drew a slow breath, and I stared at the numbers on the telephone, wondering if I'd done the right thing by coming clean. Eventually she broke the silence. 'Do you think they murdered that poor nurse because of what she told Jimmy Robinson?'

'I don't know. I think that's what he thought, at least.'

'What would make him say she was killed? How would he know that?'

'I don't know.' My head drooped against my chest. 'I keep thinking, if I'd just got to him before he died . . .'

'What about the woman he was with – he must have told her something of what he was thinking?'

'Ella Borland?'

'Yes.'

'She said they weren't close.'

'I don't believe that. He was infatuated with her, surely.

Why all the photographs otherwise?'

I hadn't thought about it that way. I kicked myself for being so blinkered. Robinson had always struck me as a lone wolf, but Ella Borland had the goods to turn any man's head. 'I got the feeling she was holding something back when we spoke, now you're making me think maybe that's it.'

'Be gentle with her, Charlie. If she does know something, she's probably afraid. If something happened to him, I mean.'

'I will.'

'If she had any feelings for Robinson at all, she'll tell you what she knows, eventually. I wouldn't want that on my conscience if I were her.'

I loved my wife for seeing the things I missed. 'I should go. I need to keep moving.'

'Charlie, wait a moment.'

'What is it?'

She was hesitant. 'I won't say come home, but please, please, be careful. If the police catch you, you'll never leave. Do you understand what I mean?'

I told her I loved her and I'd call again as soon as I could. I understood perfectly what she meant. If Cole Barrett's men caught up to me, I wouldn't likely even make it into custody.

CHAPTER TWENTY-FIVE

I didn't dare go inside the Southern Club. I was parked down the block from the entrance, watching for Ella Borland to come out, at the same time ready to bolt if I saw sign of the cops. I'd already stiffed a call to the Southern to check she was there – hanging up before the man on the other end could ask any questions. Now all I could do was wait for her to show.

An hour in, my legs were aching and I had a headache. There was enough traffic around to keep me hidden in plain sight, but I was wondering if I should move on anyway. Then she appeared, hitting the street in a plain skirt and jacket, her face showing only touches of stage makeup. She turned and walked in the opposite direction from where I was parked, so I pulled out and drove after her. As I caught up to her, I slowed to fall in step, and drew up close. 'Miss Borland.'

She stopped and I pulled over to do the same. She looked at me as if she'd been spooked by a wild animal, and I thought she was about to run. Then she came over, gazing at me through the open passenger window. 'Mr Yates, what are you doing here?'

'I need to talk to you. Would you allow me to give you a ride, please?'

'You asked me where Clay Tucker's brother lived. The last time I saw you—'

'It's not what you think. I didn't kill him.'

She stared at me and I held her eyes with mine, willing her to believe me.

Before she could say anything more, a man appeared at her side. He had his hands in his pockets, was squinting at me through the window. William Tindall.

'Everything all right here, Ella?'

She blanched, whipped around to look at him.

'Everything's fine,' I said. 'I'm just talking to the lady.'

'That right? Would've thought you'd have manners enough to step out of your car at least, eh?' He spoke with a mongrel accent, strains of Hell's Kitchen Irish crossed with British – but not the kind you heard on the Pathé films; a regional dialect, coarser. He was wearing a baggy three-piece suit, and the same newsboy cap I'd seen before, pulled low over his left eye.

'This doesn't concern you, friend,' I said. 'Move on.'

He laid one hand on the roof of the car, leaning closer. 'That's where you're wrong. You're talking to one of my girls like you're trawling for company, and that concerns me very much.'

'Mr Tindall, please, it's no trouble,' Borland said. 'This is an acquaintance of mine, he was offering to give me a ride home.'

He never took his eyes off me. 'Isn't that gallant.'

I held his look, feeling as though he was sizing me up. Despite his slight frame, he carried himself in a way that exuded power and control.

He reached down and opened the passenger door. I started to swivel in my seat, thinking he was about to come at me, but he pulled it wide and held it open for Borland. 'My apologies, then. Don't let me hold you up.'

Borland looked from me to him and back, then squeezed

around him and folded herself into the passenger seat. Tindall shut the door gently, then crouched to look at me again. 'Pay me no mind, pal. I'm protective where the fairer sex are concerned – I were raised by women, see.' There was a twinkle in his eyes as he said it, and even though his tone had softened, I still heard menace in it.

Borland smiled nervously. 'Thank you, Mr Tindall. I'll see you this evening.'

He nodded and patted the roof. 'See her to her door safe, now. You'll answer to me if not.' He winked and then watched as we drove away. Looking at him in the rearview, still staring, I couldn't shake the feeling that he knew exactly who I was.

*

Ella Borland sat as far along from me as she could get. 'You can let me out once we get around the corner. I couldn't think what else to say back there.'

'Thank you for not telling him who I was. I promise you, I didn't have anything to do with Clay Tucker's death.'

She looked at me out of the corner of her eye, then straight ahead again. 'I believe you. I wouldn't have got in the car if I didn't.'

'Where do you live? I'll drive you.'

'That won't be necessary.'

'It's no trouble.'

She flattened her skirt, turning her head to me now. 'Make a right after the next block.'

I nodded, switching lanes. 'You work for Tindall?'

'I work for the Southern.'

'And he owns it?'

'I don't know, I just dance there.' She turned a little towards me. 'I was trying to reach you, before. The man at your motel said you'd disappeared. When I heard on the radio – the killing – I assumed—'

'That I was on the lam?'

She cleared her throat and looked away again, said nothing.

'I told you, I didn't do it. I went there that morning, after I saw you, but someone else was there after me. I'm starting to think I was set up.'

'By who?'

'By whoever killed Jimmy.'

She reached into her purse, pulled out a compact. 'You say that as though you're sure now.'

'I am.'

She held it in her fingertips but made no move to open it. 'How?'

'Clay Tucker was warned about the fire before it happened.'

'What?'

'I think that's why he was killed – because he told me as much.'

'Who warned him?'

'Cole Barrett.'

The compact slipped from her grip. She moved swiftly to snatch it up from the footwell, fumbling it as she put it away again.

'Is everything all right?'

She pointed up ahead. 'You can leave me at the corner here. Thank you.'

'I'll gladly take you to your door, ma'am.'

'No.' By the look on her face, it came out firmer than she meant it to. She swallowed and when she spoke next, her voice was softer. 'Thank you, this will be fine.'

I drew up to the kerb and stopped. We were at the intersection of Orange and Ouachita, a bank on one corner, a bar opposite, businesses along both streets – not a residential neighbourhood. She thanked me again and reached for her door handle.

'Ma'am, why were you trying to call me?'

'Pardon me?'

'You said before you were trying to reach me. I was wondering why.'

She looked to the handle, then back at her lap. 'I was curious as to how you were faring in your endeavours, that was all.'

'I'm getting closer.'

She glanced up at me. 'To finding who killed Jimmy?'

'To the truth.' I put my hand on the dash. 'You're not curious about Barrett? What I told you just now?'

She took a clipped breath. 'I don't see what it matters.'

'A girl as smart as you? No sale. Now I think about it, anytime I've mentioned him, you've gone cold on me. If there's something you'd like to talk to me about . . .'

'There's nothing.'

'Doesn't it throw a new light on what happened to Jeannie Runnels? Doesn't it make you question what really happened with Barrett and Walter Glover?'

She turned her head away so she was facing the passenger window.

'Either Barrett killed Jimmy, or he knows who did. I know

213

Jimmy confronted him. What did he have?'

I could hear her breathing – shallow, rapid.

'Miss Borland?'

'I told you, I don't know.'

I took Robinson's pictures of her from the bag and dropped them on the seat between us. 'Here.'

She turned around to look. She tried to keep her features expressionless, but her eyes widened enough to betray surprise. 'Who took these?'

'They were Jimmy's.'

She picked up the image closest to her and examined it. Then a second, and a third.

'You told me you weren't close, but so far as I can tell, you're the only person Jimmy passed any time with while he was here. From the looks of these, he was holding a candle for you. Are you telling me he never once confided in you?'

She stared at the picture of her with William Tindall, and I noticed her jaw muscles tense.

'I think there's something you want to tell me,' I said. 'I think that's why you agreed to meet me in the first place, it's why you were calling me, and it's why you haven't got out of this damn car yet, even though—'

She flung the picture down onto the seat. 'Walter Glover didn't kill Jeannie.' She threw her hands to her face.

The sound of passing traffic filled the car.

I watched her, waiting, gave her some time to keep talking. My throat was tight.

Thirty seconds passed. I was about to try coaxing her when she lowered her hands. 'Jimmy told me Glover didn't kill her. Or Bess Prescott.'

I took my hands off the wheel, turned to her very slowly. 'Who did?'

'I don't know. I don't think he knew.' A tear came to her eye and she dabbed at it with her forefinger.

'How did he come to that conclusion?'

She shook her head, then met my eyes, imploring me. 'I swear to you, that's all he said.'

I tried to give her a handkerchief but she refused it. 'How long have you known?'

'Jimmy told me last week, just before the fire. I've been so unsure, I— It didn't make sense to me, I didn't know what to do. I didn't think you'd believe me.'

I said nothing, thinking it through. Walter Glover was still incarcerated when Ginny Kolkhorst was pulled out of Lake Hamilton in April. If Robinson somehow knew her killer was the same man who went on to murder Runnels and Prescott, he would have known it couldn't have been Glover.

'You don't believe me, do you?' Her eyes were burning a hole in mine.

'Don't put words in my mouth. I believe you, all right. I'd just like to know how Jimmy put it together.'

She said nothing to that, started plucking at the hem of her skirt. In the mirror, I glimpsed a Hot Springs PD prowler cruise across the intersection behind us, heading away. I inched lower in my seat, checking the intersection in front and the streets around for any others.

'Do you think Cole Barrett was behind Jeannie's death?' she asked.

I rubbed my face, thinking about all the evidence and all the dead ends, the stolen papers, everything that pointed back to him. I remembered his face when he ambushed me in my room, the speed with which he'd drawn his weapon and left me with no doubt he was capable of killing. But there was something else too, something I hadn't understood until now – his eyes showed no hatred. Almost closer to regret. His insistence that he'd tried to warn Robinson. 'I don't know. I have to make a telephone call. Let me drop you somewhere.'

She opened the door, determined that she would walk the rest of the way. 'What are you going to do now?'

I hadn't set on the decision in my head, but a surge of fear welled in me. 'Lay low a few days. If you don't hear from me in seventy-two hours, go see Samuel Masters, tell him everything you know.'

CHAPTER TWENTY-SIX

I made the call from the bus station, urgency making me break my own vow not to use the same bank of telephones twice. It felt like I was making it easy for them to find me.

The operator patched me through, and one of the staffers picked up. I gave a false name, to dupe Masters into taking the call, and a few seconds later he came on the line.

'Sam Masters.'

'It's Charlie Yates.'

He drew a breath to speak, then paused. 'Unless you're calling to tell me where you're at, I'm hanging up.'

'That's your choice, but it would be a mistake.'

'I've made worse, I'm sure of that.'

'Remember I told you Cole Barrett warned Clay Tucker in advance of the fire?'

He hesitated, deciding whether to bite. 'Yes.'

'Did you do anything with it? Did you look into it?'

'In case it escaped your attention, the only man can back your story up is dead.'

'Barrett's not, though.'

'Be serious.'

'So you just sat on it?'

'Are you questioning my methods?'

'I'm twisting in the wind here and it feels like I'm the only one gives a damn.'

'You're a goddamn murder suspect, and all I've got is your say-so. What did you expect of me?'

I gripped the receiver right in front of my mouth. 'You know what the knock is on you? That it's all just rhetoric. All your talk, that big speech you laid on me, and you don't give a damn about justice, only politics. It's true, isn't it? There're no votes to be had in figuring out who killed some out-of-town hack.'

'A wanted man taking shots at my character. Now I've heard it all.'

'Look, I've got a source telling me the night of the fire, a call was placed from Teddy Coughlin's office to the home of the fire chief. Corroborate it for me, make sure it's true. I'm betting it is, and you tell me that wouldn't warrant looking into if it is.'

The line went quiet, the roar of a bus pulling away filling the booth I was in. 'Who's your source?'

'I'm not going to answer that, but if you want to get to Coughlin, I'm giving you your chance.'

He sighed. 'We never had this conversation, understand?'

'I understand.'

'I'm serious what I said before, hand yourself in. I'll see to it you get a fair shake in the courts.'

'I'd never make it that far,' I said, and slammed down the receiver.

*

Barrett's LaSalle was parked right there on the scrub in front of his cabin.

I stopped short of his property and waited, scoping the area.

I watched the windows, didn't see anyone moving. The broken-down door on his woodshed was swinging in the breeze, banging gently against its frame.

My impulse veered towards flight – that old urge to bolt and get as far from the coming confrontation as I could.

I left the engine running and the car door ajar. A chopping sound came from somewhere behind the house, like an irregular heartbeat. I stepped into the trees next to where I'd parked and started looping towards the back of the house in a wide arc, moving from trunk to trunk for cover. I could see the brown water of the pond below, streaked with afternoon sunlight. I moved slowly, mindful of the dog I'd seen last time I was there.

Barrett came into view. He was splitting logs on a block, a pile either side of him, waiting to be chopped or stacked. He was perspiring heavily, his blue shirt wet at the arms and neck. He wasn't wearing his gun belt. There was a large metal stake in the middle of the yard, a chain attached to it, but no sign of the dog. I moved closer, stopped behind a tree near the edge of his yard. It felt like a nest of vipers had broke loose in my guts.

Barrett placed the next log on the stump and lofted the axe. He brought it down in a tight swing, cursing as it caught in the wood. He worked it free, kicked the two sections onto the pile on the right, then dropped the axe down on the grass. He turned his back to where I was hiding and walked a little way to where a pitcher was set on a rock. He took two long gulps, then splashed water over his face and neck.

I broke cover and started towards where the axe lay on the ground. Suddenly the clearing erupted – a furious barking sound. I jumped to the side in shock, flinching from the noise. I looked over, saw Barrett's dog on its hind legs, baying at me from behind the screen door. Barrett whipped around and saw me right away – nowhere to hide in the open ground.

Some reflex took over. I ran to the axe and put my foot on its neck.

Barrett hadn't moved. The pitcher hung loose in his hand. He took a few steps towards me, measured, and as he did, I saw that his gun belt was stashed behind the rock. He saw me look at it. 'You still here.'

I was breathing hard. 'Still here.'

'You thinking on picking up that axe? Better be quick if y'are.'

'Only if you make me.'

He raised the pitcher to his lips and drank. I could feel my legs bucking, tremors running up and down them. I planted my feet to gut them out.

He wiped his mouth on the back of his wrist. 'You fixing to tell me what you want, or you gonna stand there all day with your teeth rattling?'

'I want to know who killed Jeannie Runnels, Bess Prescott and Ginny Kolkhorst. I know it wasn't Walter Glover. And I want to know who started the fire.'

His free hand opened and closed again. He set the pitcher down on the ground. 'You the damnedest cuss I ever came across.'

'Jimmy Robinson found you out, didn't he? Because of the Kolkhorst girl.'

He stepped backwards and sat down on the rock, his hands on his knees, his back straight at first but then seeming to sag.

I grabbed up the axe and took a step towards him. 'Don't go for that gun, Barrett.'

He lifted his head, a sour look on his face. 'Put the damn axe down. You turned around on everything.'

'I'll keep it for now, if it's all the same.'

He flicked his fingers, the threat I posed inconsequential.

'Who killed them?' I asked.

'I don't know.'

'I don't believe you.'

'Ain't nothing I can do about that.'

'Yes there is. Convince me.'

He hung his head and a bead of sweat fell from the end of his nose. 'Your friend got killed because he came here and said the same things to me. They gonna do the same to you now.'

'Who? Who killed him?'

He ran his hand over his face. 'I ain't know who started the fire – pick a name out of a hat, you be just as close. But that ain't what you asking, is it?'

'On whose orders?'

'You said his name the last time.'

'Coughlin.'

'You shouldn't have to ask. Ain't nothing happens here without his say-so.'

'Why did he want him dead?'

He raised his eyebrows. 'You seen what he had his nose into. He was told to let it alone and he never listened.'

'Because he found out Walter Glover was your patsy and you murdered him. And they killed Jimmy to protect you.'

He shook his head once. 'Not me – the story. To protect the story.'

'You're a goddamn liar.'

He looked up and fixed his eyes on the trees behind me.

'You have any idea what it is to think you strong and find out you ain't?'

The words reopened a wound I thought had scarred over. The war, the accident, my shame. He was talking about himself, but I felt my face flush just the same. 'Is that how you excuse yourself for killing innocent people?'

'I done what I could.'

'I don't see it.'

'Goddammit, I told you, I tried to warn your friend. I tried to warn you. Ain't none of y'all sons of bitches would listen.'

'You're talking about Duke's? All you did was make a phone call when you knew the whole place was going to burn. Was that enough to ease your conscience? Hell, Tucker ended up dead in the end anyway, didn't he?'

He pointed his finger at me now, anger bringing a flicker of life to him. 'Clay Tucker was a goddamn reptile. I told him what was coming, and I told him to clear the building, but he figured he could parlay it into some relief for what he owed Teddy if he didn't interfere. A man's life goes for cheap in these parts.'

'Did you kill him on account of it?'

He lolled his head back. 'I ain't never killed anyone. Cost me everything I had because I didn't, so you get that much straight in your goddamn mind.'

'You can't even keep your own lies straight.' I pointed at him with the axe, my voice raised now. 'You killed Walter Glover so you could hang those murders on him. Who are you protecting?'

'Glover was made bad; don't waste no tears on him.'

'That doesn't make it right.'

He pushed himself off the rock and stood up. He locked his eyes on me and his lips parted as though he was about to speak, but he hesitated, ran his hand over his face. 'It wasn't me killed him.'

'What?'

He kept staring, so still I could have been looking at a statue.

I brought the axe across my chest, suddenly heavy in my hands. 'You said you did. All the newspaper stories, all the . . .'

'Teddy likes to say, "*You get along by going along.*" I always done that for him, but I drew the line when he asked me to kill a man – but it ain't like you just say no to Teddy. There's a price for that.'

My mind was racing to keep up. 'Saying you did and being feted as a hero?'

'It cost me my badge. You can't know how much of a man's pride gets tied up in that damn piece of tin.'

I stared at him standing there and saw a whole different man before me; a husk, the insides rotted away over the years until all that was left was an ossified shell, now beginning to crumble. 'Who killed those women? Tell me who Coughlin is protecting.'

'I don't know. Teddy ain't tell me and I ain't ask. That's how we worked all these past years.'

I lowered the axe and let it slip from my hand. 'You're pathetic.'

'Call me anything you like – maybe words matter where you from. Only thing matters here is power. The money and the gun.'

'Then be a man, goddammit. Go talk to Samuel Masters. He wants Coughlin, he'll cut you a deal.'

'Then I'd be as dead as you are.' He pushed his sodden hair from his forehead; he seemed to have aged just in the time we'd been talking. 'Masters is a fool. He thinks winning a few votes is gonna change things in this town. What's it gonna change? Casinos ain't just gonna up and leave, there's too much money at stake. Too many livelihoods. Even if he gets Teddy out of office, he'll be back.'

'So you're happy with your lot, hiding out here, chopping wood? Feeling sorry for yourself while more people die?'

He looked away. 'Ain't no one else needs to die if you'd just walk the hell away.'

I glanced around me, saw the dirty waters of the pond beneath us, the peeling paint on the walls of his cabin. If this was all he had left, it was still more than he deserved. 'Why the Kolkhorst girl?'

He closed his eyes, looked pained. 'It's all the same question. I ain't have no answers for you. She popped out of the lake, looked certain someone put her there against her will—'

'Why? What made you sure of that?'

'Her mouth.' He swiped his fingers across his lips. 'Someone slashed it up like they's scoring a hog.'

I closed my eyes, trying not to see it. At every turn, something worse.

Barrett didn't stop. 'But then I get the call from the boss man says, "*Cole, far as anyone's concerned, she took her own life.*" Case closed.'

My right fist balled up hard as a rock. 'You spineless son of a bitch.'

'You feel like hitting me, have at it. Didn't do your friend no good.'

I saw Robinson's ghost run across the yard to lay one on Barrett. I wished I had a measure of his temerity.

Barrett just looked at me, the way a man watched dirt being thrown onto a stranger's casket.

'What happened when he came here? Tell me.'

He dipped his head to his chest. 'He said he knew the same man murdered Kolkhorst killed Runnels and Prescott, and wasn't no way it was Walter Glover. I told him to leave, but he weren't agreeable to the idea until I let Lucy off the chain.' He nodded to the dog. 'But he came back, few days later. He was liquored up to his chops and he caught me with a cheap shot. Started whupping on me saying he was gonna kill me, till I got to my gun.'

'What did you tell him?'

He clamped the bridge of his nose with his thumb and forefinger. 'Same as I just told you. I ain't meaned to, I spilled it when he was beating on me. Few hours later, I got wind the fire was gonna happen.' He let his hand fall from his face and he looked up. 'I made the call to Tucker. I tried.'

'Don't stand there trying to sell me your remorse. Didn't stop you stealing his goddamn papers from my room.'

He was shaking his head. 'There weren't no papers in your room. The Lord as my witness.'

I didn't want to believe him, but he cut too worthless a figure not to. I thought about my suspicion I'd been framed for Tucker's murder. If that was the case, whoever killed him had to have been shadowing me that morning, to know I'd been out there. Tough for Barrett to do that and then make it back to the motel before me.

I turned and started to make my way back to the car.

'Where you going?'

I stopped, my neck tightening, thinking I'd let him fool me. I turned slowly, expecting to see him holding the gun on me.

But when I faced him, he was still standing in the same position, the gun belt untouched. 'Won't take them long to catch up to you, you know. There'll be men watching the roads. I can help you get out. There's bootlegger trails ain't no one uses by day.'

'I'll take my chances.'

'I meant what I said before about them killing you. It's a matter of time.'

'Makes me wonder why they've let you live, then.'

'Teddy don't need no more attention on what went on. It's hurt him bad already. Besides, I'm a hero, ain't you know?' There was disgust in his voice as he said it.

'Well, you tell him to take his best damn shot. Killing me won't make a difference. I'm not the only one that knows about Glover.'

His face went taut and he paled. 'Who else?'

'That's no concern of yours.'

He marched towards me. I set my feet, ready to fight – but he stopped just short. 'It damn sure is. Teddy won't leave a man alive for Masters to put on the stand.' He wiped the sweat from his face with his palm. 'Speak now, Yates. There's enough died on account of this already.'

A jolt ran through me – my last words to Ella Borland, telling her to go to Masters if she didn't hear from me. Three women dead already and no one cared; a crushing certainty that Coughlin wouldn't hesitate to have her killed too.

My eyes must have betrayed my anxiety. 'I can help,' he said.

'I can get you out – you and whoever.' He stepped closer. 'But we need to leave right now. I'll drive you, just tell me who knows and we'll go get him.'

He stood in front of me, his eyes locked on mine, no trace of deception that I could discern. They'd been a step ahead the whole time; suddenly it felt like Coughlin's men were all around me, moving through the trees, closing the net. I blinked, my guts churning, Maddened by my own inertia.

I glanced over my shoulder and found a measure of calm in the stillness of the water below. He was right in what he'd said – but it didn't mean he could be trusted.

I turned towards the car. 'Find some other way to ease your conscience.'

CHAPTER TWENTY-SEVEN

Ten miles back to town. Too far, too long, to leave Ella Borland twisting in the wind without a warning. If Barrett had any inkling about her and Robinson, he'd put it together quick enough.

I remembered seeing a filling station a mile or two before the turnoff. I drove to it as fast as I dared on the country roads, skidding on mud every time I took a bend too fine.

Barrett's expression flitted through my mind, the desperation that was evident on his face as we were talking. I believed him when he said he hadn't killed Glover. What I couldn't stomach was his self-pity, as if he'd had no choice but to take the actions he did, and that somehow absolved him of blame. I'd made decisions I wasn't proud of, same as every man – worse, even – but I carried them with me, and I bore their consequences. Barrett was too weak to do the same.

I came to the gas station and pulled up on the forecourt. I ran inside and asked for a payphone. The man behind the counter shook his head, but when I dug two dollars in change from my pocket and stacked it on the counter, he showed me through to a small office and pointed to a dilapidated hand-cranked model, partially buried by papers and a dirty rag.

The operator made the connection, but the man who answered said Ella wasn't there.

'I need to speak to her urgently. She's in danger. Where can I find her?'

He hesitated. 'You want me to pass a message to her—'

'There isn't time. I need her home number. Or her address.'

'At a guess, if she wanted you to have it, she'd have given it to you.'

'Goddammit, she doesn't know the danger she's in. Wait – call her. Tell her it's Charlie Yates and give her this number.' I read the payphone dial code out to him. 'Tell her to call me now.'

He was silent a minute, then he exhaled. 'All right, hang up so I can try her.'

I stood by the phone, knocking on the wall with my knuckle as I waited for her to call, praying I wasn't too late. I jumped when the line buzzed.

'Ella?'

'Mr Yates? What—'

'I need to speak with you.'

'Where are you? You sound out of breath. Is something wrong?'

'What we spoke about before . . .' I glanced behind me, feeling as though the owner was listening in on me, everyone a potential spy for Coughlin now. But when I looked, he'd retaken his seat behind the counter, out of earshot. 'Have you told anyone else what you told me?'

'No, of course not.'

I closed my eyes and allowed myself a breath. 'I think it would be safest if you left town anyway. Just for now.'

'Why? What's going on?'

'I should have said it before. I was wrong not to.'

'What are you— Am I in danger? What's happened?'

I scrabbled for an answer that would reassure. 'I don't know. I think this would be for best.'

The pitch of her voice rose a notch. 'I can't just leave. I have to work at midnight, and—'

'Ella, listen to me: I went to Barrett, he admitted it, exactly like you said. But it goes deeper, much deeper, and there are men who will harm you if they find out what you know.'

'Do you think I don't realise that? Why do you think I held my tongue for so long?'

'Please. The men behind this are not in the business of leaving loose ends.'

She said nothing.

'It doesn't have to be for ever,' I said. 'Just buy me enough time to get to them.'

'You're not leaving?'

'I can't. Not yet.'

She drew a sharp breath. 'Did Cole Barrett kill Jeannie?'

'No. I don't think so.'

'Did he tell you who did?'

'No. But I mean to find the man.'

She was quiet again, a long pause this time. 'Where would I go? I've got no money and no place to stay.'

'I can give you money. Enough to pay for a motel someplace.'

'I'm not in the habit of accepting charity.'

'Then call it a loan, goddammit. As long as you're on a bus today.'

I listened to her breathing, thinking. I was about to push again when she said, 'Could you call by my house?'

'Give me your address.'

'One-ten Violet Drive. It's a half-block off Ouachita.'

'I'll find it. Pack a bag, I'll be there in thirty minutes.'

CHAPTER TWENTY-EIGHT

As it was, I made the journey in twenty, expecting the cops to show up in my rearview all the time I was on the road.

Violet Drive was a narrow street of older houses, pressed up tight against each other along both sides. I found one-ten and parked outside. It was the familiar white frame structure, with a small porch and a faded red front door. The tiny yard in front of it was strewn with leaves, but otherwise bare and untended. As I set the brake, I caught a movement from the corner of my eye – maybe a drape twitching.

I looked inside my wallet. I had forty bucks on me, the last of my cash reserves. Enough to keep a roof over her head for a week or more. What came after that I'd figure out later.

I jumped out, crossed the rundown sidewalk and banged on the door. I waited, Teddy Coughlin on my mind, thinking how to get at him. The word *unassailable* kept circling in my head. The door opened a fraction and Ella peered out. She saw it was me and opened it the rest of the way, her face showing worry. She wore a simple black dress with a tie around the waist. 'Come in.'

She stepped back for me to enter. It was gloomy inside, the drapes drawn across both windows. The doorway led straight into a lounge that was cramped but homely. There were two worn-looking easy chairs in one corner with an old-model wireless next to them; in another, a small dining table held a pack of Chesterfields, a full ashtray and an empty glass. Through a doorway to my left I could see a pokey kitchen, also shaded. The door on the opposite wall was closed, presumably leading to the bedroom.

Borland crossed to the table. She took a cigarette from the pack and lit it with her back to me, taking two attempts to strike the match. 'Please, won't you have a seat?'

I shook my head. 'Are you ready?'

She sucked on her smoke, exhaling as she spoke. 'Just a moment.'

She set the cigarette in the ashtray and slipped through the bedroom door. I got a bad feeling something was off. She was nervous, which I expected, but it was as though she was afraid of me.

The bedroom door opened again and Detective Harlan Layfield stepped out of the gloom, pointing his service revolver at me. 'I thought you'd have sense enough to hand yourself in by now.'

My head sunk into my chest and it felt like someone had attached iron weights to me, everything I'd done now rendered in vain. I looked past him, trying to catch Ella's eye, but she was sitting on the bed, staring at the wall. I looked at him again. 'I didn't kill Clay Tucker.'

'Turn around and put your hands behind your back.'

'Layfield, listen to me—'

'I got no desire to fire my gun today, Yates.'

I turned slowly, keeping my hands in front of me, stole a look at the front door. It was shut, but I couldn't remember if Borland had locked it.

'Hands.'

One chance. Make a break or be taken in. I cursed myself for not remembering if the goddamn door was locked or not.

I heard him move towards me. I tensed to run.

Then Ella appeared in front of me, blocking my path to the door. I couldn't tell if she'd chosen that spot purposely or not – if she'd read my intentions. She held her cigarette in front of her mouth, flicking the butt, and it seemed as though she meant to say something, a look in her eyes I couldn't fathom.

As I searched her face, Layfield grabbed my right arm and pulled it behind me. I felt the cuff bite into my wrist, and watched as she slinked away again, the moment gone. Layfield took my other arm and jerked it back, closed the cuff on my left wrist. Ella was in the kitchen now, opening the drapes.

I heard Layfield slide his pistol back into its holster. 'Start walking.'

'Wait. My wallet's in my right pocket. There's forty dollars in there – give it to her.'

He stepped in front of me, looked from me to her and back again. 'I can't do that. Procedure.' He took a grip on my arm and started guiding me towards the door.

I turned my head as far as I could and called out to her. 'Ella, get out of town. Today.'

Layfield pulled me around by my shirt. 'You threatening her?'

I ignored him, strained my neck to look at her again. 'PLEASE. It's not safe here. Go.'

She didn't even look over. Layfield bundled me out the door.

My eyes watered coming out into the daylight again.

233

Layfield led me to a black Ford parked a little way down the street. An elderly couple on their porch stared at me as I passed. When he stopped at the car, I said, 'I want to speak to Sam Masters.'

'We'll see about all that later.'

He opened the rear door and hustled me into the car. When I sat, the position of the cuffs meant I had to lean on my arms, and my shoulders started to ache. 'My editor needs to know too. Buck Acheson, in California.' It would worry Lizzie when word reached her, but I figured the more people knew I was in custody, the less the chance of something bad happening to me.

Layfield climbed in the front and said nothing. We started to drive, crossing Ouachita onto Grand Avenue, and I thought about Ella Borland. I couldn't figure out why she'd turned me in. She'd given no hint that was on her mind when I'd seen her earlier in the day. The only notion I could come up with was that I'd spooked her by telling her to run. I jammed my head against the window in frustration.

'Settle down.'

We turned south onto Central Avenue – heading away from the police building. I watched a moment as we drove, seeing the houses and stores thin out as we got further from town, red pines and white-flowered magnolia trees along the side of the road now, glimpses of a body of water in the far distance ahead of us. 'Where are we going?'

Layfield eyed me in the rearview and said nothing.

I felt a rising tension in my chest. I tugged at the cuffs surreptitiously, but they held firm. I took a breath and waited a minute more, urging myself to be calm.

We kept travelling south, towards the water. The only buildings I could see were farmhouses now, set a long way back from the blacktop. A memory blitzed me, brought on by the land-scape – of Texarkana, the empty fields around the town; the abandoned farmhouse I'd fled from in the dead of night. Tension gave way to panic. 'Where the hell are you taking me?'

'Shut your mouth.'

I watched the sliver of his face I could see in the rearview; he kept his eyes on the road. My arms started shaking, and I yanked harder at the cuffs, felt them cut into my skin.

I clenched my teeth and waited until I was sure there wouldn't be a tremor in my voice before I spoke again. 'You're making a mistake. Take me back to the station.'

He said nothing and drove on.

We reached the lake, and a bridge carried us out over a wide channel, more land visible up ahead of us. The lake stretched for miles either side of the roadway, the sun catching the flat surface in such a way that the water looked like concrete. Reaching the other side, we passed a pleasure boat dock and small hotel on the shore.

Lake Catherine was east of town, so this had to be Lake Hamilton – the same stretch of water where Ginny Kolkhorst was found.

We followed the road across what turned out to be a small island, then onto another bridge across a narrower channel. At the far side of it, Layfield turned off onto a dirt road.

The land around the track was heavily wooded, and he drove slow. After two or three minutes, the water appeared in front of us again. A small clearing on the shoreline opened up, and he pulled the car around to a stop. A jetty on the bank ran fifteen feet out into the lake.

He climbed out and drew his gun. My heart was hammering so hard I didn't think it could keep it up for long. I could hear the engine ticking, cooling down, and bird calls coming from the trees. Nothing made sense. He opened my door. 'On your feet.'

I swung my legs around and levered myself out slowly. 'What the hell is going on?'

He gestured with his gun hand for me to walk in front of him, towards the pier. I could hear the water lapping against it quietly.

I glanced around, looking for any means of escape. Trees lined the banks either side of me, and I couldn't see any houses or buildings at all. The opposite shore was just visible across the water, at least a half-mile distant.

Layfield prodded me with his revolver. 'Move.'

I dragged my feet in the dirt, going as slowly as possible, my mind racing. The lake prompted a question. 'Did you kill Geneve Kolkhorst? Is this what happened to her?'

He didn't answer and I couldn't see his face to read his expression.

'She didn't stay down, did she?' I said, desperate. 'Think about that. What happens when my carcass washes up somewhere?'

He dug into my back again, and I kept shuffling forward. I thought of Lizzie, my heart about to burst, prayed that she wouldn't be left wondering. I started yapping quick-fire, anything that came into my head. 'Did you kill the others too? For Coughlin?' I stopped when I reached the jetty but he shoved me forward, the mud of the bank giving way to solid planks underfoot. 'You gutless son of a bitch, tell me. TELL ME.'

'Enough.' I felt the cold metal of the gun barrel touch my head. 'You know it all already, Yates. That's why we here.'

A shadow crossed my mind's eye, something reminiscent about the gun and his voice, but I didn't understand. I heard his shoes scuff on the planks as he stepped back.

I pulled at the cuffs again, but there was no give. Numbness was spreading from my shoulders, overtaking the panic I felt – an acceptance that it was always going to end this way. That I'd sealed my fate the minute I came back. Maybe long before that.

He cocked the hammer. I kept my eyes open and took in the beauty around me, my last try at defiance, and whispered a goodbye to Lizzie. *See you the next go-around.*

Then there was another noise, somewhere in the trees behind us. A car, coming down the same track we had. I stole a glance over my shoulder, saw Layfield looking around at it too. His gun was still on me, but I couldn't make a grab for it with my hands cuffed behind my back.

The car came into sight and drew up next to Layfield's Ford. My neck tensed when I recognised it – Cole Barrett's grey LaSalle. He climbed out and walked to the edge of the bank, where the jetty started. 'Hold up a minute, Harlan.'

Layfield took another step back from me, checked I hadn't moved, then turned his head to Barrett again. His mouth was ajar, his uncertainty obvious. 'What you doing here, Barrett?'

'Plan's changed. Teddy wants him alive for now. Bring him on back up.' He gestured with his head to walk me back to the bank.

Layfield hesitated. 'That a fact?' He glanced at me again, then back. 'How come?'

Barrett shrugged. 'He ain't tell me. I carry the bags, I ain't ask what's in them. C'mon.' He made a half-turn as if to go back to his car.

As he did, Layfield swung his gun around to aim at him. Barrett sensed the movement, grabbing for his weapon. They fired at the same time. I ducked, heard two, three, four shots. Barrett dropped to one knee. Layfield charged him.

I jumped up and gave chase without thinking. Layfield had his gun out in front of him, firing as he pelted along the jetty. Barrett raised his own weapon again and got another shot off, but Layfield didn't slow. When he got close, Layfield dived and speared him with a football tackle.

The sound of the gunshots echoed around the lake. I was two seconds behind Layfield. He was on top of Barrett, so I dipped my head and rammed my right shoulder into him, sending us sprawling.

My momentum carried me clear of the two men. I landed face down in the mud, no hands to break my fall. I rolled and managed to clamber to my knees, saw Layfield sit up and raise his gun. He trained it on Barrett.

Barrett was on all fours now, panting. There was blood all over his shirt. He looked up at Layfield and smiled, his eyes blazing, then lifted his gun slowly.

Layfield sprang up. He jarred his hand doing it and dropped his gun. He looked to where it lay, saw Barrett take aim, and ran instead. He ducked behind the LaSalle just as Barrett fired, the back passenger window shattering and crumbling. I heard the door of the Ford open and close and the engine start. I staggered to my feet, tried to go after him. The tyres spun and got purchase, and Layfield took off up the track.

The sound of the car faded, muffled by the trees. I looked over to Barrett, still on all fours, his head hung low. Blood was streaming from his torso to the ground, like water from a faucet. I ran over to him. 'Where're you hit?'

He grunted. He tried to push himself to his feet, but the mud was slick with his own blood and the effort was too much. He collapsed onto his side. I saw two wounds in his chest, and what looked like a third in his neck; it was hard to be certain because of the blood and dirt caking him.

'Son of a bitch.' His voice was weak.

'I'll get you out of here.' I glanced at the car, scrambling to think of a way to help him. 'My hands. I can't—'

He winced as he moved his arm, digging into his pocket. He produced a set of keys, and let them fall to the dirt. 'Cuffs. They all the same.'

I saw a small key on the ring and realised what he meant. I dropped to my knees and managed to scoop them up. Working over my shoulder, I angled the key into the lock and wrenched it until the clasp popped open. I threw the cuffs aside and spun around to face him.

Ripping off a part of my shirttail, I pressed it to one of the wounds. 'Hold it there.' I started to tear another piece, but he'd already discarded the first one. 'Goddammit—' I moved so I was positioned over his head and grasped him under the armpits, meaning to drag him to the car. 'Come on.'

He coughed, blood coming up with it, and fought to shrug me off. 'Let me rest.'

His face was the colour of milk and his shirt was soaked red. I let go of him and went to the water, scooped some up in my hand. I cupped it to his lips and poured a trickle into his mouth. Most of it ran down his cheek. His eyes were half-closed and his breath came short.

'How did you know?' I said.

'Tailed you. Had to do something.'

'Why?'

'You was right.' His face contorted in pain. 'I ain't done enough to stop it.'

'Was it Layfield? That's who Coughlin was protecting?'

He tried to say something more, but it was lost in a burst of choking coughs. He rolled his head to the side and spat. Then he spoke again, so quiet I couldn't hear it. I bent low, my ear to his mouth. He whispered, 'Run.'

His face went slack and he was still. I froze up then, stayed crouched next to his corpse for what seemed like a long time. I thought of the wife I'd seen behind him at his cabin.

When I got to my feet, I gazed out across the lake, the sunlight reflecting off it in a blaze of orange-white light. I remembered the words Heinrich Kolkhorst had spoken in irony – '*A nice place to do it at least.*' They seemed even more vicious now.

I walked over and used my handkerchief to pick up Layfield's revolver – empty. I got wise late: he knew he was out of bullets and that's why he ran. Barrett must have cottoned to it too. I put it in my jacket pocket and walked back to where Barrett lay. His gun was to one side, his set of keys the other. I pocketed both and bent down to close his eyelids.

Then I went to his car and set myself behind the wheel, seeing his blood on my hands, and the cuts on my wrists that the cuffs had left. I imagined killing Layfield. *If you gaze long into an abyss—*

My jaw shook and I gripped the wheel. I started pounding it with my palms. I kept going until I couldn't hold my arms up any longer.

I draped them over the wheel and sunk my head against my forearms, breathing hard. Barrett's corpse was still in sight, and I couldn't tear my eyes away. I wondered how much of what he'd told me was true. If he really did follow me, or if he'd known something about Layfield all along. Maybe he was always deeper into it than he could admit to himself. He talked as though he was caught up in events, as powerless as a stick in a stream, but Coughlin went a long way to protect him. Made me think Barrett was lying the whole time – to himself most of all.

My breathing started to return to normal. It was then, with the clarity release brings, that I saw a way to make sense of what happened. Why Layfield would have cause to kill Geneve Kolkhorst.

The implications were almost too big to conceive.

CHAPTER TWENTY-NINE

It took me more than five minutes to scrub the blood from my hands. The sink in the gas station washroom streaked with red when I was done.

The telephone kiosk outside overlooked the highway, a handful of cars travelling along the blacktop in the glow of the late afternoon sun. The operator connected me to the *Recorder* and I reached Dinsmore at his desk.

'I'm starting to feel like I'm at your beck and call—'

'The Kolkhorst girl. Did you look into it?' I said.

'As a matter of fact I did. And look, don't run away with this, but Cole Barrett was in charge of the investigation into her death. But that doesn't prove—'

'I already know that. I need the other thing – the trouble she had with Hot Springs PD—'

'What do you mean you already know? Why the hell have you got me running in circles?'

'Things are moving fast. This is the whole case, right here, Clyde. Did you look into it?'

'Yes, goddammit, I talked to some people, but it's thinner than the eyelashes on a fly. The nurse was accused of moonlighting in one of the hotels for extra money, if you take my meaning. The hospital management got wind of it. Guess they didn't like how it would make them look – hence they involved the cops. But the PD looked into it, talked to the girl, and they decided the allegation was baseless. Some kinda hatchet job on the part of a boy she'd given the flick to. He wanted to get her the boot from her job as revenge. That was the end of it.'

It came together in my mind like storm clouds closing on the last patch of clear sky. 'It was Harlan Layfield investigated, wasn't it?'

'How— Yes, it was. He was a beat cop at the time. Why in the hell do you keep asking me things you already know?'

Pine Street Hospital; the 'cop' who snatched Alice Anderson; Jimmy Robinson's tip-off, and the nurse who provided it. Harlan Layfield killed Geneve Kolkhorst. She knew him from her time in Hot Springs, and that's how she could identify him to Jimmy Robinson nine months later in Texarkana, when she spotted him hanging around the day Alice disappeared.

Which meant Harlan Layfield almost certainly killed Jeannie Runnels and Bess Prescott.

Which meant Harlan Layfield killed Jimmy Robinson.

Which meant—

Harlan Layfield killed Alice.

Dinsmore was still speaking, but he could have been across an ocean, he sounded so distant.

I'd sat in Layfield's car, inches away from him. I'd shaken his goddamn hand.

I doubled over and heaved, still clutching the receiver. Nothing came up.

'Yates? You hear me? How in the world is that the whole story?'

I wiped the drool from my mouth with the back of my hand. 'I'll tell you when I know the rest.'

I cut the call and re-dialled for Hot Springs PD. I asked

for Detective Layfield and was told he wasn't on shift today. I asked for his home address, and the cop on the other end got hinky, answered my question with a question. I hung up.

I dialled again, this time to Sam Masters. When he came on the line, I talked over him before he even said his name.

'Detective Harlan Layfield just tried to kill me.'

'Yates? What the—'

'Cole Barrett is dead. Layfield shot him.'

'Jesus Christ.'

'I've got the gun he used to do it. You'll find Layfield's fingerprints all over it.' I fought to keep my tone level, the anger seething just under my skin.

'Why? I don't— What in god's name is going on?'

'I was two seconds from taking a bullet. Barrett saved my life and Layfield killed him for it.'

'Why would Layfield want you dead?'

I barely knew where to start. I decided to hold back what I knew until I could make sense of it. 'No clue. Is he on Coughlin's payroll?'

'His name's never come up, but anything's possible with Teddy. Even so, these are some wild claims. You need to take a minute. I had a man look into your story, about the call from Coughlin's office on the night of the fire. It checks out.'

Dinsmore's tip, corroborated. 'Is that your way of saying you believe me?'

'Where did this all happen?'

'Lake Hamilton.' I reeled off the route we'd driven from town. 'Barrett's body is still there.'

'All right. Now if you've got the evidence like you say you have, let's get it to the proper authorities and we can start putting this thing together.'

'Is there a single damn cop in this town that isn't crooked? Someone who could bring Layfield in?'

'What? Of course, maybe, but—'

'Good. Then you set him on his tail and hope he finds him before I do.'

CHAPTER THIRTY

Barrett's face haunted me as I drove; all the blood, and still it wouldn't stop coming. I looked at my hand on the wheel, saw there was still some under my fingernails. Maybe you never can wash it all away.

I saw now that the nightmare had never stopped, but unpicking it was a different matter. Everything started with Alice; Layfield killed Kolkhorst and Robinson because they knew about his involvement in her death. Had to be. But that left more questions than answers. What did Jeannie Runnels and Bess Prescott have to do with it? Why would Coughlin protect him for their murders? And what was Layfield doing in Texarkana in the first place?

Faces mingled in my mind; Coughlin, Layfield, the two hovering like spectres. Then Barrett, Sam Masters, Alice. Ella Borland.

That last one lingered. Even though she'd turned me in, I couldn't shed my fears for her safety. What she'd done felt like a betrayal, but I looked at it from her perspective: a man wanted on a murder rap telling her to skip town because her life was in danger. And what if she hadn't called the cops? What if she'd called Layfield – knowing damn well what he intended to do? The memory of her face stayed with me, that look of guilt as she'd stood in front of me while he cuffed me – as if she was forcing herself to watch as a punishment. It sounded crazy, even to me, and I wondered if it was the product of a paranoid mind, seeing conspiracies everywhere. Another step in Robinson's shadow.

I pressed my foot down, tearing up the miles back to town. I followed Central all the way north, along Bathhouse Row to the Arlington, any pretence at moving covertly now abandoned.

I parked on Fountain Street by the side of the hotel, in a spot that afforded a view along the main drag. I took out Barrett's gun, held it in my lap and opened the cylinder. There were three bullets chambered. I remembered Ella asking me before if I was driven by revenge, and me denying it as firmly as I could. Maybe it was true then. Seemed like a memory from a different lifetime now. Alice's killer. The thought of having to tell Lizzie made me sick. I sat there terrified by my own rage, no longer sure what I was capable of.

I hunkered low, time my enemy, praying no cops would stumble across me before I could make my move. I tried to focus on what was coming, rehearsing how it would play out, hearing Sam Masters warning me against *rash undertakings* and thinking that description didn't nearly come close.

My concentration faltered. I steeled myself by going over it all in my mind. Run it back, the start: Layfield was there when Alice disappeared. Either he killed her, or he delivered her up to the men that did. Winfield Callaway as good as admitted to me he'd ordered her murder – but what the hell was his connection to Layfield? The only notion I could come up with was that Callaway had given the job to Bailey, and he'd contracted it out to Layfield – somehow known to each other on the cop grapevine. It made sense; Bailey would have needed someone who could snatch Alice from the hospital without being recognised, so an out-of-towner would fit the bill; he never could have reckoned on Ginny Kolkhorst being able to recognise Layfield. But the idea of a network of corrupt cops that reached far beyond Texarkana summoned back that urge to turn tail and run. It felt as though I'd charged into something that was bigger and deeper than even my worst fears.

That meant Layfield was the key to everything that had happened since. I remembered Cole Barrett's words, about how they killed Jimmy, *'to protect the story'* – Glover, Barrett, the whole frame-up. I believed that to be true now. Coughlin orchestrated the whole deal and the more I thought about it, the more a motive became clear: they had to kill Robinson because he was the only man cared about the cover-up. The only man could follow Layfield's string of murders all the way to Coughlin's door.

The only man apart from me.

The last of the light was fading. If Layfield was smart, he would have reported Barrett's death by now; got himself out in front of it so he could shape the investigation. He could lay out a version of events where I'd killed Barrett, and probably tried to kill him too. How we'd wound up out there by the lake would be a problem to explain, but it was his word against mine, and that was no contest. If that was the case, figure the first cop that saw me would shoot on sight. Whatever the official orders that were issued, there wasn't a lawman in the country that wanted to bring in a cop-killer alive.

That was assuming Layfield had talked. Could be he'd gone to ground and was planning to finish the job himself – that way forestalling any awkward questions about Barrett's death.

Somehow, that possibility was more unsettling – a killer lurking in the dark, waiting on his chance to put a bullet in my head. Layfield's words on the jetty came back to me: '*You know it all already.*' A taunt that I didn't understand then; now, the dread feeling that I'd been blind and people were dead on account of it.

It might not even be Layfield that came for me. I'd seen the price a life went for in this town, and it wasn't more than the coins in your pocket; any man I passed on the street could be there to stick a pistol in my stomach. No way was I going to sit around waiting for a bullet to find me. My action was justified. Layfield and Coughlin were two heads to the same serpent. But one of them was easier to get at than the other.

CHAPTER THIRTY-ONE

It was fifteen jittery minutes before Coughlin's horses came into view, their hooves clacking on the asphalt.

He slowed as he drew up in front of the building and that's when I moved. I crossed the sidewalk onto the side terrace of the hotel, then made my way along it to where it came out by the top of the staircase at the main entrance. Roman arches lined the walkway, giving me some cover. When Coughlin appeared at the top of the steps, I dipped my hand into my pocket and wrapped it around Barrett's gun. I walked up to him with my free hand extended to shake. He took it before he'd even looked at me – just another voter to glad-hand.

I leaned close, flashed the gun just long enough for him to get a glimpse. 'Walk with me or I use it. Don't make a scene.'

He kept smiling and pumping my hand. There was confusion on his face, and a flicker of disappointment made me realise I'd wanted to see his fear. An ugly thought flashed through my mind: pull the trigger. It jolted me enough I almost let go of the gun.

He dipped his gaze and then looked at me again. 'This a joke?'

I tightened my grip on his hand. 'I think you know I'm serious. This way.' I pointed back along the side terrace.

He started walking slowly, keeping the politician's smile on his face even as his eyes darted about. 'Do you really mean to kidnap me, son?'

'I already have.'

'This is my town. You harm me and you'll be dead within the hour.'

'I'm already on borrowed time.'

We made it as far as the car with no trouble, my collar damp with sweat. I opened the passenger door and ushered him inside, made him slide across behind the steering wheel, then climbed in next to him and took the gun out of my pocket to hold on him. 'Take off your hat and your jacket and put your hands on the wheel.' Any passing cop would still make Coughlin in a second, but stripping him of his signature getup at least made him harder to recognise from a distance.

He glared at me as he complied, defiant, but I saw his hand shake as he removed his hat.

I trained the gun on him, keeping it low so it couldn't be seen from outside. 'Harlan Layfield just tried to kill me, and you ordered the fire that killed my friend at Duke's. I want to know why on both counts. You can skip the part where you make like you're not involved.'

He turned his eyes to the windshield, flaring his nostrils. 'I'm expected at dinner. In five minutes, people will be tearing up the place looking for me.'

'You might not live that long.'

'Don't be ridiculous.'

'Cole Barrett is dead. Layfield killed him.' He turned his head at that, looking at me sideways with his mouth ajar. 'Figure that wasn't part of the plan.'

He looked away again.

'No sentiment for your bagman?'

I saw the muscles in his throat tighten. 'Is that true?'

'We're sitting in his car.' I pointed to my shirt where it was smeared red. 'This is his blood. I couldn't save him.'

He glanced at the stained fabric. 'That doesn't prove anything.' He lifted his chin to stretch his neck and I saw him swallow. He acted calm, but I could smell his body odour, the potent kind brought on by fear – sweat flooding his armpits and soaking his shirt. 'If there's a lick of truth to this, it sounds to me like your grievance is with Detective Layfield.'

'I'll get to him. Start talking.'

'Whatever you've been told, you're misinformed. I don't know—'

'I've had my fill with being lied to today. I know you're protecting Layfield, so you tell me the truth, or I'll put a goddamn bullet in you.'

'If you meant to kill me you'd have done it already. You're a reporter, not a killer.'

The last part almost derailed me – a veiled admission he knew damn well who I was and what was spurring my actions. Stupid of me to ever think I'd been moving unnoticed. 'Killing you isn't the only avenue open to me.' I put the gun to his knee.

He tried not to squirm in his seat. 'You don't have the first idea what you're doing.'

'That right? Try this: I've got the gun Layfield used to kill Barrett.' I swivelled towards him. 'What happens if I hand it over to Samuel Masters and his men? When they catch up with Layfield, you think he'll go along quietly? We both know you're the prize they really want. What do you think they'll offer him to start singing?'

He looked me over, took in the torn and bloodied shirt I was wearing, the red veins threading my eyes, the mud-splattered gun I was holding on him. Figure he was sizing up the chance I was bluffing. 'You've got me all wrong.'

'I don't think so.'

'What if we could help one another?'

I opened my mouth and closed it again, caught off guard.

'Layfield's been a pain in my ass for longer than I care to think about.' He looked at me again now, full in the face. His eyes were clear, his gaze steady. 'I can deliver him to you.'

For a second I was back on that jetty; I felt the tip of Layfield's gun touch my skull again, and with it, that echo of a memory I couldn't quite grasp. I blinked, dismissing it. 'It was on your say-so, goddammit.'

He was shaking his head before I even finished speaking. 'You talk as though he's my concern, but you're misguided. Cole Barrett was a good man and a fine public servant. If Layfield killed him as you say, we have a common problem. I'm offering you the chance to solve it.' He opened his hand on the wheel, flexing his fingers. 'Do we understand each other?'

His chutzpah left me reeling. The ultimate expression of his *'Get along by going along'* bullshit; shake his hand and we're on the same side. I wondered if this was how it started for Barrett, even Layfield – a dirty deal with Coughlin, borne out of anger or greed, that brought on the kind of moral decay that can never be reversed – and left them in his pocket. Even with that thought in mind, the part of me that wanted retribution on Layfield screamed to tell him yes.

'You gone quiet on me.' He cocked his head. 'Maybe not the

tough guy you thought you were. You want to run on home, instead?'

He read my self-doubt as plainly as if I'd spoken it. I understood his power then: a gift for pinpointing a man's weakness and exploiting it for himself. 'Don't sit there making out like this has nothing to do with you. You're neck deep in this.'

'Look, son, you're the man with the gun, so I'm not about to sit here and try to hoodwink you. But get your facts straight before you start making accusations. Harlan Layfield's troubles are of his own making, and he's about run out the string. Now you can do something about it, if you're so inclined.'

'You son of a bitch, you could have done something any time you wanted. You protected him, goddamn you.'

'I confess I gave him some rope. No more than that. And if Cole Barrett is dead because of that decision, then it'll sit heavy on my conscience.'

I couldn't believe what I was hearing. A jolt of panic hit me, the fear that I'd got it all wrong. 'I know what you did. You ordered the fire and you covered it up. I've got multiple sources—'

'You have evidence?' He looked at me dead on. 'Or hearsay?'

I glared at him, the jolt getting worse.

He let out a protracted breath. 'Look, I know Masters and his kind been in your ear telling you I'm responsible for everything bad happens in Hot Springs—'

'It was Barrett gave you up. Not Masters. He told me you ordered the fire. And I know you called the fire chief the night it happened. You can't wash your hands of this.'

Instead, he held them up. 'I'll never repeat it outside this automobile, but if it'll satisfy you, I'll admit to that telephone call. You're a man of the world, surely you can understand an act of political expediency.'

'Call it what you want. You had a murder written up as an accident.'

'There's an election right around the corner—'

'You trot that line out like it justifies anything.'

'That fire was Layfield's doing alone.' He stabbed his finger into his palm as he said each word. 'Whatever went on between Layfield and your friend, I wasn't a party to it. Yes, when I found out what happened, I put politics first and called in a favour to get the can kicked down the road. But walk a minute in my shoes: if I'd have went calling for an investigation into a senior detective on *my* police force, my enemies would've beat me down with it. Masters and his GI boys are relentless; you can't understand what they'll do to this town if they win. Every second man will be out of a job and the Negroes will be running wild. The Lord didn't create me perfect, but whatever decisions I made were for the civic good.'

'Letting a killer walk in the name of votes?'

'Not walk. I was fixing to deal with him after the election; all I did was forge myself a little breathing room.' He went to rub his forehead, then turned to me, uncertain, as if asking for permission to move the hands he'd already taken off the wheel – a subservient gesture that rang hollow.

I pressed the gun harder against his knee. 'Barrett told me it was on your orders.'

He winced, holding up his hand to back me off. 'Cole blamed me for the upshot of the Glover case. He felt like I sold him down the river when I bailed him out with Masters. Consider that when you're chewing on what he said.'

I locked eyes with him. It was all so plausible: Coughlin the public servant, a victim of forces beyond his control. And it made a mockery of all the people that were dead because of him. He'd made a slip without realising it, and now I had him caught in his own lies. 'I don't trust you.'

'I take exception to you looking at me like I'm the devil in a dress shirt, when you're the one holding an elected official at gunpoint. Reflect on that, young man. You've put yourself in a bind and I'm offering you a way out of it.'

It was a trap, I had no doubt of that. But I couldn't see a better way to get to Layfield than to ride it out. I looked past him, gazing into the darkness of the small park on the other side of the street, as though I was considering my options. 'You expect me to believe you'd just serve him up?'

'He has to be dealt with.'

'You'd put a bullet in me the second it was done.'

'I'm not the man you think me to be. I considered Cole Barrett a friend, even if it wasn't reciprocated at the end. Far as I'm concerned, taking Layfield off the board is doing the Lord's work.'

'What about your precious election?'

He raised his eyebrows. 'Are you offering to wait that long?'

I didn't answer.

'I thought not,' he said. 'Hell, I'm old enough to know expediency is a shifting beast by its nature.'

I kept silent a moment longer, then said, 'You know where he is?'

'No, but I can find him.'

'How?'

'I'm the goddamn mayor of this town.'

'How long?'

'Couple hours should be sufficient.'

I rubbed my neck – part for show, part because I felt as though I was burrowing into a scorpion's nest. 'Drive then. You've got calls to make.'

'Drive where? You let me go, I'll find him and tell you where he's at.'

'No. You produce Layfield, and I'll let you trade places with him. Those are my terms.'

'Are you out of your mind?' He kept his eyes on me, measuring me, then realised I was serious. He made to protest, but relented and started the engine. He acquiesced too fast; it felt like a show.

He pulled slowly away from the kerb, turning north onto Central and taking us away from Bathhouse Row. It was dark now, enough that I was confident we wouldn't be easily noticed in the car.

'Where are you heading?' I said.

'My house. I keep an office there, we won't be disturbed.'

'No one's home?'

'My wife will be at the country club till late.'

I stared hard at the side of his face. 'If this is a trap, you won't make it out of this car.'

He glanced at me. 'At some point, we gonna have to establish a level of trust here.'

I looked away.

We passed the Majestic Hotel, its name spelled out in giant letters across the roof, and after that there were no more grand buildings, only houses dotted up the embankment on the side of the road.

'What happened to Cole?' he said.

'He took a bullet that was meant for me.'

He shook his head in disbelief, taking it in. 'So he saved your life.'

I kept my eyes forward. 'Just drive.'

We rounded a shallow bend. 'Was it quick? His passing?'

I nodded so he could see, and said nothing more. But the question played on my mind. It seemed like seconds to me, but what about to Barrett? Feeling his life slip away as fast as blood spills. Did desperation and regret make the seconds stretch? Maybe the way it goes for all of us. It was unsettling to think about, given the razor's edge I was walking.

We carried on north in silence a few minutes, the air in the car thick with tension. We passed unlit residential streets and a liquor store with a green neon sign that was on the fritz. Soon we left the town behind and the darkness of the countryside enveloped us, only the occasional light from a farmhouse visible. Maybe a mile out, we turned off onto an isolated road that led up a low hill. As we climbed, he said, 'Does it trouble you that Cole took that bullet in your place?'

There was no change in his tone when he asked it, but I would have sworn he was prodding at me.

We drew up to a house – a large three-storey redbrick, recently built by the look of its pristine roof and paintwork. A turning circle took us right up to the door. He stopped the car outside it and waited. 'Well?'

I looked at the house. Two bright porch lights lit it from the outside, but all the windows were dark. I stepped out and made him do the same, keeping the gun on him all along. 'Let's go.'

He went to the front door and opened it. I followed him through the doorway into a foyer dimly illuminated by over-spill from the porch lights.

'This way.'

He led me down a tiled hallway lined with artworks I couldn't make out in the dark. At the end of it was a heavy wooden door that he unlocked and pushed open. On the other side was a long and narrow office packed with papers, files and legal texts. A mahogany desk almost blocked off one end of the room. He went around behind it, took a cigarette from a silver case on the desktop, lit it and took a drag. Then he pointed at me with the end of his smoke. 'We have an accord, you can put the gun down now.'

I nodded to the telephone. 'Make your calls. No games.'

He looked at me like a bear on a chain – resentful but scared. He picked it up and made to dial.

'Make him come alone,' I said.

'He won't come willingly. Someone'll have to hold his leash.'

I moved so I was standing by the telephone, ready to act at the first sign of trouble. 'Layfield better be the first face I see. Try to cross me and I'll make sure you catch a bullet before I do.'

He held the receiver out in front of him, as if I'd interrupted the call. 'You've made yourself clear, son. Leave it at that.' He lifted it to his ear and finished dialling.

I rubbed my temple with my knuckle, scared I was letting things freewheel out of control.

A voice answered and Coughlin spoke. 'It's me. I need to see Harlan Layfield, where's he at?'

He was silent as the voice answered him, then said, 'He made another mistake today, and I'd sure like to have a talk with him about it.' He frowned as the voice replied. He looked up at me, eyeing the gun. 'Well, go get him and we'll discuss it. Bring him by the house, I want him here within the hour.' He set the receiver back in its cradle and stood up, planted his hands on the desktop. 'It's done. Now, how about you point that thing somewhere else?'

I couldn't figure out how he'd set the trap, but he seemed satisfied with the call. Made me more certain than ever that I needed some measure of insurance. 'Not yet. How long until your wife comes home? I don't want her involved.'

He looked at the clock on the mantel opposite me. 'A few hours yet. Time enough to get him here. You can take him where you want, after that. I don't need to know no more.'

I gestured with the gun. 'Outside. The car.'

A look of confusion twisted his face. 'What for? You heard what I said – my man will have him here in—'

'Go.'

He started walking. I followed him back out through the house and to the driveway. He stopped by the car, and I opened the trunk. 'Inside.'

He glanced into the black space, incredulous. 'Are you out of your goddamn mind? There's no call for this horseshit.'

'You messed up. You made that call to the fire chief an hour before the fire. You weren't scrambling after the fact, you were laying the groundwork.' I motioned with the gun. 'Now, get in. I've got what I want, I don't need you any more. I just hope for your sake it's Layfield on his way here.'

'You son of a bitch.' He stood his ground.

I put the gun to his forehead, fretting what I'd do if he kept resisting. He took a tentative step, and it was all I needed. I bundled him the rest of the way and slammed the lid. I heard him shouting as I jogged to the driver's door.

I drove back down the hill and turned north, aware I was on the clock. At first Coughlin kept up an intermittent beat on the inside of the trunk, his shouts too muffled to make out, but after a few minutes he quit and I was left with only the sound of the engine, darkness all around me.

I stopped three times by the side of the road and climbed out of the car, slamming the door each time to make sure Coughlin heard what I was doing. The third time, I walked a dozen paces along the verge, killing a few seconds to buttress the pretence I was stashing Layfield's gun someplace. Then I picked my way back to the car, feeling the night close in on me as I thought about what was coming.

When I got back behind the wheel, I took Layfield's gun from my pocket and closed it in the glove compartment. I checked my watch. It was twenty minutes since we'd left the house. Figure fifteen to get back there and another five to make the call. Tight.

*

Coming back up the long drive, Coughlin's house was still dark – some reassurance. I stopped by the front door and jumped out, raced through the house back to the study and snatched up the phone. I tried Masters' campaign office first, hoping the proximity to the election would have kept him there at that late hour. I got lucky, and he recognised it was me right away.

'Yates? Where are you? They recovered Barrett's body.'

'What about Layfield?'

'I've got men making enquiries, but without any evidence, it's not a case of just waltzing up and arresting him. Come on in, make a full statement . . .'

I looked at my watch – almost eight. 'Meet me at ten o'clock. Drive north out of town on Park until you come to a turnoff for Big Sarn Lane. I'll be just past it, in a grey LaSalle. I've got Layfield's gun; I'll turn myself in to you personally, or not at all.'

'That's the smartest thing you've said yet. All right, ten.' He drew a sharp breath. 'Christ, I wish you'd left the gun at the scene – the evidence custody issues are going to kill me.'

'Do you want it or don't you? I'll give you an eyewitness account—'

'All right, all right, don't say anything more until I can get you on the record. Ten o'clock.'

I set the phone down and ran back outside to the car. I drove it down the hill again, turned north out of Big Sarn Lane and parked a hundred yards along on the verge. In that spot, it wouldn't be visible to anyone driving to Coughlin's house from town. I climbed out, leaving the doors unlocked, and went to free Coughlin.

When I opened the trunk, he shot his hand out to stop me closing it again. 'You stupid son of—'

'Move.' I took a step back and trained Barrett's gun on him.

He climbed out and looked around. His suit was crumpled and he'd paled. 'Where are . . .' He trailed off as he got his bearings.

'Let's go. Back to the house.'

262

'What the hell are you doing? Running around in the night – you're a madman.'

'Go.' I started pushing him back towards the house. I glanced back at the LaSalle as I walked, wondering if I'd been cautious enough. If I had the resolve to do the rest.

CHAPTER THIRTY-TWO

Coughlin was wheezing by the time we got to the top of the hill. The walk helped dissipate some of the nervous tension building in my guts. We crossed the driveway in convoy, me levelling the gun on his back the whole way.

He headed for the front door, but I pointed him away from it. The grounds immediately around the house were dense with dogwood and holly bushes, and I walked us into the thicket to the left of the house to wait out of sight. I made Coughlin sit down, then crouched behind him so I could watch the road in.

'What the hell is the meaning of this?'

'Quiet.'

The glow from the porch lights didn't reach us, so we waited in near darkness. The night air was cool and the wind had picked up enough to play tricks with my ears, but still I felt sweat collecting where my hat met my head. The anger had ebbed, draining away my grit with it, and now the fear was taking its place again. With it came doubt – a temptation to run that got more potent the longer we waited.

'You're making a mistake,' he said.

'Shut your mouth.'

I saw the headlight beams first, the wind blowing in the right direction to mask the sound of the car until it was almost in view. A dark-coloured Pontiac cruised up the turnaround and stopped by the front door, the driver's face catching in the porch lights – Layfield. I could make out the shape of another man behind him.

Layfield stepped out slow and cautious. Seeing him sent a rush of nervous energy coursing through me. He didn't have the bearing of a man who'd been dragged there against his will. He opened the rear door for his passenger, and a man stepped out. I recognised the suit even before I saw the face; cream-coloured and cut baggy enough to conceal a piece. William Tindall.

Panic welled inside of me. The waters kept getting blacker and deeper. Tindall was supposed to be retired. He was being chauffeured by the man who'd tried to kill me. I was prepared for a double-cross by Coughlin, but not for this.

Tindall folded his arms and leaned against the car as Layfield went for the doorbell. Three bullets in the gun – enough to put each of them down. The ghosts of all the dead implored me to do it. The voice of my own fear said the same – end it now and run. Truth was, I didn't have the steel. I bent low and hissed in Coughlin's ear, 'What the hell is he doing here?'

But he didn't answer me, instead calling out to them, 'Hold your fire, he's got me in the damn bushes with him. He's armed.'

Both men startled, reaching for their guns at the same time.

I whispered again. 'You're a dead man.'

He looked up at me. 'Go to hell.'

I jammed the gun to his neck.

Layfield had pressed himself into the doorway and Tindall was backing away, putting the car between us as cover. He searched the darkness of the grounds, trying to pinpoint where the voice had come from. 'That you in there, Mr Yates? Why don't you show your face, eh?'

'Put your guns down.'

'Not a chance. I don't much fancy going the way of old Winfield Callaway.'

The name was unexpected; hearing it from his mouth was like a punch to the back of the head. Black waters turning to blood.

He glanced around again, searching. 'Look, there's plenty you don't know, so stop hiding in them bushes and come out here like a man.'

'That cuts both ways.' I closed my eyes and took a breath. 'I stashed Layfield's gun, and the only man knows where it is apart from me is Samuel Masters. He's on his way to collect it in the next sixty minutes. Unless I'm alive to move it.'

I saw Layfield shoot a look at Tindall. Tindall's face didn't change.

'Bloody Masters,' Tindall said. 'All those poor bastards the Nips killed, and him not among them. That's the crime of it.'

He stepped out from behind the car and started walking slowly towards where the sound of my voice was coming from, favouring one leg. I signalled for Coughlin to stand up, ready to retreat further into the dark. Tindall stopped when he reached the edge of the driveway and lit a cigarette. 'I heard about your domestic troubles, Yates. A break-in, wasn't it?'

That stopped me cold.

'Take much, did they?'

It was impossible. Los Angeles was fifteen hundred miles away. There was no way he could— 'What the hell do you know about it?'

He took a drag from his cigarette. 'Should have taken the hint, shouldn't you? All them broken windows. Then we wouldn't have this trouble here.'

I fumbled the gun. Coughlin saw it hit the dirt and tried to swoop down to grab it, but I was faster. I stabbed the barrel into his back, panting silently, gripping his collar tighter with my other hand.

Tindall kept on. 'Problem with men like that, there's nothing to stop them coming again. Your wife – it's Lizzie, isn't it? Is she at home? I don't like involving womenfolk, but—'

I locked my arm around Coughlin's throat and dragged him into the open. 'IF YOU TOUCH HER I'LL KILL YOU.'

'Calm down, champ.' Tindall patted the air with his hand. 'Consider what's important here.' Layfield came over to stand behind him now that I was in view.

My arm shook holding the gun, my eyes locked on Layfield's. *Pull the damn trigger.* 'Alice Anderson. You killed her. That's where this started.'

Layfield stared at me and Tindall held up his hand as if signalling him to stay quiet. 'That bit about Masters and the gun, is it true?'

'Yes.' Gritted teeth strangled the word. 'Jimmy Robinson. Jeannie Runnels. Bess—'

'All right, that'll do.'

Coughlin gagged, clawing at my arm.

Tindall wrinkled his face in thought, one eye narrowing. 'Christ, this is a mess, Harlan.'

'It's nothing can't be fixed,' Layfield said. 'The gun's not as important as how I tell the story. Barrett drew on me first—'

Tindall held his hand up again to silence him. 'What is it you want, Yates?'

I swallowed, a lump in my throat that felt like it could choke me. 'I want to know why you killed all those people. And I want it to stop.'

Tindall took a breath. 'It has stopped. I've dealt with it, you have my word on that.' He half-turned towards Layfield, eyes still on me. Layfield looked away, like a scolded dog. 'But the milk's been spilt, there's nothing can be done about that.'

'Why? Goddamn you, why did they have to die?'

Coughlin struggled against me, forcing some words. 'He's ... a liability.' It was directed at Layfield. He glared back at Coughlin, and even through my rage, I sensed the rift.

Tindall closed his eyes. 'Listen, let Teddy go and take us to where the gun is and I promise you your old lady will go untroubled. On my honour.'

I kept looking at Layfield. 'You son of a bitch, tell me why.'

He dropped his eyes to the floor, almost as though he was ashamed.

Coughlin strained again and I loosened my grip a fraction to let him speak. 'He's a goddamn animal, that's why.' He said it to Layfield.

'Be quiet, Teddy,' Tindall said.

'Do something then, goddammit.'

'Mind who you're speaking to, now.' Tindall stared at Coughlin as he said it.

It felt like the air was electrified and sparking. Tindall looked about to say something to me now, but I kept my eyes on Layfield and spoke first. 'He offered me a deal to kill you, Layfield. You know that?'

Both men shot Coughlin a look.

'He had a gun on me,' Coughlin said. 'It was a ruse—'

'That's your story now, but how was I to know that?' I said. 'You were all set to send me off thinking I had your blessing to kill him. What if I'd gone ahead?'

'It would never have come to— I was trying to get rid of him, goddammit.'

'Maybe. But maybe you figured it wouldn't be so bad if I got to Layfield first. A little bit of payback for Cole Barrett.'

Coughlin bucked. 'That's not—'

'You killed his bagman,' I said to Layfield. 'You didn't expect repercussions?'

Layfield stepped towards us. 'Son of a bitch.'

Tindall put his hand on his shoulder to restrain him. 'Harlan—'

I loosened my grip a little more. 'What was it you said, Teddy? "*He's about run out the string.*" You had me convinced.'

Layfield kept coming. He spoke over his shoulder to Tindall. 'What did I tell you? This goddamn—'

'HARLAN.' Tindall jerked him back.

'Face it, he was willing to sacrifice you to save himself,' I said. 'He wanted it to go down that way, even. How's that feel?'

Tindall: 'Ignore him, he's—'

Layfield raised his gun.

I threw myself to the floor as he fired, rolling backwards. Tindall made a grab for the weapon and I scrambled into the undergrowth and flattened myself to the dirt. I glanced back, saw Coughlin was down, holding his arm. Layfield was running, tearing across the driveway towards the road out. Tindall sighted him with his gun, following his path as though he was tracking a deer. Then he sagged and lowered his arm.

He turned around and scanned the bushes. He looked in my direction, right in my eyes. I bolted into the trees, thinking only of Lizzie.

CHAPTER THIRTY-THREE

I ran until my lungs caught fire, and even then I kept staggering forward through the undergrowth. I could barely see what was in front of me, the moon all but obscured, but it was better that way, some protection in the darkness.

I stumbled up against the trunk of a red pine and clung on to keep myself upright, sucking down air as fast as I could. I looked back but the woods behind me were quiet, no sign of anyone. I couldn't square what I'd seen and what I'd heard. Didn't matter now; all I wanted was to get to a telephone before Tindall.

I took off again, Barrett's gun still locked in my grip. Best guess, I'd headed south away from Coughlin's house, and I kept going in that direction in the hope I'd come out on Park, the same road we'd taken out of town. Helped that the land sloped gently downwards – the path of least resistance.

It felt like I ran all night. Lizzie was with me all the way – but not how I wanted her to be; terrible images of hooded men seizing her in the dead of night, then of her body, snapped and broken like a discarded plaything. I remembered how Alice's corpse looked on the railroad tracks in Texarkana, and saw it now with Lizzie in her place.

There was a noise ahead, and suddenly I passed through the tree line and was on a road. My feet went from under me on the new surface and I crashed to the asphalt. I pushed myself up and tried to get my bearings, but it was a road surrounded by the woods, could've been anywhere.

Seeing no cars in either direction, I gulped down some air and started running along the verge, hoping I was heading north, back to where I'd left Barrett's LaSalle. One dread thought broke through my Lizzie nightmares: Layfield was in these woods somewhere. Running. Desperate. If he saw me first, I'd be dead before I even heard the shot.

I kept moving. After a half-mile or so, I came to the turnoff that led to Coughlin's. There were no headlamps on the lane, nothing moving as I sprinted past it. I sped up, knowing I was close now, running on empty.

I almost fell to my knees with relief when I saw the LaSalle. I leaned against the chassis, gasping for air. I lifted my head to scan the area around me, but the road and the trees and the night were still.

I got in and checked the glove compartment. Layfield's gun was still there, wrapped in my handkerchief. It felt like an empty victory; I wasn't sure it even mattered any more. One way or another, I didn't think Layfield would ever see the inside of a courtroom.

*

I redlined the engine heading back to town. The liquor store with the blinking sign was the first place I came across I thought might have a telephone. I burst through the door, startling the woman behind the counter. The blood on my shirt drew her eye as I approached. I pulled out my wallet and tossed a bill down in front of her. 'I need to make a call, my wife is in danger.' I looked over her shoulder, saw a telephone on a desk in a small room at the back.

'What on— What manner of danger?'

'Please, I don't have time.' I lifted the countertop to step inside, but she took hold of it to stop me.

'You been drinking, mister?'

'They'll kill her. There are men coming to take her—' I dipped my head, choking up. When I looked up again, my eyes were wet. 'Please, ma'am. Please. This is my only chance . . .'

She looked shocked to see me dissolve in front of her. She eyed me a second longer, then lifted the countertop herself. 'So you know, I keep a Winchester right here – case you was of a mind to take liberties.' She pointed to the rifle stashed next to her stool.

I snatched up the receiver and asked the operator to place a call to our home line in Venice Beach. The woman at the desk stared at me openly as I waited for the connection. A clock on the wall ticked the minutes away, playing on my nerves. *Pick up, pick up, pick up, pick up—*

'My apologies, sir, but there's no answer on that line.'

My insides turned to liquid. 'Try again.'

I counted off almost a minute. The operator came back, 'I'm sorry, still no—'

'Try the offices of the *Pacific Journal*. Please.' I reeled off the number.

When the call went through, it was a voice I didn't recognise that answered.

'This is Charlie Yates calling for Lizzie Yates.'

'I'm afraid she's not here, Mr Yates.'

'When did you see her last?'

'I'm not sure I could say. I believe she's off today.'

'Is Acheson there?'

'Mr Acheson is in his office.'

'Go get him.'

'Well, I don't know—'

'Go get him now. Tell him it's urgent.'

She made a clucking sound, then said, 'Very well.'

In my mind I saw them come for Lizzie, snatching her off the sidewalk as she arrived home. I told myself she was more use to them alive than dead. It was grim solace.

'Charlie?'

'Buck, I'm looking for Lizzie.'

'What's wrong, you sound frantic?'

'Buck, have you seen her? This is serious.'

'No, I haven't seen her today. You've tried the house?'

'She's not answering. I need you to send someone over there. I don't know what I've done.'

'Done to whom? Slow down and tell me—'

'Send a man, right now. If she's there, bring her back to the office and don't let her out of your sight.'

He hesitated a moment, then I heard him press the receiver against his chest as he issued a muffled instruction to one of the staff. Then he came back on the line. 'I've sent Bunny Edwards.'

It felt like I could breathe again for the first time in an hour. 'Thank you. Tell him to be careful.'

'Charlie, is this a matter for the police?'

'No. No cops.'

'Because if she's in some kind of danger . . .'

'I don't trust them to do anything.' The part I didn't say: *I don't know where this leads any more.* I asked the clerk for the

274

liquor store's number and recited it to Acheson. 'Call me back on that line as soon as you hear from Edwards.'

'What if she's not there?'

I held my face in my hand. 'Have him call you straightaway.'

*

It was a ten minute drive from the *Journal* to our apartment. I stood over the telephone, feeling like my nerves were being stripped away a fibre at a time. The clerk watched me, her curiosity obvious, but saying nothing.

I jumped when it rang. In the split second before I picked up, I tried to gauge if the time elapsed indicated good or bad news.

'Yates.'

'Charlie, it's Buck. She's not answering the door.'

I slammed my fist onto the desktop, making the clerk jump.

'Edwards said the lock has been forced. He's holding on the other line, he's asking if he should go inside.'

I felt riven. 'Yes. Tell him not to disturb anything.'

He went away and came back. 'He's doing it, he's going to call right back. Charlie, what in god's name is going on?'

'The men I'm investigating here were behind the burglary. It was a warning shot. They wanted me gone, and now they've threatened Lizzie.'

'How . . . how is that possible?'

'I don't know. I don't— Jesus, Buck, what do I do?'

'Keep your head. You don't know anything yet.'

He was right, but I had the same feeling in my gut as when Alice disappeared all those months before. One you never forgot; the feeling that she was never coming back. 'When did you see her last?'

'She was at the paper yesterday. She seemed . . . she was fine.'

Something sudden. A bad sign.

He started talking away from the receiver and I closed my eyes, waiting, gripping a fistful of my hair.

I felt a touch on my forearm, opened my eyes and saw the clerk had laid her hand there in a gesture of concern.

A telephone rang on Acheson's end. Someone shouted over to him, but I couldn't make out the words. Then he called down the line. 'There's no one there. It's empty.' The relief in his voice was evident, but I didn't feel any of it. 'Bunny says the place is a wreck, though, Charlie. I'm going to call the police, it's the only course. If someone's taken her . . .'

I said nothing, my thoughts crowded out by a barrage of brutal images. He took my silence as agreement.

'What are you going to do now?'

I put my hand on the wall, my arm trembling with adrenaline. 'I'm going to find out if they have her. Then I'm going to get her back.'

'Where can I reach you?'

'You can't. I'll call you.' I went to hang up, then thought again. 'Wait. She's got a cousin in Arizona. Phoenix.' The place she ran to after Texarkana. A shot in the dark. 'Get in touch with her, would you? Just in case. I don't know her number but her name's Clemence Anderson, she lives on Encanto Boulevard—'

'We'll track her down for you.' He couldn't hide the pity in his voice.

'Thanks, Buck.'

'Charlie?'

'What is it?'

'Try to stay calm. Don't let your fears run away with you on this.'

'It's too late for that.'

I set the receiver down, clinging to the hope that Tindall might still make a deal to spare Lizzie: Layfield's gun for her life. I didn't like the chances; easier for him to lure me with her and kill us both. Except—

Except that he let Layfield escape without firing a shot. And the same for me – maybe. I was sure he'd seen me in the bushes; he could have put a bullet in me before I ran. Just maybe that meant Layfield – and therefore the murder weapon – still had value to him. Even after he'd taken that pot-shot at Coughlin.

I picked up the telephone one more time and called the Southern Club.

A man answered. His voice was partly drowned out by the band in the background, but I could hear enough to make out his accent wasn't local – sounded more like Chicago.

'This is Yates calling for William Tindall.'

The man paused, and I thought I heard him talking to someone. The music came over clearer. A slow number – Vaughan Monroe's arrangement of 'The Things We Did Last Summer'.

'Mr Tindall isn't available for calls.' Odds on: Tindall was there, told him to say it.

'He'll want to talk to me.'

'Then he'll talk to you when he's good and ready.' The inflection in his voice said he knew all about my business.

'Listen, you son of a bitch, you tell him—'

The line went dead.

I dropped the receiver and slumped against the wall.

The clerk was looking at me, wringing her hands. She looked scared and sympathetic all at the same time. I nodded to say thanks and made my way to the door, thinking about going straight to the Southern Club to speak to Tindall. It felt like the worst play I could make, but I couldn't see an alternative.

Then another thought: get the message delivered in person. An insider. Someone who could walk right up to Tindall without suspicion. Someone who owed me.

I opened the door to a night that was bleaker than any I could remember. I felt the pull of Barrett's gun in my pocket, started shaking when I thought about what I'd done already, and the lengths I was willing to go to before the sun rose again.

CHAPTER THIRTY-FOUR

It was only a few hours since I'd left Ella Borland's house in the back of Layfield's car, but everything looked different now. I felt like I could tear it apart with my bare hands. I stopped the car in front of her yard, jumped out and ran up to her door.

I knocked once. As before, she opened it a little way to peek out, and the second it moved, I barged through. She jumped backwards, screaming. I caught the door as it rebounded on its hinges and slammed it shut. I pointed to one of the easy chairs. 'Sit down.'

She backed away from me, her eyes wide, taking in the blood and dirt all over my clothes. 'Before you do anything—'

'I said, *sit.*'

She lowered herself slowly into the chair, never taking her eyes off me, ragged breaths coming fast and hard. 'I'm sorry, I'm—'

'Where's my wife?'

She squinted at me, thrown by the question. 'What?'

'Tindall threatened my wife and now she's disappeared.'

She covered her mouth with her hand. The nail on her little finger was chewed to nothing. 'I don't know—'

'Where is she, goddamn you?'

'I swear, I don't know anything about that.'

I took Barrett's gun from my pocket. She threw her hands out in front of her. 'Wait—'

I pointed it at the floor. 'Layfield. Tindall. You set me up.'

'I had no choice. You don't understand . . .' She started to sob.

'Can the tears. Spill.'

She covered her face.

I stood over her, my head pounding. I realised that the clicking sound I could hear was my thumbnail flicking against the hammer.

'I had to. This town— This godforsaken . . .' She rubbed the tears away and looked up at me. 'There are things I haven't told you. I'm sorry.' She glanced at the pack of Chesterfields, still on the table. 'May I?'

There were two left in the pack. I took one and tossed it in her lap. She lit it, taking it from her mouth with trembling fingers. 'What happened to you?'

'He tried to kill me. But you knew that already.'

She shook her head violently. 'No, I swear. I hoped . . .'

'You hoped what?'

She took a drag of her smoke and exhaled a jagged plume. I could see her chest shaking as it rose and fell. 'I suppose I hoped he was here to arrest you.'

'Enough. You made a fool of me once already today. You knew what was going down when you called him here—'

'I never called him.'

'He just stopped by? Talk straight—'

'Mr Tindall sent him. After he saw us together earlier.'

That slowed me down. 'How did Tindall know who I was?'

'He owns this town, he knows everything that goes on.'

'You lured me here. You could have warned me.'

'How?' She leapt out of her seat. 'Layfield was standing

right next to me when you called, what else could I do?' She was leaning in close, inches from my face. She spun away in frustration. 'After I left you earlier, Pete Swinney called me—' She saw me blank on the name. 'He's one of Mr Tindall's men. He called right when I got home. He wanted to know what you said and where you went after I left you. I told him I didn't know, but he didn't believe me and he said he was sending someone over then, don't move. I was terrified, I smoked my throat raw – I thought they were coming to kill me. That's when Layfield came to the door and said I was to draw you out.'

She collapsed back into her seat and flopped her head back, aimed empty eyes at the ceiling.

I took a wooden chair from the table and set it in front of her. I sat down, the gun pressed against my thigh and pointing downward, starting to feel like I was taking my anger out on the wrong person. I looked at her again. 'What's Tindall's interest in me?'

'It's because of Jimmy. It's all because of Jimmy.'

'Talk. Everything now.'

She shook her head. 'Please. Please...'

I kept staring.

'Don't make me do this,' she said. 'If you go now, if you run—'

'They've got my wife, I can't run. Tell me, goddammit.'

She screwed her eyes shut. 'Jimmy came to me – remember that. If he'd been truthful with me from the beginning, I maybe could have done something more. Just keep that in mind.'

'What the hell did you do?'

She started in on her story and once she got going, it developed a momentum of its own – a penitent freed by the catharsis of confession. 'The first time he approached me was in the summer, asking about Jeannie's murder – he said he'd had a tip we were friends and could help with background for a story he was writing. I was still cut up about it, but I agreed to talk to him because he seemed like he gave a damn. I didn't understand what he was trying to accomplish because, at the time, I believed the story the way the papers told it – Walter Glover and all that bunk – but I didn't think anything of it.

'Jimmy kept coming by, but only at weekends, and I was fond of him. He was just . . . a whirlwind. He never seemed to stop. He knew what I did to get by, and he didn't care. He was troubled by something – anyone could see that – but he kept that part to himself. As though it was walled off. So I knew better than to ask – and so did he.

'Then, a few weeks back, he turns up where I'm working out of the blue and says he's come to town for good. The way he said it, I could tell he thought I'd be delighted. I had a clue he was soft on me, but this was the last thing I would have expected. I mean he was always talking about his work at the newspaper, back in Texarkana.

'He took that room at Duke's, and he'd keep coming by to see me – to talk. I saw a different side to him then because his mood depended on how much he'd had to drink. Sometimes he acted like we were courting – he was . . . crazy. Impossible. I got tired of him asking me about Jeannie, but he'd never let it go. He asked me the same questions over and over.

'Then just after he moved into Duke's, Pete Swinney showed up at my door. He made me a proposition – if I stuck close to Jimmy, kept them wise to what he got up to, he'd arrange a job for me at the Southern. A dancer—'

'You were spying on Jimmy? Do I have it straight?'

She flushed red and cast her eyes to the floor, two small piles of ash by her feet where her cigarette had burned away in her hand. 'I had to. It was a proposition in name only – you don't turn Mr Tindall down. I didn't see what harm it could do, it was just telling Pete where Jimmy went and who he spoke to. No great shakes.

'But then Pete started calling me every day and then it was twice a day, and oftentimes more. He came down so hard, he kept telling me to get closer to Jimmy – "*I want every word.*" I got suspicious then, because Jimmy was like a dog with a bone when it came to Jeannie and the Prescott girl, and I'm not a fool, there's no other reason why Mr Tindall would be interested in him. Or me. And I know what they're capable of.

'It went on like that for a couple weeks, and I was about ready to crack up because I was more and more certain they were involved in Jeannie's killing, but there wasn't a goddamn thing I could do about it. I was scared to death – I could barely answer the telephone. Then one night Jimmy came by and he was mad and he was drunk. I wouldn't let him in the door. I asked him to leave, but he wouldn't go – everyone along the street was looking. He started pleading, said he'd made a mistake.'

My skin prickled.

'He said he'd been by Cole Barrett's house. He called him every name under the sun. I never saw him like that before – like he could kill someone. I let him in and tried to get him to tell me what had him upset that way, but he climbed inside a bottle and clammed up.'

It chimed with what Barrett had told me – Robinson going

to his place and only leaving when Barrett set the dog on him. 'You reported that back to Tindall?'

'The next day.' She was nodding. 'I had to. Everyone knows Barrett runs bag for Teddy Coughlin. It was going to get back to them anyway.'

I saw it then. Jimmy died thinking his *mistake* was confronting Barrett; in reality, it was putting his trust in the wrong woman. 'What was their response to that?'

She looked at the floor. 'I don't know. Swinney never said much of anything to what I told him.'

'Now's the time to come clean, Ella.'

'Have you heard a word I said? They never clued me into anything, and it's not as though I was about to ask.' She brought her hands to her mouth and clamped her eyes shut, took a breath. 'But the day after, Jimmy came to me saying he was in danger. He said they'd threatened him and told him to get out of town.'

'Who had?' The answer was obvious but I wanted to hear it from her lips.

She was already shaking her head. 'He didn't say, but . . .'

'Doesn't take a lot of thinking to figure out.'

She looked down, her eyes hooded. 'Jimmy said he had help coming, someone to finish the job for him if he couldn't do it himself.'

I felt that hot feeling in my throat again, guilt filling my chest like a spurt of fresh blood. He knew they were going to come for him and he stayed anyway. If I'd have just believed him. If I'd come quicker. If—

'How in the hell could you look at him with a straight face after that?'

'How do you think I felt? I could see what was going on. They killed Jeannie.' Tears streamed from her eyes again. 'It had to be them. They killed her, and no one cared.' She doubled over, holding her face.

'Except Jimmy. And you helped them get away with it.'

She didn't reply, just sat sobbing in the chair, gasping every time she stopped long enough to draw breath.

I went to the kitchen and found a glass, filled it with water and offered it to her.

She wouldn't take it. She was muttering words now, into her hands, too quiet to hear.

'What did you say?'

'I had no choice. I never had a choice.'

'You could have told Jimmy what was going on.'

She sat up at that, her face and eyes red, couldn't look at me. 'I did tell him. I had to.'

'Told him when?'

'Right before the fire.' She picked up the glass and dropped the stub of her cigarette into it – a hiss, then the water turning dirty grey and a smell of wet ash. She set it back on the floor. 'He told me he was in love with me.'

Lovesick Jimmy; Lizzie on the money as always. 'And in return you told him you were spying on him.'

'No. Not right away.' She reached for the pack of Chester-fields. I pushed them away and she shot me a look. 'I told him he was being foolish, but he wouldn't drop it. He kept on telling me he loved me, and he knew I felt the same. And then he asked me to marry him.'

'Jesus Christ.'

'I blurted it out then – told him I had no feelings for him, that Mr Tindall made me get with him.' She was all cried out, her voice shredded. 'I never meant to hurt him, but you can't blame me for how he was. He wouldn't listen to reason.'

'That was the day of the fire, wasn't it?'

She nodded.

The day Robinson told the barman at the Keystone he wanted to die. I finally got hip – raging bull Jimmy brought to his knees not by lowlifes he was chasing but by the woman who cut his heart out. I wondered if that was what sent him charging out to Barrett's the second time – and prompted Tindall and Coughlin to decide he had to be silenced for good. 'That's why you were scared he took his own life. You knew what you did to him.'

'I never asked for his affection. I never led him on. I told him to run – begged him. I said that if they'd threatened him like I figured they had, he ought to take it seriously. That's when he told me that Walter Glover didn't kill Jeannie. I think he was looking for a way to hurt me.'

I stood up, paced over to the window and back.

'I never had a choice,' she said. 'These men kill women like me without a second thought – you *know* that to be true. If I'd lied, or if I'd run, or if I'd said no, I'd have wound up the same way as Jeannie and Bess Prescott. That's why I kept quiet when you showed up – to protect us both. And now it doesn't matter, because they'll kill me anyway.'

'What?'

'Because of you and Layfield and Jimmy. On account of what I know. Maybe not till after the election, but soon enough for sure.'

I wanted to say something to reassure her, but what she

was saying made sense. 'Why did they kill Runnels and Prescott?'

'I don't know.'

I stopped in front of her and said nothing. She looked up at me through her eyebrows. 'I have no reason to lie to you now.'

I tightened my grip on the gun, but it was for show; I wouldn't admit it, but my fury was already subsiding. My feelings didn't run as far as pity, but I could recognise a woman caught in a crossfire.

'It makes me ill thinking about what I had to do, and the people I've helped, but if Jimmy had told me from the start what he suspected about Jeannie, and what he was doing, I might've been able to warn him. Or do something different.' She stood up and made a point of looking me in the eye as she took the last Chesterfield from the pack. 'I never sought any of this out.'

'Did Tindall tell you to spy on me too?'

She took the cigarette from her mouth, unlit, and turned away from me.

A tacit admission. It left me unmoved, no surprise any more. I thought about what I needed her to do, and what it would mean. She was right; chances were they'd kill her because she knew about Layfield, and if they thought she was helping me as well, it would only make it more certain. A choice: sacrifice this woman for a shot at saving my wife. It felt like my skull was contracting around my brain.

I stood up and started across the room. 'I need to use your telephone.'

She nodded without facing me, opening her hand to indicate where it stood.

287

I asked the operator to place a call to the *Journal*. It would be futile, and I knew it, but I wanted to exhaust all the other options before making a decision.

Acheson came on the line. 'Charlie?'

'Buck, any word?'

'I spoke to the police. They're dispatching a car to take a look at your house, on account of the burglary before . . .'

'You're sitting on something, what is it?'

He grunted. 'They said it's too soon to start searching for her. That she's an adult, so she could have just taken off somewhere of her own volition. Without a specific threat against her person—'

'Did you tell them? How much more specific—'

'I told them and they laughed it off as soon as they heard me say "Arkansas". They said to leave it a day or two. I played the *bad headlines* card, but they know it's a bluff. It's department policy. And we don't rate with them, anyhow.'

'Goddammit.' I wasn't sure there was anything the cops could have done, but it smarted anyway. No help anywhere. 'What about her cousin?'

'I spoke with her. She . . .'

'Nothing?'

'Nothing. She's had no contact in months.'

I blew out a breath.

'Charlie, what do you want me to do next?'

I glanced at Ella, a dirty taste filming my throat. 'I'll take care of it. If you hear anything, call Samuel Masters. Leave word with him.'

'The Marine guy?'

'He's as close to a straight arrow as there is here.' I gave him the campaign office address to tell the operator. 'I'll talk to you.'

I rang off, feeling like I was in quicksand.

'Do you think she's still alive?'

I snapped around to look at her.

She was staring at the ceiling, her eyes unfocused. 'They all talk as though there's some code – some honour amongst thieves – that makes women untouchable, and yet we always seem to end up in the firing line.'

'Don't compare yourself to my wife.'

She lifted her head now. 'We're both at the mercy of these men.'

She was right, but she missed her mark by a hair and the indignation came off as false. Just like how she almost made a convincing Hedy Lamarr – but not quite; just like how she'd played aloof to keep me coming back with questions. Under scrutiny, it all showed up as artifice. I fished my wallet from my pocket, coming to the realisation she was forever playing a part. It made my mind up for me. 'You took the job, though. At the Southern. Dancing.' I took out what was left of the cash I'd come to give her earlier and set it on the table, holding it in place with my finger. 'Got a little something for yourself out of it, huh?'

She eyed the money, one arm folded across her stomach and the other holding her cigarette in front of her mouth. 'What would you have done?'

'Not that.' I pushed the bills towards her. 'All the rest of it I could maybe understand, but no one would have cared whether you went to dance for those men or not.'

'I've been on my own since I was ten years old. I do what I have to just to get by.'

'You can help me make amends.'

She dropped her cigarette into the glass with the other butt. 'I have no amends to make.'

'Then do it for my wife's sake. You made your choices, she has no part in this.'

She looked at the gun in my hand. 'At least they have the subtlety not to show their weapons when they threaten me.'

The words stung. I put the gun away, aware now that she wasn't the only one playing a part she couldn't carry off. 'I'm not threatening you. You take this money and you run. To-night. You can be out of the state before sunrise. All I'm asking is that you deliver a message to Tindall before you go. I won't force you, it's your decision.'

'What's the message?'

'That I've still got the gun and I'm willing to trade.'

I took my finger off the money. She reached out to take it, tentative, as though it was a trick.

The telephone rang then, cutting the silence like a Tommy gun.

She jumped, whipped around to look at it. She stepped over and answered, then turned her eyes to me, confusion on her face. 'There's a man asking for you.'

I went over and took the handset, expecting to hear Acheson's voice again. I wasn't even close.

'So we're clear from the get-go, this conversation never took place.'

Coughlin.

I was too stunned to say anything smart, words coming on reflex: 'How the hell did you know I was here?'

'Not many folks placing calls to Los Angeles right now. We

both know the switchboard operators in this town lack discretion.'

'Where's my wife?'

'I'm not a party to that. You won't believe me, but I swear it's true. Tindall has contacts in Los Angeles, and he arranged it without my knowledge.'

'Tell Tindall I want to make a deal. Tell him—'

'I'm going to say this and hang up, so listen careful: Tindall owns a motel called the Viceroy on the Malvern highway, out near the fairgrounds. He believes it to be a secret, and that's where he'll stash Layfield. Remember all he's done to you when you go there.' He listed a set of directions. 'See to this, and I'll broker a deal with him to spare your wife.'

Then he was gone.

No matter where I ran, they found me.

Ella was staring at me, the money folded tight in her fist. 'Who was that?'

'Don't go to the Southern, forget about the message. Go, now; get as far away from here as you can. Before they catch up with me.'

CHAPTER THIRTY-FIVE

I staggered out across the small yard in a daze. The car was only as far as the sidewalk, but it felt like I travelled a thousand miles in getting to it.

I climbed in and sat with my head in my hands. Layfield tried to kill Coughlin. Coughlin had every reason in the world to want revenge – and still it reeked of another trap. I'd under-estimated Coughlin once already; if I went after Layfield on his say-so now, surely it was playing into his hands.

Desperation wouldn't let me discard the notion that easy. I reasoned there was a chance Coughlin was sincere: I could only guess at the relationship between him and Tindall, but whatever the truth, it seemed like Cole Barrett's killing had driven a crowbar between the two men. Tindall let Layfield escape, and now it seemed he was giving refuge to him – two facts that had to stick in Coughlin's craw. Could be that was enough to make him cross Tindall.

And if there was a chance I could get at Layfield—

It was clear now that, even before tonight, Tindall had gone to significant trouble to protect him – the cover-up with Barrett, killing Jimmy. Layfield had some value to Tindall, and that made me think killing him would only endanger Lizzie further.

Then I realised there was another way to go about matters, and it dictated that I had to take the risk. I was willing to give up my life for Lizzie's, without hesitation. But if my hunch was right, there was a life that was more important to Tindall than mine or hers.

*

The Viceroy Motel sat on a lonely stretch of Highway 270. It was nestled among a phalanx of red pines. I'd passed a Baptist church a mile back, but nothing since then; figure the remoteness was part of its appeal.

The sign was set back from the road and concealed by the trees such that I didn't spot it until I was almost outside. I slowed some, so I could scope the place out as I passed, but I didn't want to telegraph my arrival by slamming the brakes and driving right up to the front door.

It was an L-shaped building in a clearing in the woods. It had white walls and a dark roof, maybe green – hard to tell in the night. I could make out what looked like a reception in the part of the structure nearest the road, then a line of identical doors and windows stretching back and turning the corner to form the L. There was one car parked in the lot, and a light showing from inside the room it was parked in front of.

I cursed Coughlin for luring me to this wasteland to take out his trash. It felt like I was right back where I started, running myself head first into danger to suit someone else's purposes. Except Robinson's call had turned out to be righteous; the best I could hope for this time was to come away with the means to save my wife.

That meant taking Layfield alive. He was a career cop and a stone-cold killer, with his back against the wall. All I had was surprise on my side – if Coughlin was good to his word. That, and the bottom-of-the-barrel courage that comes with being out of options.

I drove on another two hundred yards, then ditched the car on the verge and started hiking back to the motel. The grass on the roadside was long and straggly, catching and snagging my feet as I went. I ran short of breath and all the old doubts flooded back in: whether I was doing the right thing or making matters worse. Whether I had the guts to stay the course. I pushed them aside only by thinking about Lizzie – the terror she must be feeling, plunged back into a nightmare she thought had abated.

I ducked into the woods for cover as I came closer, advancing from one tree to the next as fast as I dared. I could hear branches overhead scraping against one another in the gentle breeze, and the incessant call of a whip-poor-will; I remembered the Algonquin Indian legend I'd been told as a boy that the bird's song was an omen of a soul about to depart.

I looked ahead. Nothing was moving on the motel grounds, no signs of life save that one room with a light visible in the window. It made me nervous as hell. When I reached the property line, the tangle of roots and dirt underfoot gave way to a hardscrabble lot that extended thirty yards from the building. I stopped there and hid behind the last line of trees, watching the stillness.

I was approaching the motel from the front, the long part of the L spread before me, the right-angle and shorter part of the shape off to my right, and the road to my left. The car I could see was parked outside the fourth room, counting along from the office – the one with the light showing. It had an Arkansas plate, nothing else to distinguish it particularly.

I retreated into the woods a few steps and started picking a course parallel to the line of the building. I kept glancing over to the motel as I went, pushing on until I made it to the far end. From there, I looped around so I could get a closer look at the property from behind. My heart was jumping, and a voice in my head screamed there wasn't time for this caution.

The woods came closer to the motel round back, the tree line only ten yards from the building. I fast-walked along it, surveying the scene. Each room had a single window on that side, all of them closed. There were no back doors or other means of entry or exit. I stopped a few seconds when I came level with room four. The drapes were open but the glow was dimmer on this side, as if it came from a table lamp placed near the front of the room. I stared a moment, half-expecting Layfield to appear in the glass, but everything was still.

I pressed on, and by the time I reached the road again, my nerves were shot. It was as though the place had been deserted. The car and the light said that wasn't the case.

I got the sense of being watched. My eyes played tricks on me, seeing phantom movements in the darkness, hearing footfalls behind me that weren't there. There was a malevolence that seemed to come from the building itself. My jaw started trembling then, and I could do nothing to stop it. All the money in the world wouldn't have made me go any closer. Lizzie was worth more than that.

I steeled myself and broke into a running crouch, skittering across the ground between the trees and the motel. I pulled my footfalls to tread as lightly as I could, but still they were as loud as a pickaxe hitting the gravel. When I reached the building, I flattened myself against the wall and caught my breath, the gun pressed to my thigh, listening for any sign I'd given myself away.

I was between the back of the office and the first room. I moved along the wall until I came to the first window, ducked under it, and carried on until I reached the fourth. I positioned myself next to the glass and listened for sounds from inside, but all I could hear was the flag at the front of the property flapping and tugging against its pole.

I took my hat off and craned my neck to peer through the window. Inside, I could make out an unmade bed; on the small table next to it, a quart of liquor, a mug and a bottle of pills. There was a necktie strewn over the only chair, a fedora on the seat that looked like Layfield's. The bathroom door was closed. I pulled back out of sight, my pulse seeming to spasm, listening for the sound of running water. Or anything else. Nothing.

My first instinct was to kick down his door and take my chances – but a voice buried somewhere deeper preached caution. I couldn't help Lizzie if I was dead. I wiped a line of sweat from my forehead and tried to think, feeling like every wasted minute was being taken from Lizzie's life.

Something about the scene was off. Maybe the way the drapes were open, the light inviting attention. I reasoned it out: if Coughlin sent me here as a trap, surely it should have sprung by now. He had every reason to want Layfield dead – and so far he'd proven good to his word. But still it nagged at me. There was no sign of Layfield, and it was as if it'd been left that way for me to find.

Then I tried a new spin on it: cautious Layfield – room four as a decoy, a way to buy himself a few seconds if someone caught up to him. It felt like a fit. I wondered if he was expecting me.

On instinct, I reached out and touched the glass in the window next to me – just my fingertips on the corner. It was temperate. I moved along a few steps to room three and did the same. It was cold to the touch. I retraced my steps along the wall, ducked under Layfield's window, and went to room five, reached my hand out.

Pay dirt: the glass was warmer again, barely registering on my fingertips without the temperature difference. I pressed myself to the wall. The sound of my own breathing raged in my ears, and then it warped and magnified, so much that I could swear I was hearing someone else doing the same, as though Layfield was waiting on the other side, only the width of a clapboard separating us. I closed my eyes to block it all out. A half-formed plan swirled, and I was too scared to stay still any longer.

I started moving again, heading towards the road. When I reached the highway, I crossed over to the far side and broke into a jog, certain enough I wouldn't be visible from the motel in the darkness at that distance.

When I made it back to my car, I jumped in and pulled a U-turn right across the empty highway, then sped back to the Viceroy. I kicked up a trail of dust crossing the parking lot and stopped right alongside Layfield's car.

I ran up to room four, the light still blazing inside. I set my feet, gripped the gun in front of me and told Lizzie I loved her under my breath. Then I kicked the door in.

It was flimsy and buckled easily. I charged inside, pivoted and flattened myself behind the half-open door, my gun hand next to my head. I held my breath so as not to make any noise, praying he'd take the bait.

I heard the sound of one of the other rooms being eased open, and then a man treading lightly on the path outside. I was stock-still. My heart was like a flood-pump in my chest and I was sure he'd hear it. The barrel of a pistol poked into the room, then the man stepped forward another two feet, just clear of the door. I grabbed his wrist, bringing the butt of my gun down on his head from behind, catching him near the crown. He crumpled to the floor and offered no resistance as I took his weapon from his hand.

CHAPTER THIRTY-SIX

Harlan Layfield pushed himself up so he was on all fours, the same posture as Cole Barrett just before he died. A patch of his hair was matted with blood. I stuffed his gun in my pocket and took aim at him.

He looked back and up at me, wincing. I circled around him, keeping the gun levelled on his torso.

He followed me as I went. 'How'd you find me?'

I stopped by the window and snatched a glance outside. Nothing moved. I looked to him again. 'Where's my wife?'

'What?'

'Don't make me ask again.'

'I don't know a damn thing about your woman so let's get this over with.' He lowered his head like a dog waiting to be put down.

It took all my restraint not to do as he said. 'I asked you a question.'

He lifted his eyes, his face pale and waxy like parchment. He pushed himself onto his knees so he was upright, and wiped his mouth on his shoulder. 'Bill didn't tell me nothing—'

'Don't you lie to me.'

'I swear . . .' His eyes flared.

'You're cowards, every one of you. Every goddamn one of you.' I mopped my hairline with my shirt cuff. 'Why's Tindall still helping you?'

Confusion showed on his face. 'The hell does it matter now?'

I aimed the gun at his forehead. 'The only thing keeping you alive is my inkling Tindall will deal to keep you that way. Convince me I'm right.'

'Maybe, maybe not. You ever think he just didn't want to snuff me himself?'

My nerves shorted when he said it – a prospect I hadn't considered. 'I don't buy it. He's a killer.'

'We been acquainted a long time. Makes me sick but he's the closest thing I ever had to a daddy.' He shook his head, his chin sagging against his chest. 'I hate the son of a bitch.'

I tried not to show my surprise at the emotion in his voice. 'You're talking in riddles.'

'He took me under his wing when I was seventeen years old. Caught me trying to steal a car turned out belonged to one of his men. Could've left me a smear on the sidewalk for it, but he went the other way. Can't help but have some fondness for the old bastard in them circumstances. Even considering what he made me do.'

Tremors now, getting what he was edging at. 'What he made you do? Say their names, goddamn you. Bess Prescott. Jeannie Runnels—'

'I don't remember half their damn names.'

'Alice Anderson.'

He screwed his eyes shut.

'You remember her name. Did you kill her?'

'Did I kill her…' He swallowed. 'Yeah, I did. I kill her every goddamn day, you wanna know the truth. Right here.' He tapped his forehead with the side of his finger.

300

'You son of a bitch.'

'I'll wear that. Worst goddamn thing he made me do up to then. Killing a man ain't a chore – I popped Sheriff Cooper for him in 'forty-one and Bill bought me a steak dinner. But dames are different.' He buried his face in his hands. 'There's supposed to be rules about these things.'

I feathered the trigger. One squeeze to avenge Alice and Lizzie, revenge leading me again. A selfish act that wouldn't help anything; I stopped myself. 'Tindall gave you the job?'

He nodded, dragging his hands down over his face and leaving red pressure marks. 'He did business with that high-stepper you rubbed out. Callaway. They used to move booze together under Volstead.'

My blood stopped flowing. It wasn't me killed him, but no one apart from Lizzie and Jimmy Robinson knew I'd even been in Callaway's house that night. That's what I'd thought anyway. Now the spectre that Tindall and god knew who else was clued-in.

'When it was done, I holed myself up in a room with a bottle and a gun and I put them in my mouth one after the other. Only had the stones to empty one of them, turns out.'

I wanted to kick him. 'Are you trying me for sympathy? You went right out and slaughtered Geneve Kolkhorst. You found the *stones* for that.'

'The Kraut nurse? You think I wanted to? I barely stopped shaking from the Anderson girl. I begged Bill to send someone else. I stalled him long as I could – and that was before he told me what he wanted done to her.'

'Her mouth. You cut her up.'

'Not me – Bill.'

'Tindall did it?'

His head sunk. 'No. His orders, I mean. I don't even carry a knife.'

'Why, goddamn you?'

'So wouldn't no one else in Texarkana think to speak on what they'd seen. He didn't want no comebacks on me or him after they closed the Phantom case. He told me to dump her in Lake Hamilton so Coughlin could make it go away. He didn't want no headlines, but he knew the word would get out in Texarkana. Folk knew what happened and what it meant.' His head popped up again and he held his hand out. 'I done what I could for her. Bill wanted me to cut her when she was still alive, but I spared her that.'

Desecration as an act of mercy. I wanted to kick him to a pulp. 'What about Jeannie Runnels and Bess Prescott? Why them?'

He scrabbled backwards with his heels until he found the wall and he propped himself against it, putting a hand to the back of his head. 'I can't explain them ones.'

I kicked the chair next to him, sending it flying along the wall. 'You're not about to hold out on me now.'

'I can't explain it, truly. I went with them women to chase away what I done – the usual way a man does, I mean. But once we was alone, it started eating me up, and it was like the god-damn devil took me over. I saw their faces and I remembered the expression on the other ones' faces, and then I had them by the throat and I just couldn't stop . . .' He heaved. 'Jesus Christ, it's like it was someone else did it. I swear to you, if I could take it back . . .'

'You killed them. You're responsible for everything you did.'

'No. No. The Anderson girl turned my life upside down. I couldn't stop fretting on it, it was driving me crazy. It still is. And then the nurse, and then . . . then I couldn't stop for nothing.'

My stomach knotted up at the evil in front of me, a man so far beyond redemption. Then a revelation came to me, prompted by his words, buckling my knees as it formed. 'Are there more?'

'No.'

I stepped closer. 'ARE THERE MORE?'

'NO, I swear. That's all of them.'

'It's been two months. You're telling me you couldn't stop yourself, but then you did. Pick your story, goddamn you – which is it?'

'Bill found out, he came down on me. Threatened to kill me if I didn't quit it.'

My wheels were turning now. 'So you stopped and he covered it up for you.'

'He had to. Masters started poking around in all sorts when he won that damn vote. Coughlin told Bill to kill me and be done with it, but Bill overruled him. Son of a bitch is a snake. He don't know I know that. That's why Bill made him involve Barrett – so Coughlin would have to keep his mouth shut about me.'

'Barrett killed Glover?'

'Barrett? He's worse than a woman. I drove him out there and put the gun in his hand and he said he wouldn't do it. I warned him what'd happen but he was adamant. Couldn't even bring himself to put one in a dirt-fed nigger. Glover was wailing and begging for his mama by then; I had to do it. Barrett went for my arm the first time, made me miss my goddamn shot. I had to put him on his ass so I could get it done.' He shook his head. 'Always falls into my lap. Always been that way.'

He looked up at me now and we stared at each other, his eyes wide and desperate. Even after speaking the words, he believed himself worthy of sympathy. He kept looking at me, pleading; for a bullet or forgiveness, I couldn't tell which.

'I'm not your priest, take your goddamn eyes off me.'

'You gotta know I'm sorry. If I had my time again—'

'Save it.'

I looked out the window now, planning how to get him out to the car. He was still talking, empty words about coercion and forgiveness. I figured the sob story was all in the name of getting me to lower my guard. Then I looked at him again, the pathetic figure he cut, and reconsidered that judgement.

'How did Tindall find out?'

He stopped mid-sentence. 'What?'

'About Prescott and Runnels. You said he found out.'

His mouth moved. He moistened his lips.

'You told him, didn't you? Same way you just blabbed it all out to me. You wanted him to mollify you.'

He shut his eyes. 'I told you I was going out of my mind—'

'And you told the women too. Prescott and Runnels – you confessed to them what you did in Texarkana.' It all came together at once. 'That's why you killed them – because you couldn't keep your damn mouth shut, and you couldn't leave them alive after.'

He looked away from me, across the room. I couldn't tell if he even recognised the lies he'd been selling to himself.

'You're not worth a bullet. They should leave you out for the vultures.'

'You never done something you hated yourself for?'

The line derailed me. The memories played out in Technicolor, never far from my conscious even now – the jeep crash, the hospital, the war. All those moments when we reveal our true selves, and I'd been found wanting. Texarkana as my redemption; so much self-loathing, I'd almost destroyed myself.

Then I realised that last part was the difference. 'I only ever took it out on myself.'

'I done that, believe me. It ain't always enough.' He set his eyes on the liquor bottle on the table. 'How about you hand me that whiskey?'

'Go to hell. Who started the fire at Duke's?'

'We can sit here raking over this all night, ain't no good can come of it.'

'We'll sit here as long as I goddamn say so.'

He rolled his head side to side, trying to ease it. 'I torched the place. Bill said it was my mess, so it was only right that I clear it up. Same with you.'

My hand started shaking at the last part. I switched the gun over. 'What does that mean?'

'That first day you walked into the precinct, I was sure you recognised me. I was ready to draw.'

He said it with a different inflection, and it came to me in that instant. The memory-echo he'd stirred when he put his gun to my head at Lake Hamilton – the same terror I'd felt in the abandoned farmhouse in Texarkana. Fighting for my life against a man posing as the killer. 'That was you. Under the hood that night. You ran me off the road and tried to kill me.'

He opened his hands. An admission – not proud, just

matter-of-fact. 'Could've saved us both a heap of trouble. As soon as Browning came into the squad room and said someone was asking about the fire at Duke's, I knew it was you I was gonna find waiting. Somehow had a feeling we wasn't through.'

He'd been onto me almost from the second I'd arrived. 'Were you tailing me?'

'Some. That other one, your roughneck friend, he was running in circles for weeks until Barrett spilled his guts. I wasn't sure how much he'd told you. Didn't take long to figure out not much.'

Things fell into place. 'You stole his papers from my room.'

'It was gobbledegook. That's when I knew you had nothing. Until Tucker wet his pants and opened his mouth.'

'You killed him. To make it look like it was me.'

He was shaking his head. 'That was a bonus. I killed him because I shoulda done it the night of the fire. He was supposed to be out of the pocket but he saw me leaving the back way.'

'Did you murder Robinson before the fire?'

His face went slack. 'Hell, I just helped him along. He was drinking his way out of this life anyway. I put a pillow over his face and he never even twitched.'

My jaw locked up. I looked at him down the gun barrel.

He stared right into it. 'How about we get this over with now?'

I felt hatred enough to do it. I gripped the handle so hard I worried I'd fire by accident. The thought of losing Lizzie for ever stayed my hand. 'On your feet.'

'What for?'

I kicked the sole of his shoe. 'Because I'm the man with the gun this time. Let's go.'

'Go where? Serving me up to Bill won't get you what you want.'

'You're nothing to me. If Tindall wants you, he can have you.'

'You can't be that goddamn stupid.' He pushed himself off the floor. 'Tell me how you found me here.'

'Teddy Coughlin gave you up.'

'Coughlin? He don't know about this place. Only way he could've found out is if Bill told him. I knew it as soon as I seen you – you here because Bill wants you to be.'

'Bullshit. He hid you here. If Tindall wanted you dead—'

'Wipe the mud out of your eyes, he sent you to do it for him.' He turned and took a sidelong glance out the window, a bundle of nervous energy all of a sudden. 'I had a feeling Bill was hanging me out to dry here. I knew he wouldn't do it himself, but I never reckoned on him sending you.'

The decoy with the rooms – not a defence against me; a defence against Tindall.

'He's calling the tune and you dancing right along to it.'

I tried to say something, but the sinking feeling in my chest suffocated the words. Nothing more than Tindall's pawn. Everything spinning out of control. Then one shaft of clarity cut through the storm: if Tindall didn't want Layfield, I had no bargaining chip. No way to get Lizzie back.

Layfield was glancing from one side of the room to the other, as if I was no longer a concern. He darted to the back window and peered through it from one side, taking care that he couldn't be seen. He turned to me. 'I can't spy no one, but they're here all right. They'll be waiting on you to put me under, then they'll pick you off on your way out. That's why he sent you – kill two birds with one stone.'

I kept the gun on his chest, my eyes shifting out of focus as black panic closed around my vision. 'I'm not letting you talk your way out of this.'

'You never could hide your fear, Yates. I'm right, and you only just coming to see it.' He ripped the mattress from the bed and stood it in front of the door.

My eyes flicked to the window next to it. My breathing was stunted and rapid.

'You want proof, fire a shot into the floor,' he said. 'See what happens after that when you don't come out.'

I glanced over my shoulder, wisps everywhere now.

'We ain't walking away from this one.' He reached his hand out. 'Hand me back my piece, and I give you my word I won't turn it on you. You and me can put a little hitch in their giddy-up at least.'

'Shut your mouth, goddammit.'

He stared at me, his face empty of any expression. 'They won't wait on you for ever.'

I felt like I'd stepped off a cliff. It made sense of why Tindall wouldn't take my call. Why Teddy would give up Layfield's hideout – not crossing Tindall, but conspiring with him.

I pulled Layfield's pistol from my pocket and fired into the floor in the corner of the room. The report was deafening. I moved through a swirl of gunsmoke and stood next to the front window, keeping my aim on him as I did. My mind was radio static.

I couldn't see anything out there; I let go of a breath. But then a shadow moved across the ground in the distance. It was barely visible, just a black shape blocking out the tree trunks as it passed in front of them. Then another, to the right of the first.

'You see that?'

He was looking past me, the same direction. He backed into the middle of the room, fingers curling and twitching. 'Right now, they gonna take up a spot behind that car to wait on you. There'll be a man or two covering the back as well. You gotta give me a gun.'

I opened the cylinder of his pistol, my fingers leaving sweat on the metal. One chamber empty. I flipped it shut. 'You got any more bullets?'

He shook his head.

Five left in his revolver. Three left in Barrett's gun.

I'd walked right into Tindall's trap, and now he had me. I looked at Layfield, trying to convince myself it was a trick, his last desperate play. As I did, a face appeared behind him in the back window.

'MOVE.'

He threw himself aside as I raised his gun and snapped off a shot.

The face disappeared. The window pane cracked in the top corner – the bullet flying high and wide of where the man had been. I whipped around to check the door, then the back window again. Before I had a chance to act, a shot rang out, punching through the front window. I dived to the floor.

Layfield had crawled behind the dresser against the far wall for shelter. 'Give me a gun, goddammit. You can't cover both sides.'

I tipped the table over and crouched behind it, the opposite side of the room from Layfield. Seven bullets. Could be a whole army out there.

The mattress covering the door moved – a slight judder, someone trying the knob tentatively. Then a shattering sound behind me. The back window crumbled in a shower of glass, and a rock the size of a baseball skidded across the carpet.

Goddamn, goddamn, goddamn—

I opened the cylinder of Layfield's gun and spun it to an empty chamber.

'Layfield.' He glanced over and I tossed his gun to him. 'Take the back.'

He caught it, looking shocked. I stared at him, ready to shoot if he aimed it at me. Instead, he righted it in his hand and trained it on the window.

Three more shots came through the front and slammed into the side wall. Wild shots, a distraction—

The mattress toppled towards Layfield as the front door flew open. Someone stuck a gun around the corner and fired blind into the room. The man cracked off three shots – all high – and whipped his hand away. Layfield got his foot to the door and toed it closed again. The broken lock meant it didn't stick, finished up hanging ajar. I scurried across to the mattress and shouldered it back in place. I dropped to the floor again as two shots came from behind. Layfield returned fire, his first trigger pull an empty click. I rolled so I was underneath the front window. It left me exposed to fire from the back.

'Stupid not to trust me, Yates.'

'Save your bullets, goddammit.'

'We sitting ducks.'

'They still have to get in here.'

More shots whizzed above my head. To my right, the mattress moved again – someone outside testing the door. A crazy idea—

I reached out and pushed the mattress over so it tumbled to the carpet. A man kicked the door open, but wasn't prepared for it to give so easily; his momentum carried him into the room, right in front of me. I had my gun up, but Layfield didn't hesitate, put a slug in him, point blank. The man fell hard.

'Jesus Christ—' I couldn't move for staring at the corpse.

A shout from outside: 'Shit, he's down.'

The gunman was still, his body blocking the door open. I pressed myself to the wall, trapped underneath the front window. Layfield saw the dead man's face and he glanced at me, shaken. 'He's a cop.'

My hope suffocated as the reality of Tindall's influence sank in.

There was a barrage of shouts from outside. The room was full of smoke and plaster dust, debris showered all over the floor. I inched closer to the doorway, broken glass shredding my skin, to a spot where I could just see out and along the path beyond. The angle meant I could only see one way, but there was no one on that side.

'YATES—'

Layfield shouted it. He pointed his gun in my direction and fired. I flinched, jammed my eyes shut.

The bullet never came. I opened them again; he was aiming above me. I looked up, saw a shooter had leaned through the shattered window, and now he was slumped over the ledge, motionless, half in the room and half out. His gun arm dangled loose, still clutching his pistol, the barrel inches from my head. A trickle of blood ran down the wall.

My whole body shook. Seeing everything as a blur, I snatched the revolver from the dead man's hand.

I shot Layfield a look, lost for words, but he'd faced the other way again. He yelled at me over his shoulder, 'Get back in cover.'

I threw myself behind the upturned table again, mind in tumult, trying to focus it by figuring how many bullets we had. I looked at the two revolvers I was holding; there were two in the dead gunman's, still three in Barrett's. 'How many you have left?'

He glanced over at me, held up one finger to signify he was on his last. I pointed to the corpse of the other dead gunman, face down in the doorway, gesturing to take his gun. Layfield glanced at it and shook his head, as if it was too close to the open door.

I looked at the bathroom, weighed it, figured it was the same as climbing into a casket.

Surrounded. Outgunned. Out of options.

It took a moment for me to register the charged silence that had fallen. I figured they were regrouping outside. My ears were ringing, and my hands were covered in cuts that were clogged and matted with dust. Cold air rushed through the empty window frames, swirling the dust and smoke.

Then a voice called from outside – barely audible, coming from a distance away. 'Yates, listen to me. Kill him and bring yourself out, and I'll spare your wife.'

Tindall's mongrel accent unmistakable.

Layfield closed his eyes. His mouth was ajar, resignation etched in his features.

'There's no bloody way out of there; use your head and your old lady can walk.'

I looked at the guns in my lap. My head was scrambled.

'You know what he's done to you. To them girls. What're you thinking protecting him now?' Tindall's voice had an almost singsong quality to it that belied the brutal truth of what he was saying.

Layfield opened his eyes and stared at the wall, as though part of him had already departed. Then he started yelling. 'You son of a bitch, Bill. I always done every goddamn thing you asked.'

If Tindall heard him, he didn't react, falling silent a moment before he called again. 'Do as I say, Yates. He'll only put a bullet in you if you don't.'

I looked over to Layfield. He was already watching me, and he started shaking his head in silent denial. But we both knew it was bullshit; even if some miracle got us out of there, he'd have no other choice.

I rubbed my eyes, the dirt making them tear. It should've been so easy. Layfield had never shown any mercy, and he deserved none now. But it wasn't. The idea of doing Tindall's bidding appalled me – but it was more than that. For all the certainties I'd abandoned since I first set foot in Texarkana, there was still one I clung to: that killing in cold blood was a surrender to the darkness in a man's soul. A line you crossed and couldn't come back from. I remembered something Lizzie said to me once, words from her pastor that comforted her in the wake of Alice's death: 'You can't do good by doing evil.' The memory of her saying it was vivid, and it made my heart bleed. I called out to Tindall. 'Where's my wife?'

'Still in California. She's safe enough for now. She can be tucked up in her own bed within the hour – it's for you to decide.'

He was too sincere, and my eyes spilled over at the creeping realisation he could never let her live. That no bargaining or pleading was going to secure her safety, and I was deluding myself to believe otherwise. Frustration ate me up, and I slammed my head against the table, knowing it was my own intransigence that had put her in harm's way.

I raised the revolver I'd taken from the dead gunman, aimed it at the wall along from Layfield and fired. He jerked, gaping at me at first. The single shot ripped through the silence, reverberating around the walls and out into the night beyond them.

'It's done,' I shouted. 'Let her go.'

No response came.

No spoken response—

There was the sound of a bottle smashing, and then flames leapt in all directions around me.

I shielded my face with my arm. By luck alone, the firebomb had landed on the other side of the upturned table I was sheltering behind. I looked over, saw Layfield batting at his left arm, the sleeve of his jacket alight. There were pockets of fire all around the room, the carpet, the drapes, the bedstead ablaze.

Layfield wrestled himself free of his coat and threw it across the floor, his face contorted with pain. The heat was increasing as the flames spread. There was black smoke all around the room and it triggered a bout of choking coughs in both of us. I covered my mouth with my jacket tail, but it made little difference. Layfield had slumped against the wall, holding his arm gingerly across his chest, his eyes screwed shut. I thought about Jimmy, damning myself for recognising I was on the same path as him and following it anyway. Right into the flames.

I rolled to the front window and got to my feet, sucking in

fresh air. I peeped from behind the man's body that hung there like a dead fish on a scale.

'What the hell are you doing?'

I ignored Layfield. I bobbed up and down to look, but no pot-shots came – Tindall's men content to wait us out now. I could make out a car on the far side of the parking lot, maybe twenty yards distant, and behind it, Tindall's newsboy cap out-lined in the moonlight.

I crouched again and held my breath, choking inside, think-ing their complacency was my only out. The flames were spreading across the carpet and along the skirting boards, and through the smoke I could see the roof starting to blacken. Layfield edged himself along the wall, caught between the blaz-ing dresser and the exposure of the open doorway. His face was red and covered in sweat.

To hell with waiting to die.

'I'm going after Tindall.' I shouted it, the words barely aud-ible over the fire. Layfield turned his eyes to me, but I wasn't sure he'd even heard me.

I burst out of the doorway and dived over the path, landing between Layfield's Chrysler and the LaSalle. After the heat of the room, the night air was like cold hands clamped to my skin. A shot rang out, dinging off the bodywork. I pressed my cheek into the dirt to look under the chassis of Layfield's car and saw there was a man behind a pillar outside room three, covering the doorway from the blindside. His face was jagged as lava rock. I couldn't get an angle to fire on him. He was aiming in my direction but holding his position, waiting on me.

I ran numbers. Two of Tindall's men were dead, one more on the path covering the doorway. Made four including

Tindall. At least one more around back. If they'd only brought one car, chances were that was all of them – but no way to be certain there wasn't another somewhere in the darkness.

The thought of taking Tindall spurred me. He may never have intended negotiating for Lizzie, but everything changed if I could put a gun to his head.

The man on the path was calling for me to show myself. It was a twenty-some yard dash to where Tindall stood, across open ground. A clear field of fire for the shooter. Tindall too. I didn't like my chances, but didn't see any other way to save Lizzie. I got my feet under me.

Then all hell broke loose. Layfield came flying out of the room, sprinting across the lot towards Tindall, his revolver held out in front of him. I shouted to him, but my words were lost in the sound of gunshots.

The shooter on the path had spun to track him and opened fire. Layfield stumbled as if he'd been hit, but kept going, legs pumping like a madman. I lifted my head and brought Barrett's gun up to aim at the gunman. Hand shaking, I pulled the trigger.

I saw blood spatter the pillar. Before the shooter even hit the ground, I was stumbling to my feet chasing Layfield. 'DON'T KILL HIM.'

He didn't look back.

His head start was too great. I ran after him, shouting. 'I NEED TINDALL ALIVE—'

Tindall had his gun out, a look of stunned terror on his face. He hesitated before he took his shot, and Layfield fired first. Tindall dropped out of sight behind his car.

'NO, NO, NO—'

Layfield dived across the hood of Tindall's car, to where Tindall had gone down. I ran harder.

I rounded the car and saw Layfield on top of Tindall, his fingers in Tindall's mouth to pin him down, using his other hand to hammer at his skull with the pistol butt. I hooked Layfield around the throat and pulled him away. I wrestled him backwards, his heels dragging and kicking in the gravel. Tindall wasn't moving.

Layfield threw his head back, catching me on the cheekbone. The pain made my grip falter and he spun free, then followed in with a straight right that put me down. I smashed my head on the stony ground as I landed.

I looked up at Layfield, head pounding, my vision blurred and fading. His shirt was covered with blood, as though he'd been shot, and in his eyes I saw only hate. He pointed his gun at me and fired.

There was a click. No bullets left.

He whipped back to Tindall. Before he could resume his attack, a gunshot rang out, and then another. Blood sprayed from the side of Layfield's face, and he dropped to his knees, clutching his cheek. Then he pitched over onto his face.

A red light danced around the parking lot, and I heard a screaming noise. I thought it was coming from Layfield. The shooter on the pathway outside the room staggered past a little distance from where I lay, his eyes on something across the lot. He was dragging his left leg, the barrel of his gun still smoking from the shot that felled Layfield. He opened the back door of Tindall's car and started to heft him to it. Tindall's face was a mess of blood, his eyes shining out from it like wet stones. His gaze was empty, but as the heavy dragged him to the car,

Tindall reached out his hand and his fingertips brushed against Layfield's head.

Through my daze, I realised the screaming was a siren, and the red lights were everywhere now, encircling me. Tindall's man slammed the rear door shut and dived behind the steering wheel. I battled to get to my feet and threw myself against the car. I clawed at the door handle as the driver gunned the engine. It came open, but the man stamped on the accelerator and took off, the door swinging on its hinges.

I chased after them, yelling for Lizzie.

I heard cars skidding to a halt and doors being thrown open. I kept going, tripping and lurching, my brittle legs failing me, the back lights of Tindall's car all I could see. I sensed someone on my tail – their footfalls, hard breathing. Then I was tackled from behind, brought down in a tangle of arms and legs. A voice shouted at me to be still, but I lifted my head in time to see two police cruisers pull up in front of Tindall's car, penning it in. The driver jumped out and was felled with the crack of a shotgun.

I felt a hand on the back of my neck, forcing my face into the ground. I turned my head to ease the pressure, saw the night awash with red. The edge of my vision went dark. Before I blacked out, I heard Sam Masters somewhere near me, breathless, barking an order: 'Go easy on him.'

CHAPTER THIRTY-SEVEN

I came round in a hospital bed and immediately thought I was back in Lennox Hill, the hospital where I'd spent six months after the car wreck that'd shattered my legs. Strange how that place that held only bad memories now served as the closest thing to a safe haven my brain could dredge up. It was only when the fog lifted some that I realised the surroundings were foreign to me.

I was alone in an empty ward, three beds made up with stiff white sheets along the wall opposite, and one either side of me. I could smell starch and sweat, and my head was splitting.

Then it all came back. Lizzie—

I went to get up, but as I moved, a handcuff chained to the bed rail bit into my wrist. I rattled it and tried to call out, but my voice was hoarse and weak.

A police officer in a uniform I didn't recognise appeared at the end of the room and made his way towards me, but a nurse overtook him. She rushed to my bedside and put her hand on my arm. 'Try to be calm, Mr Yates. You're quite unwell.'

'My wife— I need to get to a telephone . . .'

The cop stationed himself at the end of my bed, hands on hips. I saw the badge on his shirt, made him as Arkansas State Police. 'I'll notify the prosecuting attorney that you're awake.'

'Please. I need to make a call . . .'

'Mr Masters will be along in good time.' He marched back the way he'd come.

The nurse fussed with my pillows. My mouth was drier than desert sand, and I thought I could taste smoke. I realised that it was light outside. 'How long have I been here?'

'Twelve hours or so. They brought you in last night. Doctor says you've suffered the effects of smoke inhalation, and he suspects you suffered a serious concussion. Does your head hurt?'

I mouthed an affirmative.

'It's to be expected. Doctor may be able to give you something for the pain. Are you experiencing shortness of breath?'

'Yes.'

She nodded as if she assumed as much. 'Can you tell me what year this is?'

'Nineteen forty-six.'

'And the name of the president?'

'Truman.'

'That's good.'

'I need a telephone. Please, my wife—'

'I'm sorry, sir, I don't have the authority for that.' She turned to go. 'I'll be back with the doctor. Try to rest.'

I yanked at the cuffs again, rattling them, barely the strength to do it. The effort left me gassed, and I slumped against the bed, wondering if Lizzie was already dead.

CHAPTER THIRTY-EIGHT

When I opened my eyes again, Samuel Masters was standing over me, calling my name. The state trooper was next to him.

'I need to get to a telephone—'

'Your wife is safe.'

The words sounded sinister coming from his mouth – a matter he should have no knowledge of. A terror gripped me, the thought that he was involved in taking her somehow. Misplaced trust—

'Your boss contacted me – Mr Acheson. Your wife's with him.'

I searched his face, muddled, not sure whether to believe him.

'Did you hear what I said? I said your wife is safe and—'

'I heard you.' The explanation came back to me then – telling Acheson to leave word with Masters if he had news on Lizzie. I closed my eyes and relief flooded through me. 'I heard you. What happened to her?'

'I don't have the details. I'll see to it you get to speak with her.'

'When?'

'Let me see what I can arrange.' He wiped a line of sweat from his top lip and took his hat off. 'Quite the evening you had last night. My men found Cole Barrett's LaSalle and the gun in the glove box. It's being sent to Little Rock for testing.

Is it Layfield's like you said?'

'Yes.'

'Let's see if the analysis tells the same story you do. Officially you're still the prime suspect in the murders of Barrett, and Clay and Leland Tucker.'

'Then why haven't you had me charged yet?'

He tapped the cuff with the brim of his hat. 'I'm confident you're not going anywhere.'

'You know it wasn't me.'

He let out a breath. 'After what I saw last night, let's say I'm keeping an open mind. I want to get a formal statement on the record as soon as possible – not least because I want to know just what the hell is going on.'

I closed my eyes, seeing Tindall's face after Layfield had pulped it. 'Did you get Tindall?'

'William Tindall is dead. He suffered a gunshot wound and massive head trauma. He died at the scene.'

The words didn't move me at all – no sense of vengeance, just emptiness; another body strewn on the trail I'd been damned to walk. 'Did you know about him?' I said.

'Know what?'

'That he and Coughlin were in cahoots?'

'I don't recognise that description of the situation.' He looked to the side a moment, thinking, then back at me. 'Off the record, I was aware he was tangential to Coughlin's activities – but given my enquiries into those activities are ongoing, that's as much as I'm willing to say right now.'

A politician's answer. The thought crossed my mind that he'd ignored Tindall because he didn't hold an elected office he could make a play for. At another time it might have got my blood up, but lying in that bed, I couldn't summon the interest to care. If the worst of Masters' character was his too-ferocious desire for political power, he was still a better man than those he was trying to oust. 'I'm willing to testify against Coughlin.'

He nodded, a thin smile on his lips, but he held up his hand. 'Well, that's music to my ears, but don't say anything more for now – I don't want to leave myself open to accusations of prejudicing your testimony.'

I understood why he'd brought the trooper with him, then – a witness. Always cautious.

I touched my face, my left cheekbone tender from Layfield's punch. 'How did you find me last night?'

'An anonymous tip.'

I drew a blank at hearing it. 'Seems to happen a lot around here.'

'Man called in to say you were hiding out at the Viceroy and that a posse was on its way to punch your ticket. That's why I brought in the state police – had a feeling any Hot Springs cop would happily see you wear one because of what happened to Barrett.'

I gave a slight nod in appreciation – as much as I could manage.

'The doctor says you need some rest before we can get down to business, so I'll take my leave for a few hours. Do you want to avail yourself of an attorney?'

'I don't need an attorney. I need a telephone.'

He put his hat back on and tipped it as he left.

*

Masters was good to his word. Ten minutes after he went, the trooper appeared with a nurse pushing an empty wheelchair. He unlocked the cuff from the bed rail and motioned for me to climb in.

'I'll walk.'

'Suit yourself.' He snapped the cuff around his own wrist, chaining us together. Then he led me to an administration office outside the ward and pointed to the telephone. 'Your wife's on the line.'

I snatched up the receiver. 'Lizzie?'

'Charlie – Charlie, are you all right?'

'Where are you? Are you safe?'

'I'm at the *Journal*, Mr Acheson came to collect me himself.'

'What happened? What did they do to you?'

'They tried to take me.' There were tears on the edge of her voice. 'Two men, they were waiting to take me right off the street.'

I blinked and my vision was straight red. 'Tried? What do you mean—'

'I saw them. I'd seen them before and I put it together. It was just like Texarkana. When they were waiting for you outside the house.'

'Slow down, what do you mean you saw them? Who?'

She stole a breath. 'The day before last, I saw a car outside the *Journal* offices, and I had a feeling then. It was parked down at the corner of the block, but there was two of them in there, I saw them look at me then turn away. They all have that same type of face, they all . . .' She sounded in shock.

'Take your time.'

'When I was home yesterday morning, I kept checking the

street outside the apartment, trying to think what I should do, even though I couldn't see any sign of them. I thought— I thought I was being paranoid, but I'd been looking into it like you said; I'd put it together. Then when I came back from the grocery store last night, they were there, right across the street. There was only one of them in the car. I looked out and I couldn't see the other one. I slowed up because I just wanted to scream. And then I saw him, in the rearview, walking right towards me. Coming up on the driver's side. I knew what was happening. I knew exactly what that . . .' She swallowed quietly. 'I was shaking. I stamped on the accelerator— I ran the stop sign at the end of the block. I looked back once and saw them, standing there, just watching me go. Calm. As if they could come again anytime they wanted.

'After that I just drove. I didn't stop until I was out of the city and then I kept going – like you would. I took a room in a motel in Oxnard and just locked myself in there until I could get my wits about me. I didn't know who to call or where you were or how to contact you so I just waited there, climbing the damn walls trying to work out what to do.'

'They told me they had you. I went after the men—'

'Tindall. It was Tindall told you that, wasn't it?'

I was stunned into silence a moment, wondering just what I'd done to my wife. 'How did you know that? What did you mean you put it together?'

'Sal put me on to a man he knows at the *LA Sentinel*, Mr Booth. Sal said he was an old-timer from the New York papers who'd be able to better fill me in on Tindall from way back.'

I knew the name, not the man.

'I contacted him about Tindall and he didn't think he had

anything helpful to say, so he started telling me about all the criminal figures in Los Angeles that have connections to Tindall going back to their time in New York. I didn't recognise most of the names, but I knew Mickey Cohen, from the papers, and Benjamin Siegel. I remembered Mr Acheson saying your story had to do with Siegel making regular visits to Hot Springs and I knew then it had to be more than a coincidence. Mr Booth said they were in the same gang in New York. It had to be that he was going there to see Tindall.'

The name I'd dropped so casually to Acheson came back to haunt me now: Benjamin 'Bugsy' Siegel. His link to Hot Springs was the blaring warning sign I'd missed. He was the story all along.

'And then I thought about the burglary, and the timing of it and the fact you were out there and I just had this feeling it was all linked. It's what you always say about coincidences. I wanted to tell you what I'd learned and see what you thought, but I had no way to contact you. I tried to leave a message at the motel you were in before but they said you'd disappeared, and then I got really scared. Then when I saw that car waiting outside . . .'

She sounded exhausted and I wondered when she'd last slept without fear. 'It's done now. Tindall is dead.'

The line crackled. Then she said, 'Was it you?'

'No.'

'What happened?'

'When I get back. There are things I need to tell you, but when I see you. I'll be back as soon as they let me go.'

'Let you go? Where are you?'

'I'm fine. I found the man who killed those brothers. I can clear everything up now, I just need to tell what I know to the authorities. Have you somewhere safe to stay?'

'Mr Acheson insisted I stay with them. He's been a wonder.'

'Good. Look after yourself. I'll be there soon.'

*

When they took me back to my bed, an orderly had left a pitcher of water and a glass on my table. I picked it up to pour with my free hand, the movement made awkward by the cuffs, and realised there was an unmarked envelope leaning against it. I looked around, a sense of unease descending over me. There was no one else on the ward.

I held the envelope with my teeth and tore it open. There was a typed note inside:

> The keys to a fruitful convalescence are silence and a timely removal to the comforts of the California sunshine. With sincerest regards for the health of your good lady wife, Miss Lizzie.

It was unsigned, but the threat implied in the language meant it could only be from Coughlin. I read it again, then resisted the urge to tear it apart, instead folding it and stashing it under my pillow.

His meaning was obvious – say goose egg about him to Sam Masters. The rage came over me, and it was all I could do not to topple the bedside table to the floor. I tried to control it. I wondered if Coughlin had the juice to get to Lizzie in California – or if that connection died with Tindall. It felt like a roll of the dice by a man who knew his time was running short –

but then I remembered Masters cautioning me about Coughlin's desperation making him dangerous. I figured Lizzie was safe for now as long as she was with Acheson.

I yelled the hospital down demanding they get Masters back so I could start talking, but the doctor insisted I take some rest first. As I waited for him, I thought about Harlan Layfield and how I'd had the chance to stop him back in Texarkana. I'd walked away from the murders there thinking I'd done enough by stopping Callaway and the rest of them – but if I'd have stayed on, seen everyone involved brought to justice, then the three women would still be alive. Same for Robinson.

The guilt was bad, and it came with a chaser. When I finished raking through everything, I couldn't get away from the fact that Layfield had saved my life when he shot that gunman in the window. The shooter was inches from my head; there was no way he would have missed. Layfield's motivation might have been selfish – I was just a warm body with a gun who happened to be backed into the same corner he was – but that didn't change the fact I wouldn't be alive save for him. My heart still beating only on his intervention. It felt like a taint on my soul.

*

The doctors discharged me after twenty-four hours, under heavy pressure from Masters. He had me moved to the state police lockup in Malvern, saying he couldn't guarantee my safety if we stayed in Hot Springs. He kept me there for two days of solid questioning. A murder detective from the Little Rock division was brought in to conduct the interrogation, but

Masters was present throughout, and it was clear who was running the show.

I talked for hours – my version of the truth, Texarkana and up. I laid bare everything I knew Layfield to have done, the murders he committed and his connections to Tindall and Coughlin. Then I started lying.

I omitted the fact I was present in Winfield Callaway's house the night he and all the others died, and hoped like hell the truth went to the grave with Layfield. Turned out I could relax on that score because Masters had little interest in matters prior to Hot Springs – anything that wouldn't lead directly to Coughlin. But the flip side of that coin landed when he started asking about why I'd ditched out on the meet we'd arranged to hand over Layfield's gun to him. It got hairy, trying to keep my story straight, convincing, but I brazened it out, admitting I'd met with Coughlin at his house, but making no mention of the gun I'd used to persuade him out there.

Masters looked doubtful throughout, especially when I got to the part about Layfield shooting Coughlin, giving me a chance to escape. 'Then how come I haven't heard anything to that effect?'

The answer came the next morning when stories emerged of Teddy Coughlin being wounded in the process of foiling a robbery at his home. The *Recorder* splashed on it, carrying a picture of a defiant Coughlin with his arm in a sling, his trademark carnation pinned to it. According to the account, Coughlin had made an unscheduled return to his house having skipped a dinner engagement due to feeling unwell. Upon entering, he disturbed a masked intruder who was in the throes of ransacking his study. Coughlin was shot in the arm as he beat a retreat from the room, sustaining a serious, but non-life-threatening injury. It went on to state that, despite his wounds, Coughlin had made it to the gun safe he kept in his bedroom, armed himself, and proceeded to drive the assailant from his property. The article painted Coughlin as a hero, and the hack who wrote it speculated he'd see a surge in his electoral support as a result.

As the interviews with Masters dragged on, and the questions repeated, his initial optimism faded and his mood darkened. The truth was I had no hard evidence against Coughlin. I showed him the note I'd been sent at the hospital, and he was in agreement with me about who'd penned it – but it counted for nothing because it was clear that Masters' best shot at implicating Coughlin for his crimes had died with Cole Barrett.

CHAPTER THIRTY-NINE

Monday morning I heard the door to the cell block open, but it wasn't the usual guard came down the gangway. Instead Masters appeared, looking ashen. I jumped up from the bare cot I was sitting on, fearing it was something to do with Lizzie.

He gripped the bars and fixed me with a stare. 'I just took a call from your wife. It concerns her house in Texarkana. There was an accident last night and I'm afraid it burned down.'

'An accident?'

'Apparently so. The locals are investigating, but early indications are that there are no suspicious circumstances.'

'A goddamn accident? You're not buying that.'

He pursed his lips and looked at the floor.

'That son of a bitch Coughlin,' I said. 'You saw the note, this is him trying to convince me to stonewall you.'

He swallowed before he spoke. 'You can't make that assumption. But I'll concede, if I was a gambling man, that's where I'd lay my money.'

'Goddammit.' I smacked the wall with the flat of my hand, seeing a war without end. 'I want to speak to my wife.'

'She asked that I relate to you that she's all right.'

'I don't give a damn, I want to speak to her.'

'You'll be able to shortly. Your release papers are being drawn up. There are no charges.'

I took a deep breath at that, but the relief was rendered

meaningless by what had happened.

'I may need you to come back when I bring the case against Coughlin. That won't be until I take office in January, so for right now, I'd advise you to go home to your wife and not look back.'

'You expect me to just forget about everything he's done to me?'

'I told you when we first met: I'll get Coughlin, but I'll do it within the law. Be satisfied with that.'

*

They let me out three hours later. The desk sergeant who processed my release gave me a used pair of trousers and a creased shirt to wear in place of the denims they'd kept me in – my own threads long since disposed of. In the pocket, I found some money and a note explaining it was to cover my bus fare to Little Rock, from where I could start the journey west to California. Masters' initials were scribbled at the bottom. I appreciated the gesture, but I was pretty sure he just wanted to wash his hands of me.

As soon as I was out, I made the call to Lizzie. Her emotion bubbled over when she heard I was free and coming home, and even when I asked her about the fire, it didn't seem to dim her exuberance. She recounted what she'd been told by a fire department official in Texarkana – that the cause was uncertain, but indications were it was a result of an electrical wiring failure.

Her manner came as a surprise – she came off detached. 'I thought you'd be more upset.'

'I was at first. But the more I think about it, the more I feel as though it's a weight lifted.'

'You care to explain that to me?'

She took a breath. 'It's been playing on my mind ever since we got here. Always having that link. All the things inside that needed taking care of. Now we're free of it. We never need go back there. Pop took care of the insurance, so we won't lose out.'

I went to ask about everything that she'd lost – the photographs of her parents and Alice, items of sentimental value – and then I realised either she'd made her peace with it or at least was trying to. It wasn't for me to argue with that. 'I'm heading for the bus station now. I'll be back in two or three days, just as soon as I can be.'

It was the truth, with one omission. I squared it with myself by promising I'd tell her everything later. I hung up the telephone and went to catch a bus to Hot Springs. One last time. A risk worth taking.

*

I figured the cops wouldn't know yet that I'd been cleared of Barrett's murder, so I moved with circumspection when I got to town.

It was late afternoon when I arrived. That morning's *Recorder* carried Coughlin's campaign schedule for the day; he was due to speak at a rally at the United Methodist Church on Grand Avenue at four o'clock. Alongside it, the results of a poll taken in the wake of his injuries showed the early predictions were correct: he'd overtaken Masters' candidate for mayor, Edgar Burton, for the first time in weeks.

United Methodist was a five minute walk from Violet Drive. I took a detour on my way from Central Avenue so I could go by Ella Borland's house. I wasn't certain what my reason for going was until I got there and saw it.

The drapes were open; I cupped my eyes to the window and looked inside. The front room was mostly bare, the beginnings of a film of dust just visible on the surfaces that caught the light. There was a cup on its side on the table and an ashtray that had been spilled on the floor and left. Signs of a haphazard exit. I realised then it was what I'd wanted to see. Evidence that Ella Borland had made her choice and decided not to throw in with Tindall and his men. That whatever she'd said and done before, when she had the chance to escape, she took it.

*

I made it to the redbrick church in time for the end of Coughlin's speech. The crowd was huge, swelled by folks who wanted the chance to see the conquering hero, spilling over the grounds and onto the sidewalk. Coughlin rounded out his speech with customary vigour, waving his fedora as he soaked up the applause.

I waited off to the side of the wooden platform they'd erected for him. He climbed down the steps and shook hands with dozens of well-wishers, playing up his injury. I noticed he was shadowed from a distance now by a heavy who looked like he'd come right from a job minding the doors of one of the casinos.

Coughlin looked up and saw me through what was left of the crowd. He made eye contact, then quickly glanced at his minder, who moved to be by his side. I held up my hands to signify I was no threat, masking my anger with a half-smile. When the crowd thinned out, the two men made their way towards me.

Coughlin took in my outfit. 'Taken to wearing clothes from the goodwill box, son?'

'Still alive to wear them, at least. That must be a disappointment.'

He cocked his head. 'I don't know what you mean by that comment.'

'You sent me to die.' I eyeballed the bodyguard, watching for him to make a move, looked back at Coughlin when he kept his station. 'And then you had the gall to tell me to keep quiet about it. Make threats about my wife.'

Coughlin closed his eyes and shook his head. 'You're delusional. We have nothing more to say to one another.'

'Consider one thing: how'd it work out for Tindall when he brought my wife into it?'

'I don't know what your grievance is, son, but I think it would be best if you left town presently. Go enjoy some of that *California sunshine* I hear so much about.' He started to move off.

I stepped in front of him. 'Don't worry about me, I'm gone. I've done all my talking.'

'I heard. Except a little birdie tells me it didn't amount to much for our mutual friend in the prosecutor's office.'

Should have figured he'd have a snitch within the state police too. Didn't matter now. 'Masters is determined to get you by the book. Not everyone works that way.'

'If you're threatening me, you can save your breath.'

'I'm not threatening you. It's your associates I'd be worried about.' I scratched my chin with my thumb. 'I know exactly what Tindall was involved in, and it's my guess you're angling to replace him. Ben Siegel's been coming here for years, and before that it was Lucky Luciano. They weren't coming here on vacation – they were coming to check up on their investment. On behalf of the boys in New York and Chicago who own this town. They sent Tindall down here to oversee their operation years ago. That must have hurt your pride – having to answer to another man in your own town. No wonder you hated him. How d'you think they'd react if they knew you ratted out Bill Tindall to Masters, huh?'

He adjusted his sling.

'Took me a while to put it together, but it's amazing what a few days of thinking time does for the mind.' I knocked on my skull with my knuckle. 'No one else knew about the ambush at the Viceroy, so I figured out pretty quick it had to be you tipped Masters off. I just couldn't come up with why. And then I kicked myself for being so dumb. It's the same *why* it always is – money and power. You set me up for Tindall to kill, and then you double-crossed him, figuring Masters would catch him red-handed – or kill him. How long have you been waiting for him to make a misstep like that – years? You just waiting to pounce.' I stepped closer. 'You're slick, I'll say that for you.'

'This is poppycock.' He tried to blow it off, but a laugh died in his throat before it could reach his mouth.

'I'm leaving for Los Angeles right now. I get the first sniff of you or your hoods coming near me and my wife, and I'll drop the dime on you to Siegel's outfit.' He opened his mouth to say something, saliva stringing across the gap. I spoke first. 'And

336

in case you think you can get me before I squeal, I've already mailed a detailed statement about everything you did to three attorneys, and when I get back, I might just run to a couple more to make an even five. If my wife or me so much as miss a bus because of you, they go straight to Siegel's lawyers.'

He stepped back, his eyes pinpricks in his face now.

'I'm not finished. There's one more thing I want you to do for me: drop out of the mayoral race. Do it by the time I get back to California. Those are the terms of my silence.'

I turned and walked away, every fibre in my body tensed and shaking. From somewhere in the distance, I swore I heard Jimmy Robinson say, 'I would've killed him, New York.'

CHAPTER FORTY

When I stepped off the bus and saw Lizzie, it felt like I shed a second skin – one of fear and violence and darkness. Part of me couldn't believe I was the same man had left in the first place.

She looked drawn and I could tell she'd been skipping meals. It brought home to me the ordeal she'd been through, and a fresh wave of anger came over me – and guilt. She threw her arms around me and buried her face in my neck, and I begged the fates not to take me away from her again.

*

I finally stayed true to the promise I'd made to myself and, over the course of several days, told her everything. She'd figured out the fire at her old house in Texarkana was no accident; when I explained to her what led to it, and the measures I'd put in place to protect us, she seemed reassured. If her dispassion about losing the Texarkana house was a front, it never cracked.

It got tough when I told her about Layfield. There was little comfort for her in learning the identity of her sister's killer; she'd moved from mourning to remembrance, and giving a face and a name to the shadow she'd banished only brought it all back again. I told her I'd had the chance to kill him and that I couldn't bring myself to do it. And that he'd saved my life.

Telling her that last part was the hardest. I was scared she'd be repulsed by the thought of me being in his debt. As it was, she cut me off mid-sentence. 'You came home. That's the only thing that matters to me.'

*

I called Sam Masters the day after I got back. He skipped a greeting and got right into it.

'Teddy Coughlin dropped out of the mayoral race yesterday. Can you believe it?'

'No kidding.'

'At the eleventh goddamn hour, the son of a bitch drops out. Gave a magnanimous speech about how his injuries were more serious than first thought and he didn't feel he could govern to the fullest extent of his capacity.' He was jubilant, but the frustration in his voice was evident.

'Your man will walk it now. Can't you be happy at that?'

'We could have beaten him. Twenty years and we finally had him beat. He robbed us of that.'

'You'll get over it.'

'Maybe. I'm not letting it lie, though. I'm bringing a charge against him for misuse of public funds. If not, I'll try a charge of bribing public officials or voter fraud. I'll get him one way or another.'

I smiled at the thought – Coughlin finally brought low for something so prosaic.

'Harlan Layfield is to be posthumously charged with the murders of Jeannie Runnels, Elizabeth Prescott and the Tucker brothers, as well as Jimmy Robinson. I thought you'd want to know.'

'Appreciate you telling me. What about Geneve Kolk-horst?'

There was a pause. 'I don't have the evidence for that. I'll see to it her file remains open, but the best I can do is have it changed from suicide to unsolved.'

I thought about what it meant for the families that were left behind; closure for Robinson's sister and Sid Hansen, no such thing for Heinrich Kolkhorst and his wife. I didn't like the thought of him being left wondering, and I resolved to tell him the truth.

'How's your wife faring?' he said.

'She's bearing up. She's a fighter.'

'No doubt.' He was quiet again, and I could tell he was edging towards something. 'You feel like telling me what really happened at Teddy Coughlin's house that night?'

'Take care of yourself, Sam.'

*

We never moved back into the bungalow. The men who'd come for Lizzie had ransacked it again, a ploy to help convince me they'd managed to take her. Twice in a week was too much for anyone to bear; it wasn't ours any more. We stayed in Acheson's guesthouse for a night and then we hit the road, taking Route 1 up the coast. I told Lizzie it was a vacation, but I had it in my mind that it was best to blow town a while.

I wrote the articles I'd promised Acheson and called them in as we travelled north. They were more fiction than truth. Not because I made things up, but because of all the parts I left out: a murderous cop killing with impunity in a town

bought and paid for by mobsters on the other side of the country. Acheson knew what I was doing and tacitly approved; the
reality of the cosy relationship between gangsters and elected
officials in Hot Springs had too many parallels to the situation
in Los Angeles for comfort. He wanted the story I pitched him
– feel-good pieces about a band of GIs who came home from
the war and saved their home town in the name of democracy.
It didn't escape me that my reporting was just the same as what
had happened after Texarkana, another patchwork of lies told
to protect the square Johns from a truth they didn't want to
hear. It shocked me how easily I agreed to play my part.

At every stop, Lizzie and I took long walks on the beach,
our way of easing back into the shared life we'd started together.
We talked about our future, and it was nice to be troubled only
by everyday problems – finding someplace to live when we got
back to LA, buying another car. We even edged towards a conversation about starting a family.

But as the days went by, I could sense there was something
troubling her. I remembered the way she'd cut me off when
I told her about Layfield and I wondered if I'd been right all
along – if that truth had festered and now turned septic. One
evening, sitting on Pismo Beach, watching the breakers wash
up the sand, I asked her about it.

'It's not that. I told you, I don't care about what happened.
You did what you had to.'

I held her hand tighter. 'Tell me.'

She stared at the horizon, where the sun was fading into the
water. 'I can't keep from thinking about everything. After the
burglary, I swore I wouldn't let them chase me from my home –
not again. But they did, and next thing I knew I was on my own

in a dirty motel room not knowing if you were dead or alive. We ran all the way to the ocean and couldn't get free of it. Now we're running again. What happens when we've got nowhere left to run to?'

'We're not running. Teddy Coughlin's a busted flush – he'll have Masters all over his business for the rest of his life. And besides, we're protected. It's over.'

'Benjamin Siegel's still out there. Men like him never go away. The ones that can always find some other lowlife to pick up a knife or a gun in their name.'

I turned to look at her and I noticed she'd got some colour back in her skin and she looked healthy again. 'Siegel won't care a damn about us now Tindall's dead. He has no need to come after us. We're insignificant.'

Empty words. Even as I said it, I was bracing for the comeback I had no answer to: *So when can we go home?*

She looked at me. Her pupils were shrunken and hard from the light in a way I'd never seen them before. Half her face was in shadow. A reminder that even the brightest sunset was only the herald of night falling.

ACKNOWLEDGEMENTS

I would like to thank more people than I can list here, but in particular:

My agents, Kate Burke and Diane Banks, for all their encouragement, support and input into the book.

My editor, Angus Cargill, whose insight and advice improved the manuscript in so many ways.

The team at Faber – in particular Sophie Portas and Katie Hall – for their dedication to getting my book into as many hands as possible.

To all the bloggers and reviewers who took an interest in my writing, and in particular Liz Barnsley, whose enthusiasm for *The Dark Inside* spurred so many to read it.

To Anne and Alex Wise, and Kim and Guy White, for their phenomenal efforts in spreading the word overseas.

To all my fellow writers who've offered kind words about my work, especially Anya Lipska, Stav Sherez, Eva Dolan, Chris Ewan, Gilly Macmillan, Sarah Ward, Tim Baker, Martyn Waites, Helen Giltrow, David Young and Steph Broadribb.

To my friends who've been so generous in helping spread the word – Oliver Wheatley, Steve O'Meara, Matthew Wilkinson, Darren Sital-Singh, John Maloney, Tim Caira and Emma Callaghan.

To James Hancock and Nick Thompson – sorry about last time!

And to my family, for always believing.